D1104476

$ BLOODY MONEY $

Who Said Da Game Was Fair?

A Novel By: **Leondrei Prince**

Website: www.streetknowledgepublishing.com

$Bloody Money$®

Published by: **Street Knowledge Publishing**
Written by: **Leondrei Prince**
Edited by: **Otise Reed**
Cover design by: **Kenny Briscoe / A6 Media / www.a6media.com**
Photos by: **Shorty Wright and Charles Emory III**

For information contact:
Street Knowledge Publishing
P.O. Box 345
Wilmington,DE 19801
Email: jj@streetknowledgepublishing.com
Website: www.streetknowledgepublishing.com

ISBN: 0-9746199-0-6

Printed in Canada

Dedication

This book is dedicated to My Wife, Mrs. Prince.

You have been my best friend, the person who walked in my life and not only encouraged me, but also stood by my side when everyone else walked out. A person who despite my past believed in me, when everyone else gave up on me and counted me out. Baby I can't thank you enough for giving me a chance. I wish that I could say, "I love you," but those words are too weak to define my love and gratitude and what you really mean to me. Baby you are the truth! The total package: physically, mentally, and spiritually and I admire your strength. It takes a special person to endure what you have endured everyday. I was always told, "He who laughs last, laughs the best," and baby we're giggling.

Thank you so much baby! I love you,
Mr. Prince

R.I.P Deborah (Mommy) Prince. I DID IT!

Acknowledgments

Special Thanks to Ken Briscoe, Brandon Lewis, My ace Boon Coon, my friend & Partner Joe-Joe, my photographer Shorty Wright & Robert Bovell.

This book was written for the streets...to and for Red Brick City. (Riverside)....whass'up to my family...Mike (Mujahid) Chambers, Animal Cub, Naphie, Cousin Dog, Jerry, (Poison) Cousin Sponge, Snook, Big Little, Poop Lips, Duckworth, Teddy Bear, Mike, Mile Butter, J. Rock, My Brother from another mother Coley, (Hank Nasty), Moe & Reggie, Gator, Boog, LB Fox, Pete Rock, Thug, Dadda Boy, Jihad, Chino, Small Ball, Monk, Cousin Gurt, Sweet Momma, Lisa, Myeisha, Meena, Pooh, Vickie, Charlonda, Tish,? Curtis, The twins (La & Na), Tanya Cropper, Tish...

To My East Side Family....Murdoc, Geez, Mike Davis, Mr. C., Booka, Manny, "Harper" Gorilla, Pretty Ricky, Lil Mark, Show Tina, Lil Bruce, R.I.P, Waali, Speedoc, Jam, Stephon C.

To My West Side Family....Blick, Moe Good, Damon, Bro Malik, Sean, Funk, Skippie, Giz, Jerzey, Pop, Gus, Deverlle, Mannuel, Corey Mosley, If I forgot any one my bad!! "Oh!" how can I forget my boy Laytom, Bert, & Martin.

To My Hilltop Family...Rob (Base), Stink, Jersey, Jane Bo, Jermaine Johnson, Mil Streetz, Young Cannon, Shack, Tuck, Bruce & Brian, Darrious & Darrell & Andre, Nekt, Terelle, Fam, My cousin ES, Alfie, Smage, To The Castle; Kenny (Bin Laden), Anthony Terry, Tylynn, Ken Kent, K.B., Swaggz, Kareem, Corey, Wallace, Lil' Daddy, Rick Lewis, Rope, Cheeze, Randy, Curtis, Fresh Mally, Jaunie, The Boah "Sy;" Cousin Donald, Kev, B. Turner, Oh Shit! I almost forgot...whassup'up cousin Nurkie (Fat Cat), Goddie, Nelson, My Lil' Brothers; Lenny, Tail, and BoBo. To my Peeps; Lil' Artie, Esco, Renny Street, Meat, Den, Dog, Cousin Rosie, Cousin Jerry, Mike Smallwood, Cozzie, Sonny (The Champ), Al J., and to all my people I forgot it's truly my fault, plus the paper is almost out, but to all the rest; you know who you are.

Chapter One

The stolen black Acura Legend rode swiftly down the crowded four-lane boulevard on New Castle Ave. Dog, who was behind the steering wheel, nervously checked the mirrors in search of anyone who could be following them, and when he was sure the coast was clear he began to relax. "Nigga pass the blunt!" Dog said, veering through the rear view mirror at his boy Pretty E.

"I know nigga! Why you always babysitting the weed?" Hit Man asked.

"Fuck you two niggas! Y'all always bitchin!" replied Pretty E, as smoke escaped his mouth.

"Nigga, just pass the blunt!" Dog said, as he continued into the city limits.

The sun was just starting to set and the summer night skyline was a beautiful pink, as clouds melted away into the evening.

"Man, who we gonna get"? Asked Pretty E, as he fiddled around with the Desert Eagle pulling the duffle bag that sat behind the driver seat.

"I don't give a fuck! It's a whole bunch of nigga's on the list," Hit Man said, with assurance in his voice.

"Me either!" said Dog then paused before saying, "whass up with da boy Jamar?"

"Yeah, let's get dat nigga! I don't like his bitch ass anyway!" Hit Man spoke, still mad about the time Jamar fucked his baby's Mom.

"Yeah, let's get dat nigga!" Pretty E said, pointing the gun between the two front seats at the windshield.

"Nigga, what da fuck is you doin?" snapped Hit Man, as he leaned as far as he could towards the passenger door.

"My bad," Pretty E said, pulling the gun back to safety. Dog, Pretty E, and Hit Man were boys from back to the time they met in second grade, until they lost their virginity in middle school. They were just alike, separated only by the backgrounds of which they came from. Dog, whose real name was Michael Lollie, was from the

Clifton Park Projects. A single mom, and a dad who raised them from behind the bars of DE Correctional Center in Smyrna, Delaware, raised him and his two younger brothers. Hit Man, whose real name was Hakeeme Washington, on the other hand, had it rougher than any of the three. He had no father, and his mother was a heroin-addicted prostitute who was never around. He was the only boy of five kids and basically was raised by his sisters. Hit Man, who never really had a male role model in his life, searched the streets high and low and usually found comfort among the older guys in the projects. Consequently, he was led into a life of crime and hard knocks. He started out stealing from the local Jewel T Supermarket, but as he grew older the more serious his crimes became. Stealing cars and snatching pocket books became as common as breathing for Hit Man, until he ultimately became a drug dealer where he prospered. Pretty E, also known as Eric Davis, had it lovely all his life growing up in the upper middle class suburbs. His mother was a lawyer and his father was a doctor. Everything he needed or wanted was laid out in front of him. Pretty E had a silver spoon in his mouth, but was unhappy. His life held no excitement until he met his friends' everyday after school. As teens, and from then on he was turned out. Never again would he bear the boredom that the suburbs held for him. Dog drove the Acura over the bridge and rode into the city by way of 4th Street. Jamar was their target and he was loaded. He was one of the Nigga's in the way of their weight being pushed off to the other dealers throughout the city. Dog, Hit Man, and Pretty E were a team with a double hustle. They were killing them with the coke on the money tip, but slaughtering them in the "stick-up" game. It was the only way to fly in the two-G (2000), and they were the best.

Dog came to a slow stop on the corner of 3rd & Franklin Street and looked up and down in both directions. The open drug market was filled with crack heads and hustlers on every corner of the block.

"Yo! What chu need?" said a crack head, who approached the car as if it was a potential sell.

"Yo nigga! What da fuck is wrong wit you," said Hit Man as he rolled down the window before continuing, "Nigga do it look like I smoke crack?"

"Oh, oh, my bad family," said the crack head hearing the threat that went unsaid, "I thought y'all was somebody else."

"Yo, you see Jamar?" Hit Man asked.

"Nah, he just left. He said he had to go re-up," the crack head said, and before he could say another word, the car peeled away from the curb.

Dog sped away from the corner and made a left on 4th street headed to the Hilltop.

+   +   +   +

Jamar and his road dog Smooth pulled up in front of Sarah's house and parked one of Jamar's three luxury cars in between a trashcan and a van. Jamar reached under his seat and grabbed his glock 9mm handgun before pressing the button in his glove compartment to pop the trunk.

"Yo Nigga watch my back make sure ain't no police or nuffin watching us. You know them "stick-up" niggas ain't playin fair," said Jamar as he exited the 500 SE Benz Coupe. Smooth stood near the rear of the car shielding Jamar as he retrieved the duffle bag from the trunk.

"Shut da trunk cuz," said Jamar as he headed towards the house. Jamar and Smooth walked up the busted sidewalk ever so cautiously before they entered the dimly lit house and called Sarah's name.

Dog, Hit Man, and Pretty E had been following Jamar for weeks, and knew his every move. They were turning the corner onto Sarah's block just as Jamar and Smooth were entering the house. Dog drove slowly pass the house and parked two blocks away. Through the alley behind the row homes, they crept their way up to the side of Sarah's house. Peeping through the back window, Hit Man could see Jamar and Smooth sitting at the kitchen table. He turned to Dog and Pretty E and pointed in the direction of the front of the house, just as

they pulled on their masks. With their backs against the wall of the house, they eased their way to the front porch.

"Whass up baby!" asked Sarah excitedly, as she came walking out into the kitchen.

"Ain't nuffin," replied Jamar.

Sarah was 40 years old and still kind of cute. You could tell she was "Da Bomb" in her prime, but the drugs were beginning to take over her physical appearance. She had lost plenty of weight and her hair wasn't done yet just pulled into a dry ponytail that broke off at the edges.

"What'chu getting ready to do?" asked Sarah holding her hand up to her mouth, trying to cover up her two missing front teeth.

"Sit out here and bag dis shit up," said Jamar.

"You need me to do anything?" she asked.

"Yeah, don't let nobody in."

Smooth sat still at the table, while Jamar unlocked the lock that he had on the kitchen cabinet handles. Inside there were three kilos of crack cocaine, a scale, and some sandwich bags that sat waiting to hit the market. He grabbed one of the bricks and sat back down at the table and he and Smooth began weighing and bagging ounces in separate sandwich bags.

+   +   +   +

"Who is it?" asked Sarah, but didn't receive an answer. They knocked again and she still didn't receive an answer. She yanked the door open annoyingly expecting to see those bad ass little boys from down the street sprinting away from her door step, but was rudely greeted by the Desert Eagle Pretty E held in his hand. Sarah's heart dropped as she felt the cold steel underneath her chin. Pretty E had the barrel pushed so far up under her chin, she couldn't open her mouth to scream or talk.

"Bitch! Where they at?" spoke Pretty E in a low harsh tone of voice. All Sarah could do was point over her shoulder into the threshold of her house. The two masked men standing before her terrified her, and as she looked deeply into the eyes of the mask, she saw something she never seen before: DEATH!

"Please God, don't let these men kill me," she prayed. This was the closest she'd ever been to death, and from this moment on she promised herself and God that she'd never use drugs again. Pretty E saw the horror in her eyes, and that in itself fed his

adrenaline rush to the limit. He collared her up and led her into the house keeping the pistol under her chin. Sarah could barely walk as her knees trembled
with the idea of taking a bullet. "Please God, I'm begging you God. Please don't let them kill me," she prayed, leading them into the living room.

"Yo, stay right here with her, while I go out here to the kitchen," said Pretty E. Dog held his pistol to the small of Sarah's back, as Pretty E disappeared around the corner. Pretty E crept slowly down the hallway towards the voices he heard in the kitchen holding his gun out in front of him. He froze when a rotted out floor board squeaked, and stood still.

Jamar and Smooth sat at the table with their shirts off hanging over the back of their chairs, while they listened to a portable radio that sat on the counter. They were deeply concentrating on the drugs in front of them, as Jamar added and subtracted the drug money using a calculator.

"Yo, Nigga we came up off those last three birds some'em sweet!" said Jamar, excited.

"Dat's whass' up," responded Smooth with the blunt hanging from his lips, never lifting his head from the cocaine he was bagging. In an instant, Jamar and Smooth simultaneously cringed as they heard the floorboard squeak.

"Sarah!" called Jamar, "who was dat at the front door?"

"It was me Nigga! Now put your muthafuckin hands up!" said Pretty E as he stepped in the doorway pointing his pistol in their direction. "This is only a stick-up Nigga. Don't make dis shit no homicide!" He continued.

Jamar and Smooth sat at the table with their hands up shocked, as they watched the mask man make his way to the back door. Pretty E kept his gun on them as he fumbled with the locks. Hit Man came in carrying a duffle bag, and holding his pistol in front of him. The two gunmen made Smooth standup and back away from the table, while they forced Jamar to put the money and drugs in the duffle bag.

"If either one of you Niggas flinch wrong, Im' ma squeeze on you!" Hit Man assured them as Jamar filled the bag.

"What's dis nigga?" asked Pretty E, when he noticed the lock on the cabinets.

Jamar didn't say a word. His heart pumped rage and if only he could reach his gun he thought, "Im'ma kill one of these niggas!"

"Nigga you heard me!" said Pretty E, and smacked Jamar in the back of the head with the butt of the gun.

Jamar crumpled under with the forceful blow clutching his head in both hands. Pretty E grabbed him by his arm and pulled him to his feet. "Now open the lock nigga!" Pretty E demanded.

Pop! Pop! Pop! The pistol exploded causing Pretty E to jump. He kept his pistol on Jamar and turned to see what happened. What he saw was grotesque. Smooth was sprawled out on the floor shaking. Bullets had ripped half the side of his face off as he lay gasping for air.

"Yo! What happened?" asked Pretty E.

"Dat nigga tried to reach on me," replied Hit Man.

The outcome of Smooth reaching for his pistol had cost him his life. Blood was splattered everywhere, on the floor, the refrigerator, and the sink cabinets, and the sight made Jamar's stomach feel queasy.

"Nigga you want to be next? Well open these muthafuckin cabinets!" Pretty E snapped.

Dog bought Sarah into the kitchen when he heard the gunshots, and she screamed at the top of her lungs. The sight of Smooth lying out on the floor was too much for her to bear.

"Bitch shut da fuck up, before you be lying next to dat nigga!" Dog said.

"Yo, duct tape them two muthafuckas!" said Hit Man, and threw them the tape.

They sat Sarah on the floor next to Jamar and bound and gagged them with dishcloths, and tape. Pretty E went through Jamar's pockets until he found the keys. Once they found the keys, Pretty E opened the cabinets and their eyes grew wide with satisfaction.

"Yo come grab dis shit!" said Pretty E, when he saw the other two birds. Hit Man grabbed the half filled duffel bag and added the other kilos to their heist. "Come on lets bounce!" said Dog, hearing sirens in a distance.

"Yeah, lets do that," Hit Man added, throwing the duffel bag over his shoulder.

They were making their way out the back door when they heard Jamar mumble something under his breath.

"What chu say nigga?" asked Dog, as they all turned around. He reached down and snatched the tape from off his mouth, and asked him again.

"Pussy y'all should have killed me!" Jamar spoke with more pride than heart.

"Kill dat nigga!" said Hit Man, and Dog pulled the trigger. A bullet to the middle of Jamar's forehead, and one to his chest, clumped him over into Sarah's lap. Sarah screamed from the top of her lungs through the dishrag and tape as chunks of dark, almost black, blood oozed down her face. The masked men were gone.

+   +   +   +

Dog, Pretty E, and Hit Man darted down the alleyway with their masks still on. People were now crowding the outside of Sarah's house being nosy after hearing the gunshots. A couple of onlookers pointed down the side of Sarah's house, and gasped when they saw the three mask men running from the scene.

"Hurry up Man! Run!" yelled Pretty E, who was running in last place behind Dog and Hit Man.

They reached the car tired and out of breath and Pretty E collected the masks and placed them in a plastic bag, as Dog pulled away from the curb. Hit Man's heart began to pump even faster when he pulled the zipper back on the duffel bag, and was greeted by big faces and the three bricks of cocaine.

"Damn! This is about 50 g's, not counting the coke," said Hit Man satisfied.

"Yeah, well right now were going to stop at the Wa-Wa and get Rasul a money order," said Pretty E from the backseat. "Das the best thing you said all day, Nigga!" Dog and Hit Man spoke in unison after picking up the thousand-dollar money order from Wa-Wa. Dog continued down Route 13 headed for his apartment in Fox Run.

7

+   +   +   +

Det. Armstrong, a twenty-year veteran on the task force unit, who specialized in robberies and drug operations, was accompanied by his partner of two years Det. Cohen. When they arrived on the scene, the two made their way through the crowd of on-lookers, up the busted pavement, and onto the crime scene. Sarah sat on the plastic lawn furniture covered in a blanket shaking franticly, as officers asked questions for their reports. Det. Armstrong and Det. Cohen excused the officers in question, and asked Sarah their own slew of questions. It was useless because Sarah had no direct or concrete details of the assailants. Det. Armstrong, upset, walked away from Sarah shaking his head. Det. Cohen followed his partner across the other side of the porch where they stood alone, away from the other officers.

"What's up?" asked Det. Cohen.

"Nothing! Just a little upset that we have no eyewitnesses with anything of importance.

"That's all," replied Det. Armstrong.

"Tell me about it. It's going to be impossible to build a case with no leads," added Det. Cohen. Once inside the house, Det. Armstrong and Cohen immediately smelled the gunpowder from the assailants' guns. They walked through the house and passed several crime unit teams dusting for prints and photographing the house. A leading officer approached the two detectives and led them into the kitchen. Det. Armstrong entered the kitchen and observed the bloody scene and his reaction was just as casual as he would be when shaving his beard. While Det Cohen wasn't used to these type crime scenes yet, he entered the kitchen with his hand over his mouth, and dry heaved at the sight of the blood splattered throughout the interior of the room. Det. Armstrong stood over top of the body that was closest to the refrigerator, which was lying on his back. He knew the victim named Smooth and felt bad for his mother. Det. Armstrong had been arresting
Smooth, real name Dave Shepard, up since he was a juvenile. His mother was one of the few mothers that stood by her son after he turned towards a life of crime. He shook his head and decided at that moment he would be the one to break the news to his mother. Det.

Cohen just stood there shaking his head. There were no leads. This was the third robbery/shooting this month, but the first casualties. Det. Cohen felt a pattern beginning. He looked at his partner, and before he could speak, Det. Armstrong spoke. "Whoever is doing these robberies knows what he is doing." "I know. It's almost flawless, but they'll slip and we'll be here to catch'em," spoke Det. Cohen.

"I hope so," replied Det. Armstrong, "I hope so."

"I promise. Now come on, let's get outta here."

Chapter Two

It was the summer of 1992, and the projects in Riverside were flooded. Luxury cars lined 27th & Bower Street like a car show, as the girls stood around in "Daisy Dukes," halter-tops, and Nike Air Max trying to get a date from one of the big boys in the city. Everybody was out today, from all over Wilmington DE, a small, but fast, city. The corner was packed and a huge circle surrounded the crap game.

All the "Hustlers" were there. Mick and Huff-Nasty from the 2-6 projects, Michael and Lee from the Riverside projects, Raquan and Steve from South Bridge, G Good & B.K. also from the Bridge, and K.B., Brick and Dan from the West Side: all represented the Small Wonder. Rasul, Dog, Hit Man, and Pretty E were young bucks up and coming. The game had been a high stake one, and the pot usually exceeded 5 Gs easily. A couple of brothers from the East Side came through as the game went on. Damon, Smalls, and Rueban along with L.B. and Gig pulled up in two twins 735i BMWs' and jumped into the game. Everything was going smoothly until a couple cats from up Market St. came through on some Rah-Rah shit.

"Nigga! Your point was 8!" shouted Bugs from up Market St., as Rasul picked-up the pot totaling $6,500.00 dollars.

"Nigga my point was 6!" shouted Rasul, back at Bugs. Tempers were flaring as the two stood face-to-face arguing about the crap game. The brothers on the sideline tried to break-up what was about to happen, because they knew how Bugs got. He would try to punk the young boy out of the money or some'um, but they knew these young boys were about their work.

"Yo, AK, point seen, money loss," said Dog, from the circle.

"You ain't got nothing to do wit dis, young boy," Bugs shot back.

"You heard what he said Hoss!" Hit Man intervened.

"What? You young muthafuckas want some," Bugs asked, as his boys approached the young boys. That was the last word Bugs got to say, as a bullet tore threw his back dropping him like a fly. Rasul stood over top of him, as the crowd scattered, scurrying to their cars.

"Now what! Nigga!" said Rasul, as he pointed the gun in his face. The girls on the corner were screaming for Rasul to stop, but his mind was blank. If not for Dog, Pretty E, and Hit Man, Rasul would be doing life in jail.

Rasul jumped and sat up in his bed, as he awoke from his dream. It had been a long 8 years ago, but he remembered the day like it happened yesterday. Rasul was the other quarter of the whole. It was made up with Dog, Pretty E, and Hit Man. But, he was the one out of the four who masterminded their destiny. His 8 years sentence would be up in 30 days due to good time, and working in laundry at the prison. As he sat up in his bunk, he wondered how it was going to be when he got out.

"Chow-time!" yelled the CO from down the tier. "You got 20 minutes on the door!"

"You going to chow, Frankie?" asked Rasul, as he walked out the cell going to the bathroom to wash his face, and brush his teeth.

"Yeah, I'm going," replied Frankie, as he slipped his feet into his shower shoes.

Frankie was Rasul's cellie and mentor. He took to Rasul the first day he saw him, and showed him the ins and outs of the prison. Frankie, an old Italian man with graying hair, looked sorta like an aging Richard Grier, but for 65 yrs. old, he was well in shape. Rasul and Frankie had been cellmates for the past 5 years now and have grown a special bond, kinda like a father and son. Frankie himself has three grown daughters, and two granddaughters; but after meeting Rasul he finally got what he always wanted, a son. Frankie was fascinated at how close Rasul and his three friends were. Since the first day they brought Rasul into his cell, he never went more than three days without receiving a piece of mail or photos from them. "These boys are special," Frankie would say to himself. He told Rasul about his whole life, never concealing anything, except his position in the Mafia.

Frankie was the boss of all bosses in the Capelli Familia. Rasul kind of put things together in his own mind, but was never too sure about his thoughts. The more Frankie talked to Rasul, the more assured his plans were for Rasul. Frankie knew he had all the power in the mainstream, but with these four young boys he could control the inner city Ghettos too. The thought made Frankie smile.

Frankie and Rasul made their way across the Federal prisons compound headed to the chow hall. Rasul, carrying the afternoon's News Journal in his hands reading an article, turned to Frankie excitedly.

"Frankie look!" said Rasul then continued, "I bet this was my boys." Frankie read the headlines of the gruesome discovery of the two bodies discovered by the police. He examined every inch of the article trying to see if the police found any flaws in what the police named a robbery homicide. He felt good to have not found any mistakes, but was upset with Rasul for assuming.

"Rasul, some things are better left unsaid. Now how do you know for sure that was your boys?" asked Frankie.

"I don't," replied Rasul.

"See that's what I'm talking about. If they did do it, you just gave them away. Do you see where I'm coming from?" Before Rasul could answer Frankie started again, "The fewer that you know, the safer you are. Never give anyone any ammunition to use against you, you hear? Keep your mouth shut! That's rule number one."

"I mean I only said something cause it was you Frankie. I wouldn't say anything to anyone else," said Rasul.

"Keep it to yourself," replied Frankie, then he threw the newspaper in the trash.

+   +   +   +

After ditching the stolen Acura on Rte. 9 last night, Dog, Hit Man, and Pretty E jumped into Hit Man's Lexus LS 450 and drove to Dog's apartment in Fox Run. There, the three men sat and divided the money and put the cocaine in the safe. The apartment was empty, except for the T.V. and Play station 2 that sat in the living room. This was their stash house and the D.L. spot where they just came to relax. When everything was divided and put away, they all left and drove to Pretty E's house in Saddle Brook.

Hit Man's LS 450, Dog's station wagon Benz, and Pretty E's Cadillac Escalade pulled in front of Pretty E's two story home and parked. The three went inside and went over their books figuring out who owed them money, and who was ready to buy. They came up a long way since Rasul had went away, and they were counting the days until their boy came home where he belonged.

"Yo! We gonna throw a bash for dat nigga when he touchdown, you hear?" said Dog.

"Damn right! Dat nigga deserves a bash, after doing 8 like that, feel me?" asked Pretty E, as he broke-up buds and tossed them in the Garcia Vega shell.

"Damn right I feel you nigga! We gonna throw dat shit up at a 'Brave New World' nightclub for dat nigga."

"Yo Dog, get in touch with the boy Cholly AK up in Chester and get dat number. You know he had the boy Bleek up there last month," said Hit Man.

"Word! I forgot all about dat shit, yo! Im'ma do that. Try to get the boy Prodigy and the whole Q.B., feel me?" Dog said.

"Dem niggas probably only want like 30 G's, you know? We only want them to drop like two cuts," Pretty E added.

"Whatever them cats want nigga, we got'em. Dat's our mans' coming home, you know?" said Dog.

"I feel you said Pretty E, and held the Bic to the end of the Garci. Wait till dat nigga see how we came up," Pretty E continued as he passed the Garci to Hit Man.

Dog, Pretty E, and Rasul had come up in the game. After they all caught that little 6-month bid together on some petty shit in Ferris in '92 for conspiracy with Rasul, they were on a mission. Through selling keys, and the robberies they had been doing, they each were sitting on a cool $250,000.00 dollars a piece including Rasul. Pretty E sat back in his plush leather Lazy Boy and soaked up every inch of his earnings, as he looked around the elaborate setup in his home. The off-white carpet was setoff to a tee by the navy blue lining, and butter soft leather furniture. The glass mirror end tables and coffee table sat pretty while a crystal ball and jack occupied its space. The screen TV sat lavishly in front of the bay window, and the

Bose surround sound system thumped softly the tunes of Dave Hollister's, "One Woman Man."

"Yeah nigga, it's going to be on when Rasul hit," said Pretty E grabbing the Garci as it completed the cipher.

"Yo, whass up with those two Philly broads, Tameeka, and Tammy?" asked Hit Man.

"Oh, you know my Boo is chillin' nigga," said Pretty E, talking about Tammy.

"Whass'up wit Tameeka?" he asked again.

"I don't know nigga, I think she fuck wit her son's pop," replied Pretty E. Just then his pager went off. "Damn yo! Soon as you said some'em about dat girl, here she goes paging me," said Pretty E.

"Damn, she musta knew we was talking about her," Hit Man said, and smiled.

+   +   +   +

It was only two more days until Rasul came home, and Shelly lay awake in BoBo's bed. "Damn, what am I going to do?" she thought, as she looked over at BoBo sleeping. Rasul was her man, and now she felt as though she wasn't ready for him to come home. Her shit was all fucked up. The 8 years flew by like clockwork, and for the past two she'd been in a heavy relationship with BoBo. She always kept in touch with Dog, Pretty E, and Hit Man, and even visited Rasul sometimes when they would take her, or she used BoBo's BMW, but what now? "It has been 8 long years," she kept telling herself, but the more she thought, the more she anticipated Rasul's home coming." I just hope Dog and them don't be running their mouths," thought Shelly, as she realized just how fucked up her past had become.

Dog's girl took the kids and the Benz wagon so he drove the gold GS 300 up Chester to pick up Cholly AK. Cholly AK was standing on the corner in the "Bennett Homes Projects" when Dog turned the corner.

"Whass'up with da bull Dog?" Cholly AK said, and smiled as he approached the Lexus. "I see you finally got this shit sitting on twenties nigga!"

"Yeah, yeah. You know a nigga trying to keep up wit yo baby boy," said Dog grinning.

14

"Nigga, I'm tryin' to keep up wit Chu," Cholly AK shot back.

"Yo AK. Is you ready or what?" asked Dog.

"Yeah, but stop over dis broad's crib for me right quick. She keeps paging me like I owe her some'em, or some'em!" said Cholly AK as he jumped in the passenger seat.

"Dats what you get for being a playa nigga. You need to just lay back with the broad what's her name?" said Dog.

"Man, it's too much Cholly AK for one broad, feel me?" asked Cholly AK grabbing his crotch, smiling.

"You just like dat nigga Pretty E. Swear y'all playin," said Dog.

"Yeah. Where my nigga at anyway?" asked Cholly AK.

"He's out with Hit Man handling all the other shit for Rasul, you know. Buying the car, and getting the condo setup for that nigga for when he comes home the day after tomorrow," answered Dog.

"Yo, I ain't seen dat nigga since we was up Glen Mills in 92", said Cholly AK, then continued, "damn, dat nigga done went flat. It's the 2G," he finished, talking to no one that time, just reflecting on that long ass bid.

"Who you telling," answered Dog, as he pulled in front of the girl's house Cholly AK directed him to as they talked.

"I'll be right back," said Cholly AK, as the girl stood in the doorway. Dog took one look at the girl standing in the doorway, and got out his car as if to check the tires. "Yo AK! Where her girls at?" asked Dog.

"Here she go in here," the girl in the doorway shot back.

"Tell her to come here," said Dog.

"Nigga, I thought you was in a rush to get up the city!" yelled Cholly AK.

"Shit. If her girl look like dat, we might not be going," said Dog smiling. Dog watched as the girl strutted out of the house in her linen Gucci outfit. She looked like a dark chocolate joint, and the beige outfit set her smooth skin off like black diamonds.

"You wanted me?" she asked.

"Yeah! Whass'up wit you? Do you have a name?" asked Dog.

"Yeah! My name is Sharell, but they call me 'Sexy.' Sike! I'm just playin," she said.

"Shit. I thought you was dead serious, bad as you is," replied Dog.

"Boy shut up! You ain't gone be gassing my head up Dog," she said turning her face into a serious frown.

"How you know my name?" he asked.

"Boy, who don't know you? You probably just like your boy Pretty E", she said.

"How you know him?"

"Cause he tried to fuck me one night, after he gave me a ride home from New Alternatives up in Philly, but he was too pretty for me." Dog bagged up. He knew his boy like the back of his hand, and when she said dat, she wasn't lying. That cat took longer than women getting dressed.

"Well what happened after dat?" asked Dog.

"Nuffin, he ain't never come back," replied Sharell.

"Nah, I don't get down like dat. Just give me your number, and I'll be back when me and Cholly AK return from New York," Dog said.

"Why y'all going up there?" asked Sharell.

"Cause we gotta holler at Prodigy, and see if them niggas gone do a show for me, you know?"

"How much do they be wanting?" she asked being nosy.

"See now you asking me too many questions. Nah, I'm just playin. They probably want like 30 GS, you know?" said Dog.

"Dats too much. Shit I'll rap for that," replied Sharell.

"I bet you will," said Dog, thinking dat and a whole lot of other shit."

"Umm-Hmm. Why you say it like dat? You probably wanted to say some'em else. Here boy, get out of my face," said Sharell smiling and pushing her number in his hand. Dog pulled away from the curb as soon as Cholly AK got back in the car, as the two girls watched the Lexus bend around the corner with the system pounding.

+   +   +   +

Pretty E pulled his Escalade out of the Brandywine Condominiums and headed straight for the Benz dealership in

Cherry Hill, NJ. Everything went smoothly at the rental office, and with the extra thousand, the lady let them move in tomorrow.

"Yo Sharon. After you sign for his car, I'm going to give you like 10 G'S. I want you to go and fully furnish the condo. Don't hold back get all top notch shit! If you need more money, call me," said Pretty E, talking to his cousin.

"Alright," she said, and then tapped Hit Man on the shoulder." Baby, do you still love me?"

"Girl, go ahead with dat shit. You ain't gone keep playin wit me," said Hit Man.

"Nigga you know dat Davis broad got you sprung," added Pretty E.

"I know it too!" said Sharon rubbing his ears.

Sharon was Hit Man's ol' head. They used to mess around a couple of years ago, but she went back to her husband after about two months of messing around. Sharon was 38 and 14 years Hit Man's senior, plus she knew he was young, and didn't want to go through the games. At times though, they still got together and handled their business.

"Girl, you the one dats sprung!" Hit Man shot back at her.

"Yes, I am. But you ain't gone do right," replied Sharon, and leaned forward from the back seat, putting her arms around Hit Man's neck.

It seemed like no time and Pretty E was pulling off onto the NJ Turnpike headed into Cherry Hill. He rolled down the windows and turned the A.C. on high, spraying some cherry air freshener into the vents.

"Yo, any of y'all want to hit this blunt before I put it out?" asked Pretty E, then continued, "you know these muthafuckas ain't trying to sell a nigga shit especially if we smelling like trees, you know?"

"That's a lie," blurted out Sharon, "cause soon as these people see some cash money, they ain't worried about a damn thing."

"Word," Hit Man stated.

The Benz dealership was damn near empty, except for the cars and staff. Pretty E pulled the Black Escalade up right next to the entrance door and parked. "Come on," he told Sharon, as Hit

17

Man drove off to find a place to park. Entering the place all eyes
were on them. Sharon looked at her Lil' cousin and whispered,
"they must have saw your truck," as the employees rushed to their
assistance. It was three white men, and a sista that were
approaching.

"Nice shoes," said the sista, as she approached Sharon.

"Thank you girl," replied Sharon, and that's all it took. The
two walked off and straight out the doors to the outside display.
Pretty E looked at the three white men smiled and said, "Women!"
They gave him a phony smile and walked back to their desks.
Outside, Pretty E walked up on Sharon, Hit Man, and the sista as
they stood near a row of 600's.

"Whass'up? Which one you like? The Candy Apple Red
or this Pearl White Jawn?" Hit Man pointing at it.

"I like the Pearl White Jawn," said Pretty E.

"Me too," replied Hit Man.

"Excuse me sista," said Pretty E, cutting into Sharon and
her conversation.

"Yes," she answered.

"What they want for it?" asked Pretty E, tapping the Benz
on the hood.

"One hundred and twenty thousand," replied the sista.

"Well what do I need to do to leave the lot?" asked Pretty
E. "It depends on your credit, and place of work," responded the
sista. That was no problem and he knew it. Several years ago he
purchased a catering business from an older cat that was retiring
from the business for his cousin Sharon. She had turned the
makeshift business into a permanent and quite prosperous seafood
& soul food catering company. She hosted major events for big
companies and banks, wedding receptions, and banquets, so the
background check would go well," Pretty E thought to himself.
That was the reason why he used her for the particular thing
because her credentials were good. Once they were seated in front
of the desk inside the dealership, for the first time, Pretty E learned
her name.

"Mrs. Denise Ringgold" was written in gold letters across a
marble nameplate that sat on her desk. This is what Pretty E
wanted as he looked on her desk and at the pictures of her and her

family. "Later for dat shit", as he snapped from his thoughts. "I'm only 24 years old. I got plenty of time for dat shit, my nigga is coming home!" he thought again, as Sharon and Denise waited for the people at the credit union to finish the check on Sharon. After hanging up the phone, Denise smiled and began filling out the paperwork. "Everything went smoothly sista," said Denise to Sharon. Within minutes after signing the paperwork, Pretty E returned from the Escalade carrying a leather deposit bag containing 20 G's and handed it to Denise. Denise counted the money twice then slid the key across her desk, and said. "Thank you sista. I needed that, well… this sale to get the commission.

It's hard being a black sista doing this job, especially with it being dominated by men. On top of that, it doesn't pay all dat well anyway."

"Anytime sista. We need to have each other's backs in all situations. Even if we hadn't got off on the right foot, I wasn't dealing with those white men, especially when I seen one of my people, you know?" said Sharon.

"I heard dat," said Denise, giving her that look only a sista can give, then leading her to her new 600SL. Sharon rolled down the window and thanked Denise again before pulling off. As she left the car lot, she tooted the horn and smiled at the envious looking white men staring through the showcase window.

+   +   +   +

Jerome sat his Ford Expedition on the other side of Queens Bridge, waiting for Dog & Cholly AK. He had just hung up the phone from talking to them, and told them to meet him there in 15 minutes. Dog & Cholly AK was right on time, and followed him across Queens Bridge headed into the projects. Jerome talked to Dog from his cell phone, as he drove wildly through the city streets. Apparently, Prodigy's manager and road dog Swiff, was waiting for them at the studio ready to discuss the plans.

Cholly AK and Jerome knew each other from previous engagements, so after introducing Dog, shit started coming together.

The three men walked into the studio and sat on the leather sofa in the lobby. Queens Bridge finest Emcees' hung on the walls in huge glass picture frames and a sharp sista in business attire sat

19

behind the desk. "When you gone let me take you to dinner girl?" asked Jerome, flashing a gold fanged-out smile.

"As soon as you stop being a player," she blushed, as Jerome tapped Cholly AK's knee and smiled.

"Nigga you ain't playin," responded Cholly AK, and the two shared a chuckle. Swiff walked from behind the door in his black Armani suit and Gator boots and smiled when he saw Jerome and Cholly AK. "Whass happening' baby," he said showing his excitement seeing them.

"Whass up Cuz. This is my man's Dog, from down Delaware," Jerome said.
Dog and Swiff went to the back and handled their business, while Jerome and Cholly AK walked down the street to the Chinese store. Swiff explained that he could get Mob Deep, and C.N.N. down there to perform two songs for 20 GS, and with Nas 30. Dog said, "C.O.D.," and signed the receipt along with Swiff.

Dog handed Swiff 20 G's up-front, and 10 would be given to him after the performances on Friday night, then the two went back to the lobby.

"Y'all handle dat?" asked Cholly AK, with a mouth full of shrimp and broccoli.

"Yeah nigga, let's bounce," replied Dog.

"Alright brothers, y'all drive safe going home aw'ight?" said Jerome, "and I'll see y'all Friday," as Dog and Cholly AK left the studio.

+   +   +   +

Det. Armstrong was harassing people all month long trying to catch a wire from the streets as to who was doing the robberies. It seemed as though the dealers were just as clueless as him; he concluded after hours of interrogations. Nothing was going his way, and then it hit him. James Clark! James Clark had been a confidential reliable informant for Det. Armstrong. He pulled up to the base house on the corner of 29th and West Street, and got out of his unmarked police car.

James had been up for three days straight smoking crack, and drinking 28/20 Mad Dog. He was on his hands and knees searching for crumbs of cocaine that may have spilled into his carpet when the knock caused him to jump. From the way the

20

knock sounded, he knew it was the police. He rose to his feet looking back and forth at the front and back doors, wired from the crack: paranoid. He pulled his glass stem from his pocket and stuffed it down in the sofa before walking to the door.

"Who is it?" asked James.

"It's Det. Armstrong James. Now open the door!" demanded the detective. Det. Armstrong was taken back by the odor that escaped the house, and the appearance of James. James stood there in his soiled jeans and no shirt looking like a skeleton. His face was sunken in and so dirty it almost looked black. He smiled a rotten tooth smile and asked the detective to come in. The odor from his mouth put tears in Armstrong's eyes, which caused his tongue to touch the roof of his mouth, as if he were about to throw-up.

"No thanks," replied Det. Armstrong. I just came to ask you a few questions, that's all," he finished, reaching into his pocket pulling out a wad of money. He peeled off a 20-dollar bill and begun, "have you heard anything about the robberies that's been taking place in the city?"

"Dat depends," answered James, extending his hand. Det. Armstrong began placing twenties in his hand the more he talked. When he finished he had given James $180.00 dollars, but it was well worth it. James told Det. Armstrong everything he knew about a crew of young guys named Dog, Hit Man, and Pretty E. From what he heard, the young guys were ruthless plus major suppliers in the city, and it just seemed strange that they never had any problems. Det. Armstrong knew them all too well, and had kept his eye on them every since the shooting in 92, paralyzing a guy from Market St. He knew they were dealing, but never put the two together. Det. Armstrong left the man standing on the porch, and jumped in his car. The investigation had begun.

+   +   +   +

Yo! You hungry cuz?" asked Pretty E, as he drove back over the Delaware Memorial Bridge.

"Damn right. A nigga could go for a cheese steak right about now!" replied Hit Man, leaning back into the seats rubbing his stomach.

"Whass up? G. & P's? Asked Pretty E once again.

"Yeah, why not?" said Hit Man.

Pretty E pulled his truck in the Rite-Aid parking lot across the street from G. & P's sub shop on Market St. Pretty E got out. "Damn it's too many heads up in that muthafucka!" said Hit Man, looking at the crowd of people in the sub shop.

"Ain't nuffin nigga. All we gotta do is hit Boo off with like 10 or 20 dollars extra, so we can get our shit and bounce," said Pretty E. Det. Armstrong was just turning onto Market St., when he saw Pretty E and Hit Man going into the sub shop. He made a u-turn and pulled into the parking lot right in back of Pretty E's Cadillac truck. His mind was racing as he tried to figure out what to do next. Harassing them would be stupid he thought because he had nothing on them. Plus, he wasn't one hundred percent sure they were doing the stick-ups. He only knew one thing; they were going to tell him something.

Pretty E and Hit Man came across the street carrying their bags, and slurping on their sodas as they approached the truck. Pretty E sat behind the steering wheel and tilted it up so he could un-wrap his steak that sat in his lap. He turned the key back in the ignition, and let the C. D player melt the airwaves at a low tune.

"Damn Brother! That babe got you like dat?" said Hit man sourly, as Carl Thomas' song "I Wish" played softly.

"Hell no! I'm just on some chill shit right now," replied Pretty E. "I ain't wit dat hard shit all the time, you know?" he finished. "Man I ain't wit dat shit at all, you can save that shit for the wee-hours," said Hit Man, pressing the C.D. player and turning the volume up, as Prodigy's "Keep It Thorough" vibrated the seats. "Yeah Nigga, I rap like no-one can fuck wit me!" Hit Man emulated the song making hand gestures towards Pretty E. Pretty E just smiled and took another chunk out of his cheesesteak.

Det. Armstrong snuck up behind the truck, and crept up to the driver's side window. With his ring on his pointer finger, he tapped the glass getting Pretty E's attention.

"Yo muthafucka! What da fuck is wrong wit you, tapping your ring on my shit?" snapped Pretty E.

"Hey guys," Det. Armstrong said, ignoring Pretty E's remark. "How y'all doing today? I see life is treating y'all well," he finished with a smile.

"Man. What da fuck do you want? You wanna search the truck or some' um?" asked Pretty E, pissed that the cop was fucking wit them.

"Now, now, now, calm down, I only want to ask you a few questions, that's all. For starters where'd you get the money for this nice truck?" asked Armstrong.

"I hit the powerball muthafucka!" answered Pretty E.

"As you know, there's a lot of robberies' going on," added the Detective.

"Man. I don't know shit. Do you cuz?" asked Pretty E, turning towards Hit Man.

"I just want y'all to be careful, you dig?" asked Armstrong giving them an odd smile.

"Man. Roll da window up on that Muthafucka!" said Hit Man plainly.

"Yo Detective. What do you want?" asked Pretty E, getting angry.

"Oh! Do you really want to know? Alright, Dig this. I want you two sorry little punks to pay me a grand a week, every week or I'm coming to get all three of you muthafucka's, understood? See, I know y'all are supplying quantities of drugs to the street dealers, and one happens to be my informant," he lied.

"But I'll tell you this, give me my money, and it's like you'll have a license," he finished, with a smile, tossing a business card onto his lap.

"Gimmie a call," he said, and walked away.

+   +   +   +

It gets better, order another round
It's about to go down.
I got six model chicks, with six bottles of Cryst...
"Give it to me," by Jay Z pumped loudly through the surround sound system at Cholly AK's condo in West Chester. He and Dog stood on the side of the Jacuzzi staring, as the two girls Sharell and Janeen, kissed and played with each other passionately.

"Get in!" said Sharell, looking at Dog, then, throwing her thong at him playfully. He continued to watch as the girl Janeen poured Moet down Sharell's body, and catching it with her mouth at Sharell's crotch. Seeing this, Dog knew for sure Pretty E had

23

slayed the pussy, and Dog wasn't about to let it fly past him either. Cholly AK was two steps ahead of Dog and was already getting in the Jacuzzi, carrying a fresh bottle of Moet.

"What? I know you ain't shy!" asked Janeen, rubbing her titties at Dog teasingly.

"I know nigga! Pull dat little muthafucka out and get in," said Cholly AK.

"What little muthafucka nigga!" replied Dog, dropping his shorts and boxers all in one movement. Sharell and Janeen's eyes grew wide with satisfaction, seeing that Dog's dad blessed him well. After going some rounds freak style with the broads, Dog's cell phone rang.

+   +   +   +

"Doggie style!" answered Dog cheerfully, picking up his cell phone.

"Where you at nigga?" asked Pretty E. "Chillin' wit da boy Cholly AK and the broads Janeen and Sharell up Chester, in da Jacuzzi," replied Dog, stressin the word Jacuzzi.

"Nigga stop playin!" said Pretty E.

"Man, I'm dead serious!" said Dog.

"Nigga, you know I used to hit dat right?" Pretty E said, hyped.

"Boy. You don't know what chu missing!" assured Dog, as Sharell smiled, knowing she got da bomb shot.

"Man guess what? You know the Det. Armstrong? Well he rolled up on me and Hit Man today talking 'bout he wants a "G" a week. He said some cat we be serving is his snitch. Man that cracker is crooked as hell," said Pretty E.

"So now what?" asked Dog?

"The Nigga left a card," responded Pretty E.
"Well hold on to it, til I get there. I got some' um for that ass!" said Dog, and hung up the phone.

Chapter Three

Using one of his phone calls for the week, Frankie called the hang out spot, "Lil' Italy" and asked for Joey "The Fox," Vito." Joey "The Fox" was the next in charge and had been running the family for the past 10 years. He earned his name hands down, displaying his fox like characteristics continuously. Sly, sneaky, and silent was his forte, and he was deadly. Joey was the under boss and now as he received directions from Frankie, he didn't second-guess any of them.

"Hey Joey," began Frankie. "Listen! do you remember me saying anything about my cell-mate, the young black kid?"

"I'm not sure Boss," answered Joey.

"Well listen. I've come to love'em, you know? Like a son, and I want the best for him, understand? See, he has a crew. It's four of them and they're tuff! I mean really tuff! Never mind. Listen, call Lenny Ionni and tell him I'm sending the four of them over there for a job. I want you to keep an eye on them. Keep them outta trouble until I get my ass outta the can in 90 days, you hear?"

"Yeah Boss, but," said Joey before being cutoff.

"But nothing! Do as I say Joey, you hear? And keep them outta trouble by all means!" said Frankie as he had planned. He just jotted down the directions on that mental piece of paper in his head.

Rasul paced the floor in his cell like a caged animal. "Only eleven more hours," he thought, as plans of being with Shelly was on his mind. The radio station was doing a flashback on the life and career of the late Biggie Smalls, and flooded the airways with his music. "Damn dat nigga was tight!" exclaimed Rasul to himself, as he sung along with his favorite rapper.

"I been in this game for years, it made me an animal.
It's roles to dis shit, I wrote me a manual
A step by step booklet for you to get
Your game on track, not your wig pushed back."

"It's the 10 crack commandments!" Rasul continued to shout, pumping his fist in the air to the beat. Frankie entered the cell and turned the radio down to a murmur. "Rasul, have a seat!"

said Frankie, as he sat on his bunk and tapped a place for Rasul to sit. Rasul sat down and Frankie began. "Listen son. There have been a whole lot of things I wanted to tell you, and for starters, I've grown to love you. I love you like one of my own," said Frankie. Frankie knew there weren't any male figures in Rasul's life. So from the beginning he took on that role. "Look, I don't want you or any of your friends getting into trouble. Y'all have a lot of potential and can do some real good things for yourselves. I've set up a job for you on the streets, and I want you to go check in with some friends of mine."

"Man, I don't know none of those people, I'll just wait for you to come home in 90 days," said Rasul.

"Listen, their friends of mine, and there're going to do me a favor, by keeping y'all out of trouble. O.K.? Just trust me, I got plans for you and your boys," said Frankie. "Aw right man, but I ain't doing no working!" said Rasul.

+   +   +   +

Shelly laid the phone back on the receiver, and sat up in bed. It was 12:00 midnight Thursday, and Rasul was getting out in 9 hours. She stood up and walked over to her closet door grabbing her towel, to take a quick shower before Dog arrived. He had just told her on the phone that he'd be there in 45 minutes because it was a long ride from Wilmington, DE to Bradford, PA. Shelly stood in front of the mirror drying off, and shook her head in shame. The years had treated her body well, and she still was as beautiful as when Rasul left, but her heart and soul ached. Shelly stared deep into her eyes and for the first time realized what she had become. The streets had rinsed her clean of purity and coated her mind with material gains, and a guilty conscience. Many of nights just for money, and a want to be seen attitude, she slept with drugs dealers from Philly to Jersey. The thought made Shelly's heart thump loud in her ears. "How could I have been so stupid?" thought Shelly, beating herself up. "At least I didn't have any kids on him," she tried to compensate her mishaps.

Dog pulled up in front of Shelly's mom's house in Pretty E's Cadillac Escalade. "Damn I told this bitch to be ready!" he snapped after blowing the horn several times. Dog started disliking Shelly the moment Rasul went to jail. "That bitch don't

26

love my nigga!" he would say when he saw Shelly out in the clubs partying. He heard nearly all the rumors, and on occasions heard cats talking about how they had her and her girls at the motels and shit. He would just walk by and shake his head in disgust, but never once told Rasul anything. His reasons were not to cause any unnecessary stresses on his boy's already stressful situation.

Shelly opened up her front door and hollered out the screen door, "Here I come!" Dog stared at Shelly and for the first time lusted on her beauty. "What the fuck am I thinking?" he asked himself, as she swayed her hips provocatively. Dog, feeling guilty, still had to admit it himself, Shelly looks good. Shelly was mixed, half Black and Korean, and her light almost tan skin complimented her slanted eyes. She looked like an island woman.

"Hey Dog! You ready to go get my baby? 'Cause I can't wait!" exclaimed Shelly, who was already over zealous.

"Yeah! I can't wait to my nigga gets home!" he added, just as excited.

"Well y'all ain't going to be keepin' my baby out all night long and shit, cause I ain't havin' dat!" She smiled.

"Dat's what your mouth says!" Dog replied. "You know I got da boys from Queens Bridge coming down to "Brave New World" for his coming home party!"

"You do?" asked Shelly, wanting to go.

"Word!" replied Dog.

Shelly wanted to go to the party bad, because she knew all the ballers would be out. "Damn! I can't go up there," she thought, thinking about how many of them she had sexed. "Dat's all I need to give Rasul some'em to leave me for," she thought some more.

"Why? You commin?" asked Dog.

"Nah! Im'ma chill and let y'all do y'all's thing ,you know?" replied Shelly.

"I feel you," answered Dog, reading her mind.

+   +   +   +

Rasul packed the last of his letters and pictures in a bag, and headed out of the cell. The tier's hallway was packed with other inmates' playing cards and chess on stacked boxes. Frankie walked directly behind Rasul, as inmates said their last goodbyes and wished him well on his return to the world. Rasul sat his

27

belongings down at the tier door, and turned around embracing Frankie with a hug. It was harder than Rasul thought it would be leaving his friend/father behind in this hellhole. Frankie noticed the tears weld up in Rasul's eyes and said, "I'll be fine. I'm right behind you in 90 days, alright? Don't forget to go to Lenny's Construction Company, O.K.?" said Frankie. One word would have brought Rasul to tears, so he just nodded his head and followed the guard out the door.

McKean Federal Prison looked fabulous from the outside. The flowerbeds leading up to the gatehouse along side of the sidewalks were well kept and blossoming beautifully. "Damn! What's taking them so long?" snapped Shelly, looking at her Gucci watch that read 9:30.

"Chill girl. He'll be out in a minute. You know they have to get the paperwork right!" replied Dog.

"Well it seems to me that they should have been had dat shit right, he been here 8 years!" said Shelly. Dog caught some movement in the rear view window, as he turned to Shelly about to speak. Shelly, following his eye movement, looked too as the big steel gate began to slide open. She jumped out the truck and ran full speed towards Rasul with her arms out.

"Hey Baby Girl," said Rasul, lifting her from her feet and spinning her around.

"Hey Bay!" replied Shelly, then kissed him softly causing her panties to wet. Rasul was her first and only love: the one who took her virginity.

"Whass'up my nigga!" shouted Dog, sitting on the roof of the Caddie.

"Got damn baby! Dis how y'all ballin?" said Rasul, as he stared at the twenties sparkling on the truck.

"And you know it nigga! This ain't the half," assured Dog, smiling. The two embraced, while Shelly stood off to the side. She knows Dog, Hit Man, and Pretty E were getting money, she just didn't know how much. Looking at the truck sparked her curiosity to new levels as her hunger for money grew. All types of thoughts ran threw her head as she tried to figure a way to the money. "I know one thing, if Rasul don't start getting some money, I'm carrying my ass back to BoBo," she thought. Shelly had fallen in love with BoBo two years ago. She had him wrapped around her finger and spent his money like water. On occasion, she would go out of town and set cats up, so BoBo and his boys could rob them for extra dough, and it crossed her mind again as she watched Rasul and Dog embracing in front of the truck. In that instance, she knew money could buy her love.

"Where the keys at?" asked Rasul, holding his hand out.

"In the truck, why whass'up?" asked Dog.

"Cause nigga, I'm ready to blow this joint!" answered Rasul, "and I'm driving."

"Well let's go!" said Dog.

Rasul got behind the steering wheel and Shelly jumped up front. Dog from the backseat said, "Shelly look in the glove box, and pass me that brown paper bag." Dog grabbed the bag and got to work rolling the trees in the Garci vega's.

"Yo nigga. How you work this shit?" asked Rasul, as he fiddled with the system.

"Shelly, show him how to work dat shit. Put it on CD number 5 song number 8," said Dog, and he slobbered down the blunt.

"Oh shit! Dis my shit nigga!" said Rasul, as "Beanie Siegal's," "I Be the Truth," hammered through the box.

+   +   +   +

Rasul followed Dog's directions to Brandywine Condominiums, and pulled up to the security gate. Dog rolled his window down and called to the guard in the booth, "Yo Larry, what da deal?" Larry picked his head up from out of the Sports Illustrated magazine and spoke back to Dog, whom he'd just met yesterday. "Whass'up brother?" asked Larry.

"Can a brother get through the gate?" smiled Dog.

"No problem brother!" Larry returned the smile. The security guard pressed the button, and the gate rose. He watched as the Escalade drove onto the complex, and flattered himself with the idea of trading in his S.U.V. The minute he met Dog, Pretty E, and Hit Man yesterday furnishing their condo, he knew he'd like them, especially from the generous tip they gave him.

Shelly was surprised. This was a top-notch place to live in Wilmington and she'd been trying to get in here for years. "Dog! Who lives in here? Pretty E?" asked Shelly, being nosy. She had been trying to get BoBo to move here for about a year now, but his money just wasn't long or consistent enough.

"Nah! Rasul does," replied Dog, as he directed Rasul to a parking spot reserved for "36C." Rasul and Shelly walked hand and hand at the heels of Dog, as he led them up the corridor to the condo. Dog stopped in front of "36C" and placed the key in Rasul's hand. He opened the door and was overwhelmed with the setup. Pretty E's cousin Sharon did it up, spending nearly $18,000 on furnishing the place. The butter soft crimson leather living room set, was spaced lavishly across the polished oak wood floors. A chandelier hung perfectly over top of the mirrored dinning table, and a 50-gallon fish tank sat against the mirrored wall. These were the first things that jumped out at Shelly who stood at Rasul's side. Rasul stepped through the threshold and notices it all now. The screen TV was placed at an angle so you could watch it from the living room or dinning room. He walked over to it and stood there motionless, as he stared up at the poster sized photo above it.

"Damn nigga! Where you get this at?" asked Rasul, looking at the picture. It was of him, Dog, Pretty E, and Hit Man back in forth grade holding their blue ribbons from field day.

"Your grandmom gave it to me. I blew it up, so we could all have one. You know?" said Dog. "Come on nigga, let me show you around this piece," Dog added, taking Rasul away from his zoning moment.

The whole time they toured the three-bedroom condo, Rasul was all over Shelly, "Yo cuz! I ain't trying to see dat shit feel me? Y'all can at least wait till a nigga roll or some'em," stated Dog.

"Nigga! I been waiting 8 years for dis shit!" replied Rasul.

"Well dig dis nigga. Ya clothes is in the closet. Put some of that dress shit on 'cause we going out tonight aw'ight? Im'ma bout to roll now, 'cause I ain't wit dat lovie, dovie shit!" said Dog turning to leave.

"Hold up for a minute," Rasul said, "How Im'ma leave this place? You going to come back and get me?"

30

"Damn, I almost forgot, here nigga," Dog said, and tossed him a key to the Benz.

"What's this?" asked Rasul.

"Come on, I'll show you," said Dog, as Rasul and Shelly followed him outside. "Here! this is you," Dog said, pointing to the pearl white Benz that was sitting pretty on some twenties.

"Nigga we gotta talk!" said Rasul, lusting off his new whip.

"Yeah nigga, we do!" replied Dog.

"Look, meet me at my grandmom's crib at like 4 o'clock. She supposed to be cooking dinner," said Rasul, as Dog jumped in the Escalade.

"Come on baby!" moaned Shelly, grabbing Rasul's hand as Dog pulled off. "Let's go in the house."

Shelly sat on the foot of the bed, and stared at Rasul who stood before her in his tan federal clothes. Beneath her love for money lied a spot on her heart for Rasul. She did really love him, but her morals had been totally reversed. Love just didn't hold any weight next to her love for money; "But Im'ma try," she thought, grabbing at the snap to Rasul's pants.

Rasul looked down at Shelly and realized just how much he loved her. She had stuck by his side for 8 long years. Regardless of the fact that she had been fucking, she still stayed. Rasul loved her for that. He leaned down and kissed her forehead gently, as she tugged at his snap.

"Baby, you still love me?" asked Rasul.

"Yes, I still love you," she answered, more focused on the snap than the question. "Damn this nigga is still sharp!" Shelly thought, finally unbuckling his pants. Rasul was dark chocolate, and chiseled like the Greek God Adonis. The weights in prison definitely complimented his already natural physique. His full beard was shadowed out lightly, and the outline was done crisply with a razor, giving him a model's look. Shelly just wanted to become one with him, actually melt right into his chocolate skin. Shelly pulled his pants and boxers down around his ankles, while he stepped out of them and tossed his shirt across the room. She slowly slithered her right hand down his washboard stomach, and grabbed his half erect tool with her left hand. Up and down the

31

sides she licked, and toyed with it, bringing it to a stiffness that was almost unreal.

"Damn baby," he moaned, as Shelly continued. Rasul picked and pulled at Shelly's clothes until she was naked on the bed. He picked her up underneath the bottom of her thighs suspending her in the air, and stroked in and out of her curly softness. Shelly wrapped her arms around his neck, and looked down at his arms and chest flexing. She dug ever so deeply into her body bringing her to bliss. She rolled her head back and whined, "Ummmmmm!" as her juices flowed from her body, causing her muscles to jump. Rasul felt the reaction, and contractions on his manhood, and stroked even harder. He laid her body down on the bed so he wouldn't drop her, as 8 years exploded through his tool. Rasul laid still on top of Shelly and bit down on her shoulder, as the last of his strength dripped into her.

After showering, Shelly put back on her clothes and walked over to the closet to pick something out for Rasul to wear. It was filled with Gucci, Salvatore Ferragamo, Prada, Iceburg, and Armani with pieces of Polo here and there. Shoeboxes were stacked neatly, and behind them sat a safe. Rasul came out of the shower.

"Did you find some' um yet?" he asked causing Shelly to upspring from a squat position after eyeing the safe.

"Yeah, I found some'em," she replied, grabbing a Salvatore Ferragamo suit and black pair of gator boots.

Rasul walked over to his dresser and grabbed the jewelry box that sat next to a row of cologne. A platinum Rolex with the iced out bezel jumped out at him like a jack-in-the-box.

"What the fuck is going on?" he thought. "What are these niggas doing?" He couldn't wait to get to his grandmom's house to see what the happenings were.

"Hello," said Shelly, answering the phone. "Right here!"

"Here Baby!" said Shelly to Rasul, handing him the phone. Rasul grabbed the phone and Pretty E shouted through the other side, "Whass up nigga!? Get your ass over here cuz! Your grandmom got the grub ready and everything. Hold on, your mom wants you," he finished.

"Hey boy! How you like your condo? Ain't Pretty E and Hit Man so sweet?! Dog too! Them boys really love you. Now come on and get your behind over here 'cause mom wants to see you!" said Ms. Debbie, Rasul's mom.

Rasul stood in front of the mirror, and looked at himself in his black suit and platinum shirt and smiled like a muthafucka. How good it felt to be out of those prison tans. "Come on baby, let's go," he said, and him and Shelly left the condo.

+   +   +   +

Rasul pulled up in front of his grandmom's house in Jefferson Farms and noticed all the cars out front. A Lexus LS 450, a Benz wagon, and a Cadillac truck, all sat on chrome in front of the house, and driveway. Shelly knew about Dog's wagon, and Pretty E's truck, but the LS450 must be Hit Man's she guessed.

"Dats Pretty E's truck, Dog's wagon, and Hit Man's Lex" she answered Rasul's question that went unsaid. While he was locked
down they told him about the hustling, and few "sticks" they did, but he never imagined this. His boys had come up!

Getting out of the Benz, Rasul immediately caught a whiff of what he grew up on, which was grandmom's cooking. The aromas escaped through the screens in the windows, and Rasul knew every separate smell. "Collard greens, macaroni & cheese, pot-roast, white potatoes, carrots, and cornbread," he said aloud to himself.

"Yop!" added Shelly, agreeing to the smells as well.

"Whass-up my nigga!" Pretty E and Hit Man shouted, seeing their boy for the first time.

"What I tell y'all about using that "Got Darn" "N" word!?" shouted Grams from the kitchen.

"Grams, it's only a slang word. It's a difference between nigga, and Nigger," Pretty E shot back respectfully.

"I don't give a damn what it is! Don't use that "N" word! I went through hell trying to stop dat word from being used, and y'all use it like a damn name! Don't make no sense!" snapped grandmom again.

"Aw'ight," they all said in unison, feeling scorned.

33

They continued to embrace, while Dog looked on from the doorway in the kitchen. Holding a plate in his hand he said, "Dat's right grams tell'em!"

"Shut up nig-, I mean fat boy," Hit Man said as he caught himself, and they all fell out laughing.

Rasul walked out into the kitchen, and smiled as he watched the little old lady he loved so much do what she always did, stand overtop of that stove and throw down. "How's Mom-Mom's baby? Come here and let me look at you," she said, and reached up to pinch his cheeks. "Sit down. Let me make you a plate. I know that food in there wasn't worth a damn," she stated, and didn't know how right she was. Rasul grabbed his plate from the table and walked out into the living room taking a seat on the sofa. His mom came out the back and said, "come here boy, and give me a kiss!"

"Damn Mom, whass'up?" said Rasul, embarrassed.

"Boy I know you better come here! You ain't got no problem kissing dat big head girl!" she responded, looking at Shelly.

"Sike Shelly, you know I'm just playin," she added, and gave her son a kiss.

After everyone finished eating, and catching up over dinner, Rasul led Dog, Pretty E, and Hit Man back to his old room. They told him everything from the time he went to jail, to now. He was flabbergasted at the thought of the $280,000.00 dollars he had, but that was only the beginning. Rasul began telling them about Frankie, and some plans he had for them, but didn't know what they actually were. He told him he was sure that it was about money though. They began asking a few more questions about Frankie, but Rasul didn't have the answers. Then it hit him; "that's why he always said don't say too much." Rasul only knew what he told him and when he asked Frankie didn't answer. When they finished handling their business, they left the room and headed out of the house.

Shelly stood next to the truck, as they piled in. "So what'chu want me to do?" she asked. Rasul handed her the key to his condo, and told her to tell his mom to drop her off.

"Well when are you coming home?" asked Shelly.

"I don't know. Probably after the party," he answered.

"Don't be having my baby out there trickin', Pretty E. cause I know how you get!" said Shelly.

"Girl, he aw'ight. I got'em," he said, as Dog pulled off.

Chapter Four

A "Brave New World" nightclub parking lot was crammed with ill European cars as Pretty E pulled the Escalade into the parking lot. It was crowds of girls everywhere, and the cool summer night brought out all the latest styles. Rasul was glad Shelly had picked out the summer suite for him to wear, because it had a jacket and the way it felt right now, he knew it'll be cooler tonight. Pumps, mini-skirts, and linen dresses clothed the women, all made by top designers, as they profiled in front of the club. Rasul looked at all of them closely, but his Shelly had them all beat. "Got damn baby boy! It's off the heezy out here!" said Rasul excited.

"Nigga, wait till we get inside!" said Pretty E.

"For what nigga? You ain't got no bitches no more!" Rasul said, playing with his boy.

"Nigga, you know how I play! I still get more pussy than all you niggas!" bragged Pretty E.

Nigga, just cause you light skin with pretty hair, don't mean shit! You light skin nigga is played out!" said Dog, from the backseat.

"Is you crazy? The boy Chico & Genuine brought us back!" replied Pretty E playfully, almost causing Hit Man to spit his Hennessey out of his mouth laughing.

"Dat nigga is stupid as hell!" said Hit Man.
Once inside the club, Rasul's opinions changed, as he thought, "they musta been the homely broads." Sistas were spread-out everywhere. When the four of them stepped through the club, brothers were shouting them out from all over the club. Rasul didn't know any of them, because they were mostly from Philly & New Jersey.

"Whass happenin' nigga's," asked Rafee as he approached them.

"Peach AK, whass' happening?" said Pretty E. "Yo! dis is my nigga Rasul, we been tellin' you about."

"As Salaam-Auikum AK!" said Rafee extending his hand.

"Wa-Laikum Salaam!" Rasul shot back, as they greeted each other.

36

"This is my boy Rafee from up North Philly," finished Pretty E.

"They told me a lot about you baby boy! Hold it down out here, you heard?" Rafee said, and gave Dog & Hit Man a pound before bouncing

"Yo, Dat was my mans'. That nigga got 17th & Jefferson Street off the hook with that syrup. They said he's a millionaire," Pretty E told Rasul. Rasul looked on as the boy Rafee strutted over to the bar. His mans was at his side watching the party ever so cautiously. "Who dat nigga with him?" asked Rasul, starring at the huge brother.

"Oh, dats da boy "Muscles," his bodyguard," answered Pretty E. Rasul continued to stare at Rafee and knew one day soon, him and his boys would all be millionaires. Frankie had a plan and the goal was money, he just didn't know what the plan was. He knew Frankie was in jail for money laundering, and tax evasion, but where he got the money was the question.

Dog & Hit Man had walked over to the bar already, and were being occupied by two sistas who sat in the stools next to them, when Pretty E and Rasul approached. Pretty E was ordering a bottle of "Cristal" when Tameeka and Tammy came over. "Hey Baby!" said Tammy, wrapping her arms around Pretty E's shoulders as he sat at the bar. Rasul turned around and was overcome by the girl standing next to her. She was tall for a woman and had a dark complexion like him, but that wasn't it. Her gray eyes had enchanted him to stare. "Whass' up with your boy?" asked Tameeka, talking to Pretty E, but looking at Rasul.

"Oh! This is my boy Rasul," said Pretty E.

"Oh, this is Rasul!" said Tammy excited, "I heard so much about you!"

"What 'chu hear?" asked Rasul.

"Nothing bad!" she said assuring him.

Tameeka stood to the side, and was checking Rasul out herself now. "Damn that young boy is sharp!" she thought to herself. His suite was draped over his body perfectly, and his broad shoulders complimented his chiseled frame to a tee. He turned his attention back to Tameeka and asked, "How you doing?"

"I'm fine. How are you?" replied Tameeka.

"Aw' ight. Whass'up wit you?" asked Rasul, staring into her eyes again.

"Whass'up up with you? And why do you keep starring at my eyes like dat?" she asked, and turned away from his glare before saying," "I hate dat!"

"My fault. They just look so pretty. You know? I ain't never seen nobody as dark as you with gray eyes," said Rasul.

"I know. That's what everybody say," said Tameeka. Dog tapped Hit Man on the knee and said, "Look cuz! I think Rasul might got that," as they watched him and Tameeka talk. "Damn! And I wanted some of that too," he added.

"Hey ya'll!" said Tameeka, when she noticed Dog & Hit Man further down the bar.

"Whass'up girl," they answered at the same time.

"I see y'alls' boy is home!" she added.

"Yeah, dats him," they replied, and turned their attention back to the two ladies with them.

"I'm so glad you don't fuck wit Shelly no more," said Tammy.

"I know," added Tameeka.

"How you know I don't still fuck with her?" asked Rasul.

"Cause Pretty E told me, and if you did, well dat's a different story," said Tammy.

"What 'chu mean?" asked Rasul.

"What don't I mean, boy? She ain't right. She was fucking some boy from Jersey, named "Justice," and had her man BoBo run up in there and rob him," said Tammy.

"She is off da hook! Dat young girl is crazy!" added Tameeka.

"She was just up here last week fighting the girl "Dimples" from Sharon Hill over the boy BoBo," said Tammy, talking more to Tameeka now. The more they went on about Shelly, the further the knife dug into Rasul's heart. He was crushed, and as he thought back on earlier today he began to get mad. "Stinkin' ass bitch! She probably sucked all them cats dicks!" he thought.

Cholly AK threw his hands in the air, and yelled, "Whass' happenin' niggas," when he saw his four boys from Delaware? Pretty E tapped Rasul's shoulder and pointed to Cholly AK standing by the wall with two girls at his side. Cholly AK, always playin, was decked in a pair of burgundy gators, some mustard slacks by Armani, with a burgundy shirt to match. His iced out "Rollie" glistened from the reflection of the few lights and his pinkie ring shined like a disco ball. Janine and Sharell were at his side with their arms wrapped under each of his. They look like two "models," with their loose fitting silk, and the other playas in the club recognized the game. "What's going down playa?" a few of them said, as he made his way to the bar.

"Heeeey Dog!" said Sharell, pulling up on him and kissing his ear. "Hi, Pretty E," she continued, in a sexy voice.

"Don't get fucked-up!" Tammy shot back. Sharell paid her no mind, and just rolled her eyes.

Rasul jumped up from his stool and embraced Cholly AK with love. "Damn nigga you could have at least wrote a nigga back," said Rasul.

"Nigga, you know how it is. I'm here now baby boy," replied Cholly AK, and handed him a roll of hundreds. "I brought dat just for you."

"Good looking! Whass'up though?" asked Rasul.

"Ain't shit. Just a whole lot of police, and bitch ass niggas, feel me?" replied AK.

"I heard dat! I see you still got the broads," said Rasul.

"Oh, dats mandatory baby boy!" said Cholly AK.

+   +   +   +

"What! What!" yelled Norega, and the crowd screamed at the top of their lungs.

"It's da real!" yelled Prodigy, as Havoc, Nas, and Capone joined them on the stage. "Queen's bridge up in this muthafucka! Is Philly in da house tonight? Is Jersey up in this muthafucka? Is Delaware up in this muthafucka?" Nas shouted and the crowd erupted.

"Yo! I wanna give a special shout out to my nigga Rasul welcome home Dunn! Said Prodigy, and the base dropped.

{"Y'all need to give it up! We don't give a fuck!"}

{"What y'all niggas want, the life is mine!" }

Queens Bridge rappers did a freestyle remix to Mob Deep's song "The Life is Mine" on the stage, and ripped it. Rasul pumped his fist in the air, and bounced to the music, while Tameeka kept her eye on him the whole time. No sooner than she saw a crowd of women start to form around Rasul, she walked over and said, "I'm getting ready to leave. Are you commin' with me?" said Tameeka.

"What you say?" asked Rasul surprised.

"You heard me, Im'ma bout to bounce. Are you coming or not?" she said again, intimidating Rasul with her cockiness. "Hold on let me go holler at my boys," he said, and scooted away from the girls who had surrounded him. Tameeka looked at each of them and smirked before tossing her head back and following Rasul. "Who dat bitch think she is?" one shouted as Tameeka left, ruining the girl's plans of one of them leaving with the man of the hour.

Tameeka walked over and told Tammy to come here, as she whispered in her ear. "Girl guess what? I just told Rasul to "come on," in front of those bitches over there. They was mad as shit, but guess what? I wasn't letting any of those bitches get wit mine," said Tameeka and smiled.

"Girl, no you didn't!" said Tammy.

"The fuck I didn't!" replied Tameeka, as the two fell out laughing.

Rasul was still over there talking to Dog, Hit Man, and Pretty E when Tameeka & Tammy came up. "Come on Rasul, I'm tired," said Tameeka.

"Girl, don't hurt my boy," said Pretty E.

"Boy, all I want to do is love his sexy ass!" she shot back.

"Aw'ight then. You alright baby boy?" asked Pretty E.

"Yeah, I'm straight. But don't forget to be at my crib at 4:00 p.m. 'cause we gotta go see the boy Lenny and them," said Rasul, as Tameeka grabbed his hand and led him away.

They left the club hand-in-hand straight pass the girls from earlier. Tameeka shot them a look of promise, and held her head high taunting the females as they exited. Once outside the club, Tameeka led Rasul over to the Candy Apple Red Cadillac

Northstar parked by Pretty E's truck, and hit the alarm. "Where we going at?" asked Rasul.

"To my house," replied Tameeka.

"Where you live at?" he asked.

"Out Mount Erie," answered Tameeka, and opened the sunroof as they pulled out.

Rasul reclined his seat back and stared out the sunroof at the sky. The stars glittered brightly and Rasul hadn't realized how much he missed the little things he took for granted. Jail deprived him of all the things he didn't notice until they're taken away and looking at the stars was a moment he would savor forever. Tameeka drove to the Schuylkill Expressway and headed North to Mount Erie. She held one hand on the steering wheel and used the other hand to rub Rasul's head while he laid back.

"So, I know you're happy to be home," said Tameeka.

"Damn right. I been locked down since I was sixteen," said Rasul.

"Well how old are you now?" asked Tameeka.

"Twenty-four," answered Rasul.

"Damn! You just a baby!" replied Tameeka, surprised at his maturity.

"Well damn. How old are you?" asked Rasul.

"I'm 32," said Tameeka, not looking a day over 21.

"How many kids you got?" he asked

"Only one." she answered.

"How old?" he asked again.

"He is 15, and starting to get on my damn nerves!" answered Tameeka.

"Shit. He is a big boy. How is he supposed to act? He starting to grow up dat's all," said Rasul, and went back into his zone. Shelly had fucked his whole night up, but as he looked over at Tameeka his mind cleared.

Tameeka reached up to her sun visor and pressed the garage door opener. The electric door went up revealing the well-kept garage, and bikes lined along the wall. Getting out of the car, Rasul followed Tameeka through a door leading into the house. The room was dark, and the only sound was the humming of the fish tank's filter. Tameeka hit the light and Rasul was in awe, "damn her shit is hot!" he thought as his eyes roamed over the house. The royal blue leather furniture sat pretty on a crush white carpet. Brass end tables sat is each corner occupied by white marble lamps. The coffee table was empty of knick-knacks, but black women magazines, along with Essence covered its top. A bar with three stools sat catty corner to the wall, and wine glasses hung on a rack built from the ceiling. "Take off your shoes before you walk on my white rug," stated Tameeka, stepping out of her shoes at the door. Rasul did the same thing and when he stepped on the rug his feet sunk almost an inch. "Ain't this rug nice?" added Tameeka.

"Yeah I like this", said Rasul.

Tameeka was "the truth." She and Tammy had embezzled over a quarter million dollars from insurance companies in the last 5 years and were waiting on a suit now. After doing a year in Montgomery County for credit card fraud, she switched her hustle. Her latest scam was the sweetest. She sent Tammy to the U-Haul Company to rent a moving van. Then the two of them took it to Kensington to the Spanish boys, and had the breaks bled. As soon as they left, Tammy called the U-Haul Company and reported having problems with the breaks and that she was bringing it back. She was only two blocks away from the company, when she smashed in the back of Tameeka's Honda Accord sitting at the red light. They both sued U-Haul and were waiting on at least $65,000 dollars apiece.

Tameeka walked over to the couch and flopped down, rubbing her feet together. "Rasul could you grab my pocket book please, before you sit down," asked Tameeka, "Cause my damn feet hurt!" Rasul handed her the pocket book and sat down next to her. She pulled her legs up and laid them across his lap, as she looked through her bag. Rasul began to rub her feet, as he watched her twist some weed in some Top paper. "Why you don't use blunts," asked Rasul

"Cause I'm from the old school. Plus, I don't like dat black shit dat be coming out the back of the blunts 'cause that shit is nasty!" answered Tameeka holding the lighter to the end of her joint.

"Where you work at? Cause I know don't no regular job buy all this, unless you got some nigga taking care of you," said Rasul.

"Why some nigga gotta be taking care of me? Why I can't handle my own business?" she asked.

"I don't know. It just looks like your doing better than average," he answered.

"I am!" she said and smiled pulling on her joint.

+   +   +   +

The "Brave New World" nightclub let out around two o'clock in the morning. After paying Swiff the other 15 G's Dog and Hit Man were out. Pretty E had already left with Tammy in her Cherokee, leaving them with the truck. Once they were outside the nightclub, the parking lot was still packed. A few groupies hung around the back door aimlessly, waiting for the rappers from Queens Bridge and Dog shook his head in disgust. "Man look at them bitches! They dick-for-a-dollar-ass-broads like a muthafucka!"

"You ain't lying. Dat's why I don't trust'em now. The bitches probably got a nigga home chillin' while they out here tryin' to eat a dick!" said Hit Man as they climbed in the truck.

After sitting in the parking lot for about twenty minutes trying to catch a one-night stand, Hit Man pulled away from the club and headed home. The highway was almost empty except for a few cars, so they made it home to Delaware quicker than usual. Hit Man got off of I-495 at the Governor Printz exit, and headed to Riverside housing projects to check on his crack house.

The abandoned house was boarded up, but occupied for drug purposes. A little hole was cut into the boards for transactions, and Shay Ball and Monk handled that. Shay Ball sat at the table with his 9MM posted up next to the stack of money. He was Hit Man's lieutenant handled all the drugs that Hit Man pushed into the projects. Monk was the hustler. He was the transaction man, the one who bagged and packaged the drugs. Together the two had managed to lock the projects down in six months, and they were starting to see some money themselves. Tonight had been a good one because money was constantly

coming. They sold everything from dimes, to ounces and made
Hit Man's money faster than usual.

"Damn! We made Hit Man's thirty G's already!" said
Shay Ball, sliding the stacks of money to the side.

"How much we got left?" asked Monk.

"Almost a brick. We should see at least 18 ourselves, you
know?" said Shay Ball.

"That's cool. But, man, I'm gone stretch dat, lightin' up on
these dimes a little bit. Put 3 grams, 5.5 grams, and like 26 in the
rest of these 8-balls, quarters, and ounces, feel me? That way will
see ten a piece, instead of the nine, you know?" said Monk, always
looking to come-up.

Hit Man and Dog walked up to the house, and knocked on
the door. "Who is it?" asked Monk, trying to peer through the
blotched peek hole. "It's Hit Man," he answered. Monk slid the
board from between the step and the door, and then unlocked the
locks.

"Whass happenin' ya'll?" asked Hit Man, as he and Dog
entered the house, "Ya'll aw ight?" He finished.

"Yeah, we aw'ight, money been coming all night, we gone
need another bird for tomorrow, cause these are damn near done,"
said Monk.

"Ya'll done already?" asked Hit Man, surprised, because it
usually takes the whole weekend to move the two bricks.

"Yeah. We got your money right here," said Shay-Ball,
and passed Hit Man the stacks of money.

"Alright then call me tomorrow morning, so I can drop that
off to ya'll aw'ight?" said Hit Man, placing the money in a brown
paper bag.

Leaving the projects, Hit Man drove out to Governor Printz
and made a left headed to the Westside, to take Dog home. Dog
was bitchin' all night about how he hasn't been home with his girl
and kids, and Hit Man was glad to be taking him. "Man I'll be
glad when I drop your ass off! That girl got you sprung nigga!"
said Hit Man.

"Shit nigga your girl got you sprung! I just ain't trying to
hear her mouth, dat's all!" Replied Dog.

"Like I said my girl got you sprung!" replied Hit Man, referring to Kim.

"Whatever nigga!" Dog said, and then continued, "Yo! I think that's the vice right there," pointing to the Chevy Caprice at the red light.

Det. Armstrong and Det. Cohen were at the red light, when Armstrong noticed the Cadillac truck in his rear view. It had only been two days since he approached them with the proposition, but he hadn't heard anything back. So when the light turned green, he sat still making them drive around them.

"Damn!" said Hit Man, "I know these muthafuckas going to fuck wit us!"

"Man just don't do nuffin wrong. Drive around those muthafuckas," said Dog, as Hit Man drove around them.

Det. Armstrong was right on their bumper, as they drove past. He knew they saw him in the mirror so he just toyed with them following them around every turn. Hit Man was tired of playing the little cat and mouse game, so he pulled over to the side of the road. Det. Armstrong put the light up in the windshield, hit the siren one time, and pulled behind them. Det. Cohen looked to his partner and said, "Why'd you stop'em?"

I'm going to ask them a few questions, dat's all. See why they're leaving the projects this time of morning," replied Armstrong.

"Do you want me to come?" asked Cohen.

"Nah, it's O.K., I'll only be a minute," answered Armstrong, and he was out of the car.

Silently, he began to wish he were alone. His partner had no idea of his other side, and Armstrong wasn't about to inform him. Det. Cohen was still new to the job, and fresh from his promotion to detective. Armstrong wasn't going to risk this young punk going to the superiors on him, so he approached the truck by himself. Det. Armstrong had been crooked for the last 15 years, and before the death of his original partner, "Det. Delancy." Delancy was gunned down during one of their bribe pick-ups on the Eastside, but it wasn't enough for Armstrong to stop taking them.

"Hey guys. Whass'up?" asked Det. Armstrong as Hit Man rolled down the window. Det. Armstrong stuck his head in the truck and looked around for any more occupants, then said, "Where's Rasul? I heard he was out. I was looking forward to seeing him. Is he home?"

"You know he's home muthafucka! So what you want?" asked Hit Man annoyed.

"I wanna know why ya'll haven't called me?" replied Det. Armstrong.

"Muthafucka! Didn't you say a week!" asked Hit Man.

"Yeah I said a week, but how bout right now. Gimmie my money now smart ass!," said Det. Armstrong.

Dog reached in his pocket, and was glad he had a "G" on him. He would have hated to have to go into the money Hit Man just picked up, cause ain't no telling what Armstrong would have did. Armstrong turned his back to his car, so his partner couldn't see. Dog passed the money across the front and Armstrong tucked it in his sports jacket. "Nice doing business with you guys. See ya soon," said Armstrong smiling, before walking away.

+   +   +   +

Tameeka and Rasul sat up until the wee hours of the night getting better acquainted. The weed and drinks had mellowed them out, so talking to each other became easier. Tameeka told Rasul about her son Jaquaan, his father Jahlil and why their relationship broke-up. She told him how he had been cheating and had another family on the side. She told Rasul that she held no grudges against Jahlil, and they are still friends. "My son is over there now," she continued "Jahlil comes to get him every weekend."

"What? Is he married or some'em?" asked Rasul.

Yes. He has a wife, and two daughters," replied Tameeka.

"You're not mad?" he asked.

I used to get mad, but for what? I was young when I had Jaquaan. I have moved on with my life. I wasn't about to be stuck because of the breakup. Shit! He was happy and I wasn't. I'm not taking the back seat for no man, you know?" She replied.

"I feel you, so where are you at now?" asked Rasul.

Meaning?" asked Tameeka.

"With your relationships, where's your man?" he asked.

"If I had one, you wouldn't be here now. I haven't had any relationships or friends, male friends, in a while. See you brothers out here are too petty, and play too many games. I am a grown woman, and don't have time to play. I do enough of that with my son," said Tameeka.

What 'chu mean us guys? All of us ain't the same, feel-me? Maybe you just been looking in all the wrong places because me, personally, I wouldn't play no games especially with a woman who is so damn sexy, strong, and seems to be so self-assured about everything," Rasul said.

"Yeah right!" Tameeka said smiling, "you sound good!" They sat and continued to blow each other's mind, giving their own separate opinions on male and female's perceptions about relationships.

"So why'd you bring me here? What was your intention?" asked Rasul.

"I bought you here because for real, for real. I got kind of jealous when them girls surrounded you at the bar. So this was my only way of getting you alone," answered Tameeka.

"So why didn't we just walk off, or maybe go to your car and talk? Why did we have to come here?" asked Rasul again.

"Because I'm horny. I need some sex! You are sexy as hell, and I wasn't going to let any of those bitches enjoy what was sooner or later going to be mines anyway," all those thoughts shot through Tameeka's mind, but she said, "because I wanted your undivided attention that's why."

"So now that you have it, what?" asked Rasul, becoming more boldly with Tameeka.

"What? I got what I wanted," replied Tameeka giving Rasul the lead.

"Well I didn't," said Rasul on que and Tameeka raised her eyebrows as if to say, "and?"

"Well what did you want?" she asked.

"I wanted to holla at you too, but you had me intimated," he said.

"Why?" She asked.

47

"Because you just had some calmness about yourself, you know? Like you were confident about something nobody in the whole club knew about," he said.

Tameeka smiled and grabbed his hand. "I was confident about what I wanted. Now I'm tired, it's late, and I'm going to bed. Are you coming?" she asked, releasing his hand and heading towards the steps. Tameeka had a gait with her stuff. It could cause accidents. She looked back nonchalantly and saw Rasul behind her, and switched even more suggestively with every step. "Damn! Im'ma wear dat ass out!" he said to himself, as he watched Tameeka lustingly.

Tameeka led Rasul to the master bedroom of her three bedrooms home. The door was made of Oak and French designed. She grabbed both doorknobs and turned them at the same time saying, "don't laugh at my babies!" before walking in. The huge bed sat directly centered in the room and the mirrored headboard was full of stuffed animals.

"Are these your babies?" smiled Rasul, grabbing an old Tweetie bird.

"Yes, they are my babies. I been collecting them since I was a little girl, but I only kept the ones that I really like," she answered.

"Why? Is that funny?" asked Tameeka.

"Nah! I think it's cute," said Rasul.

"Well look, why don't you get comfortable, while I go put on my pajamas," said Tameeka.

The bathroom was connected to the master bedroom and Rasul watched Tameeka disappear through the door carrying a towel and her negligee. He walked over to the large entertainment center and grabbed the remote before flopping down on the bed. After turning on the TV, Rasul layed back and stared into the mirrored ceiling. "Damn she got it going on. I can get comfortable here," he thought, as the room welcomed him. He looked off into space and enjoyed the sound of the shower running. Being home had numbed him. No keys jingling, no walkie-talkies, no inmates hollering, just silence and the soft sound of the shower running.

    Tameeka stood in the shower and let the water beat softly down her back. The more she thought about Rasul, the harder she smiled. He had impressed her with his strong views of life and powerful conversation on relationships, and she liked that. It had been a long time since she had been stimulated mentally, and Rasul did that. "Damn and he even got a nerve to be sharp!" she thought, as she got out and toweled off. She grabbed her Vanilla "Victoria's Secret" perfume and squirted the mist on her wrist, and neck. She then stepped into her silver thong, and draped the silver-matching top over her body. Right before she walked out the door, she snapped her fingers and said, "Damn! I almost forgot!" and grabbed the perfume again. Tameeka grabbed the front of the thong, and pulled it away from her body squirting the mist one time on her womanhood. "There it goes," she said to herself and walked out the door.

    The light from the bathroom door opened causing Rasul to turn and stare. Tameeka was standing in the door profiling, with her arm up on the doorway. She walked over to the bed and stood in front of Rasul, as he looked into her eyes. Her negligee matched them perfectly, and her hedonistic body filled it completely. "Damn! Is all dat you," asked Rasul playfully.

    "Is all what me?" she asked playing along as she stepped back and ran her hands over her curves.

    Rasul reached out and grabbed her waist, pulling her towards him. He lifted the front of her negligee and kissed her navel softly. "Damn, you smell like ice cream," he said and pulled her on top of him. Lying on his back, he stared into the ceiling mirrors as he raised her negligee up around her waist. Tameeka's ass was phat, and a real pretty, smooth dark chocolate. Rasul reached down and gave it a hard squeeze one time before letting his hands finish exploring her body.

    Tameeka sat up on Rasul's crotch, and began unbuttoning his shirt. Being fresh out of prison definitely cut up his torso, and Tameeka ran her long fingernails through every crease of his six-pack. She leaned down and licked across his nipples, then blew them, sending a chill through his body. She felt the rise of Rasul's manhood against her inner thigh and smiled, grinding her hips seductively. Tameeka leaned forward and kissed him passionately, as their tongues twirled forever. She kissed his nose, his lips, and his chin, before kissing all the way down to his belt. Tameeka fiddled with his belt until she got it loose, and he pulled them off the rest of the way.

Tameeka rolled off Rasul, as he flung his pants and boxers to the floor. He rolled back over on top of her, as she peeled the negligee off of her body, and kissed her titties. Rasul did the same thing to Tameeka that she done to him, and when he reached her thong, thoughts of Frankie flooded his mind. "Rasul, you have to make a woman love you, and sometimes it causes for a little oral sex, you know?" he would always say, before giving his shoulder nudge. Rasul smiled and thought to himself, and flicked them across the room. Rasul started at her knees, licking and kissing them up until he reached her softness. With both of his hands placed on her lower abdomen, he used his thumbs to open her up.

Rasul licked and sucked at her love button with expertise, sending electricity through her body. Tameeka's legs shook uncontrollably, as she clutched the air with hands. "Oooo baby St.. St… Stop," she moaned reaching down, trying to push him away. Rasul shook his head, "no," and continued as Tameeka held his head tightly, occasionally rubbing his ears. The feeling was unbearable and when Tameeka reached her peek, her body shuddered in total bliss. "Put it in me," she cried, as Rasul rose to accommodate her. Tameeka reached down and grabbed his love muscle, and guided it into her heaven. The first stroke was hard and deep, causing Tameeka to bite down on her bottom lip. "Ou, Ou, Ouch boy!" she said, and slapped his back playfully; "dat shit hurt!"

"My fault," said Rasul, and began to grind again. Their lovemaking tonight was what poems were made of, as they met each other's stroke halfway. Tameeka felt Rasul beginning to stroke faster, and knew he was about to explode. She clutched her inner muscles around his tool and squeezed tightly, as Rasul's body stiffened, and he collapsed on top of her. "Damn Baby!" he said, and rolled off of her. They lay there starring at each other's naked bodies through the ceiling mirrors, as the sun rose on the outside world.

+   +   +   +

Chapter Five

The next day Rasul was awakened by the soft thump of the radio playing downstairs. He sat up in bed and almost couldn't remember where he was. Then it hit him all at once, "Damn! I'm home like a muthafucka!" he said, and took a deep breath. Rasul looked around the room and began to put the pieces of his drunken night together then saw his boxers on the floor "Tameeka," he said with a smile, grabbing his boxers and putting them on. He got out of bed and saw a new toothbrush sitting on top of a towel and washcloth, on the dresser and said, "Damn!" She on point!" He grabbed the things and walked into the bathroom to take a shower. Soap on and soap off was all he did in the shower. He was still conditioned for taking jail showers and when he got out; he stood at the sink and brushed his teeth.

"Good mornin', sleepy head!" said Tameeka cheerfully, walking up behind him.

"Hey baby girl. Whass'up?" asked Rasul, watching her approach him through the mirror over the sink. She gave him a strong hug from the back, squeezing his chest, before letting her nails run tenderly down his stomach.

"Come on and eat," she said smiling, "I cooked some steak, eggs and fried potatoes."

"What'chu doing? Trying to spoil me?" asked Rasul.

"No I'm not, I'm simply doing what a woman does for her man that's all, why? Them other broads ain't cook for you?" asked Tameeka.

"Sometimes," he responded.

"Well if you were my man, you'll get this everyday!" she said, assuringly.

"Well we go see if we can't work that out," he replied.

"I know we are 'cause I done already stated my claim!" said Tameeka smiling, as she left the bathroom, "come on."

Rasul got down stairs to the dinning room and his chair was pulled out at the head of the table. He sat down and nodded his head slowly, to the soft music playing on WDAS 105.3. Stevie

Wonder was singing, "Make Me Feel Like Paradise," as the radio finished up the spotlight on all of his music.

"Rasul, Pretty E said call him," said Tameeka, as she laid his plate in front of him.

"Where he at?" asked Rasul, digging into his food.

"Hold on. Let me go get my plate, and then I'll call him," said Tameeka. Tameeka sat her plate down at the other end of the table, and headed to the living room. She came back carrying the cordless phone, and the newspaper. "Just push the first button on the speed dial and he's there", said Tameeka handing him the phone.

"Where dis at? Tammy's?" asked Rasul, letting the phone rest on his ear and shoulder.

"Yeah", she said and started eating while she read the newspaper.

Pretty E was sitting on the bed getting dressed when the phone rang. "Hello," he answered.

"Whass'up nigga?" asked Rasul, with a mouth full of food.

"Whass'up wit you? You aw'ight? I heard Tameeka put the thing on you," said Pretty E, chuckling through the phone line. Rasul smiled and looked up from his plate at Tameeka. "What?" she asked.

"Nah nigga. I put the thing on her!" replied Rasul. Tameeka blushed and put her face back in the paper, "Damn Tammy got a big mouth!" she thought. Rasul stayed on the phone with Pretty E for about 10 minutes before hanging up. He looked at Tameeka and said, "Oh! So you put the thing on me huh?"

"No, not really! I ain't get to put it on you, like I wanted to!" she said.

"Not like you wanted to huh?" Well you gone get a chance to do dat" Rasul smiled, then continued, "yo, when you going to take me home?"

"Ain't Pretty E coming over here?" asked Tameeka.

"Nah. Dat nigga gotta get ready to handle some business. He's going to meet me at my crib", answered Rasul.

"Well you're going to have to take my car, because I gotta be here. Jahlil is bringing Jaquaan home today, instead of Sunday

and I don't want him in here by himself cause he'll have a house full of his boys and I just had this carpet cleaned," said Tameeka.
"Awight then," said Rasul.
After getting dressed, Rasul came down the steps and Tameeka was lying on the couch. Her long T-shirt barely reached her knees, revealing her long shapely legs. She was watching the big screen television and talking on the phone when she saw Rasul, "Hold on girl," she said then continued, "You getting ready to go?" she asked.
"Yeah. Soon as you give me the keys," he replied.
"Girl let me call you back," said Tameeka into the phone, and got up to get her pocket book. She handed Rasul the keys and walked him to the door, and asked "when you coming home?"
"I don't know. I have to handle some things today, but if you need your car, I'll get somebody to follow me up here, so I can bring it to you, said Rasul.
"Nah, I don't need it, plus Tammy has a car so if I need a ride, I'll call her," said Tameeka.
"Alright then, let me get ready to bounce," said Rasul, turning towards the door.
"Damn! Can I at least get a kiss?" said Tameeka, trying to sound mad.
"Yeah," said Rasul and pecked her lips softly tapping her ass.
"Be careful okay?" said Tameeka.
"I will," said Rasul and he left.
+   +   +   +
"Girl, he startin his dumb shit already!" said Shelly into the receiver on the phone.
"Uhm-Humm. Pretty E and them probably had him somewhere trickin! You know they're dogs!" said Rashida. Shelly had been up all night long crying. She was past that point now, because anger had overridden all of that. She paced the condo's floor waiting for Rasul and every time she heard a car start up, or pull off, she raced to the window only to find him not there.
"Girl I know I haven't been the best woman in the world, but I stuck by that muthafucka for 8 years! Eight years girl! I was

16 years old when he went to jail. What da fuck!? Did he expect
me not to grow up?" said Shelly into the phone.

"I feel you," said Rashida.

"Rashida, how do you feel me? Ain't none of them niggas
you fucked wit been to jail and when they did you ain't do the bid
with them!" snapped Shelly taking her anger out on the girl.

"Look, Im'ma bout to hang-up bitch cause I been on this
phone with you all night long! It's damn near 12 o'clock the next
day and now you wanna trip on me? Dats just why I don't do no
bids with them niggas cause you gotta go through all this shit! I'm
hanging up!" said Rashida, pissed.

"Girl, you know you my Dog!" said Shelly and they hung
up the phones. Shelly stood up from the couch and paced the floor
again, while the tears stained her cheeks. Thoughts from Dog,
Pretty, and Hit Man telling her business to Rasul, to some bitch in
the street saying something, all crossed her mind. "I know what,"
she said pumping herself up, "that muthafucka can act stupid if he
want, I'll tell BoBo to come up in this muthafucka and get that safe
out the closet then what!?" she asked herself, using more spite than
sense.

+   +   +   +

The sun was shinning brightly and the temperature was
already in the high 80's at noontime. Rasul drove the North Star
swiftly making his way in and out of the lunch hour traffic down I-
95 to Delaware. "You Know How It Gets in the Club," by Philly's
own Beenie Segal slammed through the factory car system, as the
70 MPH wind grazed the top of his head through the open sunroof.

Rasul thought to himself and visualized the brothers taking
laps around the prison compound. "I wonder what Frankie is
doing? That old muthafucka is probably somewhere playing
Dominos in the yard, cheating," he thought, smiling. Frankie
calmed Rasul down a lot, and opened his eyes up to the game of
life. How to play it, and how to live it. It was another world out
there on the outskirts of the Ghetto, and Rasul wanted to see it.
People, places, things, businesses,
property, monopolizing, making things illegal, legal, stocks, bonds,
all these things were in his reach, if he played the game right.

Rasul turned off of I-95 at the Delaware Avenue exit ramp. Dog gave him the address while he was in jail, so he knew basically where the house was. He drove until he came to Broom Street and made a left off Delaware Avenue. Rasul drove slowly down the street, eyeing the homes n the quiet section of the city, until he found Dog's house. He parked in back of the Benz Wagon that read: "KIM," on the plates and got out. The door flung open before he reached the porch and Kim came running out. "Heeey Brother!" she yelled, jumping into his arms.

"Whass'up girl?" he said holding her tight, "Damn you look good!"

"Thank you. You do too!" she answered.

"Where my niece and nephews at?" asked Rasul. He and Kim had been friends since they were kids. They were so close that they called each other brother and sister and thinking back on those days made Rasul chuckle under his breath. "So how did you and Dog hookup again? Cause I remember ya'll used to fight all the time," he said.

"I don't know. He just kept sweating me!" said Kim, laughing.

"Damn girl! You still the same," said Rasul, laughing at Kim's wild sense of humor.

They walked in the house, and the kids were sprawled out in front of the TV watching cartoons. "Look y'all," Kim said, "here goes ya'lls Uncle Rasul." The kids turned around and stared at the stranger they knew only by pictures. "Hey Uncle Rasul," they all said together.

"Uncle Rasul, didn't you just come home from jail?" the oldest one, little Michael asked.

"Nah-ahn! He just came home from the Army! Didn't you Uncle Rasul?" the middle one, Shakira said over shouting Lil' Mike.

"Yes and no," replied Rasul, picking the baby up. "Hey man! Me and you got the same name."

"I told you Lil' Mike!" shouted Shakira.

"You did not! Get out my face!" said Lil' Mike and punched his sister in the back. Shakira started crying and holding her back as she walked over to Kim. "Mommie, Lil Mike punched me again!" said Shakira, tears everywhere.

"Michael! Take your lil' ass upstairs before I kick it!" demanded Kim. "Rasul they are bad as hell," she finished.

"They'll be awight! Uncle Rasul is home now," he said, bending down to kiss Shakira on the cheek.

"Kim, Where's Mike at?" said Rasul, then continued, "I told his ass I'll be here by 1 o'clock."

"Michael! Rasul is down here waiting for you," hollered Kim.

"Here I come!" he yelled from upstairs, in his raspy voice. Dog came downstairs in his boxers with his hand in the front, and his other hand on his beard.

"Damn nigga! Do some'em wit dat gut! Dat shit ain't cut!" said Rasul, frowning his face.

"Nigga! My baby loves it. Don't you Boo?" said Dog, looking at Kim.

"You know I do!" she said, and walked over and rubbed it.

"Girl, you know you don't like dat shit!" he said smiling, and then continued, "Come on man! I told you we gotta handle some'em."

"While I go put on my clothes, call your girl nigga! She has been calling this muthafucka all night! She mad as hell," said Dog and went back up stairs.

"Man, I ain't fuckin wit her! I'm cutting her ass off, she played herself," said Rasul grabbing the phone.

"Dat's a shame, Rasul. Don't do that girl like that," said Kim empathizing with Shelly's feelings.

"It's a shame how she fucked dis nigga and dat nigga!"

"Hello. What'chu want?" he said turning his attention into the phone.

"I'm not trying to hear that shit! I'll talk to you when I get there!" he said, and slammed the phone down. Kim shook her head and said, "Michael, if you ever talk to me like dat, we fighting!"

"Girl, you ain't fighting nuffin," replied Dog, but knew her word was bond.

56

"Kim, Im'ma get wit you before I go home tonight. OK? We got a lot of catching up to do. Where dat girl Tasheena at?" he asked, as he and Dog walked to the door.

"She chillin. She be wit Tish and Rayon all the time," answered Kim.

"Tell her I said whass'up? OK?" he said, getting into the North Star.

When they reached Tameeka's Cadillac, Dog smiled "nigga was dat pussy good?" asked Dog.

"Was it? Dat pussy is like dat! Matter of fact, nigga why I'm telling you? Dat's getting ready to be my jawn." said Rasul

"My bad nigga! But yo, that will be a good move though. Her and Tammy get dat money. Them broads are slick as hell, but they take care of their niggas. At least I know Tammy takes care of Pretty E. I ain't never seen Tameeka with no nigga. I used to think she was gay or some shit!" said Dog.

"Dat's whass'up. She told me she be chillin', I think dat's why I'm digging her so much," said Rasul.

"Well! Whass'up man? Who are these people we going to meet?" asked Dog.

"My Italian peoples. We about to make some major moves, you heard," said Rasul.

"I hear you nigga. Let's do this then," said Dog.

"We gotta go meet Pretty and Hit Man first. They at my crib," said Rasul.

+   +   +   +

Pretty and Hit Man sat in Hit Man's LS 450, in the parking lot of Rasul's condo. It was almost 1:30 and Rasul was supposed to be there by 1 o'clock.

"Man, I could've been at the broads crib chillin', getting ready to watch the game, feel me?" said Hit man restless.

"What game?" asked Pretty E.

"Some new shit on ESPN 2. It's some over seas shit," replied Hit Man.

"Yo, Shelly crazy as a muthafucka, ain't she?" asked Pretty E.

"Yeah she is. I was about to slap her stupid ass!" said Hit Man, pulling slowly on the Garcia Vega.

Shelly had come out of the condo as soon as she saw the Lexus, thinking it was Rasul. When she saw it wasn't him, she started verbally bashing them like it was their fault he stayed out all night. To ignore her, they rolled the windows up, put the AC on low, and finished blowing their trees.

"Man, Rasul might have to fuck her up. I don't trust dat ho! You know she had the boy from Jersey setup! Niggas damn near killed the boy for dat cheese!" Said Pretty E with expression.

"I know, but dat bitch ain't crazy like dat! I'll kill her ass if she send a muthafucka to do something to us!" said Hit Man, dead serious. He didn't give a fuck about nobody and putting one in her head would be as easy as doing it to a stranger. The only people he cared for is, his mom, sisters, and his boys.

"Here dat nigga come now," said Pretty E, looking through the mirror in the sun visor.

Rasul pulled up next to Hit Man's Lexus and parked. Soon as he got out of the car, Shelly was coming. Her eyes were puffy and swollen from crying all night, and her face was twisted with anger. "Where da fuck you been! And who's muthafuckin' car is dis?" snapped Shelly.

"Ain't none of your muthafuckin' business whose car dis is!" replied Rasul standing next to Tameeka's car. She looked towards Pretty E, who was still in the Lexus and said, "Pretty E, I know this ain't dat bitch Tameeka's car!" She walked around the caddie and seen the Philly tags and went berzerk.

"Oh! Dat's where you stayed at last night muthafucka! Huh!" She yelled, kicking a dent in Tameeka's door.

"Yeah, that where I stayed. Why? I know you ain't mad!" he stated.

"She can't be mad," he thought, not wit all them niggas she been fuckin." Rasul stared in her face to see how his words were affecting her. Tears wailed up in Shelly's eyes, and he voice cracked as she began, "why are you doing this to me, Rasul? What have I done to you? I know I wasn't the best girl in the world, but I never left you! I was always here for you, and I'm still here. You always received mail and pictures from me and I kept money on your books. Now 'cause you home, you might've heard some shit you ain't like and you want to start acting stupid. It's all good, 'cause Im'ma be awight," finished Shelly, and headed back to the condo.

Shelly said a mouthful and it caused some feelings in Rasul. She was right, she had waited 8 years on him, but Rasul's pride was hurt. He followed her up the corridor, into the condo and shut the door.

"Yeah, I know you going to be awight! Dat nigga BoBo ain't gone let dat good head go to waste! He going to take care of you," said Rasul striking out at her mentally.

"Fuck BoBo! And fuck you Rasul! But you know what? BoBo was right, I shoulda left your ass alone soon as the judge gave you them 8 years. He told me nigga's forget where they come from when they fresh out!" responded Shelly, putting on her shoes. She was trying her best to strike back at Rasul but her words weren't powerful enough.

"Yeah. Well you shoulda listened then," he said, real slick out his mouth. Shelly was making a lot of points clear to Rasul, but he wasn't going to let her know. The more he thought about what she said, the more he second guessed his decision to leave her alone. Then, looking at her low haircut, and puffy little Korean eyes setoff by her full lips, Rasul caught some feelings. "Damn I love dis girl!" he thought.

Rasul grabbed Shelly's hand and led her to the couch, where they sat down. He used his thumbs and wiped the tears from her cheek, and gave her a hug. As delicate as he could, he explained to Shelly that he needed some space and time to think. She understood about the space, being fresh out of jail and stuff, but the time was what bothered her.

"Look baby," he began "we just going to be friends alright? I need you to know that I love you though. If you need anything, I'll be right here for you. I just need some time to think. You really hurt me," he finished.

"How much time you need to think, Rasul? And what do you mean just friends? You are, and will always be my man! Matter of fact! I'm tired of begging your ass! Fuck you Rasul! Take me da fuck home! I don't do the beg thing, you got me twisted! If that's what you want, fine! You got dat!" snarled Shelly. That was it, from that moment on Shelly's mind was made up. "I'm tellin' BoBo about the safe!" she thought to herself.

+   +   +   +

Us Guys Construction sight located in the industrial section of New Castle was owned and ran by Lenny Ionni. Lenny "Fat Boy" Ionni, a heavy set Italian man was in his mid-to-late 40's. As a wise guy, he quickly became a made man in the Cappelli Family, because of his knack for the streets. Joey "The Fox" Vito, a capo in the family at the time, took a liking to Lenny and called him a stand up guy. The next time the books were opened Lenny was made. Lenny was a muscle and had forced his way into a successful construction business in just two years. He landed major contracts with high-powered companies by putting pressure on the competition. Whether it was late night phone threats, or damaging their property, the competitors got the idea. Lenny pulled his chair up to his desk and unwrapped his Italian Sub., as he awaited for the arrival of Rasul, Dog, Pretty, and Hit Man.

Rasul and Dog were in Tameeka's car followed by Hit Man and Pretty E in the Lexus sped through the city pressed for time. Dropping Shelly off had taken longer than Rasul expected. It was two o'clock already, time for the meeting and they were late. They swerved through traffic and ran red lights at their own discretion, making up exceptionally good time. Breaking the city limits and entering into New Castle, Rasul made a left under the overpass and drove to Us Guys Construction. The sight was fenced off and a few trailers were sprinkled over the grounds surrounded by dump trucks. A huge gravel pit sat in the middle and several men were at work aimlessly, removing rocks with cranes and forklifts.

Rasul, Dog, Pretty E, and Hit Man walked up to the trailer that had the sign "Front Office" on the door, and went in. The secretary, a beautiful blond with long hair and eyelashes greeted them when they entered.

"Good afternoon. May I help you?" asked Lucy the secretary, when Rasul approached her desk.

"Yes. We have a two o'clock appointment with Mr. Ionni," said Rasul.

"What is your name?" asked Lucy, picking up the office phone.

"Rasul," he answered.

"Lenny, you have a Mr. Rasul here to see you," said Lucy, through the phone.

Lenny was back in the private office, stuffing his face with the last of his Italian Sub., when the phone rang. He chased the bite down with a swallow of Pepsi, and belched when he answered. "OK send them in," he said then continued, "Do you have any antacids?"

"Yes," she replied.

"Well send them in with Rasul, because I think these hot peppers gave me heart burn," said Lenny.

"Whatever you say," replied Lucy, sarcastically.

Lucy hung up the phone and grabbed the TUMS from her purse, and handed them to Rasul. Directing them to the back office, she noticed them for the first time. Rasul, Dog, Pretty E, and Hit Man were all sharply dressed, silk shirts, pants, and Gator boots decked them all, and big chunks of jewelry decorated their hands and neck. Lucy made mental notes. These four young black men weren't here for a job, it was something much bigger.

Rasul, Dog, Pretty E and Hit Man entered the small room converted into an office and saw the fat man sitting behind the desk. His cheeks were chubby and his neck wasn't visible to the eye because of his double chin. His large potbelly under the t-shirt disabled his shirt to button up, so it hung open. Lenny stood up from his chair and stepped around his desk when they entered; he stood 6 foot 5 inches into the air.

"Good afternoon. Which one of you's is Rasul?" asked Lenny, extending his hand in greetings.

"I am," answered Rasul, shaking the huge man's hand.

"I've heard a lot about you. Frankie says you're a real close friend of his," said Lenny.

"Yeah! He's like a father to me," said Rasul.

"Good, Good, Good, nice to hear that. Who are your friends?" asked Lenny.

"This is Dog, Pretty E, and Hit Man," said Rasul pointing to each of his friends.

"Hit Man huh? I like that name," smiled Lenny, and then told them to have a seat.

Sitting down in the small office the four felt awkward.
Lenny sensed their uneasiness and tried to relax them by starting
up casual conversation. He explained to them that they would be
getting started as soon as Joey gets there. The name Joey rang a
bell in Rasul's head. Frankie told Rasul all about Joey and how
crazy he was. Hearing all those stories about Joey actually painted
a picture of the guys' face in his mind. Dog, Hit Man, and Pretty E
sat on the couch uninterested in the conversation because they
didn't know any of the people Lenny and Rasul were talking about.
      "Yo! Is this them?" interrupted Dog, pointing out of the
window at the limousine approaching the trailer.
      "Yeah, that's them," answered Lenny.
The limousine pulled in front of the trailer and came to a slow halt.
The driver got out of the car and walked to the back to open the
rear doors. Joey "The Fox" Vito, dressed in a navy blue Salvatore
Bonfi suit stepped out looking dapper. His gold round toe,
crocodile shoes matched perfectly with the suspenders and his salt
and pepper hair was combed neatly in place. He stood on the side
of the limousine looked up at the trailer, then out over the
construction sight at the men at work. Joey was reminded of his
younger days as he watched the men bust their asses for a decent
living. He knew long ago that his life would be different, because
working was never on his list of things to do. As a teenager he and
his friends were considered young thugs in the always tuff
neighborhood of "Lil Italy." They were into everything, and with
Joey's quick wit, and master planning skills he became the
ringleader.
      Frankie "Fingers" Maraachi, boss of the "Capelli" family
was faced with a decision. The community was complaining about
the young thugs, and they wanted the neighborhood cleaned.
Frankie sent the word. When Joey received word that Frankie
wanted to see him he was overwhelmed with fear and confusion.
"Why me?" he thought. Joey was determined. This was his
chance to impress the man who he so heavily admired. Later on
that same day, Joey, along with his two best friends Rick and Nikki
Stango, went to meet Frankie. The rest is history.

Frankie took an immediate liking to Joey and his friends and to everyone's surprise the three young men became made on each of
their twenty-first birthdays. Joey was a soldier in the family from day one, and like his friends Ricky and Nikki Stango, he carried a mean reputation. Joey was sly and stealth in his actions and kept his name "The Fox."

Nikki, "Snake Eyes," Stango, the older brother of Ricky stepped out of the limo next. He was dressed in jeans and a t-shirt, and his 6 foot 3 inch frame bulged from underneath the t-shirt like an armored vest. Nikki had a dark olive complexion and he didn't look a day over 30, although he was 40 years old. He sorta looked like a young Robert DeNiro, but his eyes were beady and unmistakable, and earned him the name "Snake Eyes."

Last to exit the limo was Ricky. Richard, "Richy Cheeks," Stango was short and almost fat, the direct opposite of his brother except for the olive complexion. Out of the three men, he was the worst of them all when it came to his temper. Rick was a killer. He and his brother together were accountable for more than half the hits the family made over the past 15 years. He stepped out of the limo draped in an Armani suite, and spit before firing up the Cuban cigar squished between his chubby fingers.

      +   +   +   +

Shelly sat in the living room of her mom's house trying to get her lies together. She didn't know where to begin, because she didn't have any excuses for not returning BoBo's pages. He had beeped her all night long, but she was so worried about Rasul she ignored them. "How could I have been so stupid!" she scorned herself. Her mind was racing with thoughts of BoBo in the lead and she knew she had a lot of explaining to do. BoBo was a real some-timey type of person and she hoped she hadn't lost him for being so stupid. For the past 8 years Shelly had doubts about waiting for Rasul. She knew he would want to put his thing down in the streets, but thought her love for him would allow her to deal with it. She was wrong. Shelly's love for Rasul was nothing compared to her newfound love for money. And after her encounter with Rasul, she felt she should have gone along with her doubts all along. Shelly knew Rasul really did love her, but now revenge was on her mind. Her heart felt as though an invisible hand was squeezing and pulling the life right out of her chest, and she wanted him to feel that same way.

Through all of her relationships she never gave her heart away, because it always belonged to Rasul and that's what kept her cold. She was able to back out of them with ease and not feel anything behind it, but now it was different. She couldn't just walk away from Rasul; however, she wanted him to hurt. Right before she grabbed the phone to call BoBo, the doorbell rang.

                +   +   +   +

Joey "The Fox" led the way as, "Richy Cheeks" and "Snake Eyes" entered the trailer.

"Good afternoon Mr. Vito. Lenny is expecting you," said Lucy upon their entrance.

"Where's he at?" asked Joey.

"In his office," replied Lucy.

Entering the small office, Lenny stood up from behind his desk to greet the acting boss and his capos with hugs. As the four men hugged and patted each other's backs Hit Man tapped Pretty E's leg and chuckled.

"Who da fuck does he think he is?" asked Hit Man in a low tone of voice, referring to the arrogant man Lenny called Joey.

"I think he's the boss on some' ol mob shit," replied Pretty E quietly.

Rasul, Dog, Pretty E and Hit Man continued to watch the four Italian men greet and get situated in the small office, awaiting the meeting to begin. Lenny introduced Joey to the four of them, while the Stango brothers stood-off to the side observing each one of them carefully. Hit Man not liking to be grilled spoke up, "yo, why are these two dudes staring at me and shit?"

"Who, them?" asked Joey, turning towards his friends.

"Yeah" answered Hit Man, then continued, "they act like they got a beef or some shit."

"Oh no, there's no beef at all. In fact," said Joey, motioning Ricky and Nikki over to them "let me introduce y'all to them. This is Ricky and Nikki close friends of Frankie."

Hit Man, feeling bad vibes from Ricky and Nikki, hesitated to shake their already extended hands, until Rasul shot him a crazy look. After the handshake, the meeting began.

"I guess I should be getting started then," said Joey, and then continued. "Listen, your not here for a job or anything like that. You're simply here to have a front. I have been given a direct order to give you pay stubs weekly, and cover for you if any of y'all needs covering. Lenny will explain to whomever, that he's your boss. If you need any cash just call. In the meantime, be careful at whatever it is that y'all do. If you run into any problems, I mean any, don't hesitate to call me, not Lenny, me. There's almost nothing I can't fix," he finished and handed them each a card.

"Any questions?" asked Joey. The meeting was over.

Leaving the small office made Rasul, Dog, Pretty E, and Hit Man feel secure. They had a new connect and the most powerful connect of them all: "The Mob." Pretty E who trailed the four stopped at the desk and talked to Lucy.

"Lucy right?" asked Pretty E.

"Yes, that's right," she answered, looking at the handsome young black man in front of her.

"I'm Pretty E," he spoke extending his hand before going on "you sure are looking good today. Your man is a lucky guy."

"Thank you. But I'm a happy single woman."

"Is that so?" he asked.

"Yes. It's so, why do you ask?" asked Lucy, feeling she was being hit on.

"Since you put it like dat, why don't we talk more over dinner?" he shot back.

"Nah! I think I'll pass on that," smiled Lucy intrigued by his forwardness.

"OK, then maybe next time," said Pretty E and winked. Lucy blushed and couldn't understand why she felt giddy, and before Pretty E could say another word Rasul was pulling him away.

"You have to excuse my boy," said Rasul, as he pulled Pretty E out the door.

"I'm a big girl. I can handle myself," she responded. Lucy shook her head and smiled, as Pretty E was being pulled out the door. She was still trying to put a finger on her giddiness, and realized she was attracted to him.

+   +   +   +

Det. Armstrong's heart raced. He couldn't believe what he was seeing through his binoculars, as he watched from the highways overpass that ran overtop of the construction site. Following the four
young men Rasul, Dog, Pretty E, and Hit Man couldn't have went any better. Us Guys Construction site was a major construction company in the Tri-State area, with ties to the mob. Det. Armstrong didn't know what was happening but it had to be of some importance he reasoned, especially seeing the limo arrive. For an hour, Det. Armstrong sat patiently until the men exited. "So," he thought, "this is y'alls source, huh?" he asked as if the four men were there. His heart thumped loud inside his chest, neck, and ears as he literally shook with excitement. "I can see it now!" he said to himself again then continued. "The headlines will read. Det. Armstrong twenty-year veteran nets huge drugs, weapons, and homicide bust connecting the mob, and young African American thugs in Delaware."

Filled with the excitement of receiving nationwide publicity, Det. Armstrong jumped in his car and peeled away from this post, seeing the young men pull away in the Lexus and Cadillac.

Chapter Six

It was no surprise to see BoBo on the other side of the door when she answered it. Putting on a fake smile she said, "Hey baby. I was just about to call," and moved to the side, so he could get in.

"Damn. You just now was 'bout to call?" he asked sourly.

"Yeah, why?" she asked dumbfounded.

"Girl, don't start playing stupid. You know damn well I been paging you all night, and I even called your cell phone," he said, walking towards her pocketbook on the couch.

"Damn", she said to herself, as BoBo grabbed the pager from inside the couch bag. "I forgot to clear the numbers!"

"Come here! Why da fuck you always playin' wit me!?" BoBo said, grabbing her face and holding the pager in front of it.

"Stop boy! My mom is upstairs," she said, and snatched it away from him making him angry.

"Where da fuck was you at last night and don't lie! 'Cause I already know da boy Rasul came home."

Shelly walked over to the couch and sat down. If she wanted to lie she couldn't because BoBo knew Rasul was home, and the look on her face gave her away.

"Ok, I did stay at Rasul's last night, but we didn't do nuffin," she lied. "He had a party up in Philly last night and never came back."

"Well what da fuck was you doin' dere anyway?" he asked.

"I don't know, I guess I just wanted to see him, dat's all," she said.

"Bitch! You know what? You shoulda stayed yo'ass wit dat nigga 'cause I'm tired of your shit!" he said.

"Think fast Shelly! Think fast!" she thought before saying; "Baby, you know what? After I saw him, it wasn't even the same. I thought it would be different, but I ain't even feeling him like dat no more. But I do got some good news," she said smiling, and stood on her tiptoes in front of him. Kissing him softly on the lips she said, "He got a safe."

"Is some'em in it?"

67

"You know it is. His boys are Pretty E and them," she answered. Pretty E's name rung like a cash register in BoBo's ears. He and his boys Dog and Hit Man had shit locked down and on occasion BoBo bought weight off them himself. BoBo, caught up in the moment as Shelly mentioned Pretty E's name, forgot he was even mad. He loved Shelly, and she loved him too, or so he thought.

"So where does he live?" asked BoBo.

"Brandywine Condo's, #36C," replied Shelly.

"Where he at?"

"I don't know."

"Alright then, listen baby go to the house and wait for me to call or get there ok? I love you hear?" he said kissing her forehead before leaving.

"You too," she said, as he walked out the door.

+   +   +   +

The sun was blazin' hot and shining down on the world, as if through a magnifying glass. The two luxury sedans were parked parallel in the driveway of Pretty E and Hit Man's two-story home in Saddle Brook as they stepped across the freshly manicured grass up to the front door.

"Yo, what time is it?" asked Dog, following Pretty E into the house.

"Almost 3:30 p.m. Why?" responded Pretty E.

"Cause I want to start getting this shit ready, so we can handle this business tonight," answered Dog.

The four of them sat down on the couches and took it from the top, explaining to Rasul all the "work" they missed out on yesterday. The drugs, money, robberies, and people on the list to get were the main topics. The more they explained, the more Rasul couldn't believe it. His boys were holding it down, and had been for the past 8 years. The only problem was that they had no idea of what to do, or what direction to go in with the money. See, the prisons walls have a way of making a blind man see the world and all that is in it.

Rasul had educated himself in ways that still sometimes surprised him today. He didn't know everything, but he knew a lot about a lot of things, and cleaning up this money and investing it

was the only thing that mattered right now. His plans of becoming a
millionaire would come together sooner than he thought. He
didn't know this much money was involved, or that it had become
so easy to touch this kind of cash today. Back in 92, before he
went to jail it
was hard to see even 25 thousand dollars. "Then again," he
thought, "we were young and dumb." Spending money on non-
sense like motel rooms, hair-do's, and Reeboks for the young girls
added up." He smiled at the past.

 "So, when are we going to do this?" asked Rasul about the
robbery of a dealer on the North Side of town.

 "Soon as the sun starts setting," answered Dog.

 "Well let me call Tameeka and let her know. I'll be later
than I thought," he said, to no one in particular.

 The answering machine picked up on the first ring, and
Rasul dialed again. It ran several more times before the deep and
heavy voice picked-up.

 "Hello. Is Tameeka there?" asked Rasul.

 "Yeah, who dis?" the deep voiced man asked.

 "It's Rasul."

 "Oh," the man said, "hold on for a minute."
Rasul heard the phone being sat down, then heard that same voice
holler, "Mommie! Rasul's on the phone!" Rasul chuckled at
himself for the thoughts that raced through his head, as he waited
for Tameeka to pickup the phone.

 "What da fuck did I tell you about screening my damn calls
boy?" Rasul heard, before hearing the sweet tones of Tameeka's
voice.

 "Hey baby!" she said, gingerly.

 "Hey. What'chu doing?" asked Rasul, just as gingerly.

 "Nuffin' upstairs folding clothes thinking about you.
Where you at? Still in Delaware?" asked Tameeka.

 "Yeah!"

 "Did you do what you were supposed to do?" she asked
him again.

 "Yeah, I handled it, but I think Im'ma be a little later than I
thought getting back up there though," he said.

"Why?"

"Cause some'em came up, but I won't be too late. I should be there about 9:00 though aw'ight?" he said.

"Alright," responded Tameeka.

"Tameeka! Was that Jaquaan?"

"Yeah! He gets on my nerves though, thinking he's my daddy or some shit."

"I was the same way. He's only looking out for his mom, that's all."

"I'm grown! I can handle me."

"They said you'd say dat."

"I can."

"Did you cook?"

"I started not to, but since Jaquaan was coming home I did. This boy is greedy as shit."

"What'chu cook?"

"Pepper steak, rice, and baked potatoes. I was hoping you be here when we ate, but it's aw'ight though," said Tameeka, trying to make Rasul feel a little guilty.

"Why yo say it like dat?"

"Like what?" she asked.

"You know. Like you trying to make me feel bad or something."

"I wasn't trying to make you feel bad baby, I know you have things to catch-up on. I ain't trippin', you just better have your butt here by 10:00," she said laughing.

"I will Mom," said Rasul teasing.

"Aw'ight den, handle your business."

"Aw'ight give me a kiss," said Rasul. They each made kissing sounds into the phone, and hung up. Soon as the phone hit the receiver, Pretty E started.

"Damn nigga! They said the first shot of good pussy a nigga get when he get outta jail, springs dat ass out!" he said, and Dog and Hit Man fell out laughing.

"Fuck you nigga!" said Rasul blushing and embarrassed by his boys laughing.

+   +   +   +

70

BoBo, excited about the news Shelly just gave him about the boy Rasul, drove his 535i quickly across town to Read Street where his boys were. He pulled his BMW up to the corner of Lancaster and Franklin Street and parked in front of the drive-thru liquor store, getting out to find his boys Rock and Dino. BoBo's heart raced with the thought of all the money that was soon to be split between him and his boys, despite who it was coming from. He knew Dog, Pretty E, and Hit Man was dangerous, but so was he. Money was the mission and he knew they blessed Rasul with a lump sum. Money, power, and respect was what the world was based on, fuck who was the holder, as long as it was possible to knock him or them off. As BoBo rounded the corner, he walked towards Read Street watching their money being made. When BoBo rounded the corner walking towards Read Street, his mind was made up. All systems were a go, and he knew his boys would be up for the Caper, they always were.

Dino and Rock sat in Rock's Yukon Denali behind the liquor store on Read Street watching their money being made, when BoBo approached.

"Whass' going down, nigga?" Rock asked, when BoBo got to the truck.

"Ain't nuffin. Whass'up wit y'all? Is the young boys handling business?" asked BoBo, turning his attention to the youngin's on the corner.

"Yeah! They doin' aw'ight, but, the police been hot all day!" he answered.

"Whass' up wit'chu Dino? You aw' ight nigga?" asked BoBo.

"Yeah! I'm straight. A nigga just fucked up right now. That Dro (Hydro) got a nigga twisted, feel me?" said Dino, in a slurred voice.

"I feel you. But yo! I got some'em real sweet for us. Do you remember the boy Rasul that Shelly used to fuck wit? Well anyway, she went to holler at the nigga on some' ol how you been type shit, and found out da nigga got a safe full of dough."

"How da fuck she know?" asked Rock.

71

"Damn! Let me finish nigga! Look, the boy Pretty E and, what's them other two nigga's name?"

"Who? Dog and Hit Man," asked Dino.

"Yeah! Dat's them nigga's. Anyway, they done copped dat nigga a brand new 600 SE, a condo, and some other shit, so you know they smashed that nigga wit some cake!"

"Right." Rock nodded his head and said.

"So whass' up? Y'all wanna check dis shit out? I know it's at least six figures up in that muthafucka! 'Cause da boy Pretty E and Dog got shit locked. I know them niggas is worth six, if not, seven figures."

"Man, them niggas ain't like dat!" said Rock.

"Man, Shit! I don't know why they ain't. Them niggas had a run," agreed Dino.

"Well it's on then! You know I'm down wit whatever involves a come-up," said Rock.

"Well let's go check this shit out then," said BoBo, getting in the back seat of the truck. Rock called his young boys to the truck and handed them a brown paper bag. "Look, dat's the rest of that bird in here aw' ight? Soon as y'all knock that shit off, do that one too, aw'ight?" he said, referring to the bag he just gave them.

"Yeah! We got it. How long you goin' to be?" one of the young boys asked.

"Not long, about an hour," he said and pulled off headed towards the condo.

Brandywine Condominiums was beefed up with security. There was a guard who sat in a Sally Port at the entrance controlling the gate, while two cars patrolled the inner area of the complex. Rock pulled his truck in across the street from the complex in a strip mall, and the three eyed the target for about 30 minutes. They all were focused on different things about the complex, Dino eyed the Sally Port, Rock timed the security patrol cars circling the complex, and BoBo studied the outer fence surrounding the condos.

"Yo! Drive around there for a minute Rock!" BoBo said from the backseat, noticing the gap between the fence and tree line.

Whass' around there?" he asked.

"I don't know? We about to find out though, 'cause I don't think it's a fence around there. Look at those trees," BoBo said pointing.

Rock drove slowly around the complex and sure enough there was no fence separating people from entering the premises.

"Yo, dat's probably whey them cars keep circling around like they do, to keep an eye out on this side, you know?" said Dino but, BoBo had already drew that conclusion.

"Yeah! I was thinking the same thing," replied BoBo.

"Yo, them cars circle this joint every three minutes. Do you think it's enough time to get to the condo from here?" asked Rock.

"I don't know? Now all we have to do is find out where #36C is," said BoBo.

Rock pulled away from the curb driving around to the entrance. The security guard Larry was inside the Sally port talking on the phone when they approached the gate. Larry sat the phone down on the desk and asked through the plexiglass, "Identification card please?"

"Nah! We just here to see somebody, dat's all," said Rock.

"Well, I just can't let you in like that," said Larry, before being propositioned.

"Look man. We're only going to be a minute. I'll tell you what, how about this?" said Rock, holding out a hundred dollar bill.

"In that case, go ahead," Larry said, taking the money and lifting the gate.

Rock drove into the complex in search of number 36C and to their benefit it was right next to the tree line.

"Bingo!" said BoBo, adrenaline pumping.

+   +   +   +

Rasul, Rod, Pretty E, and Hit Man sat smoking blunt after blunt while gambling with each other on the Sony PlayStation. They hadn't realized time had elapsed like it did until Dog glanced at the clock. It was 5:30 p.m., and the sky was already dimming into what would soon be darkness, and they hadn't even begun putting together their mission.

"Yo, let's start getting ready to handle this "BI" 'cause it's getting late," Dog said, as the last of the blunt smoke escaped his lungs.

"Yeah. 'Cause I gotta drive all the way up to Philly," Rasul added standing up to stretch his legs.

"Yo. How we goin' to do this shit again?" asked Hit Man making sure everyone was on the same page.

Pretty E and Dog went over the plans one more time from the top. The plan was to stick Malik and Shawn up for everything at their stash house on the North Side. Over the past couple of months, Malik
and Shawn came from outta nowhere, splurging on to the drug scene causing a shortage to their money being made, and that was no good. Dog, Pretty E, and Hit Man laid low and watched their every move. That was their thing! Watching and waiting for new dealers to make a move in the game, so they could knock them off. It was called capitalism. An idea they thought of long ago. "Why should we risk going to jail for pumping hand to hand on some street corner, when we can let the next muthafucka get da gravy, and we take it! Feel me?" Hit Man said, during one of their many get togethers, and it stuck, they lived by it.

Leaving the house, they piled in Tameeka's Cadillac and headed to the city. Rasul drove around each side of town, tooting the horn at people he hadn't seen in years, trying to waste time so they can begin. Around 8:30 p.m., it was totally black outside with the exception of the streetlights. Time to begin! Rasul drove the car to a nice residential area of Wilmington's small city on 38th and Van Buren Street. The quiet row homes that lined the block were considered middle class living, a place where people were financially stable. As he drove up and down the streets within a four-block radius, he thought back to the days when he, Dog and Hit Man would walk up here from the projects to go swimming at P.S. Dupont School. It was like entering a new world to them as kids, and was one of their many dreams to own one of the mansions. Now, as an adult he realized the homes weren't at all mansions, but merely row homes in a good neighborhood, he smiled.

Pulling into one of the alleyways behind a row of homes, Rasul hit the lights. He eased up the alleyway coasting with just his foot off the brake, until he pulled up next to a Ford Explorer and stopped. Hit Man, the car thief from their younger days, went into action. In a matter of seconds, he was sliding the pulley down into the door's window frame, and unlocking the door to enter. Just like that, the jeep came to life and Hit Man was leading the Cadillac out of the alley.

+   +   +   +

"Damn! Where are they going?" Det. Armstrong asked himself, as he followed the Cadillac around in circles. He hadn't let them out of his sight since earlier today at Us Guys Construction sight because his gut feeling said not to. He had a feeling something was
going down, and now as he sat two alleyways behind Rasul, Dog, Hit Man, and Pretty E he found out his intuition was right. He fought the urge to run up on them now but decided to wait. He watched anxiously as Hit Man went into action, and followed as they left. Two blocks away from the petty car theft crime scene, Det. Armstrong cut on the flashers in his unmarked car stopping the Cadillac.

"Man this muthafucka is a nuisance!" Dog said, as he turned in his seat watching Armstrong approach through the rear window.

"Hey guys. Looks like grand auto theft is a hobby of y'alls, huh?" he asked with a sinister grin.

"What auto theft? This car is registered and insured," said Rasul.

"Was the jeep?" Armstrong shot back.

"Damn nigga! How long you been following us?" Dog snapped, and then continued, "We already paid you!"

"Long enough to know something is going down tonight and I want in. Now what are the plans guys?"

Dog's mind was racing as he watched the curiosity of the crooked cop's eyes. He was trying to read the detective's whole demeanor and greed was most definitely something he saw.

"I got it!" Dog said to himself then, asked the detective, "What are you doing tonight?"

"Why?" asked Armstrong.

"Never mind." Dog said, throwing the bait to the detective.

"No! Why?" asked Armstrong, in a more greedy tone.

"Because something big is about to go down, feel me? I'm talking four kilos' and fifty-thousand or more understand and by you holding us the fuck up, you fucking up the plans!" Dog said. Pretty E and Rasul looked at Dog like he was crazy.

"Yo man! What da fuck!" Pretty E said, tapping Dog's shoulder from the backseat. He turned briefly and gave them a look that it was all good, and turned back to the detective.

"What plans?" Armstrong asked, in disbelief overtaken by the words, "fifty-thousand."

"Look, we don't have time to explain, but if you want in you're in. Just let us go and we'll break you off, before we don't get nuffin' cause we missed them," Dog said, impatiently.

"I'm in!" Armstrong said, catching the bait like a fish. His mind was in frenzy and his first thought was keeping it all." Who are they going to tell? Hell! I'm a cop for God's sake, no one would believe I'd ever been in such a thing," he managed to reason with himself.

"Well come on then," Dog said uninterested that the detective decided to come instead of just collecting his share. That made Det. Armstrong even more willing, hearing the disappointment in Dog's voice. "Yeah! Im'ma keep all the shit!" Det. Armstrong thought, as he stared in the car at the young Bucks.

Hit Man saw the detective's car pull Rasul over and he kept going as planned. He parked on the side of Haynes Park and waited patiently on the arrival of his boys, knowing it wouldn't be long before they pulled up. Starring out of the rear view mirror he saw the Cadillac turn the corner followed by the detective. "What da fuck are they doing?" he asked himself, as the detective parked behind the Cadillac.

"Whass' up?" asked Hit Man, as they approached the Explorer.

"Everything is cool," Dog said, and right as everyone was getting in the Explorer, he stepped closer and whispered to Hit Man," this is the last time this muthafucka is going to fuck with us! Feel me?"

"Word!" replied Hit Man catching on.

    +   +   +   +

Malik and Shawn sat in the young girls house on the North Side playing their usual Big Willie style, as Rita, Myra, and Dawn sat back smoking their weed up. Malik had been fucking Rita for the past six months. He ran her babies' daddy away for putting his hands on her. Rita was 19 years old and one of the baddest young jawns in the city. Malik's boys always got on his shit, saying the girl was too young for him and his 32 years. Malik listened and heard everything they said, but Rita's small compact body, coated with cinnamon skin spinned him the minute he saw her. He had to have her. Since then, shit has been going fine and they were expecting a baby in another two or three months.

"Girl , what I tell you? Didn't I say don't be smokin no weed with my baby inside of you!" Malik snapped as Dawn passed her the blunt.

"Boy, she only going' talk two pulls, damn! Why you bugging?" Myra said, adding her two cents.

"She ain't taking no pulls!" he replied, taking the weed from her and taking a couple pulls himself.

"You get on my nerves thinking you all dat!" Myra said, rolling her eyes.

Rita wanted to say something herself, but being stupid wasn't what she wanted to do. The money was too long and her girls could say or think what they wanted to. She wasn't about to lose Malik. That's why she's in a house paying a mortgage and they're still in the projects. What she didn't know was forgetting where she came from. She'd soon be reminded.

Malik got up from the couch and walked out into the kitchen to grab a Corona before calling Shawn and heading down into the basement. The basement, done up like a living room, was plush. The drop ceiling hung just enough to reach up to touch it with a fully extended arm and the screen TV sat back customized into the wall. Black leather furniture lined the walls and a billiard sized pool table sat squarely in the center of the floor. Malik grabbed the remote and the wall slid open revealing a Bose Surround Sound system. He pressed the play button and Big Pun's CD pounded the walls:

Big Pun be the largest thing
Coming out of the projects
And Dat's How We Ro-o-oll

He nodded his head to the chorus and grabbed two snack trays from behind the bar, and sat them in front of the couch where he and Shawn were sitting. Then, walking over to a large picture of Malcolm X on the wall, he took it down revealing a safe. Shit had been butter sweet for him and Shawn the past year, and they were enjoying he benefits. Malik opened the safe and seven neatly stacked bricks of cocaine sat next to a large amount of cash.

"Look Cuz!" Malik said, smiling and stepped back so Shawn could see the contents of the safe.

Malik reached in grabbing two bricks and the triple beam scales, and placed them on a piece of the snack tray.

"Come on man, let's bag dis shit up and get it on the market!" said Shawn excitedly.

+   +   +   +

Niggas will find ya bitch
Ta Find ya bricks
See if you love ya chick
or love ya chips
4-4 Desert Eagle
Puttin holes in ya whip
Beanie Siegel, Desert Eagle
I love this thug shit!

Beanie Siegel
"What A Thug About"

Beanie Siegel' s CD played roughly through the factory system as the Explorer pulled away from the curb. Inside the jeep Pretty E reached in the duffle bag he was carrying, and handed everyone a mask and surgical gloves. Det. Armstrong sat in silence amazed as he watched the four young men work. They did everything with precision, always covering every step in case of a breakdown or fault. It only took two minutes of watching them work for the detective to close every case of open robberies in his head. He knew they were responsible for them all. Driving away from the park, Hit Man slowly drove to 25th & Madison Street cautiously zoned out in the lyrics of Beanie Siegel. Somehow,

someway the music pumped them up before all their missions.
Rasul observed the street thoroughly; glad to see it was empty of
people because the job would be a lot easier. Hit Man was excited
to see Malik's S-Type Jaguar parked out front of the house. He
almost stopped on sight, but continued up the street and parked on
the corner. Slipping into their masks and gloves they exited the
Explorer like a SWAT team, swiftly moving onto Rita's porch.

     Rita barely heard the knock on the door over the thump of
the stereo playing down the basement. Lazy, she asked Myra to
answer the door and sat still. Myra sucked her teeth. She was tired
and lazy
herself from all of the weed but got up to answer it. Without
looking through the peep hole or asking whom it was, she snatched
the door open. To her surprise there stood five masked men. Her
first instinct was to scream, but terror gripped her and she stood
wide-eyed. Dog was the first one to enter the house, brushing pass
Myra with his pistol in front of him. Rita and Dawn were half
asleep, nodding out on the couch, and never saw it coming. They
were awakened by the heavy footsteps and the sight wasn't pretty.
In front of them stood a masked gunman holding his finger to his
lips in a hush position.

     Armstrong followed Dog into the house and Pretty E,
Rasul, and Hit Man followed them, escorting Myra at gunpoint.
Sitting them all on the couch next to each other, they duct taped
their arms together behind their backs and their feet too. "Where
they at!?" Dog asked. "Down in the basement," stuttered Rita
before her mouth was taped shut.

+   +   +   +

     Bagging up the last of the two kilos, Malik looked at
Shawn and smiled. Feeling satisfied, he yelled over the bass in the
loud music, "You ready?"

     "What?" replied Shawn.

     "I said, are you ready?"

     Still not able to hear Malik clearly, he shook his head
anyway and began taking down his snack tray when he caught a
glimpse of a shadow coming down the stairs. He paid it no mind
figuring it was Rita and continued cleaning up. Just like that a
forceful blow caught the top of his head from behind, staggering

79

him into the wall causing Malik to jump. It was too late, three of
the masked men held them at gunpoint. Aghast, Malik stood still
scared to move for fear of his life. His nightmare had come true;
he had been caught with his pants down.

"Turn this muthafuckin music down nigga!" snapped Hit
Man, collaring up Malik by the shirt. Malik grabbed the remote
and cut the stereo system off, then, was led to the couch and seated
next to Shawn. Dog pulled the duct tape out and taped them up,
and then the three of them began ransacking the basement. Hit
Man grabbed the bagged up bricks Malik and Shawn had sat on the
pool table and Det. Armstrong, with police instincts, searched the
remainder of the basement thoroughly. Behind tables, lamps,
furniture, under the rugs,
and in the drop ceiling he searched until stumbling upon the safe
behind the picture. "I found it!" he said excitedly calling Dog.

"What?"

"The safe!" Armstrong said.

Dog snatched Malik up from the couch and walked him
over to where the detective stood in front of the safe.

"Open da safe nigga!" demanded Dog.

Without the slightest defiance, Malik followed every rule
figuring if he cooperates he'd still live to see another day. What he
didn't know was that everything he strived so hard for would cost
him his life. Malik entered the combination to the safe and stepped
back. He watched almost sick to his stomach, as the masked filled
the duffle bag with his $150,000 dollars and other five kilos. Dog
watched Armstrong load the duffle bag and by looking at the bulks
of money he knew it was more than he expected would be there.

Armstrong's heart pounded with greed and satisfaction as
he filled the bag. It was the most cash money he'd ever held in his
hands at one time in his entire life. "This is why!" he thought
about his decision on becoming a crooked officer, the money was
plentiful. There was no way he'd earn these type dividends by
being a straight forth officer, and he needed the money more than
ever at this time of his life. Gambling had gripped him by the neck
like a dope fiend monkey on his back and now as he held the cash
in his hands there was no doubt he was keeping it. There was
enough money here to save his marriage, pay his debts, and hit the

Casino's in Atlantic City, which had become his second home. A sudden fear overcame him as he zipped up the duffle bag with "his" money, then instinct said turn around. Dog lifted the .45 caliber, and the last thing Armstrong saw in this cruel and sometimes cold world was a quick spark of fire. He never felt a thing. The bullet tore through the middle of his eye, plastering his brain into the inside of what was just an empty safe.

Armstrong slithered lifelessly to the floor, leaving a streak of fresh blood on the wall. Dog turned to Malik without an ounce of remorse, then raised the gun again and fired. Malik was dead before he hit the ground. Moving quickly now, Dog placed the duffle bag on his shoulder and turned to leave. Hit Man turned to Shawn, who was still duct taped on the couch, and smiled a cold smile as he had done when Dog shot Malik. He literally shook with an evil excitement, as he watched the fear on Shawn's face. The minute he saw Dog grab the duffle bag and turn to leave, he raised his gun and fired.

+   +   +   +

As they parked in the Strip Mall across from the Condos, Rock, BoBo, and Dino exited the Yukon. Watching patiently and waiting for the security car to pass, they were in their own little zone. After the car passed, running toward the Condos in a squat position, they made their move.

+   +   +   +

Dog darted up the stairs, his heart racing, filled with a rush of excitement. This was what he yearned for: "The Payoff." And when he reached the top step, it was almost orgasmic. "Where's Hit Man," Pretty E asked in a whisper when Dog approached. "He should be coming."

Hit Man was downstairs cleaning his tracks. He grabbed the gun from Armstrong's waist, placed his own in Armstrong's hand and turned to Malik. He raised the gun and shot four more rounds into the already dead Malik and moved the body facing it towards Armstrong. He stood there for a minute and realized something was wrong. He put Det. Armstrong's gun back in his hand and placed his gun in Malik's hand. "Yeah" he thought, and headed up the stairs.

81

Pretty E moved quickly towards the basement door when he heard the shots. An uneasy feeling crossed his mind. "Damn Nigga, what happened?" Pretty E asked. "I was cleaning up, dat's all. Now, let's get the fuck outta here," Hit Man replied.

Rita, Myra, and Dawn watched in fear as the four masked men stood before them; one whose gun still smoked. They didn't know what was going to happen, but they all prayed a silent prayer to be rescued. Tears started to flow down Rita's cheeks as she thought the worst! Malik is dead! She looked at one of the masked men; her eyes slanted in rage and mumbled something through her taped mouth. Pretty E was the masked man. He smiled beneath the mask and walked over to her. Just then, sirens sounded in a distance. Her prayers were answered.

"Come on Nigga," Dog said from the doorway. Pretty E bent down and kissed Rita's cheek, sending a creepy, disturbing feeling up her spine, before he turned to leave. The four masked men darted

from the house, two of which carried duffle gags. Hit Man led the way and jumped behind the wheel off the Explorer and brought it to life. "Here they come," Rasul said, as they all piled in. He was still a little nervous, not yet

adjusted to the streets thoroughly. Hit Man mashed the gas causing the wheels to screech, leaving about 10 feet of skid marks as they headed up the one-way street.

+   +   +   +

Det. Cohen was in an unmarked car. He watched from four cars back as the masked men ran from the house to an awaiting get-away jeep. With patrol cars behind the jeep, he was sure they'd be run down, so he stopped at the house. Det. Cohen, along with three other detectives, and several uniformed officers entered the house on 25th and Madison Street. The first thing they saw was the three young ladies duct taped, bound, and gagged on the sofa. A familiar scene for Det. Cohen, as he thought back to Jamar, Smooth, and Sarah. Instantly, he knew the same people were responsible. He waited for the uniformed officers to cut the ladies loose, and then he started asking questions. "Who was it"? How many was it? Where'd they go? Why were they here? Is anybody else in the house? No, you're not being arrested."

After the slew of questions, Det. Cohen learned a lot. Five masked men had came, four of them left. There were seven or eight shots fired downstairs. It was what they all expected; three lifeless bodies sprawled out on the basement floor. Automatically, Det. Cohen pulled out his cell phone and called the coroner, and then his partner. There was no answer!

+   +   +   +

Hit Man rounded the bend at almost 75 miles an hour, causing them to slide in their seats, but the assault never stopped. One of their slugs hit dead center of the driver's side window. The cop never felt a thing as he slumped over the steering wheel, the car still moving rapidly. His partner in the passenger seat tried to grab the steering wheel, but to no avail; the car crashed into the guardrail, blocking the road where the other two cars were. The officers in the two cars could do nothing but watch as the Explorer disappeared down the highway.

+   +   +   +

The crime scene was taped off and Det. Cohen stood off to the side observing as the fingerprint unit and the Coroner checked the bodies. It looks like one of the victims and one of the masked men apparently shot one another during the robbery. Forensics experts found traces of drugs, along with a substance call "Manotol," usually used for the cutting and blending of cocaine. Det. Cohen walked over to the lifeless masked man, and wondered what was taking his partner so long to return his calls and pages. He bent over and peeled the mask off of the body and saw the unthinkable! Everything stopped, the whole room stirred in disbelief! Det. Armstrong was one of the robbers!

Chapter Seven

Hit Man drove on I-95 rapidly in and out of the lanes, sometimes even riding the shoulder. He knew that he had to be off the Interstate before the helicopters were called and he was relieved as he reached the Pennsylvania Ave. exit. The Explorer stopped at the light and Hit Man decided to ditch the vehicle at the Reservoir, which was only a block away from Dog's house. Pulling up at the Reservoir, they exited the jeep quickly. It was pitch black and the streets were clear. This made everything more relaxing. Hit Man ran around to the back of the jeep, and dowsed the interior with a can of gas he found in the trunk. The rest of them stood off to the side as lookouts, as Hit Man threw the match and the jeep went up into flames.

The grandfather clock in Dog's living room read 12:45 a.m. Hit Man, the last one to enter the house, eased the door shut so he wouldn't wake Kim or the kids up. They all walked into the dinning room and sat around the large marble table. Dog emptied his duffle bag, as did Hit Man. The sight was a beautiful one, stacks of big faces tied in rubber bands, and ounces of cocaine occupied its mass. The four friends evenly split the cash, giving them equally forty-three thousand, seven hundred and fifty-dollars apiece.

"Look, Pretty E and I will drop this code off at the Stash house on our way to the crib," Hit Man said, as he placed the kilos back into the duffle bag.

"All right then," Dog said. "Well look Nigga, take me to my car so I can head up Philly," Rasul said to Dog. "Damn! Dat's right!" Dog said.
"Rasul, if Tammy ask where I'm at, tell her I'll be there in the morning," Pretty E said, "All right," Rasul answered, and they all left the house together.

Rasul drove the North Star up I-95 headed to Philly. In the southbound lanes, he saw fire trucks and police cars headed in the direction of the stolen jeep, or so he thought. There weren't many cars on the interstate, so Rasul drove cautiously, staying in the center land. Occasionally, he'd glanced over at the brown paper bag on the passenger seat and thought about what he was going to do with the money. Riding past the Philadelphia International Airport, he looked over and saw planes running down the runway, and decided a trip was definitely a must. He turned up the radio and began to think of Tameeka as the sound of Tina Marie's "Dear Lover" blew softly through the Bose speakers.

+   +   +   +

BoBo just dropped Dino and Rock off at their car. He was still dumb-founded about what he found in the safe. "A quarter mil," he kept saying over and over in his head as he pulled up to his apartment complex in Christiana: "The Harbor Club." He parked his 53S in its usual spot, and walked up to the door of the apartment carrying his new fortune, eighty-three thousand. He couldn't wait to see Shelly. She is going to get loved down like never before. BoBo walked in the apartment and saw Shelly's pocketbook and keys on the counter. He then looked down the hallway and saw the light from the TV playing in the bedroom. As he made his way down the hall, he smiled. "Damn, I love this girl." He thought.

Shelly heard BoBo when he came in. She had just finished taking a shower only moments before, and still smelled of berries from the Herbal Essence soap she used. She had hoped all day that BoBo would be safe going into Rasul's condo, and that the safe was still full of money. She loved Rasul to death, but her love for money meant more to her than anything or anyone. What she didn't know was that her love for money would cost her and BoBo their lives.

"Hey baby," Shelly whined as BoBo entered the room. "Was everything OK?" "Baby, it couldn't have been sweeter," he said, and dumped the money on the bed.

Shelly sat up on her knees and threw lumps of money up into the air playfully. BoBo dived on the bed and did the same thing. Before they knew it, they were in each other's arms naked and making love like two savage beasts.

+   +   +   +

Rasul pulled into the garage damn near four hours late, and went through the door. "Damn! I almost forgot," he said to himself, as he kicked off his Timbs, before walking on the carpet.

He walked down the hallway into the threshold of the house and there she was asleep on the couch, in her t-shirt and panties.

"Get up Baby," Rasul said, leaning down to kiss her lips. Tameeka was wide-awake, and had been all night. She had just finished watching an old episode of the "Jefferson's," and was waiting for "Good Times" to come on, when Rasul came in. She stretched out, moaned, and then, said in an almost whisper; "I'm up." "Baby, warm me up something to eat. I'm starving," he said. "I should make you do it since you don't know how to come home on time," she replied. "I was handling some business." "Well, I'm sleeping" Tameeka said. "Come on Baby, please!" He said, kissing and grabbing at her. "Boy, get out of my face!" She smiled.

Tameeka got up off the couch and walked toward the kitchen. Rasul sat there and stared at all that ass, as it shook uncontrollable like Jell-O as her panties jammed up into one cheek. "I'm'ma wear dat ass out!" Since she wanted to talk shit to Tammy he thought. Just then, Tameeka ran her fingers along the lining of her panties to pull the jam out.

"Ee'el girl! Wash your hands before you go fuckin wit my food. All in yo'ass and shit!"

"You ain't say dat last night when your face was all in it!" She shot back! Tameeka came back carrying a plate of steaming hot pepper steak and a bottle of soy sauce. She placed it on the coffee table in front of him, and then asked, "What's in the bag?"

"A couple of dollars, why? You need some money or some em?"

"Boy, I'm, straight. I don't need your money, I got my own!"

"Why you say it like dat?"
"Like what?"
"Like you was being smart or some 'um."
"Baby, if I need some money, you'd be the first person I'd asked, OK?" Tameeka said.
"It better be me!" Rasul said.

+   +   +   +

Det. Cohen was at a lost for words when his partner's wife, Mrs. Armstrong, answered the phone the next morning. It was too late last night to wake her up with such horrendous news, so he waited. He couldn't even get the words out. She already knew. She just had that feeling. "My husband is dead, isn't he?" "Yes, I'm afraid so," answered Det. Cohen. That was the last words they spoke, then he heard the dial tone. Det. Cohen walked into the locker room area, and all eyes were on him. He stood at his partner's locker and began to empty it out. "What the fuck is this? Who put this shit here," he snapped, as he held a mask in his hand. The other officers snickered and turned their heads the other way. "Fine! Fuck all you!" Det. Cohen yelled. From that moment on, he vowed that nothing would stop him from getting whoever was behind the robberies.

+   +   +   +

Rasul woke up the next morning bright and early. Tameeka had already gotten up and he could smell the breakfast being cooked. After brushing his teeth and washing his face, he headed downstairs.

Tameeka and Jaquaan were both in the kitchen when Rasul walked in. Jaquaan was a spitting image of his mother. "Good morning Baby," Tameeka said cheerfully, "This is Jaquaan!" "Hey whass'up young'in! How you doing?" Rasul said. "I'm cool," said Jaquaan, really not at all interested in any conversation.

Rasul felt the vibe and smiled. He probably would have felt the same way about his mom's boyfriend the first time meeting him, but she never brought any of them around. Tameeka placed her plates on the table in front of them and she sat down to join them. Rasul started the conversation.

"Do you like sports?"

"Yeah, I play ball at the F.L.C." Jaquaan said.

"Do you start?"

"Yeah, I start Varsity, and I'm only a sophomore." Jaquaaan said.

"Oh, so your game is like dat?"

"I'm the man! Nigga's can't hold me!" Jaquaan said.

"What da fuck did I tell you about your mouth? "Do you want me to smack your damn teeth down your throat," Tameeka interrupted.

"No." Jaquaan said.

"Well, watch what da hell you say, 'cause you ain't grown!" Rasul started the conversation right back up, and Tameeka just sat there and smiled. She was glad to see her son interacting with her new man. She knew if Jaquaan accepted Rasul, the better their chances were at keeping their relationship together.

"So whass'up Man? You hanging wit me today," Rasul asked Jaquaan?

"If my Mom lets me!" Jaquaan said.

"I got you," Rasul said, and shot a wink of his eye across the table at her.

Inside the car, Jaquaan was messing with the stereo system, and asking a ton of questions. Rasul just drove, answering most of them with one-liner responses.

"Where we going?" Jaquaan asked.

"Delaware!"

"Dat's where you from?" Jaquaan said.

"Yeah!"

"What is it like down there?" Jaquaan asked.

"You'll see!"

"Oh…. Do you gotta car?" Jaquaan asked Rasul.

"Yeah!"

"What kind?" Jaquaan said with curiosity.

"A 600 SE Benz!"

"For real, can I drive?" Jaquaan said excitedly.

"Do you drive"?

"Yeah, me and my boys be stealing cars. My mom doesn't know though." Jaquaan said with a hint of pride.

"Let me tell you something young brother, I started out stealing cars and ended up doing 8 years of my life in a Federal prison. That ain't the way to go. Keep playing your basketball. If you want to take your girl out or some 'em, and need a car, all you gotta do is ask me. I'll let you use mine. I just don't want to see you go to jail, or hurt yourself. That'll kill your Mom! You hear?"

"Yeah! But don't tell her!" Jaquaan said. "Tell her what?" Rasul asked. "About me stealing cars!" Jaquaan said with intensity.

"Alright but you better not take another one, cause then you gotta

deal wit me…. I can't stand any liars." Rasul said and looked over
at Jaquaan. "Aw'ight." Jaquaan said.

They hit the Delaware State line in no time, and Jaquaan
just looked out the window eyeing the scenery. He knew his way
to Delaware, but just not around Delaware. Rasul kept on driving
and
told Jaquaan they would ride around later. First, they had to shoot
to his crib, Brandywine Condos.

As Rasul pulled into the complex, something in the air
didn't feel right. "Oh shit! Dat shit is hot! Is that yours?"
Jaquaan asked as they pulled up next to the Benz." "Yeah, dat's
mine." Rasul got out of the car and Jaquaan followed him up the
corridor to his condo door. Rasul put his key in the hole and the
whole door fell off the hedges. He reached back with one hand
and pushed Jaquaan up against the wall. "Go back and get in the
car," Rasul said. Jaquaan did what he was told, but glanced over
his shoulder, his heart racing, as he saw Rasul pull out a gun from
the small of his back. Rasul walked into the condo and it was in
total disarray. Furniture was flipped over, pictures were snatched
from the walls, and shit was thrown all over the place. He walked
back to his bedroom slowly with his gun raised in front of him, and
saw the empty closet. The safe was gone!

Rasul attempted to call Dog. "Please hold while the next
Nextel subscriber you're trying to reach is located," the automated
voice said twice before the phone rung. Dog answered on the
second ring and Rasul began telling him how the door to his unit
just fell in, his condo had been ransacked and his safe was gone!

"Your safe is gone?" asked Dog not believing what he had
just heard. "Yeah, it's gone, but I ain't worried about that though,
wasn't nuffin in it, was it?" "Nigga, what chu mean you ain't
worried about it? Nigga, your quarter mil was in that safe!" "I
thought y'all all had it! "Nah man, look don't move. Im'ma call
Pretty E and Hit Man, and we're on our way."

Rasul and Jaquaan sat in the Caddie waiting for his boys to
come. He was talking on the car phone to Tameeka, but never told
her what went down. He even made sure Jaquaan wouldn't say
anything about it either by peeling him off a hundred-dollar bill.

On that note, Dog's Escalade pulled up behind him, followed by Pretty E's crop top SC 400 Lexus Coupe. "Yo, what happened?" Hit Man said, as the four of them stood behind the cars. "Man, I came home, and my shit had been shooed down," Rasul said. That was all he had to say. Hit Man knew from the door, as did Dog and Pretty E, that Shelly was behind this shit. "Man, the only person who knows where you live besides us is da bitch Shelly," Hit Man responded. I didn't think she'd do no shit like this to me," Rasul said! "Nigga, you don't know Shelly. That's her M.O. but she fucked wit da right nigga this time, though! We got her ass, Hit Man said!"

Rasul gave his keys to Jaquaan and told him to take his car up to Philly and put it in the garage. "I know you going to ride around, just be careful, and don't crash my shit." "Aw'ight," Jaquaan said, almost too excited. "And tell your Mom I'll call her later." They all piled in the Escalade and led Jaquaan to the highway before they went to handle their business. They didn't want to put too much pressure on Shelly, they wanted her to come to them and they knew just how to lure her into a setup.

+   +   +   +

BoBo and Shelly were just turning over at noon from a long night of passion and love making, on stacks of money. Shelly jumped up like it was Christmas in the dead summer, as she realized it wasn't a dream. It was real and to make sure she grabbed a handful of money and smelled it. BoBo watched, as Shelly stood nude in front of the mirror on the dresser, and decided he was going to do something special for her. "Baby, he called gaining attention, "Let's get married." Shelly, not sure of what she just heard, asked, "what did you just say" yet smiling from ear to ear. "I said, let's get married!" BoBo said with confidence. "I thought that's what you said! Yes! I'll marry you!" She shouted, and dived onto the bed with him.

The two of them took a long shower and then Shelly called Rashida. She couldn't wait to tell her the news. "Yeah girl, and he asked me to marry him! For real!" Rashida said shocked. "Yeah!" Shelly said with arrogance. "So whass'up with Rasul?" Rashida asked trying to start something. "Girl, I don't know…. I love him,

but shit! A bitch trying to get married and settle down, you
know!" Shelly said trying to convince herself that marrying BoBo
was what she really wanted. "Well do that shit then," Rashida said!
"So whass'up? You're trying to go out and celebrate?" Rashida
asked. "Yeah girl, whass going down!" Shelly said. "Nuffin!
Let's just go to the Casbar or some'em. It's Saturday night too, so
you know it's going to be packed." Rashida said to Shelly.
"Awight... well, let me
call you a little later then so I can go to the Mall!" Shelly said with
excitement. "Awight then bitch and you better call!" Rashida said,
and hung up the phone.

+   +   +   +

     The Casbar, located on New Castle Ave., in the bottom of
the South Bridge Projects, was a little hole in the wall joint that
stayed packed. Everybody who was somebody hung there, and
tonight everyone was out. Shelly and Rashida sat at the bar with
their backs to the door sipping Apple Martinis while eyeing the
crowd. The boys, Hoss and Dunn, from the Bridge Projects, held
their Moet gobblets in the air, and toasted they're together,
celebrating Dunn's release from Gander Hill Prison. The mood
was straight. Females strutted in the latest fashions, and the
brothers just sat thugged out in t-shirts, jeans and Timbs.

     Beast and his crew, full of young boys from Riverside
Projects, stepped in and all eyes soon turned to them. Beast sat at
the bar next to Hoss and Dunn, and his crew stood closely behind
him. The Beast was the name he earned, as he muscled his way to
the top of the "Game." Him and his road dog Bud had the North
East Side of the City in an uproar, and now that their big cousin
Rasul was home, they had even more power.

     "Hey Beast, where Bud at?" the young girl, Sharrie asked.
"I don't know Bitch! It looks like he is in my pocket," he said
rudely! "You ain't' have to say it like dat," she said smiling, not
even affected by the harsh way he said it." "Well, why are you
still here?" Beast asked. She walked away. "Damn! These Bitches
phat as a muthafucka," Dunn said. "Man, fuck these Bitches! All
they trying to do is freak a nigga, and get their bills paid!" Hoss
shot back. "Well, Im'ma pay them then! Dunn said laughing and

91

him and Hoss smacked hands! "Yo, my people been in here yet?
Beast asked. "Who? Hoss asked, 'Rasul!'"
"Hoss and Dunn didn't actually know Rasul personally, but they
had heard mad shit about him. They knew his boys were Dog,
Pretty E, and Hit Man. Rumors had it that they were all
millionaires. In fact, Hoss did a lot of his business with Pretty E.
"Nah, we ain't' seen him," Hoss answered. "Well, Im'ma
introduce y'all to dat Nigga. I know he's getting ready to do some
big things 'cause he always does, Beast said. "Yo, ain't that da
broad, Shelly," asked Dunn? "Yeah,
dat's her, answered Hoss. "Man, dat's her!" answered Hoss!
"Man, dat Bitch sharp as a muthafucka!" Dunn said. "Yeah, but da
bitch think she all dat! I tried to holler at her one time. She told
me, if I ain't have six figure digits, I ain't have a shot!" One of the
boys with Beast said. "Man, dat Bitch love my people! He came
home a couple of weeks ago and he ain't even fuckin wit her, dat's
why she still fuckin wit da nigga, BoBo," Beast stated.

+   +   +   +

Outside, Rasul had just landed in Delaware from Philly. It
was 12:30 a.m., and outside the Casbar cars were lined on both
sides of the street. People who weren't inside the bar and lounge
stood outside blowing trees and sipping beers, when Rasul pulled
up. The pearl white 600 SE Coupe came to a smooth stop, and the
people stood wide-eyed with their mouths open. Rasul put his
hazard lights on, and got out carrying his cell phone. "Ooh shit!
Whass happening Nigga!" Dwight said excitedly when he saw
Rasul.
"Hey Baby Boy! Whass' going down Nagga?" Rasul said,
just as excited. Dwight was his boy from back in the day; they
used to live next door to each other and Rasul had a secret crush on
his older sister.
"Aw man, ain't shit. Just maintaining, that's all. How bout
you?" Dwight said. "Man, I don't know. You know me; I'm
always making moves. Feel me!" Rasul said. "I see Nigga! So,
whass up?" Dwight said. "Give me your number and shit, some
big things are getting ready to happen. You wit me?" Rasul asked.
"You know I am!" Dwight said, handing him his number on an old
napkin he just picked up. Dwight's consign, "Im'ma get wit you

92

then." Oh, and tell your Mom and them, Im'ma stop by and see them," Rasul said, and Dwight walked away!

Rasul called Dog, Hit Man, and Pretty E at the house in Saddle Brook, and everything was ready to go. He double-parked his Benz, then, stepped into the Casbar. The music was loud and cigarette smoke filled the air, burning Rasul's eyes as he stepped through the door. He didn't notice Shelly at first, because her back was turned to him, but he did see his Lil' cousin Beast who was at the other end of the bar. Whispers spread throughout the bar when people noticed Rasul, and the girls' became fidgety sitting on their stools hoping to get his attention. Rasul threw his hand up into the air, and the lights bounced off his Presidential Rolex like a disco ball. Breast, Hoss, and Dunn did the same thing, then, got off their stools to meet him.

Shelly's heart pounded so hard, she felt the beat in her ears, when she saw Rasul. He had walked right past her, but she knew he had seen her when he turned around. He didn't know I had anything to do with it, she convinced herself, but felt even more relieved when BoBo and them came in. BoBo stood next to Shelly and she pointed Rasul out to him. Immediately, he felt inferior to Rasul because he knew Shelly would never love him like she loved that Nigga.

"Yo cousin, the broad Shelly just pointed you out to the boy BoBo," said Beast! Rasul turned around and smiled. He looked Shelly straight in the face and blew her a kiss. BoBo was infuriated when he saw her drop her head and blush. "What Nigga," he yelled from the bar! Rasul paid him no attention as Beast, Hoss, and Dunn stood up and yelled back! Before he knew it, they were headed his way. "Meet me at the house, Baby," BoBo said, and directed Shelly and Rashida to the door.

All hell broke loose at the Casbar as people trampled over each other trying to get out! Somehow, throughout all the commotion, Shelly got separated from Rashida. She stood outside by herself. Rasul never got involved with the fight, but Beast, Hoss and Dunn went heads up with BoBo and a couple of other cats, as he slipped out the door. His plan was going perfectly as the commotion continued. Shelly stood at the end of the block unnoticed. The tumbling carried out into the streets. People were

scrambling to their cars, as Rasul made a U-turn and eased down
the street.

"Come on," he said to Shelly through a half-cracked
window. "I'm waiting on Rashida!" Shelly said sternly. "Girl,
why you frontin? Get in the car," He said again. "I said, I'm
waiting on Rashida!" Shelly said agitated. "You know I love you
right!" Rasul said trying to play on Shelly's emotions. "No the
fuck you don't!" Shelly said. "Are you getting in or what?" Rasul
asked getting impatient. Shelly didn't think twice as she looked up
and down the street making sure nobody saw her getting in. "And
I'm engaged," she chuckled to herself as she pulled the door shut.
"Girl, why you trying to play hard?" Rasul asked. "Cause, you
tried to play me like I was some lame Bitch or some'EM! I stuck
by your ass 8 long years.
What? Was my life supposed to stop?" She asked. "Nah, but at
least you could of respected yourself...matter of fact, let's talk
about something else." Rasul said. "About what?" Shelly asked.
"About you coming wit me and we working through our lil'
problems, you know." Rasul said. "I have to be home by 3:00
A.M.," she said, looking at the clock on the dashboard, thinking
about BoBo. "Why?" Rasul asked. "Never mind!" Shelly said.
Shelly didn't give a fuck about the time or BoBo, she loved Rasul,
and the more she glanced at him sitting behind the wheel, the more
she wanted him. He set off a fire between her thighs that only he
could extinguish, and she knew tonight would be perfect. She
daydreamed about what she was going to do with him. Deep down
inside, he really did love her, and he couldn't understand how or
why she would send someone to rob him. It hurt him to his heart
to know that she didn't love him the way he loved her! "Damn, I
hope she didn't have nuffin to do with my shit getting robbed," he
thought as he looked at Shelly, while they sat at the red light.
Shelly was fine! She had her hair pulled back into a ponytail, with
a pair of tight jeans and a shirt with the back out.

Shelly felt Rasul's eyes roaming all over her body and her
crotch got wet at the feeling. This nigga got me fucked up, she
thought! But then she felt bad. She knew what she did was wrong
and now she realized the money really didn't matter not compared

to Rasul anyway! Instincts made her lean over and kiss Rasul on the cheek. "Baby, I love you," she whispered! It was too late.

+   +   +   +

Rasul pulled up to the Saddle Brook house in New Castle and all the lights were out. He led Shelly up the walkway and put his key in the door. As he pushed it open, he stood to the side and directed Shelly to enter first. "Go ahead, he said." Shelly was hesitant about going into the dark house, but stepped in anyway. The next thing she felt was a hard push in her back causing her to stumble into the house. She spun around on her heels and at the top of her voice yelled, "What da fuck is you doing, boy!" Then the lights came on. Dog, Pretty E, and Hit Man were sitting in the living room.

"Bitch! "Who da fuck did you send up in my people spot? Hit Man snapped, as he got from the couch and walked toward her. "I ain't tellin," and before she finished her lie, Hit Man smacked her viciously across the face causing her to fall down to her knees. The smack was powerful! The sound sent chills up Rasul's spine. "Bitch, Im'ma ask you one more time! Who the fuck did you send up in my people's spot?" Shelly didn't answer. She knew they weren't going to do anything out of the ordinary, like shoot or kill her, so she kept her mouth shut. Another smack. She said nothing. Another smack. She said nothing. Rasul couldn't watch! It was too much for him to watch! His first love was being brutally beaten. He turned his face when Shelly's eyes met his. He wanted to help but this was the "game." This was the price you paid when you did dirt. Shelly couldn't believe Rasul! He was letting Hit Man abuse her and a hatred she didn't know exited overcame her. "I swear to God when I get da fuck outta here, all these muthafucka's are going to jail," she said to herself, as the abuse continued. After about ten minutes of getting her ass beaten, she still didn't break. Hit Man was getting frustrated and tired of the way Shelly persisted. So he thought of something else.

"Open up that muthafuckin basement door!" Hit Man said to Rasul, as he picked Shelly up by her hair. Hit Man dragged Shelly down the steps to an awaiting chair where he, Pretty E and Dog tied her up to it. Hit Man went back upstairs, and Pretty E and Dog stayed downstairs with Shelly. "Nigga, whass wrong

with you, Hit Man asked as Rasul sat long faced on the couch?
"I'm straight!" Rasul answered sporting a mad look.

"Fuck dat Bitch down stairs! She don't give a fuck about
you Nigga! Man! Dat Bitch got da game all fucked up! She don't
even give a fuck about herself" Hit Man, said, but Rasul still felt
bad.

Hit Man walked through the kitchen out into the backyard
and in no time returned to the house walking "Rude Boy," his pit
bull. He turned to look at Rasul when he approached the basement
door, and said, "Man, fuck dat Bitch! He then disappeared down
the steps.

The sound of paws tapping down the steps brought Shelly
back from an almost unconscious state. She sat battered and
bruised from the assaults, and didn't know how much longer she
could take the abuse before she would break. Hit Man came down
the steps followed by Rude Boy, his pit bull, foaming at the mouth.
Shelly's eyes grew wide when she saw the pit bull drooling at the
mouth. Shouting, she said, "please, don't sick that dog on me!"
"Well, whom did you tell," Hit Man asked! "I ain't tell nobody,"
she said. Then Hit Man let the dog loose. Rude Boy lunged and
clamped
down on Shelly's kneecap. Shelly started shaking uncontrollably
and the pain was too much. She then let out a scream.

"All right! All right! All right! I'll tell you!" Shelly
screamed. Hit Man pried the dog's jaws loose and Pretty E
snatched him off, as blood gushed from the bite wound.
"Who was it, Hit Man asked?
"It was BoBo and them," she said, through swollen lips.
"Where's he at? Hit Man asked.
"He lives in Harbor Club Apartments, building 12, number
3." Shelly said. That was all they needed!

+   +   +   +

BoBo drove across town in a rage. He hoped, actually
prayed, that the fight over at the Casbar would still be going on.
He stopped off at one of his base houses. The woman opened the
door glad to see BoBo, certain that he would have some drugs on
him. But, he brushed right by her and went into the house. BoBo
grabbed a chair that sat near the kitchen table. He stood on top of

it to check above the drop ceiling for his pistol. He pulled a shiny chrome 45.cali from out of the panels, which was in a purple Crown Royal bag and placed it in the small of his back, then, he left for the door. Before the woman could say anything, BoBo said, "I'll be back," then, he left the house.

       He pulled up in front of the Casbar and the police were everywhere. They had the block surrounded and were escorting people to clear out the area, so he drove right pass. Still frustrated, he decided to wait. "Im'ma catch them Niggas slippin," he told himself, heading down the highway to go home.

       Once on I-95 south, heading to Newark, he grabbed the half of blunt of Hydro that sat in the ashtray and sparked it up. The first drag he took instantly took effect, as he blew the thick smoke through his nostrils. He was still coughing and gagging as he pulled into his complex's parking lot. He placed the pistol under the passenger side of the seat and got out heading up the sidewalk to the apartment doors. He took one more drag off of the blunt and threw it down because the fire had burned his fingertips. He thought about the half of a turkey sub he had left in the refrigerator. "I know Shelly better not have ate my sub," he said to himself as he turned the key in the door.

       The apartment was dark as always except for the light from the TV in the bedroom. He stepped into the kitchen and looked into the refrigerator for his sub. While standing in the doorway of the refrigerator, he unwrapped it and took a huge bite before letting the door shut as he headed down the hall. "Shelly," he called, with a mouth filled with food, but there was no answer. She must be sleeping, he thought, and continued towards the bedroom, not knowing he was about to stumble upon his own death.

       He heard the "click, click" sound of the gun gauge being cocked as the lights came on! BoBo stood stunned! He felt like a statue unable to move as he stared down the barrel of the twelve-gauge gun Hit Man held in his hands. Pretty E stood off to the side, leaning up against the dresser, holding a pillowcase. He reached in and grabbed a wad of money.

"Look familiar," he asked while holding the stack toward BoBo. There was nothing he could say!

Hit Man got off of BoBo's bed and with one swift motion, the barrel of the gun gauge smashed against his jaw. Pretty E caught him as he fell unconsciously in his arms, while pulling the rope from his pocket. After laying BoBo on the floor, Pretty E tied his wrists together. BoBo moaned, he was still groggy from the blow. Pulling him up on his feet, they dragged him down the hallway towards the front door.

"Yo, put this jacket over his arms so the neighbors don't see his arms tied," Hit Man said as they headed out the door. "Pop the trunk," Pretty E said when he saw the coast was clear.

+   +   +   +

Det. Cohen was lost. He had always been a straight up cop and never knew about the secret life his partner had been living. He tried and tried to get the facts straight. It couldn't have been his partner behind crime sprees, but then, why was he found dead at the scene? How was his high priced house and car that was out of the range of their salary being paid for? Things just weren't adding up. He knew of only one place to start.

+   +   +   +

Rasul, Pretty E, and Hit Man stood in the living room after pacing the floor aimlessly trying to find out what to do with Shelly and BoBo, who were tied up in the basement. They came to several conclusions. Unfortunately, there was always an uneasy feeling about the outcome. Either they weren't quite sure of how sound proof their plans were or whether the risk was too great of getting caught. At one point, they even thought of letting them go, but changed their minds quickly, knowing that they would run straight to the Police. "I got it," Rasul said, as he leaped up from the couch and grabbed the phone!

"Yeah, whada' ya want," the heavy accented Italian man answered on the first ring.

"Hello, may I speak to Mr. Vito, Rasul asked? "This is he."

"Hey, this is Rasul! Uh, I came across a little jam."
"Listen, call me on this number," Joey, "The Fox" Vito said, and then gave him a private number. The private number was ringing before he could get the regular phone on its hook.

"Hello," he answered on the first ring. What's your problem?" Joey, "The Fox" Vito asked. "Well, a couple of days ago, someone broke into my house and took my safe. It had two hundred and fifty thousand dollars in there. So, me and the boys found out who it was and snatched them up." Rasul said. "Wha ya mean?" Joey, "The Fox" Vito asked. "We kidnapped them." Rasul said. "Where's the money?" Joey, "The Fox" Vito asked. "We got some of it back, but not all of it." Rasul said. "They took $250,000 dollars, Joey asked confused." "Yeah!" Rasul said. "Well, where are the people y'all kidnapped at?" Joey, "The Fox" Vito asked. "Right here in the basement." Rasul said. "Did anyone see y'all grab the people?" Joey, "The Fox" Vito asked. "Nah, ain't nobody see shit!" Rasul said. "Are you certain?" Joey, "The Fox" Vito asked with concern. "I'm positive." Rasul said. "Give me the address where y'all are, and don't move. I'll have it taken care of," Joey, "The Fox" Vito said then Rasul hung up the phone.

"What he say?" Dog asked, over hearing the conversation Rasul had with Joey. "He said just chill, and it'll be handled! "He's sending Ricky and Nikki," Rasul answered. "Ricky and Nikki?" Hit Man asked. "I can't stand them two muthafucka's. I just don't trust em. It's some'em about them." The four of them sat around the living room, thinking separately. Each one of them was thinking about what
was getting ready to happen. Rasul felt the most uncomfortable because of Shelly. He still loved her, and couldn't believe she actually turned against him for money. He just didn't understand how or why she went there, when she could've had it all, once he actually settled down. "Man, fuck her," he said to himself the more he thought about it. "She don't give a fuck about me!" Rasul said.

"Rasul, you aw'ight Nigga," Pretty E asked, noticing the pain in his face. "Yeah, I'm straight." Rasul said. "Here, spark dis up then, Pretty E said, as he handed him the Garci Vega.

+   +   +   +

Off in the distance, siren's sounds caught their attention. It seemed as though it was right outside the door. Rasul got up off the couch and walked over to the window, and looked out. The flashing light lit up the neighborhood as an ambulance stopped right in front of the house. "Man, what the fuck is going on!" Hit Man asked, looking over Rasul's shoulder. "Man, I don't know." Rasul said confused.

The ambulance doors opened up, and Ricky and Nikki, dressed in paramedic's uniforms, got out and walked to the back of the vehicle and grabbed two stretchers. They each pushed a stretcher up the walkway toward the front door, and before they could knock, the door opened up. "Whass' up, Rasul asked," but Ricky and Nikki didn't respond. They just pushed right pass them and went into the house. Once inside, Ricky turned to Rasul and asked, "where are they at?" "Down in the basement," Rasul answered, as they disappeared through the door leading to the basement.

The lights came on. Shelly heard footsteps as she squinted her eyes trying to adjust to the light. She looked down at her feet and BoBo was lying on the floor duct taped and gagged. Her heart thumped so hard that she could actually feel the beat in her neck. She saw a huge Italian man with hairy hands approaching her. He was so big she didn't even notice the short chubby man standing next to him with the doctor's bag in his hand.

"Who are ya'll? Are ya'll the paramedics? Did the neighbors call the cops? I sure hope so cause I want to press charges on all their asses," Shelly said.

Ricky sat the doctor's bag on the floor and peeled the zipper back. He reached inside the bag and grabbed a rag, pouring a liquid onto it as he walked towards Shelly. He grabbed her by the back of the neck and held the rag over her nose and mouth. In seconds, she was out and unconscious, slumped forward in the chair.

BoBo was watching the whole thing. He tried with every ounce of strength he had to break free of the duct tape. Nikki, noticing the struggle, kicked him in the stomach, balling him up into a fetal position just as Ricky prepared the rag for him. In seconds, he too was knocked out. Ricky and Nikki began to work more swiftly now as they freed Shelly and BoBo of the duct tape. After they were freed, Ricky reached back in the duffle bag and got a clean rag and cleaned them up as best he could. Satisfied, he put everything back in his doctor's bag and zipped it up. Nodding to Nikki, he reached down and placed Shelly over his shoulder, and Nikki did the same with BoBo, and they headed upstairs.

Ricky and Nikki came through the door of the basement carrying Shelly and BoBo on their shoulders and placed them on the stretchers. They pulled sheets over both of them, leaving only their heads uncovered. Rasul, Dog, Pretty E, and Hit Man watched in almost a horrified state. They each were in their own thoughts, but thinking the exact same thing. "What are they going to do with them," as they led the stretcher out the front door to go to the ambulance. Whatever they did, they all knew it wouldn't be pretty, but no one said anything. They just stood in the doorway dumbfounded, and with fear of the unknown as the ambulance pulled off.

Chapter Eight

The stretch white limousine was in the same spot now for almost an hour, awaiting the release of Frankie Maraachi. A few news crew people were outside setting up equipment. And all of them tried to get a glimpse of the Mob boss's release. Many people speculated and the word was that "age," along with the "time inside" the prison walls, had done damage to the once flamboyant, handsome man. McKean Federal Prison's front gate slide open and cameras began to flash, as the Boss of the notorious Capelli family walked out. It was much different than everyone expected. The man looked marvelous. Being sixty-five, he didn't look a day over forty, and his head, full of graying hair, was groomed perfectly.

"Hi Frankie," a news reporter yelled! "Can we get a smile for the cameras", he asked, smiling at him? "How about a word or two," another one yelled? They got nothing from Frankie Maraachi. Nothing at all, not even get a nod of the head as the limo drove off.

+   +   +   +

"Wise Guys" a bar and lounge located on Union and 6th Street in the Little Italy section of the city, was jammed for Frank's coming home party. The two-story building smelled of all kinds of sauces and Italian dishes prepared by the chef in the kitchen. The music played loudly over the rumble of voices in the lounge. The club was decorated simply, but tastefully, as large photographs of Babe Ruth, and the "Great One," Al Capone, hung on the walls. The dance floor was average, and beautiful tables of marble surrounded by leather chairs, occupied the rest of the space. Joey, "The Fox Vito," was seated at the rear of the club at a large table surrounded by people who looked as important as him, along with Ricky, Nikki, and the beautiful Lucy. When Rasul, Pretty E, Dog, and Hit Man entered, Joey stood up and immediately directed them to the table, while the other patrons looked on confused because they were the only Black people in the club.

"Everyone, these are Frankie's adopted sons, Rasul, Eric (Pretty E), Michael (Dog), and Hakeeme (Hit Man)," said Joey as the four shook everyone's hands. "Hey, how are you guys? I'm Johnny and a friend of Frankie's, is a friend of mines," he said, as he handed them all business cards. "Don't ever be afraid to use the number, he finished." This went on for a few more minutes. Everyone else of any sort of importance said the same thing, so they ended up with more business cards than they were expecting.

"Hey beautiful," Pretty E said, staring at Lucy. He could tell he had an effect on her because she dropped her head, and blushed heavily. "How are you Eric?" Lucy didn't know what it was about Pretty E, but he intrigued her. She had seen some good looking black man on several occasions, but was never really physically attracted to them like she was to Pretty E. Her curiosity was arousing secretly. She had fantasized about black men. She wanted to know if it was true what they say that black men were excellent lovers! "I'm fine and yourself!" Pretty E said. "I guess I'm fine too." Lucy said. "I see somebody has the hots for Lucy here," Joey said, as the people at table broke into slight chuckles. "Don't feel bad, she's had that affect on each one of us," he assured him. "Yeah, she's something special," Pretty E, said. Rasul shook his head, as if to say, he just don't stop. Dog and Hit Man had the same thought.

The table where they were sitting was facing the entrance door. When it opened, someone yelled! "Hey, everybody! It's Frankie!" A cheer broke out, as people stood on their feet anxious to greet the "Boss" of all Bosses. Frankie stepped through the door wearing a tailor made milk white suit by Salvatore Bonfi, soft Italian leather shoes designed by Maury, and his trademark, a Cuban cigar resting in his lips. He peered through the crowd then made his way toward the back where he spotted Rasul. He stopped only to shake a few hands, and said a couple hellos. He got to Rasul rather quickly. With his arms wide open, he said, "hey son." "Whass up Pop, Rasul responded. This was something they started in prison. "Hey Joey!" Frankie said. "Hey Boss!" Joey said. "Ricky and Nikki!" Frankie said and nodded his head. "Hey Boss!" Johnny, Big Sal, Petro, and Mikey said as Frankie acknowledged them with handshakes! "And who is this," Frankie asked, starring at the striking blond. "This is Lucy!

"Lucy, this is the Boss," Joey said, introducing them.
"Yeah, she's my wife," Pretty E joked back!

After getting acquainted with everyone and eating a meal fit for a king, Frankie fell right back into the groove of things. It felt like he never left a year and a half ago! But it sure felt good to be back! He sat at the head of the table and eyed his four adopted sons with persistent stares trying to find something wrong or unsettling. There was nothing. In fact, the more he studied them, the more he enjoyed what he saw. They showed loyalty, and they presented an air of greatness. Hit Man, he felt was the more serious one, while Dog was more observing. Rasul was a natural born leader, while Pretty E well, he was a business-oriented lady's man. But that wasn't hard to tell. The way he and Lucy was all over one another giggling and touchy feely all night long.

Frankie's plan was coming together like clockwork, and soon he'd have control over the inner city's drug market along with the mainstreams shipping and docking down the waterfront. The Capelli family was already moving up fast in rank with the other 5 families in New York, as well as in Philadelphia. Their muscle game had netted millions over the years, and they bo-guarded their way into building contracts with major companies such as MBNA and Dupont. It was time for business.

Frankie gathered the men's attention by banging his spoon against his glass, and then gave orders. All of them followed him into the back towards the door that read "Members Only," while Lucy jotted down all the notes for the conversations at dinner. She smiled and waved her hand at the waiter and asked for an Apple Martini, once the men got up to leave.

Inside the private room sat only a few poker tables and one large round table. Each man grabbed a seat, and Frankie sat at the head of the round table, while Joey "The Fox" walked over to the file cabinet and retrieved the most recent books. Frankie flicked through the pages of the books containing everything from bookying, to building. He did so thoroughly, and everything was in tact, all except the drugs and the fact that Lenny "Fat Boy" Ionni was being ratted out for racketeering. He turned to Rasul and asked, "I have a little problem, can you handle it?"

"Yeah, whass' up?" Rasul said.

"There's a guy named Johnny Valentino that owns an auto body shop on Lincoln St. He's going to testify against "Fat Boy" next month on racketeering charges. He doesn't think we know, but our sources are always correct. "We need to make sure he doesn't show up for court."

"No problem." Rasul said.

"Good. Then there's the drugs, can y'all move em?" Frankie asked.

"No problem." Rasul said.

"Then it's set," Frankie said confidently.

The meeting was over...

+   +   +   +

Lucy was at the bar downing her third Martini when Pretty E approached her from behind. "Hi," she spoke more excited than she wanted to seem, but she didn't want her invitation to be unnoticed. "My, aren't we cheerful?" Pretty E responded, noticing the welcome. Lucy giggled.

The Martini's were starting to take effect on Lucy and she noticed just how handsome Pretty E was. Pretty E was tall; around 6'2'' with light browned skin. He had a curly little Afro with the temples tapered and when he spoke his lusciously full lips overcame Lucy.

"So, how many did you have?" Pretty E asked, grabbing her glass, only an olive left inside.

"Only a couple, Why? Would you like one? My treat." She responded.

"No, but I would like to take you home. You know? You shouldn't be driving." Pretty E said trying to act concerned for her safety.

"Oh, I'm not. I rode with Joey." Lucy said.

"Well, you're leaving with me." Pretty E said showing his persistence.

"My, aren't we demanding?" Lucy loved it. It had almost been two whole years since she had been involved romantically, due to
work and as she talked to Pretty E she realized just how much she missed the act.

105

"Yeah I'm demanding, especially when it comes to you. I've wanted you from the first moment I saw you. You are sexy as hell!" he said, meaning every word.

Lucy was speechless. Pretty E had no idea the power or the effect his words had on her. She was actually rubbing her legs together under the bar, wet with secretions.

"You think so? Am I really that sexy?" She asked playing along. "You know you are," he responded, then, Rasul interrupted them.

"Hey Lucy, can you excuse us for a moment?" Rasul asked, as he pulled Pretty E to the side. "Yo, whass up?" Pretty E asked. "Man, we getting ready to bounce, you ready?" Rasul asked.

"Man, I'm chillin. I'm getting ready to go over to the broads crib. I'm trying to fuck, feel me?" Pretty E said. "Man that broad ain't giving you no pussy." Rasul said.

"Man, that broad a freak!" Pretty E said convinced.

"Alright then. We getting ready to roll, so hit me up tomorrow so we can handle our business." Rasul said.

"One Love" Pretty E said.

"One Love" Rasul said.

"Is everything alright?" Lucy asked, when he returned.

"Yeah, everything's straight. You ready to blow this joint?" Pretty E asked Lucy.

"Yes, I'm ready to blow this joint." She said, mockingly.

Leaving "Wise Guys" Bar & Lounge, Pretty E and Lucy were greeted by a change in weather. The once beautiful clear sky was now darkened by night and heavy clouds, as rain poured down in floods. Pretty E told Lucy to stand under the foyer as he ran to get the car, and pull it up to the door where she stood. When he returned, Lucy placed her pocketbook on her head and darted out into the rain, as he held the door open.

"Wow! It's pouring out there," She said, shaking the water from her pocketbook and arms onto the floor.

"Yeah, and I didn't even know it was supposed to rain," he replied, as a streak of lightning lit the sky, followed by a tremendous boom of thunder. Pretty E pulled his S.C. 400 Lexus Coupe away from the curb in route to I-95 by way of Union St. He turned on 4th

Street taking it all the way down onto the ramp, and asked; "where do you live again?"

"In Newark, on Old New London Road," she answered, as the car escaped into traffic.

"Well let me know where to get off at," he said, leaning back into his seat. Lucy still couldn't believe she was actually going through with it, allowing Pretty E to accompany her. This was a first for her. She usually was so conservative and straight up that she was often taken as a no non-sense type of person, but tonight was different.   Lucy felt daring, and was getting excited just at the thought of how the rest of the night would go. She glanced out the corner of her eye at Pretty E and imagined him laying on top of her, as they had passionate, consensual sex; nothing more! Lucy just wanted to be fucked tonight, and fucked good for the first time in what seemed to be an eternity for her. She directed Pretty E off of the highway bringing them only minutes away from her apartment complex.

"Do you mind stopping there?" she asked, referring to the liquor store straight up ahead of them. "I'd like to get some wine to cap off our night."

"No, I don't mind. I could stand some too," he replied. The rain was still pouring down hard, but Pretty E didn't notice, as he jumped out of the car and ran into the store. His mind was too busy occupied by the thought of Lucy, and how she probably was a freak; all white girls were. He couldn't wait to tell his boys about it, as he stood at the counter looking out into the car as the man grabbed the Moet from the shelf. Lucy was one fine ass white broad. Her long blonde hair and wide set blue eyes gave her a Pamela Anderson look, just more conservative, but it was close enough. He grabbed the wine from the counter after paying the man, and headed back out to the car and pulled off.

The apartment complex where Lucy lived looked high maintenance and uppity from the structure and expensive cars that occupied the parking spaces. Building 227 was right in the front of the complex off to the left, where Lucy lived. The two of them exited the car and ran through the apartment building front door as fast as they could as the thunder still boomed occasionally off in the distance.

"Well here we are, at my little domain," Lucy said, turning the key.

Inside, the apartment was decorated simple. It almost had the exact look a furniture store display would have. Pretty E concluded that she'd brought the exact same lay out she saw and liked, and got it all at once. The only thing that stood out about the apartment was all of the many roses throughout the place.

"Why all the flowers?" he asked.

"Oh, these were presents. My birthday was two days ago," she answered.

"I wish I would've known. I would have given you a belated gift or some'em." Pretty E said.

"Oh, that's no problem. I plan on receiving your gift tonight." She said, and walked off before he could reply. He caught the whole message, and the sway in her hips, as she strutted down the hallway.

"Well, are you going to just stand there, or accompany me to my room?" Lucy said, getting bolder and bolder, as the night progressed. She loved it too, because she felt naughty, almost trashy, a way she had secretly always wanted to be, at least once in her life.

Pretty E followed Lucy into her bedroom and sat on the bed holding the bottle of wine. He popped the cork and kicked off his shoes, as a few bubbles ran down the neck of the bottle onto the floor. "I'll be right back," Lucy said, and left the room returning with two glasses.

"Here," she said fix us up a couple of drinks while I go shower up."

"OK, but don't take too long. I'll miss you," he whined.

"Promise," she said kissing his cheek before leaving the room.

As soon as Pretty E heard the shower running he jumped up off the bed, and raced out into the living room. He grabbed two handfuls of roses, and ran back into the bedroom pulling the sheets back off the bed.

Shaking and banging the roses together he caused the pedals to spread across the waterbed's mattress and then lit the two candles on the dresser. Next, he poured two glasses of wine and stepped out of his clothes, only in his boxers. Then he sprawled across the bed on top of the rose pedals.

Lucy came back into the bedroom wrapped only in a towel, surprised at how much Pretty E went through to paint a romantic picture of the evening. She smiled as she stepped towards him holding a hand on her towel, and a hand out to grab the glass he held. They toasted their drinks because so far they had been having a good evening; they drank and Lucy sat down next to him as rain beat up against the window.

Pretty E removed the glass from Lucy's hand and placed it on the nightstand. He lifted the window above the bed's headboard and the rain bounced through the screen like a mist, as he lay down next to Lucy. The two of them embraced and rolled around on the bed kissing hungrily, Lucy's towel coming undone revealing her tanning lines. Pretty E looked at her body and instantly became erect as Lucy grabbed him and stroked him slowly. She rolled him over on his back and kissed him down his body, placing him inside her mouth, as he squirmed from the heat. Up and down Lucy worked her neck, as Pretty E tangled his fingers in her hair, caressing other parts of her body at the same time, the rain totally drenching them now. Pretty E pulled Lucy up and she straddled him, as he played with her hair and stared at the ceiling. Biting her bottom lip, she let out soft cries of ecstasy as he went into the very depths of her. Red stains, and streaks from the petal covered their bodies and still clung to their skin, as they reached total bliss. Lucy was startled.

Her mind was going crazy as Pretty E showered. "How could I? What have I done?" Lucy thought. She never mixed business with pleasure and now she knew why. What she just experienced wasn't supposed to feel like that. It wasn't supposed to make her catch feelings but it did. Lucy shook away the remaining grogginess she had in her head from the drinking and jumped up putting on her robe as Pretty E came back from the shower

"What's wrong?" he asked noticing her sudden mood swing. "I didn't do anything wrong, did I?"

"No. It's just, just that I. I don't know? I think you should be leaving right now."

"Really" he asked. "For what?"

"I don't know Eric; I just really need to be alone right now."

"Alright then, I guess I'll be going," he said, putting on his clothes.

Lucy stood off to the side leaning on the dresser while Pretty E dressed. She didn't want him to go but he had to. She needed time to think. Her body was saying stay, almost still trembling from the events just moments ago but her mind knew better. She knew her emotions would override her intellect if he stayed.

"But damn!" she thought, I don't want him to feel that I'm pushing him away because I do want him. I just need time to think and with him being here I can't.

"Damn. Are you at least going to walk me to the door?"

"Of course I am." She answered, sensing his attitude, "Listen, Eric I never done anything like this before. I'm just really confused right now. I didn't plan on what we did, to have so much of an effect on me. It was different. I mean you-you made me feel. I don't know, just give me time to think," she finished, as they stood at the door.

"I understand," he replied coldly, not really effected at all. He was just ready to bounce. He had already done what he wanted, so leaving wasn't a problem.

"Do you?" She asked, he didn't respond. "Thanks," she said, and kissed him as he walked out the door.

Lucy ran over to the kitchen counter and grabbed a pen and pad. She raced back to the front window in the living room and watched as Pretty E got in the car. As soon as he pulled off Lucy got a good look at his plates. "Pretty!" she jotted down on the pad and placed it in her robe jacket. Lucy was a Federal Agent working undercover inside the "Capelli family" for the past two years. She was on the verge of cracking them wide open. However, now with

Pretty E, Rasul, Dog, and Hit Man, and the return of Frankie she was back at square one.

+   +   +   +

Two weeks had passed since Frankie's release, and it was only days away from Lenny "Fat Boy" Ionni's trial on racketeering charges. Rasul, Dog, Pretty E, and Hit Man went over their drill several times until it was perfect, then decided it was time. Rasul drove the busted up "Delta 88" and Dog, Pretty E, and Hit Man followed him in a stolen Honda Accord. They parked two blocks away with a perfect view of the shop; ran and owned by Johnny "The Rat." Frankie had given him that name as soon as he caught wind of him testifying against Lenny. Rasul pulled up in front of the auto shop and parked across the street. It was 12:30 in the afternoon and the streets were busy, crammed with people hurrying back to their jobs from lunch break, just as they planned. Rasul got out of the car and walked right into the shop through an open garage door.

"Hey. Who's in charge here?" Rasul asked.

"I am," he heard a man say, as he slid from beneath a car on a rolling board.

"Johnny?" Rasul asked.

"Yeah, and you are?" Johnny said with caution.

"I'm Dave. My boss, Joey, referred me to you. I work at the US Guys Construction Company."

"Oh, sure! What can I do for you buddy?" Johnny asked, as Rasul smiled. The guy was clueless, but Rasul sensed his slimy demeanor; he knew from the gate that this guy was a snitch.

"My car sounds terrible, it's really knocking. I think I may need an oil change."

"Let's go take a look at it then," Johnny said, and the two of them went outside.

Dog, Pretty E, and Hit Man saw Rasul and the guy they automatically took for Johnny, leaving the shop. Rasul gave the signal by rubbing his hand across his head and they waited.

"Turn her on, and pop the hood," Johnny said, grabbing an oily rag from his jumpsuit.

Rasul got in and popped the hood looking out the rear view mirror, before turning the ignition. He pumped the brakes twice

111

giving them the go ahead, and they were in motion. Rasul got out
of the car and stood to the side while Johnny worked underneath
the hood. Just then, Hit Man brought the stolen Honda Accord to a
screeching stop right next to the cars. Johnny jumped up from
beneath the hood to see, but it was too late. Pretty E and Dog was
already pulling the triggers. The first shot caught him in the throat
throwing
him backwards, the rest of the bullets spun him around leaving him
slumped over the still running engine. Rasul jumped in the Honda
and they were gone, just like that, in broad daylight, as pedestrians
screamed and ran for cover.

+   +   +   +

   News cameras and crews, along with the police had the
whole block taped off. Johnny Valentino a known made man in the
"Capelli Family" was gunned down. It was a media frenzy and
they were on it like a flock of hungry buzzards. Mike Sampson, the
leading anchorman in the Tri-State Area, was the first to arrive.
   "Hi, I'm Mike Sampson and I'm standing in front of the
auto shop ran and owned by Johnny Valentino, who was shot
fatally today by a group of assassins. Witnesses who saw the event
take place say it happened around 12:51 this afternoon. So far it
looks like a robbery attempt, but sources say it could have been a
calculated mob hit. Just in a few days, Johnny Valentino was
supposed to testify in a trial against Lenny "Fat Boy" Ionni, and
somehow police and special mob units think their information
leaked out. I'll bring you more on this and other stories tonight at
eleven.
   " I'm Mike Sampson Channel Ten News"

+   +   +   +

   Det. Cohen's new partner Reynolds accompanied him to
the crime scene. They arrived at the scene several minutes after the
actual shooting, and began questioning witness after witness, when
Det. Cohen got a feeling of dejavu. Witnesses said it was four
black guys, who did the shooting, yet the victim was a Mafia
member. Coincidence: he doubted it. Det. Cohen sat on the hood
of his car, as the coroner and police continued to comb the scene
for evidence. With both index fingers massaging his temple he
tried to then remember his partner Armstrong saying something

112

about the mob. He just couldn't remember. Something else stood out about this afternoon, it was just too flawless, something that frustrated Det. Cohen many times before. He knew of only one crew of black men he assumed to be behind this type of work, but could never prove it, and somehow he thought they were connected to this too. If they weren't then so be it, but he was damn sure going to start there.

+   +   +   +

Lucy was still on her lunch break when her cell phone rung. She reached over in the passenger seat and grabbed it on the third ring.

"Hello," She answered.

"Lucy, where are you at?" her Superior Capt. McMichaels asked.

"On my lunch break, why? Is there a problem?"

"Yes, and a big one at that," he replied.

"What is it?"

"Our star witness is dead," he said then he heard a silence on the other end of the phone.

"Lucy, are you still there?"

"Yes, I'm here."

"We don't know exactly what happened, but we think robbery. Four black men, early to mid 20's," he said as Lucy's mouth went dry.

"Well let me call you tonight, when I leave the office. Maybe Lenny will slip up and say something." Lucy said.

"Alright then, you handle your end, I'll handle mine," Captain McMichaels as the line went dead.

Lucy's heart was pounding in her chest, neck, and ears. She reached up into her sun visor and grabbed her pack of Marlboro Lights, pulling aimlessly on the cigarette as she drove to her job. "Pretty E," she thought matter-of-factly. She remembered the night at "Wise Guys" when they had a private meeting together with Frankie. There she assumed the Hit was planned. Lucy's job was important to her, but so were her feelings. The night she and Pretty E spent together was special to her, as were the others that followed. She had fallen in love with Pretty E. She had gotten to know him personally, and from the stories he told of him and his

113

friends her heart ached. She understood why they sold drugs for a living. Pretty E actually made her understand the struggles of a black male a lot better than what she thought. She realized that the world had been designed for people like her, not people like Pretty E. And it was especially designed for the black male to fail. Racism, discrimination, and the lack of ownership of their own businesses kept them unemployed and frustrated. Drugs controlled their communities; liquor stores were on every corner forcing them to fight a constant uphill battle. Some were fortunate; able to withstand pressure better than others, some just gave up early, figuring it just wasn't going to get any better, and some just put faith in God. Lucy had to think of something, but she knew turning them in was out of the question.

Chapter Nine

Frankie sat on his porch awaiting the arrival of his four adopted sons. He was proud of them and their job today, and wanted to let them know about it face to face. "Honey!" he called to his wife. "Can you please bring me a glass of Iced Tea?" Frankie still couldn't believe he was home. It never occurred to him until his prison stint, how beautiful it is to just be relaxing on his porch overlooking his five acres of land. Frankie took the glass of tea from his wife and strolled over to the horses stable and watched, as his thoroughbred "Wise Guys Prize" galloped around behind the mare he brought for him to stud. Frankie leaned on the fence and shook his glass rattling the cubes, when he heard the car pulling up the driveway.

"Hey Guys!" he called out, when he saw Rasul, Pretty E, Dog, and Hit Man getting out walking towards the house: "Over here," he finished.

"Damn! What's that smell?" Dog asked," I'm hungry as a motherfucka!"

"Damn Nigga you just ate! Man, you just a greedy muthafucka." Hit Man said to Dog. Frankie tried to make out what they were saying, but just couldn't quite make out the words.

"What did you say?" He asked.

"I said, what the hell smells so good? We smelled dat shit before we even got up here," Dog answered.

"Oh, that? That's just my wife's home made Italian bread and Chicken Alfredo; can't forget the clams in white sauce," he said proudly, as they joined him at the wood fence to watch the horses.

Frankie began, "I built this horse stable for my little girls when they were children. "Daddy," they would say, "We want some ponies." "Hell, when I was a kid my Pa was a butcher, I couldn't even get a dog. I was just like you guys to a degree, the only advantage was my skin color, but I was poor too. I remember like it was yesterday how my Pa would bring home extra meat from the market, and how he stressed the importance of hard work. Then there was my uncle Sal, he and Pa would fight all the time

115

about him not working, yet uncle Sal never wanted for nothing. He was my favorite uncle, and the neighbors loved him too. I wanted to be like uncle Sal. He'd

always come to my room and drop money in my piggy bank, and I didn't know till later that they were hundred dollar bills. We were crying broke, yet I had over two thousand dollars in my bank." He smiled as if remembering the day then he continued. "You four guys remind me of myself: young, ambitious, and hungry. What I admire the most is that you guys are all for one and one for all. I have big plans for you all," he finished, and then added, "Let's go inside" as he led the way to the house.

Entering the house, the smell from the kitchen was almost so overwhelming that you could taste the food through your nose. Frankie grabbed the remote and pressed the button, spinning one of the bookshelves around revealing a large flat screen television.

"I want y'all to see this," he said, as a pre-recorded tape of Mike Sampson played, talking about the robbery/murder earlier today. When the segment went off, he turned to them and smiled.

"Perfect," he said, "You guys did a perfect job. My inside source down at the station says that they are in a total disarray, that's why I called you over. Had they thought it was related, I probably wouldn't have seen you guys for a couple of days, but for now we're clear. So relax, but here's the real reason you guy's are here. I wanted to talk to y'all about the drugs. See, me myself, well, I don't deal in drugs. I just don't like to be involved, that's why we're stuck with loads of them. A few of my guys down at the Port of Wilmington, on several occasions have come across shit loads of the stuff, leaving me with well, more than enough. That's where you guys come in."

"What do you need us to do?" Rasul asked, as if he didn't know.

"I need you's to move the shit. Ten grand a kilo, that's it," Frankie answered.

"How many is it?" Dog asked.

"We'll just have to see, won't we?" Frankie was saying, when Mrs. Maraachi wheeled in a tray full of food.

"I'm not interrupting, am I? I figured you's a bit hungry," She said.

116

"Thanks honey, we'll make our own plates." Frankie said as she begun to prepare.

"Oh!" she responded, catching her husband's glare. She knew that look meant she was in the way of business, so she excused herself.

"Now, where were we?" Frankie asked.

+   +   +   +

Twelve o'clock midnight the very next night, Rasul, Pretty E, Dog, and Hit Man were pulling up to the warehouse right off of Rte. 273. The huge brightly lit warehouse was the center of everything the "Capelli Family" had their hand in. From the legit business to the crooked wholesales, they had monthly access to items they either stole, or high-jacked from the port, airport, or tractor-trailers they shook down randomly. Hit Man parked his I.S. 400 next to Joey "The Fox's" Lincoln Towne Car, and a van labeled *Us Guys*. They made their way up the steps to the main entrance.

Walking through the doors they were greeted by the hustle and bustle of the workers scurrying around trying to get there jobs done. It took almost five minutes of exploring the isles before they recognized someone they knew.

"Hey Kevin! You seen Joey?" Rasul asked, when he noticed one of the drivers from the construction site.

"He's over there!" He pointed, yelling over the forklifts and loud crashing sounds of crates and boxes being moved around.

"Thanks," Rasul replied, then wondered how many of the men and women knew their every day's job was actually ran by the mob.

Rasul led the way over to Joey and as they approached him, he was giving orders to a woman driving a forklift full of boxes. He pointed them in the direction of his office, and went back to instructing the woman on the forklift as they walked off. When they entered the office, Frankie was laid back in the chair with his feet up on the desk, talking on the phone. He nodded his head to them and held up a finger as if to say, one minute, as they took their seats.

"Whass' up guys?" he asked, placing the phone on the receiver.

"Ain't nothing," they spoke in harmony.

"Well, are you guys ready to see the goods?" He asked, and got up not waiting for their answers.

Frankie led them down a hallway to another part of the warehouse that was sectioned off. Inside the area was nothing except some crates stacked in piles almost ceiling high. One particular one was on the ground with a crowbar leaning against it. Grabbing the crowbar, Frankie popped the crate open displaying a weighty amount of cocaine bricks, as Rasul, Pretty E, Dog and Hit Man's eyes grew wide with desire.

"So how many do y'all want?" Frankie asked, smiling, as he handed Rasul, Dog, Pretty E and Hit Man a kilo apiece.

"Can you move em all?" he finished.

"Yeah we can move em all. Just let us do the foot work, get the word out that we got it, and they'll be moved," Rasul said.

"Fine," Frankie said, "cause there all yours anyway. Y'all are about to become some very rich young men."

"You ain't lying." Dog said, interrupting, estimating approximately fifty kilo's.

"Rasul I'll give you the keys to this particular part of the warehouse, so you'll always have access. Now let me get back to work," Frankie said, leaving them alone.

"God Damn!" Dog said, unable to hide his emotions, as he stood and turned in circles looking at all the crates.

"Man, it got ta be twenty-five hundred kilos here!" "At least twenty-five hundred!" Pretty E said, just as excited. "Man, dis shit only happens in da movies nigga!" Hit Man said, still not believing what was happening.

"Well look, we ain't just going to sit here and bullshit, nigga'z! It's real, this ain't no movie, and nigga'z we about to be rich as a muthafucka! Yeah we sitting pretty now, but I'm talking about being rich! Nigga ain't nuffin getting sold unless it's our shit. Nigga'z ain't gotta go to the city no more." Rasul said, meaning every word. This was the break he'd been looking for all his life, from day one in the game: a chance to be a millionaire, to get out, and help out around the hood. He knew by pushing the drugs through the community it was doing more damage, causing

118

more death, but everybody did. He had plans to help out once he was able, but right now this was the
only way. Wasn't nobody going to give him shit, and he knew that. "Come on," let's bounce, he said.

+   +   +   +

I'm out for short term goals, so when the weather fold
Put away the leathers, and put ice on the gold
Chilly, with enough bail money to free a big Willie
High stakes I got more real estate than Phil.
Shoppin Spree's Copin 3's.
Fully loaded, yes!
Bouncin' in a Lex Luger
Tie and smoke like Buddah
50 G's to da crapshooter
Can't fade me!
"Jay Z" Can't knock da hustle!...

Rasul, Pretty E, Dog, and Hit man put in two weeks of heavy recruiting and had big plans when they were done. They played the city close because, not only were the streets watching, but they were also talking now too. Renting a two-story house on Vanderver Avenue gave them an easy transportation spot, because it was the city's dead center. They did the footwork hollering at almost everyone they knew who was pushing weight, but they weren't the focus. The focus was the young boys barely flipping ounces, because they were the ones who were hungry. Pretty E scanned the east and West Sides looking for a crew of hungry young boys. Besides their regulars, they had managed to recruit ten strong, who they thought fit the bill to push the drugs non-stop. Just twenty more minutes and the house would be full with the crew that would make them all millionaires.

    Rasul's little cousin Beast was the first to arrive. He wasn't there to be put on the team. He was there to do business. He had already, along with his boys Bud & Toots, managed to lock the projects down with their own little crew so looking for work was out. Beast was there strictly to cut the rise of reeing-up. If the price was right and the coke was butter, then why risk going to Florida, California, and New York, it was just that simple.

    "Hey cousin! Whass' up?" Rasul said, opening the door.

119

"You tell me," Beast asked.

"Come on in, let's get off the porch. I'll holla at you in here." Rasul said, stepping back into the house.

"Damn! Where's the furniture at in this muthafucka!" Beast asked when he saw Pretty E, Dog, and Hit Man sitting around the living room in fold up chairs.

"Ain't none nigga! Dis house ain't for dat shit. Only furniture up in this muthafucka is a bed, and dat's for when a nigga find some strange "Pussy," feel me?" Rasul responded, slapping his boys' hands.

"I feel you cousin, but whass' up wit dat other thing?" Beast asked.

"I got em for you, since you my favorite aunt's son, just give me 15 G's a kilo."

"Say word, nigga." Beast said.

"Word!"

"Is it butter? Man cause I don't want no bullshit coke, then can't move dat shit." Beast asked.

"Nigga! You think your peeps would sell you some bullshit?"

"Nah, I'm just saying." Beast said.

"Hold on for a minute. Let me show you some' em." Rasul spoke and walked into the kitchen. He grabbed the keys from out of his pocket and unlocked the lock they put on the cabinets handles overtop of the stove. Inside, sat the fifteen kilos they brought from the warehouse the night before that he planned on giving the squad later on today. Rasul grabbed one of the kilos heavily wrapped in wax paper, and went back into the living room.

"Here nigga!" Rasul said, tossing the brick to his cousin. Beast pulled his keys out and dug into the corner of the brick to better see the product. As soon as the seal was cracked, the already strong smelling drug smelled even stronger, almost like a gas or glue smell.

"God damn cousin! You got some' em here. Look, let me go get right, and Im'ma holla back later, I want five of them joints."

"Aw' ight den, let me know when your ready."

"Aw' ight," Beast said, slapping hands with everybody as he walked out the door.

Right after Beast left, the crew of young boys started coming in, not all ten of them, the main six, one from every set except Riverside because Shay-Ball and Monk represented there. The boah Zoop-Loop represented South Bridge Projects, Mikeavelli represented the East Side, the boah Juan represented New Castle, and the boah

Skipper represented the West Side. The crew was assembled; now the only thing left to do was put the plan in action.

"Check it out," Rasul began, "Nigga'z is ready to blow!" He emphasized. "We got whatever the hand calls for, you feel me? It don't matter. I don't care if a nigga want ten bricks, we got it. Listen, every one of y'all is assigned to y'alls own set. I want, well, we want y'all to get y'all own separate little crews feel me? I know some of y'all been beefin, Zoop Loop and Skipper, so y'all need to squash dat shit! It's about dat money now you heard?"

"Man, fuck dat nigga! I ain't gotta fuck wit dat nigga to get no cheese, feel me?" Zoop Loop said.

"Man, fuck you too!" Skipper said.

"Well what den nigga?" Zoop Loop said standing up.

"Look man. Both of you nigga's chill da fuck out before I start snapping in this muthafucka!" Hit Man stated seriously, both of them know his work.

"I'm just sayin'," Skipper replied.

"What chu sayin'?" Hit Man inquired.

"Nuffin!" Skipper said.

"Now like I was sayin' Juan you and Mikeavelli report to Pretty E, Shay-Ball & Monk, y'all already know what time it is, Zoop-Loop and Skipper, y'all report to me aw' ight? Now look, this is how it's going down. We're about to go hard on these nigga'z, feel me? We got them things for 18 thousand, you heard? For y'all it's 17, even when we front them to y'all, so y'all coming either way, feel me? Look, the faster y'all move them shits, the faster we all get rich. We don't want no bullshit. So if you ain't feelin' the rules, then don't bother, cause once you take em they yours," Rasul finished.

"Yeah we don't want to bullshit!" Hit Man convinced them.

Rasul went on and on. Pretty E, Dog, and Hit Man adding their comments when needed. The tone was set, and the crew was intact, now the money would start rolling.

+   +   +   +

The house on Vanderver Ave. had become a gold mine in less than a month. Rasul, Pretty E, Dog, and Hit Man had barricaded the house off like a fort, doubling up the front and back doors, barring the windows, and having some crooked cable guys add surveillance on the telephone poles, giving them and eye on a two-block radius. The house was nearly impossible to penetrate, and if it was penetrated, the drugs would already be destroyed. They worked in shifts, Dog & Hit Man from 8 in the morning till 8 at night, and Rasul and Pretty E, from 8 at night till 8 in the morning. After every rest day, Sunday, they'd start the new week by changing shifts. In a month, with the help of the crew, they knocked off nearly 25 kilos clearing almost a half of million dollars. The word was out. Hustlers from everywhere Philly, New Jersey, Chester, PA., and even New York were coming down on the regular. The goal was to clear a million a month and at the rate they were going they knew it was attainable, that's why they put in around the clock hours. Even through all the long hours they still managed to maintain their social lives, all except Pretty E. Lucy and Tammy had him drained, not counting all the other ones he was juggling on the daily basis, and it was beginning to show through his words.

"Man, I'm getting tired of these bitches cousin. They be bugging, trying to stress a nigga out and shit. Im'ma have to cut some of them Broads off, feel me?" He asked Rasul as soon as they settled and after relieving Dog and Hit Man at the house.

"I feel you, but you do the shit to yourself. Nigga, you always did. How you gone!"

"Then the babe Michelle is on some dumb ass shit talking bout she pregnant. I only hit the thing like, three times!" He added cutting Rasul off, as if not hearing a word he said.

"Is she?"

"I don't know, but if she is and Tammy gets wind to da shit, I'm done! She's a crazy muthafucka! I love her ass though, I just sometimes wish she was like Tameeka, cause she on some' ol chill shit. Whass' up wit-chall anyway? I heard she might be pregnant."

"I don't know, she might be. She goes to the doctor's today, so we'll know some' em soon, you know? Who told you she was pregnant, Tammy?"

"You know she did!" Pretty E confirmed.

"I knew she told Tammy, and she has a nerve to tell me don't say nothing until we were sure." Rasul said.

"And you didn't?" Pretty E asked.

"Didn't what?" Rasul asked.

"Didn't say nuffin nigga! Dat's crazy cousin, you ain't even tell us nigga! Damn! She got you like dat?!" Pretty E said, throwing a guilt trip at him, then, smiling.

"Nigga fuck you!" Rasul said, and laughed. "I think I'm going to ask her to marry me, you know?"

"Nigga! Say word!" Pretty E said.

"Word. You know that's my baby." Rasul said.

"Yeah, she loves your crazy ass like a muthafucka. I heard dat. I know I'm da best man right? Especially, since I hooked y'alls thing up!" Pretty E said.

"I don't know, y'all might have to pick a number or some shit, cause I can't choose, you know? I might have three best men."

"I feel you, but you at least gotta let me throw the bachelor party. Shit you know them nigga's can't pick up broads. I mean Dog's girl, cousin Kim now she's right, but you be seeing what type of bitches he be fucking. He fuck's thug bitches, ugly bitches, broke bitches. He just don't give a fuck! Now Hit!" He exclaimed before going on, "dat nigga is crazy!" He finished, and they laughed since Hit Man only fucked with big girls.

"Yeah, I think you better do that!" Rasul said.

"Bet, on that note let's get shit set up, so we can get dis money," Pretty E said, and went to the cabinets to see how much work was left.

By twelve o'clock midnight, four hours after they got there they had knocked off a brick and a half. Rasul put the play station Dog and Hit Man had brought for the house on pause and picked up the real estate paper.

"Yo man, we gotta get ready and clean up some more of this money, cause I'm about ready to buy a new house and a club or some shit. How about you?" He asked Pretty E.

"I was thinking about buying a house myself. I might even cop my young jawn Michelle a beauty salon or some' um."

"Who?"

"My young jawn, nigga! Man, dat pussy is off da hook, plus she a good girl."

Rasul didn't answer he just shook his head. Wasn't even an hour ago, nigga was talking about cutting her off, now he talking about spending forty or fifty G's on her for a shop. "Fuck it! It's his money," Rasul said to himself, thinking about exactly how much money he wanted to clean up. Since tomorrow was Sunday, rest day. He, Pretty E, Dog, and Hit Man cleaned their money up at least twice a month, in a way that people rarely did. They each would take their own separate money, maybe 50 or 60 thousand up to Atlantic City, NJ. Once they got there, they would break the money up by taking 10 or 15 thousand apiece to different Casino's and get chips. After that, they'd gamble away maybe a grand or so and cash in the chips. Instead of getting the money back they'd ask for a check. The checks would be stamped by whatever Casino it came from, so when they deposited them into the banks, there wasn't any question about how or where they came from. That kept the Fed's at bay. Sometimes the checks came by way of one of the many businesses the "Capelli" family ran. Also, the business cards they got from "Wise Guys" Bar & Lounge the night Frankie came home, sure came in handy.

Chapter Ten

... Super Nintendo, Sega Genesis
When I was dead broke man
I couldn't picture this!
Juicy Biggie Smalls

In a year's time, Rasul had accomplished everything he dreamed of when he was confined to the walls of McLean Federal Penitentiary. His bank account had reached a million dollars, as did his boys Dog, Pretty E, and Hit Man, and it was still growing rapidly. Each one of them had invested into some real estate by purchasing homes and small businesses such as roofing, landscaping, and concrete laying. Their most successful ventures were the houses, which they rented out to Section 8 occupants, and "Ballers," a two-story nightclub for the High Rollers and Heavy Weighters.

Rasul rolled over and smiled as his baby Tameeka cuddled up against him. Her stomach was beginning to show, and her face and feet were getting fat. He kissed her forehead gently, causing her to open and shut her eyes, and then she cuddled up even closer to him.

"Ahn Ahn, back up off me! You always trying to be stuck all up underneath a nigga and shit!" Rasul said, as he playfully pulled away from her, nearly rolling out of bed.

"So what? I know I can, can't I?" She said, holding on to him even tighter.

"You know you can baby. I'm just playing." Rasul said.

"You better be! You know Jaquaan's birthday is Saturday, right?" Tameeka asked.

"Yeah, I know. He keeps crying about a car ever since he got his license." Rasul said.

"Shit! Who gone buy it?" Tameeka said.

"I think Im'ma go' head and get him one, you know?" Rasul said.

"For what? He drives yours or mines all the time. Plus it's about time for me to get a new one. You know me and Tammy are getting ready to settle." Tameeka said.

"Settle what?" Rasul asked.

125

"You remember that time with the u-haul truck." Tameeka said.

"Oh, I forgot all about dat," He laughed.

"Whass' funny?" Tameeka asked.

"Yall crazy as a muthafucka," he said, then, the door flew open. Rasul said.

"What da fuck did I tell you about dat shit? Didn't I tell your ass to knock on my door first?" Tameeka snapped, as Jaquaan walked into the house unannounced.

"My fault, I forgot mom," Jaquaan replied.

"Forgot my ass! Now, what if we ain't have no damn clothes on? Huh?" She asked.

"I don't know?" Jaquaan said.

"I would have fucked you up, dat's what! Now what the fuck do you want!" Tameeka snapped.

"Never mind," he said, his feelings bruised.

"Boyyyyy, stop playing wit me! What did you want?" Tameeka said sternly.

"I was going to ask Rasul could I use his car?"

"Hell no!" Tameeka said.

"But Mom." Jaquaan pleaded.

"But Mom shit!" she said, then, got checked by Rasul.

"Chill the fuck out, Damn! Why da fuck you always yelling at the boy? He ain't even do shit!" Rasul snapped at Tameeka.

"Dat's my son! Don't tell me..." Tameeka said but was cut off.

"Man, shut da fuck up sometimes ... Dat's my son too, now what! Matter of fact, look downstairs on the table, or on the kitchen counter and get my keys. You can take the car." Rasul said.

"You better not!" Tameeka said sternly.

"Man take the car, I got dis!" Rasul said certainly.

"Thanks Rasul," Jaquaan said. He knew exactly what he was doing by asking for the car while Rasul was there, and almost smiled when he saw his mom's face tore up. He decided to bounce out the room as soon as he got his answer.

126

"Get off me!" Tameeka said, pulling away as Rasul grabbed at her.

"I know I can, can't I?" He said, and she couldn't do nothing but laugh.

"Boy, you make me sick! Im'ma still kick Jaquaan's ass though, you watch." Tameeka said.

"And Im'ma kick yours."

Tameeka picked up the phone and called Tammy while Rasul was in the shower to make sure she didn't leave her to go to the lawyer's office because Rasul needed her car. He explained to her that he had a meeting with some real estate people for some reason or another, but she didn't understand. She just shook her head and acted like she did because whatever it was she knew her man could handle it. Sometimes she had to remind herself that she was eight years his senior.

Rasul got out of the shower and started getting dressed. Today was business, so he dressed in a blue, pinstriped Armani suit, with suede and leather blue gator shoes and matching belt, and then called Frankie. He wanted to make sure everything was a go, and the realtors would be on time, before heading down to Delaware.

He loved it living up in Philly and Mt. Erie, but he was too large now. The homes were beautiful, he just wanted more. He was a millionaire now, and was ready to start living like one. He knew of several places in his hometown in Delaware that were excellent living areas, and when the realtors said they had one in Greenville, he jumped on it. The house was a beautiful six-bedroom, three-and-a-half bathroom, three-car garage: a mini mansion. It was just minutes away from boxing promoter Butch Lewis and a block away from the middleweight champion of the world Bernard "The Executioner" Hopkins. It was the perfect place to ask Tameeka to marry him. Not to mention a perfect gift for her also.

+   +   +   +

Lucy walked out of the kitchen in just a T-shirt, no panties, carrying breakfast on a tray. She was whipped. Pretty E was sexing her like crazy, and her rational thinking was being altered each time she came. Lucy was cum drunk from all the fucking and sucking and was slowly slipping on her notes for the investigation.

Her real job as a Federal Agent was almost non-existent, she was too wrapped up in
Pretty E. Pretty E was a perfect gentleman to Lucy. He was always flattering her with comments about what she wore, or how she looked, and on occasion the boxes from "Tiffany's" really made her feel appreciated. He always listened too, and that was important to her being though she was living a lie. She was a totally different person with a new identity, in a world of isolation, with no friends, no family, nobody. She was alone until meeting Pretty E. He gave her what every person in the world needed, and intense affections that were sincere. Everybody needs somebody, and by him being there she almost on more times than one gave herself away by telling the truth and alleviating the weight of the lie from her shoulders.

Lucy walked into the bedroom carrying the tray, and blushed when Pretty E looked her in the eyes and smiled. Giddy, she dropped her head and thought; "Damn, I feel so high schoolish," as she walked over to the bed. She placed the tray on his lap and sat down on the bed next to him as he ate, with her legs open. He thanked her as he grabbed the tray and was almost unable to eat because he was distracted. The blonde strip of hair on Lucy's prize was almost impossible to resist.

+   +   +   +

Dog and Hit Man were at their last stop for the morning and was glad it was almost over. Their first two stops at the roofing and landscaping offices were routine going over the books and making sure everything was running smoothly. They pulled up to "Ballers" Night Club at 10:30 a.m., a half an hour late to meet with Sharon and the builders. They were supposed to be there to discuss adding another section on to the kitchen, as an expansion for Sharon's catering business, and as a expansion of the menu that just served soul food. With the addition of the an extended menu which included seafood, the kitchen would be a major plus to the money already being made at the door and bar.

"Hey y'all. Whass up?" Sharon, Pretty E's cousin asked, stepping out of her BMW when she saw Hit Man and Dog.

"Whass happenin'?" they replied.

"Ain't nuffin, just out here waiting on these damn builders to get here. They was supposed to be here at ten, but said the designer wasn't there yet, so they didn't have an estimate of the costs, but they're on their way now. I just hung up with them."

"That's whass up." Dog said.

"Uhm-hmm. Whass' up wit Chu Hakeeme? What? You can't speak?"

"I spoke." Hit Man said.

"No you didn't!" She said, rolling her eyes.

"I did too. I said whass up? Soon as we got out the car", he said, tongue-tied. Sharon had always had that affect on him, and he hated the fact that she used him for a rebound, but he understood. When they first connected and got together everything was already established. He had a girl and she was separated from her husband, so they were just friends who happened to fuck on occasion.

"Well, you need to make yourself clear then. You need to say, "Hey Sharon, on some' ol individual type time. Shit I do it to you, even when I'm wit my husband, so don't play!" she said, flatly.

"You got dat," He said, as the builders pulled up.

+   +   +   +

"Girl, you are carrying that baby low. You know it's going to be a girl, right?" Tammy said, as they walked down Center City, Philadelphia towards the lawyer's office.

"Girl, don't say that! I don't need no hot ass little girl, they are too much. I want another little boy. Let somebody else worry about pregnancy, feel me? I mean, if Jaquaan gets some girl pregnant, he's damn sure going to take care of it, I'm just saying, I don't want mines coming home pregnant, you know what I'm sayin'?"

"Mmm-Hmm girl, causes guess what? You gon' be the one taking care of the baby."

"I know dat's right!" Tameeka said, as they entered the lawyer's office.

"Grossberg & Grossberg" a personal injuries law firm known for getting you the best money for your injuries, was in the dead center of Center City, Philadelphia. Tameeka and Tammy

both had used them before and the results were good. They walked
into the office and were greeted by the coolness of the air
conditioner as they took a seat and waited for the secretary to assist
them.

"Good afternoon, Mrs. Grossberg will see you now." The
secretary said, after filing some paperwork in the cabinets, and
buzzing Mrs. Grossberg's office.

"Thank you," they said in unison, walking into the office.
Mrs. Grossberg, a forty something year old white woman, sat
behind her desk staring out of her window overlooking the city.
She spun around in her swivel chair and greeted them with a smile.
"Have a seat," she said, and went through the folders on her desk."
I have two checks here, one for you Tammy and one for you
Tameeka. I want y'all to look at them and see if y'all approve.
They are made out for what you'll receive. My fee is already
deducted. If you disapprove with the amount, I'll just send the
check and we'll probably have to wait almost another year, but I
don't think it'll be that much more. However if that's what y'all
wanna do, we'll do it." She said, and slid the two checks across the
desktop.

Tammy's check was for sixty-five thousand, and
Tameeka's was for fifty-five thousand. They looked at each other
both surprised, but concealed their approval. They both were only
expecting maybe twenty to twenty-five thousand, but this was way
out of the range they expected.

"This is fine by me!" Tameeka said happily.

"Me too!" Tammy added, and the rest was history. They
left the office of Grossberg & Grossberg fifty & sixty thousand
dollars richer.

"Come on girl, let's go to lunch on South Street, my treat,"
Tammy said, switching her hips gingerly as they walked down the
street.

"Girl, you so crazy!" Tameeka laughed.

                    +   +   +   +

Patterson & Swartz real estate agents were there when
Rasul arrived. He stepped out of the Cadillac looking exactly like
he was money. His whole appearance from his suite, tie, and gator
shoes, to his fifteen hundred dollar gold shades, spoke money. He

stood next to the car as he took off the suit jacket, and tossed it back into the car, then turned to meet the realtors at the front door.

"Good afternoon Mr. Jefferies, how do you like what you see so far?" Troy, one of the realtors, spoke.

"Impressive! Very impressive!" Rasul answered nonchalantly.

"Well let us show you the rest of the house, follow me," the other one, Steve said.

Steve and Troy took Rasul on a tour of the beautiful mini-mansion, pointing out every detail of the house. They led Rasul through the house explaining the grade of the solid oak floors. The back door leading to the patio was oak too, and paved in a Buckhorn Charcoal Flagstone. Banded in brick sat the second patio, a 5 X 6 foot brick wall fish pond marked the junction between the patio closest to the house, and the one they were standing on.

"This here was revamped by the old owners. The pump that used to run the old hot tub is now used to put circulating water into the fish pond." Steve explained.

"I see," said Rasul.

"See right here, the patio steps out onto your lawn, bordered by trees and shrubs; well each step is a single piece of flagstone. The house is a marvelous buy!" Troy spoke, as they headed in to look at the rest of the house.

"Here you have plain picture style cabinet doors and drawers that echo your window trim, and your counters are polished marble. Your double bowl sink is stainless steal, and here is your grill and 12 range stove." Steve explained, as they looked at the kitchen.

"Impressive." Rasul inquired.

"Great! Let's see the rest." Steve said again and they toured for the next hour and a half. Rasul saw the game room, the three-car garage and driveway with lights that ran all the way up to the house from the street, and the other five bedrooms.

"Let's talk a price." Rasul said standing in the master bedroom, the one part of the house he liked the most.

The master bedroom was laced with everything from a moon roof skylight with a cover, to a fireplace that was designed with rock, not brick. The conjoined bathroom was huge, equipped with a Jacuzzi, steam room, and a huge circular bathtub made of marble with
gold swirls. The faucet, with hot and cold-water handles, was solid gold, with mirrors surrounded the walls. It was perfect.

"The old owner was a huge Al Pachino fan, and the idea for the tub came from the movie Scarface, did you see it?" Steve asked.

"How much?" Rasul asked again.

"One point five," Troy answered.

"One point two," Rasul shot back.

"Come on Mr. Jefferies. You have a luxurious 6 bedroom, 3 bathroom home with a pond, a pool, a hot tub, a game room, a few acres, and multiple fireplaces; one point five is a steal!" Troy said.

"I get your point, but I'm only willing to pay one point two, that's it. No more, no less. I'm sure someone's willing to take my million." Rasul said, not budging.

+   +   +   +

Baller's Nightclub was the newest rising hot spot in the tri-state area. It was a renovated warehouse on the East Side of Wilmington, right off of Church Street. Thursday night was ladies night and the two-dollar drink special that ran until eleven, helped the door reach its quota for the night, and it wasn't even mid-night yet. Rasul, Pretty E, Dog, and Hit Man sat in the V.I.P. on a balcony overlooking the club's dance floor taking pleasure in what they started. They smiled to themselves as people filled the club to capacity. Just seven months ago they were robbing and killing to pump petty amounts of cocaine through the city, now they were millionaires.

Baller's was their pride and joy, a plan they had thought of way before they even had the money to afford it. It came second only to the love they had for each other and their families. Actually, it was like family, because it had a life of its own. They put a lot of ideas, time, and money into the old warehouse by giving it a total makeover and renovating it from top to bottom. The results were prodigious.

The bar was double sided and oval with three bartenders, which sat in the middle of the club surrounded by the dance floor. So when you danced you were actually dancing around the bar. The D.J. sat perched on the stage at the rear of the club, elevated above the crowd, as he spun the latest tracks, and a lounge was set up for the partygoers to relax. Plushly carpeted and furnished with leather, the lounge gave the club a touch of home feeling, which made it unique.

Upstairs, sectioned off from the V.I.P., was a social club's atmosphere. Tables and chairs with a small stage engrossed with a mic and mic stand occupied its space. This was where every Monday and Sunday night "Ballers" held an open mic night for poets, and local rappers trying to make it big in the industry. With the addition of Sharon's catered seafood menu, and the already popular soul food menu, "Ballers" was surely ready to compete with the big name hot spots on the entire Eastern Coast.

"Yo, Im'ma bout to go downstairs and see if I can't catch some em strange for tonight." Pretty E said, getting up from the table carrying a bottle of Cristal.

"Hold up cousin, I'm coming too." Dog said, as he staggered off behind him.

"Yo, them two nigga'z is crazy." Hit Man said, answering his cell phone.

"You ain't lying," said Rasul, as he watched Hit Man curse out whoever was on the other end of the phone.

"Look, I said I'll be home in the morning. I'm outta town, that's where! I know I been gone for two days and I miss them too! Listen, I ain't trying to be arguing with you right now, so I'll see you in the morning." Hit Man spoke into the phone to Trina, his kid's mom.

"Who was dat, Trina?" asked Rasul.

"You know it was, she stay trippin."

"I'd be trippin too nigga, especially if you ain't been home in two days." Rasul said to Hit Man.

"I told her I was outta town and the bitch still snapping!"

"Nigga she knows you ain't outta town!" Rasul said.

"How she know? If I say I'm outta town, dat's all it is."

"Well she gonna to know tonight you ain't outta town, wit all these nosy muthafuckas in here, and I still can't believe you bought the broad Angie up in here wit Chu! Nigga, you slippin." Rasul said.

You act like I planned on staying or some shit. I only came for a couple drinks, and to check on y'all. I ain't know you nigga'z was goin' to talk a nigga'z head off. Matter of fact let me get up outta here before some dumb shit do happen."

"Yeah, cause big Trina will snap, and I'll hate to see dat!" Rasul said.

"Man, she ain't going to do shit!" Smiled Hit Man.

+   +   +   +

Trina just put the kids to bed and was running her bath water when the phone rang. She almost didn't hear it though, because she was in the back and had the stereo playing not loudly, but just enough to hear while she was bathing with the door open. She ran out front into the living room and answered it on the third ring, and wished now that she' da let the answering machine pick it up.

"Uhm-hmm girl...Right here posted up at the bar with the Big Bitch, Angie." Lyneeka said stressing the words Big Bitch, as she looked across the bar.

"Girl is you sure? Cause I just now got off the phone with him and he's outta town." Trina said not believing the words herself, as they left her mouth.

"Girl, I'm looking at his ass right now!"

"I'm on my way! Don't let them muthafuckas go nowhere." Trina said.

"Awight girl. You know da bitch think we half ass cool." Lyneeka said.

"Ahhn–Huhn. Well keep da big bitch right there, cause I'm going to beat her ass!" Trina said, and hung up.

Trina couldn't believe what she just heard. Her heart dropped to her stomach and she felt faint the more she thought about Hakeeme and Angie together. She ran into the bedroom and put back on her "D.K.N.Y." sweat suit and sneakers, then darted into the bathroom when she realized she left the water running. After cutting the water off she stood overtop the sink, and grabbed a rubber band from the cabinet behind the mirror, and literally shook as she pulled her shoulder length hair into a ponytail.

"Im'ma beat this bitch's ass!" She said to herself, as she went into the kids' room to get them up.

"Boy, I said get up!" She yelled the second time, as she stood over her son, with the baby in her arms. Little Hakeeme stumbled out
of bed half asleep, but not fast enough for his mom and he soon knew it.

"Didn't I say, come on?" She yelled again, this time snatching him by the arm. "Here boy! Put your damn shoes on!" She snapped holding a sneaker to his foot. No sooner than he stepped in his shoes, Trina was dragging him off down the hall, carrying the baby in her arms, heading out the door to the truck.

"Latoya?" She said into her cell phone, as she put the kids in the Excursion. "Girl be at the door when I get there. I need you to watch my kids, while I go beat this Bitch's ass!" she said, backing out of the driveway.

"Who? Girl" asked Latoya.

"Da Bitch Angie, from over Market Street," she answered, and hung up.

The lounge area in the club was cluttered with people, and the waiters were moving frantically to keep everyone satisfied with their orders from the kitchen and the bar. Pretty E, as usual was posted up on one of the couches with his girls Myeisha, Aunt Rhonda, Georgina, and Sheena trying to convince Myeisha to come home with him.

"Oh, so you can't come with me? Is dat how we ballin?" he asked Myeisha.

"Boy, if you don't go head somewhere, all drunk! Don't make me call my cousin and tell him you fuckin' with his favorite baby cousin," she said.

"Rasul already knows, tell her aunt Rhonda. He knows I got a thing for your sexy ass, wit cha black self."

"Dat's what your mouth say." Myeisha said.

135

"I do. Plus dat lame ass nigga you fuckin wit ain't shit anyway. What can he do for you that I can't? I heard he ain't right no way." Pretty E said.

"Why you hatin?" Myeisha said.

"I ain't, I'm just sayin, and da nigga ain't been to jail yet!" Pretty E said.

"So what!?" Myeisha said.

"Damn! You ain't gotta get all mad and shit. I'm just fuckin wit chu." Pretty E said, turning his attention to the entrance of the lounge, as his boy Cholly AK came in.

"Whass happenin, nigga? I see you posted up wit da ladies. How y'all doin?" Cholly AK said, before saying," I know you going to introduce a nigga?"

"Yo, this is my man's from Chester, PA, Cholly AK. AK, these are my babies Myeisha, Aunt Rhonda, Georgina, and Sheena," Pretty E said.

"I ain't your baby, either!" Myeisha said, frontin.

"Well who's dis?" Cholly AK asked, looking at Aunt Rhonda.

"I can talk, you can ask me about me," she answered for Pretty E, liking what she saw.

Cholly AK had always been a pretty boy in whatever he wore, but his red Roc-A-Wear sweat suit, gold Gucci frames, and butter Timbs gave him a hard, pretty look. The red in the sweat suit complimented his caramel complexion, and his platinum chain hung down to his navel, while his diamond-flooded charm matched perfectly with his wristband-sized bracelet.

"Oh. My bad, whass' up wit chu then, since it's like dat?" He asked Rhonda.

"You," she said, moving over so he could sit down next to her.

Angie sat at the bar and sipped politely at her White Russian looking dapper in her linen Liz Claiborne pants set. She took pride in being a plus sized independent woman, and you could tell by the way she held her
head high. She knew she was big, but with her height she carried her two hundred and forty pounds almost unnoticeable. "Hey Girl!" she yelled, across the bar over the music to Lynneeka when

she spotted her at the other end, putting her cell phone in her Coach bag.

Lynneeka saw Angie throw her hands up in the air, and tried her best to muster up a smile. "She must really think we like dat, huh?" She asked herself, picking up her drink in motion towards her. Lynneeka and Angie were cool, but Trina was her Ace-Boon-Coon, and she would be damned if she was going to sit back and not do nothing.

"Hey girl, whass up? Who you here wit?" Lynneeka asked, knowing the answer already.

"A friend of mine." Angie said.

"I heard dat. Are you still doing nails over at Renee's?"

"Uhm-hmm girl, I ain't going no where." Angie said.

"Oh, dat's whass' up. I think me and my girl Trina goin' to stop by tomorrow and get our shit done, then, you remember Trina don't you? My girl, the one whose man owns this club. The one dat got da kids by Hit Man?" Lyneeka said, as she watched Angie squirm in her stool.

"They ain't still together are they?" Angie asked, disbelievingly.

"Yeah girl, they getting ready to get married. You know they just had a little girl." Lynneeka said, rubbing it in.

Angie was pissed, not at Hit Man, but at herself because she knew in her gut that he was still fucking with Trina. Her instincts told her to stop fucking with him, but her loneliness had mistaken her to believe it was love. "Shit, she would tell herself, it's hard to find a decent man being a big girl; especially one that was nice looking and paid." To her it seemed as though every man she ran into either had four or five kids, got high, was jobless, tried to use her, or was just plain ugly. So fuck what she knew to be true, she acted off of emotion, and once again was holding the shitty end of the stick. Hit Man had been lying to her the whole time.

"No I didn't know they just had a little girl but if you'll excuse me, I'm ready to leave," Angie said, stepping off with an attitude.

+   +   +   +

137

Trina slammed on the brakes right in front of the club's entrance, causing the people on the sidewalk to jump. She jumped out of her Excursion mad as hell, as Trina's "Da Baddest Bitch" escaped through the truck's speakers out into the night's air. Trina stomped up to the door pushing through the people who were waiting in line, "Excuse me!" She barked at those not moving fast enough.

"Trina!" Latoya yelled stopping Trina at the door. "Girl, Im'ma go park dis truck and stay out here wit da kids, cause they don't need to be around all this shit."

Trina entered the club storming past the bouncers and pay desk without stopping. The girl Bonita working the door knew her, and by the way she looked she knew not to even speak to her. Trina
squinted her eyes adjusting them to the dark and scanned the club's bar and dance floor looking for Lynneeka or the girl Angie. Her anger became rage instantly when she saw Hit Man and Angie standing near the back of the club having what seemed to be an argument. "This muthafucka been lying the whole time." She thought as she stepped to him. She loved Hit Man, but the countless cheating, and lying were beginning to wear on her. This was the last straw. She was tired of playing the fool, and no matter how much he cried, begged, or pleaded, she was leaving his ass tonight.

"What da fuck is dis, Hakeeme?" She asked, smacking the side of his head. "Answer me muthafucka! I thought you was outta town!"

"Baby, hold up. Not right here, not in the club. Let's go out here," he said, trying to avoid making a scene.

"I'm not going no where! And bitch, who da fuck is you!?" Trina said to Angie, as a group of on lookers began to build.

Angie was big, but Trina was just as big, if not bigger, and the look on her face said she was ready to go to blows for her man. Angie tried her best not to say the wrong thing hoping to settle this dispute like grown women, but as soon as she opened her mouth to speak Lynneeka said, "Yeah! Trina, dat's da bitch right there!" And before Angie could speak up, Trina was on her.

"Bitch!, I bet chu won't fuck another bitch's man! Will you, you fat bitch!" Trina said, throwing blows between words.

The first punch was the worst blow because it caught Angie off guard. She tried to grab at Trina's hair, but by it being in a ponytail it was worthless. The only thing she could do was ball up and try to defend herself from the barrage of punches that followed. The excitement of the two women fighting caused the onlookers to get a little rowdy, however they were quickly settled down by the bouncers who pulled the women apart and cleared the instigating onlookers before something bigger transpired.

Trina couldn't believe what just happened, or the way Hit Man had acted. It wasn't the actual fight that had her in disbelief, it was the fact that not one time had Hit Man stood up for her, or put the other girl in check. This in itself was a slap in Trina's face, and he didn't even care. That was it; that put the icing on the cake. She looked at him through her slanted eyes and meant every word that came out her mouth next.

"And you, you mother fucker! You might as well stay wit da fat bitch, cause you don't have a home anymore! You no good bastard!" She yelled, before storming out of the club with Lynneeka in tow.

Hit Man was at a lost for words because never once in the five years they'd been together had she talked to him like that, and watching her storm out of the club was a hurting feeling. His heart told him to chase her
down, but his mind said leave her alone, for the reason that she was still angry. He turned to Angie and the way she looked reflected his own feelings, but he really felt bad when she spoke.

"Why couldn't you be honest with me, Hakeeme? Why did it have to come to this?" She asked with tears welled up in her eyes from the embarrassment, and hurt she felt.

"About what?" he asked, benumbed.

"See, that's what I'm talking about Hakeeme. Everything has just come out, and you still can't be honest. All the things you told me, it was all game. You are one big game Hakeeme, Hit Man, whoever you are. I can't believe I fell for it, even though my heart knew the truth. I should have just listened to myself when I noticed how you acted whenever I asked about her. I knew y'all were still together. Hakeeme, just take me home, I'm ready to leave. You got dat; I fell for it like a sucker, never again! Look, can you please take me home?" She said, talking more to herself than anything else.

"Angie! Angie! Come 'ere girl!" he called, but she kept right on walking out the door as he followed. "Damn!" he thought to himself.

Rasul sat in the V.I.P. and watched the whole thing transpire shaking his head as he thought, "Dat nigga do some dumb shit."

Rasul learned one thing in jail if he didn't learn anything else, and that was the importance of having a good woman. Eight long years of loneliness was way more than enough time to realize that fact. He knew and understood that good woman was the only thing holding a man away from his own destruction. That's why as he sat shaking his head he just couldn't understand Hit Man's choices and his unthought of decisions. It was more of a petty shake than disgust because he knew Trina would be scorned, then he realized just how blessed he was to have found Tameeka. With just the thought of Tameeka on his mind he gathered himself and was ready to leave. Everything he had planned in those eight years of solitude was coming true. The only thing left to do was give up "Da Game" and he was well on his way to doing so. "Just a couple more mil and I'm done," he thought and headed downstairs.

"Yo, ya'll gon' be alright?" Rasul asked Dog and Pretty E once he reached downstairs.

"Yeah! We straight, why? Whass'up?" Pretty E asked.

"Im'ma bout to bounce and I just want to make sure y'all nigga's don't forget about tomorrow. This shit is important to me and I want everything to be alright, you know? I'm trying to have the whole house furnished and slept in by Saturday night. We got all day tomorrow and half a day Saturday to get the shit done. I'm going to get Jaquaan's truck in the morning because it's his birthday, so we goin' to have to be moving by Saturday night. I'm goin' to need y'all to help transport all Tameeka's people down here from up in Philly. I want everybody to already be there and for the bar-b-que to be jumpin when I pop the question.

"You dead serious ain't you nigga?" Dog asked.

"About what?" Rasul asked.

"About getting married nigga! Dat's what! Is you goin' crazy?"

"Nah I ain't goin' crazy I'm blessed. Listen y'all, don't forget that Saturday night all Tameeka's people is coming down, her Mom, Grandmom, Cousins, Sister, all of em."

"Alright man! Got damn! How many times you goin' to tell us? Damn! Relax cousin we got your back," Pretty E said cutting him off.

"I'm just saying if y'all goin' to be blowing tree's do that shit outside, cause I don't want "Grams" smelling no tree's and shit."

"Come on now Cousin, you goin' overboard. You know damn well nigga's ain't goin' to disrespect like Dat. I wish you just relax." Dog said.

"I know Cuz relax. Matter of fact, come' ere and give a nigga a hug." Pretty E teased then continued, "Congratulations!"

"Congratulations shit! She didn't even say "Yeah" Yet nigga, and she might not nigga as paranoid as you is," Dog joked then said, "Nah, I'm just bullshittin Cuz. Congratulations on going back to jail!" and they fell out laughing.

+   +   +   +

By Saturday evening, everything was going according to plans. The house was completely furnished by interior decorators and Jaquaan's truck would be done by seven o'clock at Persian's Auto. It was funny what cold cash money could do and Rasul remembered the days without it, as Dog drove to pick up the Yukon Denali.

"Yo man. Ain't it crazy what money can do?" Rasul said.

"Why you say dat?" Dog asked.

"Cause man look at how fast I got all this shit done. I mean at first I was getting the run around. But when I told them muthafucka's I got cash, and was willing to pay a little extra, their couple of weeks went to how fast I need it done, feel me?"

"You know that's how they get down. You just better be glad it got done."

"I heard dat. I'm just hoping Pretty E and Tammy got everybody together by now and they're headed to the house."

141

"Everything is cool. I just talked to him and Big Trina and they said Tammy just called them and said they were on their way. I think she said your mom and grandmom was already there so chill out."

"Whass'up wit Hit Man and Big Trina?"

"I don't know? I still think they ain't talking, but she ain't goin' nowhere and neither is he. Pretty E called me last night and said that nigga called and left like a hundred messages on their phone
crying and shit", chuckled Dog and Rasul, as they pulled into Persian's Auto on Broad St., in Philadelphia.

"Got damn Baby Boy is dat da truck you brought him right there!?" Dog asked.

"Yeah dat's it."

"Shit I might get rid of the Escalade and get one of them shits. Then again I love my Baby and if Im'ma get one of them, she staying too."

"Nigga you need to get rid of that thing, you had it since they first came out. In fact I think you picked me up from jail in that shit."

"I know huh? That shit is hot!" Dog exclaimed, as they looked at the Burgundy Denali sitting plushly on twenty-two's.

"Yeah dat muthafucka is hot huh?" Rasul asked.

"Damn right! Dat lil' nigga ain't goin' to know how to act. He already thinks he's a pretty boy."

"Yeah, dat's my lil' man's for real," Rasul said as they entered the store. "Yo Craig, is she done yet?"

"Yeah, I just finished her. She would a been done earlier, but I blew a tweeter and had to replace it," he said as he stood behind the counter. Craig, a little frail white man with glasses and a pocket protector, tried his hardest to be cool, but couldn't disguise his inability to do so, as he rocked his fitted hat backwards and tied his Timbs up way too tight." The system is astounding! The aquatics in the truck help upgrade the sound like crazy! Wait'll you hear it!" he said, excitedly leading them back out into the lot.

Outside in the lot, Craig pressed the alarm button on the key chain and the lights flickered the same time the locks popped open. He jumped behind the wheel and cut the radio on cranking it to the max as Cam' Ron's "Oh Boy" pounded the pavement that they stood on. Rasul looked at Dog and the two of them cringed their faces with approval as they nodded their heads to the clarity of the music.

"You like it!?" Craig yelled over the bass.

"Yeah I like dat nigga! Now get your funny lookin' ass out so I can pay you! I still think you tryin' to work me!"

"Work you? Hell, you got da money, wit'cha funny lookin' self!" Craig responded with a laugh of his own, as they went into the store.

After paying Craig the money, Dog followed Rasul in the Benz towards Mt. Erie turning the heads of the Temple University students as they rode by. He called Tameeka on his cell phone and told her he'd be there in a few minutes, and then hung up to call the house.

"Hello," an unfamiliar voice answered on the first ring.

"Hello. Who is this?" Rasul asked.

"This is Ms. Helen, Tameeka's grandmother. Who is this?"

"This is Rasul."

"Oh, Hi Baby! Where you at?"

"I'm in Philly. I was just calling to make sure y'all made it down there safe, that's all."

"Yes Baby we're all here and this house is beautiful! I bet you paid a pretty penny didn't you?"

"Yeah, but not too much."

"Where's my grandbaby at?"

"She's at home. I'm on my way there now so I can give Jaquaan his birthday present."

"What'cha get him?" Ms. Helen asked, trying her best not to sound nosy.

"You'll see it later on when he gets there, I don't want to tell you and spoil the surprise." Rasul said.

"O.K. Baby, I see. You said y'all will be here tomorrow right?"

"Yes, but Jaquaan will be there tonight." Rasul said.

"Do you want me to get someone else on the phone for you?"

"Nah, that's alright. I'll see y'all tomorrow." Rasul said.

"O.K. Baby, see ya then."

"O.K." Rasul said and hung up as he pulled up to the house.

Rasul turned the radio all the way down and pulled into the driveway as stealth as possible. He didn't want to take a chance on Jaquaan hearing him pull up and blowing the surprise he had for him. Then, it was almost destroyed when Dog pulled up seconds behind him. Rasul jumped out of the truck with his hands waving rapidly at Dog for him to turn down the box or cut it off.

"Whass'up nigga?" Dog asked, sticking his head out of the window.

"Turn the box down nigga," I'm tryin to surprise my lil' man's," Rasul answered.

"Oh! My bad nigga you should a said some'em. I ain't know you was tryin to surprise dat lil' nigga."

"Yeah nigga it's a surprise," Rasul said, as they headed into the house.

Tameeka was on the couch with her feet up on the coffee table watching the Wheel of Fortune trying to figure out the last puzzle when they walked in. The music from upstairs in Jaquaan's room was so loud that you only heard the thud of the bass even though the door was shut. He knew right then that Jaquaan didn't hear them come in.

"I know y'all better take them raggedy ass "Timbs" off on my damn white rug!" Tameeka snapped, forgetting all about the game show.

"Girl, ain't nobody thinking about this cheap ass rug! I'll get it cleaned." Dog said, then continued, "wit'cha fat ass!"

"Fuck you! I ain't goin' to be fat for long." She said, scooping a spoon full of pickles, ice cream, and potato chips she had crunched up in one bowl.

"Baby, who is Jaquaan upstairs with?" Rasul asked.

"His shadow." Tameeka said.

"Who Corky?" Rasul asked.

"You know it." Tameeka confirmed.

"Well let me get up here so I can give him his present, cause I know he wanna go out tonight, and the first thing he gonna

say is, Rasul can I use your car? But now he got his own shit."
Rasul said, dangling the keys to the Yukon.

"You brought him a car anyway?" Tameeka asked.

"Nah, I brought him a truck. Go outside and look at it while
I run upstairs." Rasul said.

The music coming from inside Jaquaan's room was so loud
that Rasul had to pound on the door. It took at least three hard
pounds before the music went down and Jaquaan snatched open
the door.

"Whass' wrong wit'chu Boy? Shouldn't you be happy on
your birthday?" Rasul asked.

"When you get here?" Jaquaan asked.

"About ten minutes ago why? Whass'up?"

"Cause man, my mom gets on my nerves sometimes. It's
my birthday and she won't even let me use the car. Man she ain't
even goin' nowhere. Can I use yours cause me and Corky tryin' to
go out?" Jaquaan asked.

"Nah man you can't use mine, but you can use yours.
Happy Birthday Baby Boy!" Rasul said, and tossed him the keys.

"For real?!" Jaquaan said surprised.

"Yeah Baby Boy. Happy Birthday!" Rasul said.

"Yo man, I love you Rasul you treat me better than my own
pop." he said, and hugged him.

Rasul smiled on that note gaining a joy like never before as
he hugged Jaquaan. Just seeing his face light up, and the way he
had changed over a year by Rasul just being there, showed him
how important it was to have a male figure in your life growing up.
Jaquaan's grades went up from D's to C's and was one of the main
reasons Rasul got the truck, not to mention that Corky and the rest
of his boys were still stealing cars and sooner or later they'd be in
jail. No matter how much he preached to Jaquaan about joy riding
in them stolen cars he knew he was going to do it anyway. That
was the icing on the cake, the real reason he brought the car.
Besides, he didn't want Jaquaan to blow his chance at getting a
scholarship from Germantown High.

When they got outside, Tameeka was sitting in the truck
going over the upholstery shaking her head with her lips turned up.

She looked at Rasul disgusted and he knew he was in for some
heavy tongue lashing

when they were alone, but it didn't matter because Jaquaan was
siked. His eyes lit up like a new born baby's seeing Christmas
lights on a tree for the first time, as he ran to the truck with his boy
Corky right behind him.

     "Rasul come'ere." Tameeka said, grabbing him by the arm
and pulling him off to the side." Baby why would you buy that boy
a
truck like that? He does not need it. Shit, he would a been just as
happy if you brought his ass a squatter."

     "Baby he aw'ight. I did dat for a reason. I did for him what
I was neglected as a child. My pop couldn't afford to get me no
shit like dat, and if he could he wouldn't have. Shit dat nigga
didn't even
buy me a pair of sneaks, feel me? So don't spoil my moment,
cause I'm just as happy as him."

     "Yeah I feel you now! You feel me. The first time his ass
fucks up he ain't driving it!" she said.

     "You got dat," Rasul responded to her sarcasm, then called
out to Jaquaan who was already backing out the driveway. He
walked over to the driver side window away from Tameeka and
leaned in explaining to Jaquaan about the new house and
engagement party and asked, "What do you think?"

     "Word? Dat's whass'up man for real cause I ain't never
seen my mom dis happy."

     "Thanks Baby Boy. But here's what I need you to do. I
need you to cancel your plans for tonight. I know it's your
birthday, but I need you to take Dog home, well to the new house
with everybody else. Your grandmom and all of them are down
there already waiting for tomorrow when I surprise your Mom, so
you especially need to be there feel me? Corky you can go too just
make sure you let your mom know first."

     "Aw'ight then. What time y'all coming tomorrow?"
     "About twelve."
     "Aw'ight dat's whass'up. Dog you ready?"

"Yeah, here I come young buck," he said and turned to Tameeka. "Yeah, I'm hanging wit the young bucks tonight," you got a problem wit dat?"

"Don't get my Son in no shit Dog! He's a good boy, he ain't like y'all," Tameeka said.

"Yeah right. Dis lil' nigga is off da hook! Nah I'm just playin, you know I got'em. He is in good hands." He smiled as Jaquaan turned up the box and backed out the driveway.

"Jaquaan!" Dog yelled over the system. "Go to the strippers on Broad St. Happy Birthday Nigga! My treat!"

+   +   +   +

Rasul rolled over in bed and squinted his eyes, as a ray of sunlight crept through the window and perched perfectly on his face. The love making he and Tameeka made last night was the main reason he was still groggy, and having the best sleep he'd had in months. Since the pregnancy, the lovemaking had become almost non-existent due to Tameeka's constant mood swings, plus the more her stomach grew the harder it became to position themselves. Doggy Style was getting old, but last night was beautiful, almost animalistic. Tameeka initiated the whole thing and had taken charge from the door, which was surprising, as they went hard nearly to the crack of dawn. That's why when Rasul looked at the clock on the nightstand, he sprung up. It was already 11:30 a.m., and it didn't seem like he'd even been sleep, but for twenty minutes.

"Come on, Baby. Get up," Rasul said, jumping out of bed.

"Why Baby? Let's just lie here all day and cuddle. I just want you to hold me," she responded.

"Nah, come on Boo. We got things to do. We gotta be somewhere in like an hour."

"See, that's why I can't wait to have this baby. What? I ain't attractive to you no more? Why can't we just lay here?" she asked, as Rasul saw the mood swing coming.

"Cause we have somewhere to be, that's why. Why you always going there?" Rasul said.

"Cause, you don't spend no time with me anymore dat's why," she said directly, tears welled in her eyes.

147

"Look man, why you always trippin'? Just get da fuck up and come on, damn!" Rasul said, feeling himself getting frustrated.

"Whatever!" she said, sucking her teeth as she stomped off into the bathroom.

By 12:30 p.m., they were dressed and headed to Delaware, and though Tameeka questioned nonstop about where they were going, he was able to change the subject. Rasul was anxious and nervous about what he was about to do and once again he ran his hand slightly across his pants pocket checking to make sure the ring was there. When he felt it, he smiled and had many pleasant thoughts going through his head. He knew this was the day, the first day of the
start of his family. He made a silent vow to himself this very moment, and promised himself that he was going to be a real man; husband, father, and friend, then he placed his hand on Tameeka's knee.

Something was going on, but Tameeka just couldn't place her finger on it. All morning long Rasul had been anxious and rushing to get out of the house and the more she thought about it the more curious she became. He just wasn't telling her anything. "What is it?" she asked herself, racking her brain trying to remember each and everything he might have said that would bring her closer to finding out. There was nothing else she could have thought about. She hated being left in the dark, or being surprised. She tried to use her best reverse psychology and played mad, slapping his hand from her knee. When that didn't work she really got mad, not at him, but at herself for pretending to be mad, cause now she was.

"Whass wrong wit'chu?" Rasul asked, turning off of I-95 to Delaware Ave's exit in Wilmington.

"Nuffin," she said, and broke out laughing. She just couldn't hold it in anymore. She felt stupid as hell for trying to play mad and had gotten mad for real, and it didn't even work.

"Whass funny?" Rasul asked, beginning to laugh himself.

"Nothing, just get me wherever it is that you're taking me. You make me sick cause I can't even stay mad at you," she said, finally giving in. She was ready to get the suspense over and to find out what was going on.

+   +   +   +

The six-bedroom mini-mansion was full of life, as both Rasul and Tameeka's family bar-b-qued and partied in the backyard, while the kids ran around going bezerk in all the many rooms they had to play in. Dog,

Pretty E, Hit Man, Jaquaan, Corky, and that one drunken Uncle every black family has, James-Earl, played bat mitten arguing the whole time.

"James-Earl! Why the fuck every time we go somewhere it always gotta be you the only one showing off?" his wife, Tameeka's Aunt Joyce, yelled.

"Aw hell Joyce. This is the men playin' Why the hell you always over here in our shit? Shouldn't you be havin' yo ass over there fixin' some potato salad or some shit?" He slurred, and then stumbled, as Pretty E and them bagged up laughing.

"I know you ain't showing off Earl?" she snapped, irritated by their laughs.

"I know you ain't showin' off Joyce! Don't make me really act a fool!" he stated, seeming as if he sobered up that fast.

"Joyce! Come on over here and leave them alone!" Tameeka's grandmom, Ms. Helen yelled across the yard by the pond, trying to stop the kids from throwing rocks in it.

"Dat's right Mom! Ya better get her," James-Earl yelled, while no one was really paying any attention.

"Now dat's enough Earl! You don't want Mom Helen to snap." Just like that it was over. The whole incident went unnoticed.

Both Tameeka and Rasul's mothers, along with some cousins, brothers, sisters, aunts, uncles, and friends, sat around one of the picnic tables. Each one of them was sharing a story about Tameeka or Rasul. It was crazy, because if you didn't know, you would have thought that the families knew each other for a lifetime, and not just a night. It was plain chemistry. They were getting along great. There were even a few disagreements, some even had disputes, but there was nothing major. However, they did agree on one thing, and it was that Tameeka and Rasul made a storybook couple.

+   +   +   +

Only minutes away from the biggest question of his life, Rasul's heart was in his stomach. He pulled the car over to the side of the road and reached into the glove compartment grabbing a red heart-shaped blindfold. Tameeka frowned her face up, tired about all of the games, but Rasul paid her no mind and asked her to put it on.

"For what, Rasul? What are you up to?" she asked, and then started to smile; thinking that it was what she thought it was, but really was not sure.

"Baby just do it, O.K.?" he replied, watching her pull it over her eyes trying not to mess up her hair, as he pulled back onto the road.

"Where are we going, Rasul?" Tameeka asked.

"It's a surprise." Rasul said.

"Why you can't tell me? Im'ma be just as surprised if you tell me now." Tameeka said.

"Nah Baby, you'll spoil it." Rasul said.

"Spoil what?" she tried to make him slip.

"Nuffin." Rasul said not falling for the trap.

Rasul pulled the car up in front of the new home he purchased and stopped at the bottom of the driveway. There were so many cars out in front of the house, and in the driveway that he barely found a place to park, and he squeezed in behind Jaquaan's truck. He looked over to Tameeka and said, "Baby, take it off."

Tameeka was glad when the car came to its final stop, because her curiosities were killing her. The mystery of the unknown was almost unbearable, as a million thoughts raced through her head. "The main thought was of Rasul asking her to marry him, because for the past three or four months he'd been hinting around to it, but then again, he hadn't said anything to her lately. Or maybe it was the house she asked for repeatedly?" She didn't know, but when he told her to take off the blindfold, she gasped.

"Ra-Rasul," she stuttered," Is this?" she asked wide eyed, hands over her face, as she stared in awe at the three story mini-mansion.

"Yes Baby, it's all yours!" he answered, and she leaped across the seats smothering his cheeks with kisses. "Damn! Is this all I had to do to get a little affection?" He teased.

"Ooooo Baby! Thank you! I love you so much!" she said, still holding him around the neck.

"Anything for you Baby! Now come on so we can look at it, plus we got all these people waiting on us," he said, opening the car door.

Rasul lead Tameeka through the front door and they could hear the music and laughter coming from the backyard. The house was breath taking, occupied by Italian leather furniture, beautiful paintings and sculptures of African Heritage. Two huge African masks hung oddly on the wall overtop of a wooden statue of an African king with a spear. Three glass elephants were in each corner of the living room. Rasul lead Tameeka through to the game room/library and she was once again in awe at the sight of the computer lab he had set up just for her.

"Baby, this house is beautiful!" she marveled.

"We're not done," he said and was ready to show her the rest of the house when Jaquaan saw them.

"Mom! Dis house is da shi…! I mean da bomb, ain't it!?" Jaquaan said.

"You better had caught yourself and, yes, the house is the bomb!"

"Mom, you should see the baby's room and my room! Oh, Mom! We even got a pond!" Jaquaan said, happy as a kid at the ice cream truck.

"A pond?" Tameeka said surprised.

"Yeah mom. A pond!"

"Rasul?"

"Yeah baby, a pond. I went all out for you," he smiled. With Jaquaan leading the way they toured the rest of the house, but not like Tameeka wanted to, she'd do that later. Right now she wanted to host the guest at the bar-b-que especially since everyone was rushing them to get outside once they knew they were there. As soon as they got outside on the back deck, they were spotted.

"Hey Baby! How's my grandbaby and great grandbaby?" Mom-Mom Helen asked, and rubbed Tameeka's belly.

"We're fine Mom-Mom."

"Well you know this lil' baby goin' to be a girl, don't you?" Mom-Mom Helen said, still feeling her stomach.

"Don't say that Mom-Mom. That's the same thing Tammy and Erica said. I think they're tryin' to jinx me," Tameeka said, gazing out over her luxurious backyard. "Baby, where you going? She asked Rasul, as he headed down the deck steps into the yard.

"Down here to make me a plate, I'm hungry. Why? You want me to make you one?" he asked.

"No, Im'ma eat some of yours." Tameeka said.

"Damn! All this food and shit and you still want to pick off my plate!?" Rasul said.

"Boy shut-up! I know I can, right?" Tameeka said.

"You won't pick off this one!"

"Dat's what'cha mouth says." Tameeka said.

"You'll see," he said, and stepped off heading towards the grill.

Tameeka sat right next to Rasul and picked through his plate, just like she said she was, as the two families sat down to eat. This was the first time each family had gotten to really meet either Tameeka or Rasul other than seeing them out in the car, or just speaking to them on the phone when they called looking for the other one. But, everyone seemed to honestly like one another. Tameeka was so busy running her mouth that she didn't even notice Rasul getting up and standing beside her.

"Can I have everyone's attention?" Rasul interrupted as Dog stopped the music. "As y'all all know, me and Tameeka are having a baby soon, that's why I went out and brought this house. This is sorta like a house

warming for us, but it's really for our families to get to know each other. Kinda become connected through our love," he said, and dropped to one knee.

Rasul pulled out the diamond ring box from Tiffany's and revealed a rock so big and perfectly cut that the women all held their breath. "Tameeka," he continued, holding the ring out towards her, as tears stained her cheeks. "Baby, from the first

night we shared together, I knew I wanted to share every night that followed after that with you, and I did. You are my love, my life, and you give me strength. Baby, you are something special. You gave me the support and strength I needed to become who I am today, and you're still not done, because
now you're about to give me the best gift of all, a child. I know I can never do anything that will amount to that, but I can for what it's worth, love you the rest of my existence. Baby—will you marry me?"

Chapter Eleven

The Double Tree's Presidential Suite on Broad St. in Center City Philadelphia was the location of Rasul's surprise bachelor party. Pretty E had booked ten dancers from the ghetto fabulous "N.O.B." *Night on Broad's* strip club to give him a show he'd never forget. The girls were already there setting up when Pretty E walked through the door.

"Hey Baby, whass'up?" Fantasia, the one who supplied the girls asked.

"Ain't nuffin' Y'all alright up in here?" he asked, starring at the red-bone with the blonde wig, see through halter-top, and mini-skirt.

"Yeah, we straight. When the rest of them coming?" she asked.

"In about an hour. I just came early to make sure y'all were straight, you know?" he said, as several of the girls came from the back room.

"Hey Boo!" Ms. Thang whined when she saw Pretty E, "Whass'up? Me and you tonight?" she asked, biting her bottom lip.

"You know it is!" he shot back at her, walking towards her. He and Ms. Thang had hooked up on several occasions, and each time had been a memorable one.

"Ahn-Ahn! How you goin' to go there and I'm standing right here, boy?" Co-Co asked, hands on her hips revealing that huge round ass of hers, with the balloons tattooed on it.

"Oh shit! Hey Baby Girl, you know me, I can handle the whole weight," he said, as Co-Co and Ms. Thang laughed.

"You so damn nasty!" Co-Co said, remembering the time her and Ms. Thang gave him a ménage-a-trois.

"Ain't he!?" Ms. Thang added, thinking the same thing.

Pretty E pulled out his cell phone and called the house on Vanderver Ave. hoping to catch Dog, Hit Man, and Rasul before they left Delaware and, to see if the crew had gotten there yet. He was glad when Dog answered the phone on the second ring, because he needed them to make a few stops on the way up.

"Whass' happenin' nigga? Everybody there?" Pretty E asked.

"Nah, we still waiting on Cholly AK to get here. The babe Aunt Shonda got dat nigga spinning, you heard me?" Dog answered.

"Well who's all there so far?"

"Me, Rasul, Hit Man, Zoop-Loop, Skipper, Floss, Dunn, Monk, and Shay Ball. Yo, who's dat in da background?"

"That's the dancers." Pretty E said.

"Yo, is my baby Extasy there?" Dog asked.

"Yeah, she here." Pretty E said.

"Tell 'er I'm on my way up," Dog said, excited.

"Damn nigga! Where's Rasul? He can't hear you can he?" Pretty E asked.

"Nah, nigga! What? You think I'm stupid or some shit? Dat nigga way out in the kitchen." Dog said.

"Oh! Well look. When y'all on y'all way up, I need y'all to stop and get some liquor and shit, I forgot. Oh yeah! And, look upstairs in da closet in da hallway and grab dat weed. I got a pound of Purple Haze in there." Pretty E said.

"Aw'ight nigga, we got it." Dog said.

"Aw'ight then, peace." Pretty E said.

"One!" and they both hung up.

+   +   +   +

"Girl, you know they havin' one! We should try and find it," Tammy said, talking about the bachelor party.

"I know girl. Let's raid dat muthafucka," Erica, Tameeka's sister said.

"Girl, they probably goin' be fuckin' them nasty bitches and everything," Trina said, planting seeds in Tameeka's head.

"Nah, Ahn. Not Rasul. He don't get down like dat!" Tameeka responded, second-guessing her own self.

"Bitch, screw my head back on when you finish! Dat nigga is getting ready to marry you. Don't you know this is his last night of freedom? Girl, he goin' to fuck some'em I'm tellin' you!" Erica said, and that was it, Tameeka was on her way out the door.

"Come on y'all!" Tameeka said.

"Dat's right! Let's go raid dat muthafucka!" Tammy said, "and I hope I catch Pretty E's ass, cause Im'ma fuck his ass up!" she

155

finished, checking for her pepper spray as they left the house. Then they all piled up in Trina's Excursion and were out. Where? They didn't know.

+   +   +   +

Dog, Hit Man, and Rasul, along with their crew of young boys, stepped off the elevator on the seventh floor, and walked down the Double Tree's elaborate hallway towards Room 716. The Presidential Suite was at the end of the hallway and as they neared it, they could hear the music coming from beyond the doors like the party had already started. Dog stood before the door carrying two cases of Corona's, and because his hands were occupied, he kicked at the door for someone to answer.

"Whass' happenin' niggas? About time y'all here!" he said, stepping to the side so they could come through the door.

"Yeah-Yeah! Now, where's the party at, nigga?" Dog asked, sitting the cases on the table next to the window.

"It couldn't start till the man of the hour got here, ain't dat right Rasul?" Fantasia said, as they got comfortable in the living room. "This is your night Baby! Now let me go get the girls together," she finished, and disappeared down the hallway.

In less than five minutes, Fantasia lead the first girl out into the living room, and the party began. Discreet jumped up on the table in a full body suit with her titties and crotch cut out, and began to dance. Her tall slender frame revealed her curved body, and a gap that made men's' faces cringe. Running her hands across her body, swaying her hips provocatively, she dropped into a split and bounced her ass up and down against the table.

"Got damn baby! I bet'chu can't do dat wit all dis up in you!" Zoop-Loop shouted, and threw a fifty up on the table, as he grabbed his crotch.

"Dat's right! Y'all need to be real generous up in here tonight," Fantasia said, encouraging them to keep tossing the money, as she scooped it up for her dancer.

"Where's the man that's about to give up all this for the married life?" Discreet asked, fingering herself gently to the music.

"There he go! Dat's dat nigga right there!" Pretty E said, pointing to Rasul who was sitting in a love seat by himself.

156

"Discreet slithered off the table like a snake and crawled over to Rasul on her hands and knees. Rubbing his thighs with her hands, she undid his pants with her teeth, and placed a rubber in her mouth. In one swift motion she put the rubber on his dick with her lips and got up. Smiling, she stood before him and turned her back to face him, and shook her ass as she bent down and grabbed her ankles. She blew Rasul a kiss through her legs and winked her eye, then walked away when the music went off.

"That's right! Give it up for my girl, Discreet," Fantasia said, as the guys gave it up for the girl who just danced, by clapping and barking. "These next two girls are off the hook, and sexy as hell! So, I need y'all to really be generous with the dough, cause their definitely going to give y'all y'all's money worth!" she finished, and disappeared down the hallway.

"You aw'ight nigga? You ain't second guessing is you?" Dog asked Rasul, who was still smiling as he took off the rubber.

"Nah nigga, I'm straight," he said, as Co-Co and Ms. Thang walked out.

Co-Co and Ms. Thang turned it out from the gate, as they fondled each other roughly, snatching off one another's Velcro lined outfits leaving them bare in just thongs. They sprawled out on the floor and Ms. Thang reached for her duffel bag, and pulled out a double-headed dildo. Sitting in front of each other, they both cocked
their legs up and pulled their thongs to the side, and ran the heads of the dildo up and down their pussy lips. After about five minutes of that, they maneuvered into the sixty-nine and Dog and them went crazy.

"Oh shit! Dat's right homegirl eat dat shit!" Shay-Ball yelled, and threw a wad of five dollars bills on the floor next to them.

"Damn! Can I taste it!" Cholly AK shouted.

Co-Co and Ms. Thang performed like that for two whole songs, and on the third one they each grabbed a Corona bottle and made the nozzles disappear in their pussies. They looked at each other as if to give a secret signal and just like that with no hands, they spit the bottles out causing them to hit the floor.

"Now dat's pussy control!" Monk said, as a cloud of purple haze smoke escaped his mouth.

The next six girls performed one at a time in almost the same manner and when they all had performed separately, Fantasia brought them all back out.

"Fantasia, let me holla at you for a minute," Pretty E asked, as the girls performed lap dances for Rasul and them.

"Whass' up Pretty?" she asked.

"Yo, how much you goin' charge me?" Pretty E asked.

"For what? It all depends." Fantasia said.

"I'm tryin' to have an all out Orgy in this muthafucka. Give my boy some'em to remember forever—feel me?"

"I feel you. Let me go holla at my girls and I'll let you know some'em aw'ight?" she said, and walked off.

Pretty E watched Fantasia as she went from girl to girl and negotiated something with them separately. Whatever the cost, he decided wasn't a concern, because he was going to pay whatever to make his boy's bachelor party a night to remember. It was just getting the girls to go for it that was his concern.

"So whass'up?" Pretty E asked when she came back.

"5 G's and it's on! Dat'll give us all $500.00 a piece," she said.

"Well it's on then," Pretty E said, and walked over to Dog and Hit Man to get the rest of the money.

+   +   +   +

It had been almost two whole hours of searching each and every hotel and motel in Wilmington and New Castle, before Tammy received the call she was waiting on. She answered her cell phone and was given the whole run down by her girl Mecca, who worked at the strip club "Pony Tails" on weekends.

"Hey girlfriend, whass'up? I ain't trying to be nosy or some shit, this is just a question," Mecca said.

"O.K. Whass'up?" Tammy asked.

"Ain't Tameeka getting ready to marry Pretty E's boy?"

"Yeah, why? Whass'up?"

"Cause the babe Tywana called me last night and asked me if I wanted to do a bachelor party with her, for some dudes from Delaware. I was like, yeah, then I was like, Nah Girl, he knows me, plus that's my girl's man—feel me? Plus the girl Tywana gets down like dat, she does dates and everything!"

"Well where they at?" Tammy asked, stomach turning.

"Up here at the Double Tree on Broad, in Center City."

"Thanks Mecca, girl let me call you later girl and give you the run down on everything, cause we about to crash dat muthafucka!"

"Alright girl, don't forget to call me." Mecca said.

"I won't," she said, and hung up the phone. "Trina," she continued, "How fast can you get dis truck up to Philly?"

"How fast you need me to get there?"

"Now! I just found out where those sorry muthafuckas at!"

"Where?" Tameeka asked.

"Da Double Tree on Broad St," Tammy said, and Trina mashed the gas, leaving about five feet of skid marks on the street, as she pulled away from the motel parking lot headed towards I-495, to Philly.

+   +   +   +

Fantasia and the girls stepped off the elevator dressed in their regular street clothes, carrying gym bags on their shoulders. "Girl, it's hot as shit!" Co-Co said, wiping the sweat soaked hair away from her cheek, and pulling it behind her ears out of her face. "Girl, they were off da hook!" Ms. Thang shouted as she laughed about what just took place.

"Shit girl. Did you see how little dat young boys dick was!? He coulda kept dat muthafucka in his pants!" Co-Co clowned.

"Yeah girl! He had a dick like a three-year old!" Discreet added, and they all fell out laughing.

+   +   +   +

Trina made it to Philly in record time, mainly because she wanted to catch Hit Man in the act of doing some shit he wasn't supposed to be doing." It ain't even been two weeks yet, and that muthafucka is back at it." She thought, cursing herself out as she pulled up in front of the Double Tree Hotel. The truck hadn't even come to a full stop yet, and Tammy and Erica had their doors open ready to jump out. Trina threw on her hazard lights and parked in front of the entrance in the fire lane and they all jumped out. No sooner than they stepped through the main entrance door of the lobby, Tammy spotted Fantasia and her crew of girls laughing coming towards them.

"There! Dem bitches go right dere!" Tammy said, walking towards them hearing every word they said.

+   +   +   +

"Mmm-Hmm girl, dat muthafucka is sharp! I coulda sucked his dick all night!" Discreet said.

"Who girl?" Co-Co asked.

"The boah Ra-" and before she could get his name out, Fantasia nudged her in the ribs with her elbow.

"Hey girl! Whass'up?" Fantasia spoke, when she saw Tammy.

"Ain't nuffin. Whass'up wit'chu Tywana? What'chall doing here?" Tammy asked, giving each one of her girls a sharp look.

"Nuffin' just finished doing a show for some dudes from Delaware."

"Do you know them?" she asked.

"I know one of them," Co-Co said, missing the look that Fantasia gave her, his name is Pretty E.

"Pretty E? Do you know what room they was in?" Tammy asked, wanting to jump down this bitch throat.

"Why? You know him or some'em?" Co-Co asked, putting her hands on her hips.

"Yeah I know him real well. He's my man," Tammy shot back with confidence.

"Your man? Oh shit y'all! Pretty E got a woman," Co-Co said smartly, as her and her girls laughed at the unsaid joke.

"Bitch what da fuck is dat supposed to mean?" Tammy asked one step away from swinging on this bitch with all the sarcasm.

"You tell me, dat's your man, Bitch!" she said, ready for whatever.

"Fantasia, you better check your girl for she get fucked up," Tammy said.

160

"Tammy girl, don't worry about her. Dat bitch is drunk! I think they in room 716, ain't they Chocolate?" Fantasia asked.

"Thanks girl. Let me go for I have to whip dis bitch's ass!" Tammy said, and walked away.

"Fuck you Bitch!" Co-Co said, still running off at the mouth." I see you ain't handling your business at home, cause he damn sure don't know how to act! In fact, when you get up there make sure you tell him to get my hair out his teeth, Bitch!"

"What bitch?" Tammy said, turning on her heels.

"You heard me!" Co-Co said.

"What?" and Tammy charged at her.

The two of them latched on the each other's hair and pulled and tugged, but that was about all that went down, because security had rushed the altercation before it got ugly. "Bitch! Im'ma beat dat ass!" Co-Co snapped, as they were pulled apart. Trina grabbed a hold of Tammy, and Fantasia and Ms. Thang grabbed Co-Co, then the security led them though the lobby. Tammy was hot. Co-Co had pushed her past her limit. She couldn't believe that bitch had told her to tell her man to get the hair out of his teeth. The more she thought about what that bitch had said, the madder she became. She couldn't imagine Pretty E eating none of those nasty bitches' pussies, but the thought of it is what hurt the most.

"Girl, im'ma bout to fuck up that no good bastard!" Tammy said, her voice cracking as she boarded the elevator with her girls.

"Don't pay dat bitch no mind. You know damn well he ain't eat dat bitch's pussy," Trina said.

"I don't know girl. Them muthafuckas will do anything with a drink up in'em!" Erica said, adding fuel to the fire.

They stepped off the elevator and stormed straight towards room 716. Outside the door they couldn't hear anything, and was beginning to think Fantasia had told them a bold face lie, but Tammy knocked anyway. The door swung open and Floss stood there in his boxers and socks.

"Yo, whass'up?" he asked, the party is over."

"Where's Pretty E at?" Tammy asked.

"He in there sleeping home girl, why whass'up?" he asked, not knowing who the four females in front of him were.

"Can you tell him his woman is out here, and Rasul's fiancée is with her? Oh, and so is Hit Man's wife," she said, motioning her neck in a way only a sista could.

"Oh shit, Yo, could you hold on for a minute?" he said, wide-eyed not knowing how guilty he looked, as he shut the door.

Floss moved frantically through the Hotel suites living room picking up the towels that were flung around on the floor, and waking up his boys at the same time.

"Yo, Pretty E! Get up man! Yo! Get up!" he said, tapping Pretty E on the shoulder, as he lay on the couch knocked out.

"Yo, whass'up? Whass' happenin'?" Pretty E asked groggily, as he turned his back to Floss.

"Yo, man! Your girl is at da door!" Floss said.

"Say word! She out there?"

"Word!"

Pretty E jumped up from the couch a nervous wreck, his whole high blown away, as he tried to gather himself." Damn! Where's Rasul at?" he asked, then heard the pounding on the door.

"Open this damn door!" Tammy hollered.

"Hold on, here I come!" he yelled back, and turned to Floss. "Yo, go get Rasul, Dog, and Hit Man up, while I put on my shorts and get the door.

Pretty E opened the door and was damn near trampled as Tammy barged in with Tameeka, Erica, and Trina right on her heels.

"What da fuck is going on Eric?" Tammy demanded, pushing Pretty E in his chest, as she glanced at the empty beer bottles and blunt roaches in the ashtrays.

"Ain't nuffin' going on! Why da fuck is you buggin'!'" he snapped.

"Ahh-Huhn! Just like I thought, you nasty dick muthafucka's!" Trina said. Where da fuck is Hakeeme at!"

"I can't believe y'all was in here fucking those nasty bitches!" Erica said, instigating the matter.

"Why don't you mind your muthafuckin' business! You always in some'em!" Pretty E said, directing his attention to Erica.

"Dis is my business! My sister about to marry one of y'all no good asses!" she replied.

"Girl, just shut up for a minute," Tameeka said, holding her hand up to silence her sister. "Where's Rasul at?"

"He uhm, in da back," Floss answered.

I wasn't talking to you," Tameeka said sarcastically, as Rasul came down the hall pissy drunk.

"Hey! Whass'up baby?" Rasul said, stumbling towards her.

"You tell me. I wanna know what da fuck was going on in here tonight!"

"Nuffin' baby. Pretty E and them just threw me a bachelor party dat's all. I know you ain't mad are you? I told you you coulda had a bachelorette party."

"Well why is it rubbers and shit all over the place? Did you fuck any of those stripper bitch's, Rasul?"

"No girl! You know I ain't goin' out like dat! Why would you ask me some shit like dat?" he lied through his teeth.

"Why would they lie Rasul, I know you fucked'em.

"I did not! Them bitch's might say anything."

"Yeah, well if I do find out you fucked them bitches, we won't be getting married," she said, trying to be hard." Now get'cha shit, and come on, wit'cha drunk ass!"

Rasul, Pretty E, Dog and Hit Man breathed a sigh of relief the moment they realized they were cool. Yeah, Tammy, Tameeka, and Trina were mad, but it was their own fault. Had they never come looking for the party, they would of never knew what went down at the parties, and woulda still been stuck on assumptions of what goes down. Nothing they saw in the room could be held against them, because at bachelor parties these things happen. So, as they left the room with their girls they felt no way in the wrong, but they did know they'll be in the dog house for a while.

+   +   +   +

Det. Cohen answered his desk phone on the first ring and was greeted by a voice that had become all too familiar to him. It was Rashida, the best friend of the missing girl Shelly, who had disappeared more than a year and a half ago. Every time he heard Rashida's voice his heart went out to her, because her pain was only a mirror reflection of the pain he felt his own self. There hasn't been a day gone by where he didn't feel pain, and it would never go away until he found the people responsible for murdering his partner.

"Det. Cohen," Rashida began, "Is there any new leads?"

"Nothing! See it's very difficult to gain any leads when you have no eyewitnesses, or crime scene. I mean, she just disappeared into thin air, and in a public place at that" he answered.

"Well did you check on her ex-boyfriend, Rasul? I know he had something to do with it!" she said.

"How do you know?"

"Cause, the boy BoBo who's missing was Shelly's new boyfriend and—and—"

"And what?" he encouraged her.

"And he robbed Rasul just the day or two before they both became missing. That's why I know he had some'em to do with it!"

"Thank you Rashida for just giving me a motive. I'll keep my eye on him, because I have reason to believe he's involved in a lot more than just this. Rashida, as soon as I hear something you'll be the first to know, as will her mother, so just be strong o.k.?" he said, more to himself than her, and hung up the phone.

Det. Cohen got that feeling all over again. That pain that's almost so unbearable it causes his mouth to dry up and makes him break out in a cold sweat. He knew in his gut that the four men he called "Young Punks" were behind his partner's death, and Shelly's disappearance. He got up from his desk and walked over to the file cabinet where he kept all of Armstrong's things, and there they were. "How could I have overlooked this?" he said to himself, and slammed the file cabinet shut.

+   +   +   +

Lucy stood up from the large conference table and stormed out of the room causing the pictures and the large eagle that hung on the wall to shake. As she slammed the door, she said to herself "I'm about tired of this shit!" as her shoes clicked loudly down the hallway of the Federal Building. "Who the fuck do they think they are?" She asked herself of her superiors. I'm the best damn agent this building has ever seen!"

Lucy graduated at the top of her class when she went to college and decided to join the academy thereafter. Lucy was a natural at it and in her first year as an agent, she netted one of the largest cocaine busts on the East Coast sending her up the scale of ranks. In two years on the force, Lucy went undercover and remained that way, cracking major drug rings throughout the United States. The case she was on now, with the Capelli Family, was totally different. They were one of the fastest rising mobsters the "Feds" had
seen since the early eighties, and they were advanced, and up on technology. It was hard for Lucy to actually gain enough concrete evidence on them to build a strong case in court, and she was becoming frustrated. Today was one of those days.

Lucy got behind the wheel of her 2001 Maxima and headed out of the parking garage in a hurry, trying to get as far away from the day's stress as soon as possible. She reached for her Marlboro Lights in the sun visor, and plucked one out of the pack as she sat at the red light. Pulling hard on the cigarette, Lucy filled her lungs with the smoke and actually felt the tension of the day ease, as she exhaled blowing the smoke out of the driver's side window. She started thinking about Pretty E and the things that went down between them. Pretty E had totally made her fall head over hills in love with him. The sneaking around and age difference was also an attraction for Lucy. She felt giddy, like a high school girl with a crush on the star quarterback, and the thought made her smile. She couldn't wait to get home. Tonight was their night to spend together, and it was going to be a good one. "Im'ma make sure of it!" she said to herself.

+   +   +   +

The sun was shining brightly in a cloud free sky overtop of Rasul and Tameeka's mini-mansion. It was their wedding day and cars lined the driveway and both sides of the street as more than two hundred guests made up of family and close friends filled the backyard of the estate. The yard was elaborately setup with white and red roses lining the outer limits of where the large wooden white fold up chairs sat in rows along side the yard where an altar was built up on a platform. The Reverend stood on the altar next to the pianist talking to members of Rasul and Tameeka's family's. The pianist played several songs as the guests settled in their seats and waited for the wedding to begin.

Tameeka was a nervous wreck as she watched the people pile into their seats, from the window of her master bedroom.

"Girl, I wish you sit down somewhere! Shit, you making me nervous," Tammy said, getting up from the bed to accompany Tameeka at the window.

"Girl, look at all those people! I'm nervous as hell. What if Rasul freezes up and don't want to be married? Girl, you know I'm nine years his senior, what if some young girl his age comes along?" Tameeka asked herself, looking more at Tammy.

"Girl, dat boy loves you! Look!" Tammy assured her grabbing Tameeka's hand making her look at the rock on her finger. "Girl look around you!" she continued, "Would a brother not sure of himself have you and your son up in a damn mansion!? Bitch please! If you don't calm down and relax, you won't even be able to enjoy the best day of your life."

"Girl, I don't know what I'd do without your ass," Tameeka said smiling, as she stood before the mirror. "Do I look fat?"

"No girl, you look good as hell! That gown makes your pregnant ass look beautiful," And it did.

Tameeka was absolutely perfect and the gown complimented every feature of her body, and even though she was 7 months pregnant, the gown still hugged her curves like a candy wrapper.

"Are y'all almost ready?" Trina asked, sticking her head in the door from out in the hallway, where all the other bridesmaids were.

"Yeah, we'll be there in a minute," she said, and Trina shut the door.

"Well girl, this is it," Tammy said, starring into her best friend's eyes, "You ready?"

"Yeah, I'm ready," Tameeka said, and the two embraced. It was all love.

+   +   +   +

     Rasul, Dog, Hit Man, and Pretty E sat isolated in the game room away from all the happenings throughout the house. In a corner
of the room away from his boys, Rasul stood alone gazing out of the window in deep thought, while his boys cracked funnies about him tying the knot. However, it wasn't a laughing matter to him. Over the past year and a half, almost two, Rasul had worked hard to get where he was. He had dreams, plans, and goals to fulfill when he left the confines of McKean Federal Prison, and he accomplished them all. Rasul was a millionaire, and as he stood staring out of the window, he knew he was blessed. Never being one to be a real spiritual buff, for that moment he thanked God and made a promise to be done with da game after the marriage.

     Rasul felt the time was now to give up the game. He had done well in no time and accomplished what people have chased for a lifetime. He knew the game had a limit and he reached his already; it was just explaining to his boys that he was done that concerned him. He didn't know how they would act towards him giving the game up, especially since they were at the top of it. The money was rolling in from all avenues, the businesses were booming, the real estate was profitable, and Ballers Night Club was premiere, stopping the drugs would be the best move he reasoned. It was senseless to continue with the drugs because everything was legal, and Rasul couldn't think of one reason to risk jeopardizing all that they accomplished. That's why he was getting out; it was the best thing for him and his boys he decided.

     "Yo! Whass' happenin' nigga? You aw'ight?" Dog asked.

     "I know nigga. You ain't got cold feet do you?" Pretty E joked.

     "A lil' some'em, but I'm cool. I just was over here thinking, dat's all," Rasul replied.

     "Thinking about what?" Hit Man asked concerned, hearing the seriousness in his voice.

     "About life cousin, about all this shit! I mean, when I came home from jail I had plans. Nigga was trying to get rich and chill, but after I got rich man shit got addictive. Feel me? Now I'm about to be a dad, a husband, a best friend…Yo, it's a lot of muthafucka's depending on me, on us for that matter. I'm just saying. Yo, we can't take care of shit dead or in jail, feel me? I think it's time for us to get out, you know?" Rasul said.

"Awwww shit! Dat nigga on some crazy shit already. Damn cousin, you ain't even married yet and you got soft!" Pretty E said, not catching the meaning of what was just said.

Rasul wanted to snap and cuss his ass out, but he bit his tongue. He knew Pretty E was from a different walk of life and had to remind himself of that sometimes. Pretty E had just always had all his life, whereas Rasul, Dog, and Hit Man never had. He thought that becoming rich was something that was pre-destined to happen, or supposed to happen because his parents were both rich. He never knew struggle first-hand like his boys, so he couldn't comprehend. Rasul smiled at the thought and his anger was gone that fast. He looked at his boy and said," Nah cousin, I ain't get soft, I got wise!" I'll explain it to you more when I get back from my honeymoon, cousin."

"Whatever nigga!" Pretty E said, still not getting it.

"I feel you cousin!" Hit Man said to Rasul.

"Me too," added Dog.

"Damn, all y'all niggas got soft!" Pretty E said, and then someone knocked on the door.

"Aw'ight, here we come," Rasul said.

Rasul turned to face his boys and the group hugged in the middle of the floor, and just like clockwork they stepped back and said, "Damn we sharp!" and fell out laughing.

+   +   +   +

Rasul stood at the altar in his milk white tailor made Armani tuxedo with his boys Dog, Pretty E, and Hit Man. They were draped in powder blue matching tuxes and white gators awaiting the arrival of the bride. Rasul peered through the crowd and saw faces of friends and family members he hadn't seen in years, but he lit up when he saw Frankie and Joey "The Fox" Vito. He felt like a proud son, and by the way Frankie looked, he felt the same way only he was a proud father. As soon as the pianist began to play and the crowd stood in ovation for the bride, Rasul's heart sunk into his stomach. Then came the surprise of a lifetime; Musiq Soul child walked down the isle on the red carpet singing "love", and the crowd was in awe. Rasul, the shock still evident on his face, turned to Dog.

"It was Cholly AK's idea," he said, nodding his head in the direction of his seat. Rasul looked through the crowd for him. As usual, he was dipped in money and adorned with a green Versace suit
with matching shoes and accompanied by two females; he raised his hands and smiled.

Tameeka's heart pounded so hard it was like a drum in her ears as she made the longest walk of her life. Her father turned to her right before they walked out the back door and asked, "Pumpkin, are you alright?" she shook her head and they headed out. Tameeka's knees trembled so bad that she cuffed her gown around the thigh area with one hand, lifting it up a little bit, cautious not to trip over it, as the flower girls led the way. This was her day, one big dream come true, and seeing Musiq at her wedding was the icing on the cake.

Rasul took her by the hand after shaking her father's hand, and pulled her close to him as they intertwined fingers. "Baby I love you," he said, and tears streamed down her face.

"I love you too," she managed to say through a cracked voice, then, the ceremony began. The Reverend went through the vows and just like that, they were pronounced husband and wife.

"You may kiss your bride!" the Reverend said, and Rasul and Tameeka kissed for what seemed to be an eternity, as the guests clapped and cheered them on in congratulations.

+   +   +   +

Chapter Twelve

What's beef!?
Beef is when you roll no less than 30 deep.
Beef is when ya moms ain't safe up in da streets.
Beef is when I see you, guaranteed to be in I.C.U.
       Biggie Smalls: What's Beef!

      Sixth and Madison Street on the West Side of town was a gold mind and tension between Skipper and the New York boy Cee-lo and his crew was at a boiling head. Neither one of them was willing to budge because the block was just too poppin'. Skipper, along with his crew of four, was profiting nearly a hundred grand a week on the block, and being bo-guarded off the block where they grew up all their life wasn't going down.

      "Man, I'm tired of these bitch ass niggas!" Skipper said, staring at the boy Cee-lo standing on the steps in front of the broad Chantel's house. "I'm tired of these sorry ass bitches too! Keep fuckin' wit these outta town ass niggas!" He finished, getting madder as he spoke.

      "I feel you cousin," Littles said.

      "Man these niggas gotta roll! Come on!" Skipper said, and got up off the steps he was on, and headed across the street. "Yo, let me holla at you right quick," he said, calling Cee-lo out to the sideway where he stood.

      "Yo son, what da deal?" he asked, stepping down off the steps.

      "You! Yo cousin, ain't no more pumpin' on dis block. Y'all niggas gotta take dat shit up the block, or around da corner or some'em! Cause dis block right here," he said, motioning his arms, "Is mine."

      "Yo son, "Cee-lo said, through a smirk," I ain't goin' nowhere! You ain't runnin' nuffin'!" he said, stepping in Skippers face.

      "Why don't you chill wit dat shit!" Chantel yelled from the doorway, sensing the fight about to start up.

      "Fuck you bitch! It's bitches like you that be havin' these punk muthafuckas down here!" Skipper said, then slipped the punch the boy Cee-lo tried to sneak in, and countered with a left cross. Cee-lo threw his hands up and moved them around wildly trying to confuse Skipper but it didn't work. Skipper, who boxed at the center for years, and won golden gloves twice, wasn't pleased at all. He stood calmly and waited to throw his shit soon as he saw an opening, he caught Cee-lo with a stiff straight jab that caused him to stumble back. Once he saw that Cee-lo was weak, he went on the attack catching him with everything he threw, and dropped him. Skipper stood up overtop of him and said, "Yeah Pussy! You getting the fuck up outta here!" He and Littles walked off, leaving Cee-lo bloody and lumped up on the sidewalk.

"Damn he whipped his ass!" they heard someone say, as they got in Skipper's C.L.K. 430 and mashed out.

+   +   +   +

Dog, Pretty E, and Hit Man had the house on Vanderver Ave. under control along with everything else, such as the Club and businesses. Rasul had been gone on his honeymoon for two weeks now in the Ivory Coast over in Africa, and they missed his presence, but he'd be back in two days. They sat at the table in the house on Vanderver Ave. and counted the weeks taken from all six of their lieutenants, and smiled. Combined, they reached almost seven hundred fifty thousand dollars in profit.

"Yo, ain't it crazy how we was only making like 10 thousand a week when we first started, now we making like damn near a mil?" Pretty E said, with a blunt dangling from his lips.

"Damn right. I remember when we weren't even making dat!" Hit Man said.

"Who you tellin?" Dog complied, putting the money in a briefcase.

The three of them bagged up all the work that was left in the house and put it in duffle bags, then left in separate cars to go drop off to all of their Lieutenants on each side of town.

+   +   +   +

Skipper sat on the steps in front of the base house him and his crew pumped drugs out of eating a bag of potato chips and drinking a quart of water he brought down at the corner store. Sixth and Madison Street was swarming with crack heads and dope fiends headed nowhere in life, but this is what society refused to recognize. These were the people whose dreams were disappearing in the smoke of their crack pipes and the venom injected through their syringes. That is what the government allows into this country everyday. Skipper shook his head in shame because these were his people, Black people, who were targeted the most, but realized this was his only means of survival. Trying to make himself feel a little better about the situation, he told himself, "Shit, these muthafuckas won't give me no job paying decent money, so I gotta do what I gotta do!"

He looked up and down at the block and for the first time in his life he actually saw the ghetto that many people had seen for years. He saw the thousands of Black people just in his neighborhood, oppressed by the unseen arms of the government. Empty coke bags, broken bottles, used needles, and trash littered all over the street decorating it like the fresh lawns, and neatly trimmed bushes in the upper and middle class neighborhoods of Amerikkka. For some reason, Skipper was just seeing everything for what it was. Maybe it was because of the fight he had earlier, that had him in this state. Maybe it was just a mood swing that opened his eyes. Whatever the reason, he was wide-awake and still felt like he was dreaming a nightmare.

The voice of a little boy crying brought him back to the present moment, and when he looked and saw the little boy chasing behind his mother, anger overcame him. Skipper remembered just like yesterday when his own mom ran from house to house trying to find a fix at a local heroin spot. He knew what she was doing was wrong, and in his heart he wished she would stop, but he was only a child. There was nothing he could do but wait until she finished, then, maybe she would take him to get some'em to eat.

Skipper knew the woman named Roshell, a local prostitute, or in street terms, Trick Bitch, from the block. He also knew from experience that the little boy Tyreek was going through the same shit he did as a kid. Skipper stopped Roshell and explained how he felt,
and advised her on what she needed to do, but she simply brushed it off by saying, "I'm grown!"

"Well at least take him to get some'em to eat," Skipper said, and handed her a twenty-dollar bill. Roshell took the money and started to walk away when he stopped her. "Here," he said, while the little man wasn't looking, and slid her a six-tenth of rock.

"I'm only doin' this shit so you don't spend my money on no drugs. That right there should be enough to hold you for a while. Now take him down 4th Street to McDonalds and get him some'em to eat. If I find out you ain't feed him, you can't ever get a muthafuckin' thing from me! I mean dat shit!" he stated, and walked away. When he got back to the step he felt good inside knowing that the "lil'" guy would go to sleep with a full stomach.

While Skipper got comfortable on the step, a crap game on the corner across the street between a few hustlers from the block nearly went unnoticed by him. He was on point and didn't want to be caught lunching in case the boy "Cee-lo'" returned with his crew to retaliate. He wiggled his fingers around the cast that he had put on his hand earlier, after breaking it on Cee-lo's jaw today, and with his good hand adjusted the 40 Cal. he had in the small of his back. Skipper watched as his workers ran from car to car, person to person, offering the package like it was legal, while he waited on Pretty E to come.

"Yo Littles, how much work is left?" he asked, when Littles came back from making a transaction.

"About a bird. Why, whass'up?" Littles answered.

"Nah, I'm checking that's all, cause peoples is on his way and I think he droppin' some'em off, so I need to know whass left, feel me?"

"Yeah, it's about a bird."

"Shit. The way the money coming right now, we'll be done with dat shit in a couple hours, Huh? What's dat, like four bricks dis week?" Skipper asked.

"Nah, like almost four and a half." Littles said.

"See dat's what I'm talking about. We shoulda been moving dat a long time ago. That's why I ran dat nigga the fuck outta here,
feel me?" he said, stopping in mid-sentence when he saw Beverly. "A, Yo Bev, you got some trees?" he yelled, down the street.

"Yeah, why? Whass'up?" she yelled back.

"Come 'ere then let me holla at you for a minute!" he said, reaching in his pocket with his good hand. "Yo, do me a favor. Take 80 dollars out of there and give it to Bev for me," he said, passing his money to Littles.

Skipper didn't even get a chance to smell the weed Beverly put in his hand, because no sooner as she passed off, an all black Crown Victoria came to a speedy halt freezing the block. "Damn!" Skipper thought, trying to cuff the weed, "I'm going to jail, I got this gun on me," he assumed, thinking it was a vice car. He was wrong, and realized it too late, when all four doors on the Sedan opened up at the same time. The shots that rang out that night, which left Skipper, Littles, and Bev dead in pools of blood, would ring forever in the ears of the city.   +   +   +   +

Pretty E was making his last drop off of the night, when he noticed police cars speeding up in his rear view mirror. Staying calm, he continued heading towards the West Side and breathed a sigh of relief when they shot past him. "Damn!" he said relieved, knowing the five-kilo's in the trunk was enough to lay him down for a long time. "I wasn't going out like dat!" he told himself, clutching the Desert Eagle in his lap, and he meant it. Pretty E turned off of 4th Street onto Madison Street, and pulled over on 5th Street when he saw all the police cars on 6th Street. "Damn I hope Skipper ain't get in no shit!" he said, to himself getting out of the car and heading towards the commotion. He didn't even get a chance to get up the block good, before T-Dot one of Skipper's workers came running up to him.

"Yo Pretty E! The New York boys just killed Skipper!" he said.

"What New York boys?" Pretty E asked, as his heart sank to his stomach.

"The boy Cee-lo and them!"

"Cee-lo!" he asked, his heart pumping rage now.

"Yeah. Tall dark-skinned nigga!"

Pretty E couldn't believe what he was hearing. Skipper was like a little brother to him, he couldn't be dead. He had to see it for himself, so he continued up the block. Once he reached the crime scene, all his fears, doubts, and uneasiness were confirmed by rage, when he seen the coroner pulling the sheet up over Skipper's face.

"Yo! Where da fuck them nigga's at?" he turned and asked T-Dot.

"I don't know cousin? I wasn't out here, I just got here right before you did, but all them was out here," he answered, pointing to the dudes on the corner.

"Yo! Who was out here when my peoples got shot?" He asked, as he walked over to the dudes on the corner.

"We was all out here, but dat shit happened so fast, that Skipper and them couldn't even move!" one of them said.

"Well who knows where them nigga's be at? I got a brick for whoever finds out where them nigga's at!" Pretty E said.

"His baby's mom live right dere," another one said, hoping that was enough to get him the brick.

"Right where?"

"Right there."

Pretty E walked across the street and knocked on the door only a few feet away from where the police had the block taped off at, and the girl Chantel answered the door.

"Yeah?" she asked, standing behind the screen door.

"You fuck wit da boah Cee-lo right?"

"No, not like dat," she answered, fear evident on her face.

"Well, you know where he be at, right?" he asked.

"No, he could be anywhere?"

"Well look, go get me a piece paper and pen, so I can give you this number," Pretty E said, and waited for her to come back, when she disappeared into the house. "Listen, if you here from that nigga find out where he's at and call me. I know dat nigga is going to call, so don't act like he didn't, ain't, won't or wouldn't. If I have to come back and check on you before you call me, it's going to be ugly. You heard? You see dat tape and shit?" he said, pointing to the crime scene. "Dat nigga killed my little brother!" _ He stated, and walked away, as she stood in the doorway literally shaking with fear.

Pretty E walked back by the crime scene headed back to his car, and took a long hard stare at the scene. Police were everywhere. Detectives were going door to door interviewing people, plain suit cops were looking for evidence, the coroner was zipping up the body bags, and blue and white officers held the crowd of bystanders at bay. "I'm'ma kill dat nigga!" Pretty E thought, as he stood dazed with anger, and filled with revenge, as he watched them work, then he focused in on a familiar face. He couldn't quite remember where he knew the Detective from, but he was sure he knew him, and when they made eye contact he remembered. The two of them took a long stare at one another, but no words were exchanged. They spoke with their eyes, and the conversation wasn't mutual.

Det. Cohen smiled.

+   +   +   +

Rasul, Pretty E, Dog, and Hit Man all sat in the game room of Rasul's house contemplating their next move. Rasul had only been gone for two weeks and a major loss had overcome him and his boys. Skipper was the top lieutenant on their team of dealers, and he was going to be sadly missed, but Rasul had already charged it to "the game." He realized that these things happened, so retaliating was really not what he wanted to do. They had come too far to loose everything off of emotion, and he expressed it.

"Man, that's the problem now! Nigga's think we got soft cause we making dough!" Pretty E snapped.

"Man nigga's know we ain't soft!" Dog said, taking offense to being called soft.

"Well why the fuck nigga's keep trying to play us then?" Pretty E asked again.

"Listen to what you're saying Cuz. We on some bigger shit now. Nigga's got kids, homes, businesses, all that shit. Why da fuck would you want to jeopardize all that, when all we gotta do is have Frankie handle it?" Rasul asked Pretty E.

"Because man, I'm tired of havin' to keep running to them nigga's! We been handling our own shit, so why is this so different? Them punk muthafuckas killed my lil' brother. Dat lil' nigga was like a lil' brother to me and I want to be responsible for killing dat
nigga! Feel me? How da fuck am I supposed to look his son in the eyes knowing I ain't handle my business, like I'm some bitch or some'em!" Pretty E replied, becoming emotional.

"Yo! Fuck dis shit! Check this out I'm tired of you two muthafuckas crying bout whass' next! What da fuck you want to do Pretty E?" Hit Man asked, getting hyper himself.

"I want to handle this shit."

"Well let's handle it then. I need some wreck (rec.) anyway!" Hit Man replied.

"Fuck it! If dat's what y'all wanna do, let's do it! I'm wit'chu!" Rasul said.

"Well it's official then," Dog said, and for the first time in over a year, they were going back to the streets.

+   +   +   +

Colony North apartments lay at the bottom of Market Street, right off of Lea Blvd. It was where the New York boy Cee-lo was hiding. In just two days, his baby's mom Chantel called about his whereabouts as soon as she found out he was staying with another broad. Pretty E, Rasul, Dog, and Hit Man were on their way. Even though this was their first time putting in work in over a year, their adrenaline pumped liked they never stopped. Hit Man drove the stolen Monte Carlo carefully up Gov. Printz Blvd onto Lea Blvd. and crept up on the premises.

"I don't need no mask nigga! Cause I ain't leaving any witnesses!" Hit Man said, as he eased the car up to the last building with the lights out. "I'm killing everything moving!" He said, getting out of the car. "Just give me some gloves!"

"Me too," Dog said, following Hit Man towards the building.

"Which apartment is it again?" Rasul asked.

"B-12," Hit Man said, as all four of them crept up the steps to the apartment's front door.

Whass'up Son,
I heard they got you on the run
For a Body
Now it's time to stash da gun
Give me a hot second I won't speak long
It's all fucked up some bodies snitching on da crew
Word is they got pictures of you….
                   Temperatures Rising
                      Mobb Deep

Cee-lo and his boys Snow, Shorty, and Diesel sat around in the apartment smoking 'Ls' and sipping Hennessey as "Mobb Deep" thumped through the house system's speakers. None of them were overreacting to the fact that Cee-lo had caught body just days ago, because it was nothing new. In the past three years they had all caught bodies in Brooklyn, Virginia, and Baltimore, so they were taking the same approach about this body, it was no different. The only thing now was that they were trying to figure out where they wanted to go next.

"How about North Carolina? You know Whitehead and them is in Durham," Snow suggested.

"Yo, Son! I was thinking Atlanta. My peoples in Stone Mountain, plus they doin' there thing out in College Park," Shorty said.

"Yo! I was thinking Atlanta too Son," Cee-lo said, then, continued, "That's where all the black people is at, feel me? Nigga's can blend right in, you know?"

"Yo, you hear dat Son?" Diesel asked, turning down the system.

"Yo kid! Why you buggin?" Shorty asked.

"Nah Son! On some real shit, I think I heard some'em."

"Nah man, we straight. Don't nobody know we here. Nigga's think we outta town by now," Cee-lo said.

"Man I don't know?" Diesel said, and got up to check the door.

+   +   +   +

Hit Man stood in front of the door and heard music coming from inside the apartment, then, it suddenly stopped. He put his finger up to his lips signaling Rasul, Pretty E, and Dog to be quiet, and took a step back from the door. In one swift motion he kicked the door off the hinges, busting Diesel in the face knocking him to the floor, as the four of them, barreled into the apartment. Hit Man stepped through first clutching his 45 Cal., and Cee-lo's eyes grew wide with fear as he leaped from the couch and ran down the hallway. Hit Man pulled the trigger but missed, as dry wall exploded from the walls leaving baseball sized holes that you could see through the other rooms.

178

Pretty E, Dog, and Rasul all stepped in the apartment right behind Hit Man and unloaded, as Shorty, Diesel, and Snow all dove behind the couches trying to escape the gun fire. There was nothing they could do as the bullets and buckshots from Dog and Rasul's Desert Eagle's and Pretty E's shotgun tore through the cushions of the furniture, splattering their remains all over the walls.

"Yo! Go make sure them muthafuckas is dead!" Rasul said, as Dog pulled the couches. The sight of the three lifeless bodies literally cut to pieces by the bullets, almost caused Dog to get sick on the stomach. He squinted his face up and turned back to Rasul and said, "Yeah Cousin, them muthafuckas is done!" then they heard the shot.

Hit Man chased Cee-lo down the hallway, but didn't see which room he ran into. He stood in the doorway of the master bedroom with his gun out in front of him, and scanned the room carefully before stepping in. Looking around, Hit Man noticed the closet door on a crack and tip toed over to it, recklessly snatching it open. Cee-lo, who was laying under a pile of clothes, jumped up and fired a single shot dropping Hit Man to his knees. Laying lifelessly in a fetal position, Hit Man fell unconscious, and Cee-lo ran out of the room.

Pretty E, hearing the shot, immediately ran towards it to check on Hit Man, but was on a straight path towards Cee-lo. Cee-lo was frozen in his tracks when he saw the barrel of the gauge, but raised his gun to shoot when he realized death was standing before him. Pretty E gritted his teeth and squeeze the trigger as the buckshot's splashed his white T-shirt, turning it almost a black-red. The power of the 12 gauge 'Shoty' lifted Cee-lo from his feet throwing him back into the bedroom, and Pretty E stood overtop of him. Pretty E looked down at the motionless body at his feet gasping for air, and smiled of sweet revenge. He placed the barrel of the gauge against Cee-lo's forehead and squeezed, blowing the back out, as it bounced against the carpet.

"Dat's for my lil' brother nigga!" he said, then, ran to Hit Man who was laying in a fetal position in front of the closet.

"Hold on Cousin! You gonna be aw'ight. We gotta get you to the hospital!" Pretty E said, almost frantically.

"I can't breathe Cousin," Hit Man mumbled, as Pretty E kneeled down beside him.

"Yo! Rasul! Come' ere man! Hit Man got shot!" Pretty E called.

Rasul ran in the bedroom and stooped down next to Pretty E.

"Yo man, we gotta get him outta here!" Pretty E said, as Hit Man went in and out of consciousness.

"Come on then! Let's get him outta here!" Rasul said, moving quickly now as they each placed one of Hit Man's arms around their shoulders and stood him up.

"Yo! I hear some sirens y'all. It's time to bounce," Dog said, helping them with Hit Man out the door.

The sirens were approaching fast as Dog went to get the car and Rasul and Pretty E stumbled down the apartment's steps with Hit Man. Four or five different people were looking out of their apartment windows and Dog saw them. He jumped from behind the wheel of the car, and let rounds off into every window he saw people looking out of, as the potential witnesses ducked and hid. In the next few seconds they were loaded in the car and leaving the complex, driving right pass the police who were entering the complex.

+   +   +   +

Det. Cohen walked into the living room and what he saw was indescribable. It was the nastiest scene he'd ever seen on the side of his partner, Armstrong, nearly two years ago. There wasn't a doubt in his mind after finding no leads, that this was the work of the same thugs who killed his partner. Det. Cohen walked around forensic experts, coroners, and other D.T.'s shaking his head in disgust, then, remembered what he found in his file cabinet. The two-page report written by his partner was shocking to him, but kept a secret by him. No way would he allow his superiors to get wind of it, because then they'll know the truth about Armstrong. Armstrong was as crooked as the letter 'S', but Cohen still loved him. He taught him everything about the ins and outs of being a good officer, and he admired Armstrong's, do it his way approach.

Cohen promised himself that he'd never air Armstrong's dirty laundry, then thought about the report and what it said:

Tuesday, July 19th 2000 Time: 1100 hrs.

Today I observed Rasul, Eric, Hakeeme, and Michael (Aliases) Rasul, Pretty E, Hit Man, and Dog) go into Us Guys Construction sight. Several minutes later a limousine arrived. I followed and pulled them over, after they left the premises.

Friday, July 22, 2000 Time: 1400 hrs.

Today I received my first pay off $1,000.00 Dollars.

Det. Cohen was brought back to the present tense when he heard one of the forensic experts yell, "I got something here!" and wave for someone to assist him. Det. Cohen stood at his side with his counterparts, and listened as the forensic guy explained.

"Here we have four bodies, and five different blood samples," he said, holding up five test tubes. "There has to be a fifth person. Either he's another victim or he's the assailant," he stated. Everyone's attention level was in high gear, then, came the break over the walkie-talkies.

"Attention all units, please be advised that there has been a gun shot victim escorted to Riverside Hospital, by unknown men. Victim is in stable, but critical, condition," then there was static.

"I'm on it!" Cohen claimed, and ran towards the door. "Whoever this person is, he's who I want. I know it!" he thought, as he burned rubber down the street of the complex headed to the hospital.

+   +   +   +

Dog sped the stolen Monte Carlo up Lea Blvd across Market St., and headed straight towards Riverside Hospital. Irregardless to any traffic lights, he dodged in and out of the traffic lanes in hysteria, as Hit Man fell in and out of consciousness.

"Come on man! Drive this muthafucka!" Pretty E exclaimed.

"I am nigga! What da fuck you expect me to do?" Dog snapped.

"Yo! Calm da fuck down, he's going to be alright. Just keep driving Dog," Rasul said, and they were at the hospital in minutes.

Dog pulled the car up to the Emergency Room entrance and Pretty E was already jumping out of the car. Rasul, who was in the back seat with Hit Man, lifted him out of the car as gently as he could, and the two of them carried him through the doors.

"Yo! We need some help!" Pretty E shouted, to the nurse behind the station.

"Hurry up! He's been shot!" Rasul added, as the nurse took her time.

The nurse jumped up and called some type of code, and nurses came running from everywhere. Two doctors, followed by several nurses, placed Hit Man on the stretcher and wheeled him into the "Trauma Unit," as Pretty E and Rasul slid out the door. When the nurse turned around to ask for the victim's information, his friends were gone.

Chapter Thirteen

Det. Cohen was ecstatic when he hung up the phone. The hospital officials had just confirmed the match of blood found on the scene, to the patient brought in last night. "I knew it!" he said to himself, jumping up from his desk. Det. Cohen had worked around the clock last night going over case after case of unsolved murders; robberies in the city over the past three years, and what stood out the most were the similarities. In every case of this magnitude, there was a pattern, plus there was no evidence. They were always perfectly done, no witnesses, no evidence, no trails of any sort, but last night a crucial mistake was made, they left behind D.N.A. There was no doubt in Det. Cohen's mind that the person or persons who done this, were responsible for his partners murder. He looked down at the picture on his desk, as he put on his overcoat and smiled a sinister smile. "It was you muthafucka's, wasn't it?!" he said, like they could hear him, as he folded the folder on the photographs of Rasul, Pretty E, Hit Man, and Dog that he found in Armstrong's files.

It took Det. Cohen absolutely no time at all to reach the hospital, as he drove with the flashers on in his unmarked car. He walked through the doors and headed straight to the Intensive Care Unit, stopping only at the information station on the floor.

"Excuse me," he asked the nurse, flashing his badge. "I'm Det. Cohen and I'm here to see the patient that was brought in last night with a gunshot wound to the stomach. Could you please tell me the room number?"

"Weren't you here last night? I'm sure the doctors notified you last night that the patient wasn't able to have visitors or be questioned right now. He was in surgery last night, and I'm sure he's still heavily sedated, and," Det. Cohen cut her off.

"I received a call this morning from a Doctor, "Uh!""

"Dr. Zwanky?"

"Yes, Zwanky. He explained everything to me, and said the patient is fine now, just a little groggy."

"Well I'll have to check," she said, glancing down at a clipboard, then, picking up the phone. "He's in room 1111" she

said, when she hung up the phone, and then pointed in the
direction.

"Thank you," Det. Cohen said, and headed down the
hallway towards the room.

+   +   +   +

Lucy rolled over in bed and stared at Pretty E who was
stark naked and snoring like a baby. "Gosh, I love this man," she
said to herself, before kissing his forehead gently. Last night, Lucy
saw a side of Pretty E she never seen before, as she tried to
comfort him from crying. It was devastating that Hit Man got shot,
but it was an opportunity for her to close the case on the "Capelli
Family." She knew with the right pressure, he

would easily fold, and help her out to save himself and his boys.
Lucy got out of bed and went into the bathroom carrying the
cordless phone, and shut the door behind her. She turned on the
shower water, and sink faucets, then, dialed the hospital.

"Yes. This is Federal Agent Jennifer Vault and I'm calling
on the condition, or any information you have on a patient brought
in last night with a gunshot wound. A mister called Hakeeme. H
as in Harry, A as in Alice, K as in Kathy, E, E, M as in Michael,
and E. Last name Stewart.

"Can you please hold?" the nurse asked, clicking on the
elevator music Lucy hated so much.

"Ms. Vault," she asked, coming back on the line. "Yes we
have a Mr. Stewart here and he's fine. He's alert, and stable in
I.C.U. In fact, there's some officers here talking to him."

"Damn!" Lucy said.

"Is there a problem?" the nurse asked.

"No, there's not a problem. O.K., thanks a lot," Lucy said,
and hung up the phone tossing it on the toilet seat. "Damn I have to
stop those cops from ruining my investigation!" she thought, and
turned to dart out the door.

"Damn what? Who was that?" Pretty E asked, nearly being
run over by Lucy trying to get out the door.

"Oh! You scared me baby," Lucy said startled. "That was
nobody. Just Lenny asking me to come in early, that's all," she
said, then asked, "Are you alright?"

"Yeah, I'm alright. Just thinking about my boy, I feel like I'm responsible, you know?" he answered.

"Why would you feel responsible? What happened?" she asked, trying to get more information out of him.

"Nothing. It's a long story," he said.

"I have time." Lucy said.

"I don't. I have some shit to take care of today. Why don't you walk me to the door," he said, and turned to leave.

Lucy gave him a kiss at the door, then, rushed herself to get dressed. "I gotta get to this hospital," she reminded herself, as she locked the door behind her.

+   +   +   +

Det. Cohen walked into room 1111 and was happy to see the patient was Hit Man. "Suffer you Bastard!" he said to himself, as he looked at the tubes in his nose and mouth. Hit Man opened his eyes and frowned his face, when he saw the Detective sitting at his bedside.

"What da fuck are you doing here?" he asked.

"Don't play stupid Hakeeme. I know and you know that you shot and killed four people last night. You're going away for a long time, you no good muthafucka!" Det. Cohen said, his emotions beginning to override his intellect.

"I don't know what you're talking about?" Hit Man said in a voice barely above a whisper.

"You will know what I'm talking about and so will the Judge and jury. I have your D.N.A. at the crime scene, and it places you there. Now you have two choices to make. Either you tell me who your accomplices were, or get the death penalty. What's it going to be?"

"I need my lawyer."

"Fine. Johnny Cochran couldn't get you outta this one! Your ass is gone to fry!" Det. Cohen said.

"Excuse me! Why are you badgering this witness? Who are you anyway?" Lucy demanded, catching the tail end of the conversation.

"I'm Det. Cohen head officer on this case, who are you?"

185

"I'm Federal Agent Jennifer Vault, and these are my partners Agents Williams and Satterfield. We're taking over here, so if you'll excuse us," Lucy advised.

"Over my dead body! This is my case!" Det. Cohen stated adamantly.

"No this is ours, so I'd advise you to leave before your job is in jeopardy. Yours and your supervisors!" Agent Williams, a forty something year old black male stated, towering over the detective.

Cohen stood up from the bedside and glared at the three Federal Agents, before exiting the room. He was pissed, but there was nothing he could do. The 'Feds' had the power, but he was sure going to give his Captain a mouth full, once he got back to the station.

Lucy walked over to Hit Man's bedside and placed her hand over her mouth. Seeing him lying there, tubes everywhere, was almost too much to bear especially, since this person was so close to Pretty E. Lucy loved Pretty E so much; she actually felt his pain, as she looked on at Hit Man. What happened next was unexpected, as Hit Man shouted, "Bitch you're a cop! How? You're fuckin...," and before he could get it all out, Lucy was smashing her hand down on his wound. The pressure on his staples stopped him in mid-sentence. There was no way Lucy was going to let her partners hear, what she was sure was going to be said next about her love affair with Pretty E.

"Shhhh! Shhhh!" she shushed him, then, turned to her partners.

"Fellas can I get a moment alone with the suspect?"

"Sure", they said in unison, and exited the room.

"Hit Man," Lucy said, when her partners left the room, "I know this may come as a shock to you, but I'm a Federal Agent. I've been working undercover for the last four years trying to bring down the Capelli Family. I never meant to fall in love with Eric, it just happened. I never mixed my work with my love life before, this was a first, but I'm not the issue. Hit Man you are in some very deep

trouble. The police have four dead bodies and your blood at the crime scene. I stepped in because I can help, but only if you help me. I'm sure the prosecutors are going to push for the death penalty, but it can be avoided."

"How?" he asked.

"By testifying in court against Frankie, Joey, Lenny, Ricky and Nikki."

"I can't do that," he said.

"You have to. Listen, I have enough information to tie you in with them too. You and your friends, but I don't want that. You don't either. If you promise me right now that you'll testify, and give

me everything you know about the Capelli Family, you and your friends will go free. I'll make sure of that, but if you don't, well, I have to do my job."

"Are you sure?" he asked, weighing his options.

"I'm positive," she assured him.

For more than two hours Hit Man laid in bed, and gave up everything he knew, while Lucy and her partners taped his statements. Hit Man went all the way back to the day he first met the Capelli's, to the time Ricky and Nikki came and got Shelly and BoBo. He told of the hit they did on the snitch at the auto body shop, and the kilo's of cocaine at the warehouse. Lucy and her partners were at awe about all of the information Hit Man had to dispense. He had given them enough information to bring up more charges of racketeering, murder, and even a new one, drug distribution. Now all they had to do was protect the star witness, because even though they had the tapes of confession, without him they were inadmissible in court, because the jury could rule that the tapes had been co-hearsed.

Lucy got on the phone and called her Captain to explain everything that Hit Man just told her. She also said that due to the nature of the charges, and who they were against, Hit Man would need to be put in a safe house until she could get the entire case together, and that could take a month or two. So together, they both decided that he would also need a new identity to go along with the new location, until they could get a trial date.

"Yes, that'll be fine," Lucy, said.

"O.K., then tomorrow I'll have everything together," the Captain said.

"Tomorrow is great, the sooner the better and I'll make sure there are no visitors, and an officer at the door."

"Perfect!"

"See ya later," she said, and hung up the phone.

"What?" Hit Man asked concerned.

"You'll have a whole new identity tomorrow, and you'll be relocated to a safe house until trial. No one will know where you're at, not even your family," Lucy said.

"Well, can I use the phone?"

"No, not now. Maybe later," Lucy said.

+   +   +   +

Rasul could hardly sleep last night thinking about Hit Man, and was up roaming the house when Tameeka came downstairs.

"Good morning baby!" she said gingerly, when she saw him pacing the floor.

"Hey Boo, whass'up?" he answered.

"Nuffin, I couldn't get back to sleep when I noticed you gone. You know I can't sleep if I'm not all cuddled up underneath you," she said smiling, then, continued, "Have you heard anything about Hit Man yet? I know Trina is worried sick. Don't you know we went out there last night, and they had the nerve to tell us we couldn't see him?"

"Who?" he asked.

"The police! They act like he did some'um, or some'em," Tameeka said naively.

"Yeah, they do that when people get shot," Rasul said.

"You want something to eat? I'm hungry," she said, Rasul following her into the kitchen.

"Nah, I'm straight."

"Ooooo! Baby come' ere, hurry up! Come feel the baby, it's kicking like crazy! She must be hungry," Tameeka said, lifting her T-shirt for him to come feel her stomach.

Rasul put his hands on both sides of Tameeka's belly and rubbed it, as the baby kicked wildly.

"Damn Baby! Does that hurt?" he asked Tameeka.

"No, only when she is in my ribs. I hate dat," she answered.

"Hey Baby Girl! What'cha doing in there?" Da-Da can't wait till you come outta there." Rasul spoke into Tameeka's belly button.

"Boy you are crazy!" she giggled.

"Nah-Ahn!! The Doctor said she could hear me when I do that."

"Whatever," she smiled, sucking her teeth, as she reached for the eggs in the refrigerator.

"Baby, do me a favor."

"What?"

"Call the hospital and see how Hit Man is doing for me." You know what to say, right? You gotta tell'em you Hit Man's sister or some'em."

"Boy I'm not stupid! You act like I'm dumb or some shit! I got dis! Just give me the damn phone, you make me sick wit dat dumb shit!" she snapped, snatching the phone out of his hand.

"Damn! I only said call the hospital," he said, feeling scorned, but used to it. Every since she got pregnant her mood swings became more and more erratic, so it was becoming a regular to him.

Tameeka talked back and forth on the phone from one Doctor to another trying to get information on Hit Man. "I said I'm his sister!" Tameeka snapped, becoming more and more frustrated. "I mean, y'all act like y'all can't tell me nothing about my brother. All I want to know is what da fuck is going on! Don't make me come down there!" she finished.

"That wouldn't be good Miss," the doctor said, "The police have taken over, and they said no visitors. It has become a police matter. We did our job, he's stable, the surgery went well, and he's going to be fine, and that's all I can tell you."

"Fine!" she said, slamming the phone's receiver down.

"What happen Baby? What they say?" Rasul asked.

"Them muthafucka's is crazy! He's alright, but they act like he's under arrest or something!"

"Why you say dat?"

"Cause! The police got his room guarded and everything!"

Hearing that, Rasul was mad as shit. He paced the floor back and forth cursing under his breath because he knew he shoulda followed his first instinct. There was no way they were supposed to risk everything they worked so hard to get, and now he knew why." The police probably trying to charge him with that shit from last night," he thought, bringing his pacing to a stand still.

"Baby, why is the police there?" Tameeka asked.

"It's a long story. I'll tell you about it later, right now I gotta go get with Dog and Pretty E. I gotta see what da fuck is going on!" he said, and gave her a kiss before leaving.

"Be careful," she said, as he shut the door behind him.

+   +   +   +

Rasul, Pretty E, and Dog sat in the house on Vanderver Ave. talking about everything that happened last night at the apartment. They went over every detail repeatedly trying to find out what went wrong, and kept coming up with the same thing, they never should have went. Pretty E was feeling the blame the most, because it was him who made the decision to go. They had done this same thing plenty of times before and nothing went wrong, so he had the same perception of what would happen this time. They would go in and handle business, then leave, but that wasn't the case this time. Hit Man was laid up in the hospital near death and the police were all over him.

"Man, I told you muthafucka's we shouldn't have went!" Rasul said upset, shaking his head.

"Man, we goin' be aw'ight. Hit Man is a soldier," Dog said.

"Man, I hope so...It's a different story when them muthafuckas start talking life in da joint. I just hope he don't crack," Rasul said.

"Life for what? They ain't got nuffin' on him," Pretty E said.

"They must do, they there ain't they?! Them muthafuckas got some'em!" Rasul assured him.

"The only way they could have some'em on him, is if some of his blood was on the scene after he got shot," Dog said, and their minds raced.

"Damn!" Rasul said, "That nigga was leaking like a muthafucka!"

190

"Do you think some dripped on the floor somewhere?" Pretty E asked.

"Nigga, didn't you just hear me say, he was leaking like a muthafucka? I knew we shouldn't went!" Rasul said, and then his cell phone rang.

"Calm down Cuz. It might not have been none," Dog said, as Rasul answered his phone.

"Man, I seen da blood right there! Hello," he said, into the phone.

"Rasul? Where are you's guys at? I need to see yous's right now! I can't believe you's done some'em so stupid!" Frankie spoke.

"What?" Rasul asked, hoping Frankie didn't know.

"Don't play stupid Rasul. You know good and well what I'm talking about. That shit you's pulled last night, has stirred up a lot of shit! I'll talk to you's when you get here," Frankie said, and the line went dead.

"Who was dat?" Dog asked.

"Frankie," Rasul answered.

"Whass'up?" Pretty E asked.

"I don't know? He wants to see us. He said some'em about last night," Rasul said, and they got up to leave.

+   +   +   +

Frankie hung up the phone. "They're on their way."

"I knew we shoulda never done business with those Moolians they're all the same. They self-destruct. They're jealous of one another, either they're telling on one another, or they're just plain at one another's throats for some Pussy. Either way they end up killing or hurting one another for something less than that," Joey "The Fox" spoke to his Boss.

"Yeah! In most cases that's right, but Rasul and I have an unbreakable bond you or nobody else' can understand. He's like my own blood, do you understand?" He paused, "I knew you wouldn't. But as for the rest of them, I'd kill'em without a single thought," Frankie spoke, and they waited.

When Rasul, Pretty E, and Dog arrived at Frankie's ranch style home on the outskirts, Mrs. Maraachi led them down the hallway to where Frankie and his under boss Joey "The Fox" Vito

191

awaited them. Their faces showed disgust and their eyes were
piercing when they took their seats, and for the first five minutes
no one said anything. Frankie got up from his chair at the head of
the round table and walked over to the phone stand, bringing the
answering machine back and sitting it on the table in front of them.

"Listen," Frankie said, pressing the play button and the tape
began.

"Frankie, Hey Boss. This is officer Dinarro and we got a
problem. I don't know who this guy is, but he sure knows a lot
about you. His name is Hakeeme Stewart, and he's running his
mouth at the hospital to the Feds like he's one of them. Last night
he was brought to the hospital by two or three people, we know it
was two for sure. Anyhow he was shot once in the stomach, and
later charged with four bodies at an apartment complex. I think
they shook him up pretty bad. Anyway, the Feds have taken over
and they're placing him in a witness protection program until they
can gather up a strong enough case, then they're coming to arrest
you. Without him there's no case, so as soon as I find out his
whereabouts I'll let you know. Until then lay low, and stay clean.
I'll call you tomorrow" and the recording stopped.

Pretty E and Dog looked to Rasul who gave them an "I-
told-you so," look when the machine stopped. If they hadn't heard
it themselves they wouldn't have believed it, but they did. It wasn't
them who had turned police, but what Hit Man had done had sure
enough made them look just as bad as him. They looked to Frankie
as if to say, what are we supposed to do, and lowered their heads in
shame.

"There's one thing in this lousy world I just don't tolerate!
I hate it more than a child hates spinach and that's a rat! I know
this guy is a friend of y'alls, but he has to be taken care of,"
Frankie said, and checked their facial expression before he
continued. "That sorry son of a bitch isn't going to be the cause of
me, or anyone of you's to go inside of that filthy can! He'll meet
his fuckin' maker before I see the can again! You hear me?" he
said, pounding his fist on the table. "I can't believe this shit! What
da fuck was you's thinking? Why didn't yous's call me? I could've
handled everything, now we're all in a freakin' jam! What was
you's thinking about, huh?"

"We were going to call, but the problem was ours. We wanted to handle it ourselves," Rasul spoke for the three.

"Your problem is my problem," Frankie responded.

"We wanted to handle it. They killed one of our Lieutenant," Pretty E spoke.

"How many times have I told you's guys that emotions can cost you your life!? You're just not thinking when you're emotional, so don't act off emotions. You'll regret it more times than none. Listen, I want everyone to go home and relax. Go home to family and rest. I have to figure out how to get us outta this jam. You's knows you's really fucked up this time. Really fucked up!" Frankie said.

+   +   +   +

The loud ring of her phone and the alarm clock going off at the same time awakened Lucy. "Fuck!" she said through a yawn and a stretch, and sat up to grab it off the nightstand next to her bed. "Hello.., Uhm-Hmm, yes, that's good. When? Well let me get ready. I'll meet you and the Marshall there at noon then, O.K.? I'll see you then. Bye". Lucy sat the phone down on the receiver and thought about what her Captain said about Hakeeme. They'd found him a house in Harrisburg, PA. in a small rural section near the city. His new name was Mark Johnson, and they'd be moving him today. Lucy got up and walked to the bathroom to shower.

As she stood under the hot water lathering up her hair with 'Pert,' her mind took a journey. She thought about how her life had turned out thus far, and was rather proud of her accomplishments. She graduated at the top of her college class, the top woman in the Academy, and earned her degree in Law, but then she became depressed. This wasn't her life. It was her parents, her brothers and sisters, not hers. Lucy had followed their footsteps. Her father was a judge, her mother a prosecutor, along with her brothers and sisters being lawyers. "This isn't my life," she thought. "I'm supposed to be a defense attorney. I hate being anything like them." All her life being the youngest of five, she had to follow their rules. Everyone wanted Lucy to be so perfect. Flawless, because they had made mistakes and it was too much pressure, so she bucked against them. She became a wild teen who lost her virginity early, hung

193

out, drank, and even smoked marijuana. She did it all. But then came the pressure again from her family, being an outcast by them, and it eventually won, turning her into one of them. Ms. Perfect, the nerd, and Ms. Can't do no wrong, then the tears started. She tried to tell

herself it was the shampoo burning her eyes, but it wasn't; it was the pain. The pain of not being able to be herself and the agony of always feeling like an outsider throughout the years really hurt Lucy. Then, she thought about Eric (Pretty E) and how doing something like sleeping with him, a black man, was totally against everything her family stood for. The feeling that brought to her, sleeping with a black man, was wonderful, she was free and it was defiance against her family, but also something she wanted to do.

Being in the presence of Pretty E had done just that, gave her freedom. Freedom from her parents and family, freedom from her job, and made her feel whole, complete, like she was finally living her life her way. Then there was the feeling she felt from his touch. The way his hands made her body sing, the way she felt while he explored her insides, the way she cuddled against him, and then she realized she was masturbating.

Lucy got out of the shower and dressed in a sweat suit Pretty E had brought her. She didn't' actually know the fashion statement it made, but it looked great. The symbol on the chest, and the word "Roc-a-Wear" on the sleeve in blue, against its gray fabric was perfect with her Nike cross-trainers. Pretty E was all over her mind, and she knew she wasn't going to let anything happen to him. Her job was no comparison to the love she felt for him. "I have given them everything they need to close the case against the Capelli's. My job here is done," she said to herself. "That's it! I'm resigning," she made up her mind. Lucy grabbed a tablet of paper from out of her closet, and walked out into the dining room, and sat at the table. Then she began the letter.
"My Dearest Pretty E",

Where do I begin? Who knows? But I would first like to apologize for lying to you like I did. I deceived you, and I never should have kept a secret from you. I'll understand if you never want to speak to me again, but I have to come clean to you. My love, I'm a Federal Agent. My name isn't Lucy. It's Jennifer Vault. I've been working undercover for four years in the Capelli Family. Pretty E baby; I'm so sorry. I've been living one big, too good to be true, great old-American lifestyle until I met you. You made me see and understand another side of life I only saw on T.V., or read in a book. I have always been sheltered away from people and society by my family, so I never actually got to meet real people. People who weren't on the same status level of my family or the people we knew. I only knew about your type of people from what my parents told me. Not the actual race issue thing, but the struggle, and the people who were living it. I was always taught that the financially bound people were lazy, and robbed, hurt, and stole from people for spite, or because they was too lazy to work. Baby it's a long story, but when I met you, my views changed. My whole outlook on life changed. You made me see that people, the ones financially bound, probably more times than none are doing what they do because they have to, not because they don't care or they want to. My love, what I am trying to say is who's to say that selling drugs is wrong, that stealing is wrong, and that robbing is wrong? Especially when it's for a purpose. I blame the economy and the government for the woes of the people, for the crime rate, and why the people are jobless and struggling.

Baby I love you more than you'll ever imagine and that's why I'm resigning from the Bureau. Hit Man is going to be fine, I made sure of it. You, Dog, and Rasul will be fine too. I only wanted the Capelli family, and I finally got them. Now I'm going to pursue my dream as a Defense Attorney. So, my love if you're ever in need of a lawyer that'll give her blood, sweat, and tears in court to defend you, I'm the person. Baby you made me love the bad guys, the good bad guys that is ☺ and I'll never be so judgmental again. Eric I love you sooo much, I just wish we were both at the same spot in our lives. I mean, you're young, and you're so damn gorgeous, ladies run to you, you'll never settle for me, at least not now anyway, so I have to say, "Good Bye." Eric I love U. (P.S) here's how to reach me:

1-800-777-9191

Be careful!   Love ya ☺ !

Love,

195

Lucy
A.K.A.
Jennifer Vault

    Lucy finished the letter, but couldn't stop the tears. She got up, licked the back of the envelope shut, and put it in her jacket pocket. Once she reached her Maxima, she did her ritual, and grabbed
her Marlboro Lights from the sun visor. She looked at the clock on her dashboard that read 10:45 a.m. "Plenty of time," she
thought, fixing her make-up in the rear view mirror. Lucy cut on the car and tuned her radio to her favorite station 99.5 WJBR and the soft sounds of DiDo seeped through her Bose Audio System, as she sung along:

    Tears gone cold I'm wondering why?
    I got out of bed at all.
    Morning rain clouds up my window,
    And I can't see at all.
    And even if I could, it'll all be gray
    With your picture on my wall
    It reminds me, it's not so bad, It's not so bad

                Dido

                Tears Gone Cold.

    Her tears started again…

Chapter Fourteen

Hit Man lay in his hospital bed and stared at all the "Feds" scrambling around his room trying to get things together, while Lucy sat at his side. It was like a dream, he couldn't believe this was happening to him. Lucy tried her best to console him and keep his mind off of what was happening, but he wouldn't allow her comfort. He had become a snitch, and it ate at him like nothing else he had ever felt. Just the thought of him being up on the stand testifying made him feel like a sucker. Not because of what people would think, but because of what he would think about himself. Then there was Rasul, Dog, and Pretty E, the only people in the world besides his mother and sisters, wife and kids that he loved. What would they think, what would all of them think?

"Listen Hakeeme, your new name will be Mark Johnson," Lucy said, handing him a picture I.D. with the photo she took last night. "We're moving you to Harrisburg, PA. Agent Williams and Agent Satterfield will be the only people in contact with you. If you need anything at all, anything—you contact either one of them. They are going to supply you with transportation, clothing, and dividends. I don't actually know how long you will be in this particular place, but I'm sure that after the trial you will be moved, and reunited with your family."

"What? You mean I'm going to be moved again after this?"

"You'll have to be in the witness protection program for the rest of your life. This is the Mafia we're dealing with."

"Look, if I gotta go through this shit for the rest of my life, I'm done. Fuck dat deal. Y'all gotta do what'cha'll gotta do," he said seriously.

"Fine! If you want the needle I can't stop you. I just thought you were a lot brighter than that." Lucy said agitated and got up. "Captain! Call it off and let Wilmington PD. handle this shit of a case. I don't care anymore! Let this piece of shit get the needle!" she said, pointing her finger towards Hit Man, winking her eye. She knew deep down inside that Hit Man wanted to live, that he was just uncertain. The whole situation was difficult, it would be difficult for anyone who's lived a certain lifestyle all of their life, and now suddenly has to be asked to be a different way.

"What do you mean, call it off," the Captain asked, catching Lucy's wink. The wink itself was a signal that most law enforcement officers used as a code to get on the same page, so when the Captain saw it he played along.

"He doesn't want to testify now, and we're not going to beg him. It's his life, let him get what he wants," Lucy said, continuing with the reverse psychology.

"Wait a minute! Hold up. I'll do it. I don't want to die like that, I wanna see my kids grow," Hit Man said, after pondering on the outcome.

"Good for you," Lucy said.

"But why do I have to call them?" he said, motioning to Agents Williams and Satterfield.

"Because they're in charge of you," she answered.

"Where will you be?" he asked.

"I'll be in touch," she said, Hit Man didn't respond.

The walk to the cars and jeeps parallel parked in front of the hospital was hell for Hit Man. The walker that the doctors had given him had his unused arm muscles burning and his back ached from being hunched over, not to mention it hurt every time he breathed. He just came out of surgery a day ago, from getting the bullet removed from its lodging place in the tissue of his abdomen, so his face twisted with pain with every step. He flopped down in the backseat of the Crown Victoria after walking nearly a mile so it seemed, and asked the Marshall's for a cigarette. "They didn't smoke was their answer," he sighed, "Damn I need a cigarette." Lucy walked over to the car smiled, and reassured Hit Man that he'll be fine. He looked lost and his face showed worry, and again she tried to comfort him.

"I told Eric and the rest of them they'll be fine too," she said, this time getting a smile from him. "Don't worry about anything Hakeeme. Keep a clear head and ready yourself for trial. Your kids and family will be taken care of also, so before I leave is there anything you need to ask me?"

"Yeah, give me a cigarette."

Hit Man was numbed with disbelief, and as sure as he was in the backseat of a Marshall's car heading God knows where, he still couldn't believe it. He stared out the backseat window at the trees, the street signs, license plates, and pedestrians of the place he called home all his life, and wondered would he ever see it again. For the first time since Hit Man was a child, a teardrop stung his cheek, and emotions overwhelmed him. He couldn't believe he had become what so many so-called thugs, ballers, and Big Willie's all over the hoods of Amerikkka had become, a snitch. He shook his head as if to shake out the thoughts, but the more he heard the C-B's crackling static through the air, saw their freshly shaved faces, and smelled their cheap cologne, the deeper the wound in his soul became.

+   +   +   +

The sun was setting overtop of the Federal Building when Lucy and her Captain finished up the paperwork. Her head was pounding at the temples to the sound of the computers keys being tapped, and her eyes were heavy from the lack of sleep she got last night. The anxiety and excitement of Hit Man agreeing to cooperate had kept her up tossing and turning most of the night. It was the most unexpected lead she'd hope to receive, but it was the most concrete. The information that Hit Man had given them last night closed almost every open case she had on the Capelli's. From the hit on Johnny at the Auto Body Shop, to the muscling of merchandise down at the docks at the Port of Wilmington, Hit Man's statements closed them all. Now all she had to do was keep him alive until they could make the arrests of Frankie, Joey, Ricky, and Nikki, and that could take several days.

Lucy closed her folder on the desk in front of her and looked across the room into the Captain's office. Captain Bailey was sitting in his plush leather office chair behind his solid oak desk talking on the phone, while she was trying to build up the nerve to do what she planned on doing from the start. All day long she contemplated on her decision to resign looking for reasons not

to, but there wasn't any. Pretty E had changed her views on life forever. Lucy swallowed the
last gulp of coffee she had in her cup, got up, and headed into the Captain's office.

"Captain Bailey, we need to talk," Lucy said, walking uninvited into the Captain's office.

"Hey Lucy, I mean Jenny. I've become so accustomed to calling you Lucy, I nearly forgot you real name," he chuckled. "What can I do for you?" he asked, hanging up the phone.

"I really don't know if there is or not. We just need to talk," she said.

"Is there a problem? Everything's fine with the case, right?" he asked, detecting a problem.

"Yes, everything is fine with the case. Hit Man is safe in Harrisburg, Williams and Satterfield are on their way back here, and I've closed all the open cases we had on the Capelli's. With Hit Man's testimony at trial we'll get all the more serious convictions. You know the murders, racketeering, loan sharking, manufacturing cocaine, delivery, weapons, and robbery charges. We'll get convictions on all of that, but that's not why I came in here."

"Continue," the Captain said.

"Captain Bailey I've been in this line of work for over eleven years. I've made some of the largest busts on the East Coast. I've been undercover on this particular case longer than any other case in my career, and you know what? It gave me time to think. Captain this job has been my life. Outside of my work, I don't even have any friends. I don't have any children, no husband, no social life, nothing. Life is much more than this job to me today. I'm tired of being lonely. I want a husband, I want kids, I want all of those things and my biological clock is ticking. I went to college, earned a degree in law, but for what? I haven't had time to use it. Captain, I guess what I'm trying to say is it's time for me to move on, change careers, become an attorney and open my own practice. This job just no longer fulfills me. Do you understand what I'm trying to say?"

"I understand Jenny, but what about the case?" Captain Bailey asked.

"The case is open and shut. I've given you everything you need to bury the Capelli's. You no longer need me on this case, and really, I don't feel like the whole trial thing. I'm ready to move on, so I'm handing you my verbal resignation. This is my last day here. I'm sorry Captain," Lucy said, turning her gaze to the floor.

"Jenny there's no need to feel sorry. If that's what you feel you need to do go ahead. You have my full support. It's a somber moment right now to see you want to go, but that's my own selfishness. I don't want to hold you back at fulfilling your obligations to yourself. I'm quite sure you thought this decision over thoroughly before you made it, and I know you're going to do just fine at whatever you decide to do, you're just that kind of person. I just want to let you know that you'll be missed dearly by all of us," Captain Bailey said, and before Lucy could turn to leave he said, "Thanks Jenny, for everything."

Lucy left her Captain's office, went to her desk, and packed her belongings. She fought back the tears of her departure with every piece she packed away in the boxes, but knew this was what she had to do in order to gain some type of social life, and find her own identity. Several of her co-workers stopped by her desk as she packed to wish her well, and offer their assistance in any way they could, but she kindly refused. The last thing she wanted or needed was a hand out, besides, with the money she had accumulated in her savings account she was more than well off. When she finished packing, she took one more long look at the people she called family, and the place she called home for the last eleven years, and picked up her boxes and left.

Lucy drove her Maxima through the city taking in the scene of Wilmington's small town for the last time. She was going home back to Oxen Hills, Maryland the place where she grew up. Riding down King St. she made a left onto 4th Street and headed to Pretty E, Dog, Hit Man, and Rasul's nightclub, "Ballers". She parked in front of the entrance, got out of her car, and slid her letter under the door that read good bye to a true friend and lover. What she didn't know was that in a year, she'd be the mother of a three-month-old inter-racial love child. Lucy got back in the car and drove to the I-95 ramp and headed south. She drove fast, but not necessarily speeding, as her emotions rose and an unending tear streaked eyeliner down her face.

She drove through the easy pass, placed her arm out the window and waved good-bye to another chapter in her book called life.

+   +   +   +

Frankie, Joey 'The Fox' Vito, Ricky, Nikki Stango, and a host of other made men and wise guys sat around the bar at "Lil' Italy's" Bar & Lounge, half drunk and going mad because the Yankee's were down 4 to 2 in the top of the eighth inning. Frankie drummed his fingers against the bar nervously as Derrick Jeter stepped up to bat then was interrupted by the bartender; a baby faced Italian man in his early twenties. "Hey Frankie, telephone," he yelled. He held the phone out and hunched his shoulders in an apologetic manner sorry to have interrupted the Boss, and said, "It's a Mister Dinarro. He says it's important." Frankie got up from his barstool grabbed the phone and stepped around the corner for some privacy. With his free hand he covered his ear and spoke into the phone. "Hello. Dinarro?"

"Yeah, hey Boss, good news! That young kid, Hakeeme Stewart, I finally have a location on him."

The call couldn't have come at a better time if it was planned. Frankie had been uptight and pressuring Dinarro for two weeks for the information on Hit Man and it finally came. Dinarro told Frankie that Hit Man was in Harrisburg, PA on 2615 Hemming Way Rd., in a rural area of the city. There was no security there with him, the house was a one level duplex on a road with only seven other homes, and it would be easy to take care of business, and go unnoticed. Frankie, sighed with relief, thanked Dinarro and hung up the phone. Frankie knew he'd have to move fast and have Hit Man whacked immediately, because it would be any day now before the Feds came knocking. Without Hit Man's testimony, he wouldn't spend a day in jail, and with him dead, they probably wouldn't even arrest him. A loud cheer erupted from around the corner and Frankie shot around it to look. "What happened?" he asked.

"Jason Giambi just smashed a two run homer!" Joey "The Fox'" answered.

"Yeah, took Randy Johnson deep center!" Nikki added.

"How many outs?" Frankie asked.

"None!" Joey replied.

"Good. Real good," Frankie said, deciding to wait until the game was over to tell the clean-up crew, Ricky and Nikki, about their new job.

+   +   +   +

Rasul, Pretty E, and Dog sat around the living room at Hit Man's house with Tameeka, Tammy, and Kim trying to keep Trina calm. She had been hysterical from the moment Hit Man got shot, but not being able to see him or talk to him had her going in circles. Trina was a pretty girl, if you liked big women, but that opinion was arguable, because in just three days she had totally let herself go. Her hair was matted down to one side of her head and the bags under her eyes were terrible, not to mention the house. The house was filthy, dishes were everywhere from where the kids left them, and clothes were all over the place. Rasul took one look at Trina and knew she hadn't been sleep since she heard Hit Man had been shot. Tammy and Kim, off instinct, just started cleaning up the house because filth wasn't one of their closest friends, Tameeka's either. In fact, it was her idea to start picking up first, but they made her sit down because her belly had her wobbling all over the place.

"Trina girl. You need to get it together, this ain't even you! Everything is going to be fine, ain't that what that cop said?" Tameeka asked.

"He said they got him put up somewhere, but he didn't say where. He just said that he's fine and not to worry," Trina answered, and started crying again.

Rasul looked to Dog on that remark, who was already looking at him and shook his head. They knew where Hit Man was at, not the exact location, but they knew he was in a Federal Witness Protection Program, and Trina's remark just verified it. Pretty E sat on the loveseat by himself feeling like shit. He couldn't stop blaming himself for Hit Man getting shot, but him turning Police witness was unthinkable. He couldn't understand it, none of them could, and just like always they were all thinking the same thing. "How? Why? and what's going to happen to them?"

203

+   +   +   +

Hit Man slammed the phone down on the receiver and threw the whole thing across the room, smashing it against the wall. For
two whole weeks, every hour on the hour, he tried to call Trina or Rasul, but the Feds blocked all outgoing calls to Delaware, except for their officers. Hunched over in his walker, he walked to the front door and hobbled out on the porch. "If only I had a ride up outta this muthafuckas!" he said to himself, staring at a tractor out on the farm of his next-door neighbors. "I can't believe those muthafucka's got me way out on some damn farm!" he said, getting angrier the more he talked. He wished like hell he could start all over, take it all back, never step foot into that apartment that night, but he couldn't. The damage was done and there was no turning back now. He plucked a Newport from his pack and pulled on the brown tip hard, filling his lungs with smoke before blowing it out of his nose. Instead of calming his nerves, it felt like a ton of bricks came crashing down on him. He was a snitch, the Police, a cop ass nigga and he knew it, and however, he didn't have to be. For the next half hour he looked out over the pasture and pondered over his next move, until the sun started to set and the mosquitoes came out. Flicking the butt of his fourth cigarette out into the front lawn, he turned and struggled back into the house. He grabbed his Sprite from off the coffee table and flopped down on the same Lazy Boy he'd been sitting in for the last two weeks, and said, "I ain't going out like no sucker!" as he flipped through the channels of the T.V.

Chapter Fifteen

Ricky's small stubby hands wrapped in black leather gloves with the knuckles cut out gripped the steering wheel of the Lincoln Town Car as it cruised at a steady 68 mph on cruise control. Frank Sinatra's classic: "New York State of Mind" played softly through the speakers, as they floated up the Interstate North to Harrisburg, P.A. Ricky Stango sung along with Frank Sinatra, while his brother Nikki nodded out to the soft music as they made the trip. Their job was ordered and like so many others, they were going to fill it. Hakeeme Stewart was the mark that had to be whacked, the one Nikki referred to as a "Lil' Punk" from the day they met at "Us Guys," so it was going to be fun for him.

"Hey Nikki!" Ricky said, waking his brother from a nod. "I just love ol'blue eyes. His music just makes my dick hard to kill a freakin' rat!"

"My dick is always hard to kill a freakin' rat!" Nikki said, and they shared a laugh.

"I knew from the first time we met those freakin' Miolies that they were going to be a problem," Ricky said.

"I kind of like that Dog guy though. He's my kind of freakin' guy. Doesn't say too much, but you know he's there. Reminds me of myself," Nikki said, "But that Hit Man guy! I wanted to kill his ass the day we met him over at Lenny's."

"Looks like you got your wish."

"Fuckin Ay I did. Im'ma slice dat piece of shit rat's throat while he squeals like a little bitch," Nikki said, motioning his finger from right to left across his huge neck.

From the moment they received the order from Frankie, they were ready. This was their job they were killers from the heart. It was the main reason Frankie kept them in the position they were in, because they wouldn't hesitate to kill any member in the family if need be. Ricky and Nikki Stango were emotionlessly cold as a December morning, savoring love for only one other person in this world, Frankie. They had no wives, no children, and no family here in the states since their parents died; they only had each other. Ricky and Nikki kept to themselves, they were loners, quiet, and secretive, and

that kept the Capelli's Family members on edge, something
Frankie enjoyed. He enjoyed the fear they gave off, the fear of the
unknown, just being able to not figure someone out kept you leery,
and the "Stango" brothers were the poster boys of fear. Frankie
met Ricky and Nikki back in the old neighborhood the day they
moved to the United States from Italy. They were just kids then,
but when they reached middle school they lost both their parents in
a car accident. With no family here in the States, they moved in
with their best friend, Frankie, and they were forever grateful. To
show their gratitude to Frankie, they made a bond with him that
would last forever. One day while out playing in the rain, the three

of them raced Popsicle sticks down the gutters on the street,
laughing and talking about their futures. Ricky came across a
broken coke bottle and stopped.

"Hey y'all! Let's be blood brothers!" he said.

"Blood brothers?" Nikki asked, "We are blood brothers!"

"But Frankie's not," Ricky replied.

"I know I'm not, and there's no way it can happen. We
don't have the same mom and dad," Frankie said.

"We do now," Ricky replied.

"But y'all were adopted by my mom and dad."

"But we can still be blood brothers."

"How?"

"Like this," Ricky said, and sliced the palm of his hand.
"Here do it," he said, passing the piece of glass to Frankie. After
all three of them slit their palms they shook hands passing one
another's blood through each other's wounds.

"See? Now we're blood brothers!" and it was the best day
of their lives.

Ricky remembered that day like it was yesterday. He
looked to his brother and asked," Hey Nikki, do you remember that
shit we did as kids, that made us blood brothers with Frankie?"

"Yeah, I remember that shit….I still got the damn scar on
my hand," he said smiling at the good memory.

"Yeah, those were the good ol' days," Ricky said,
continuing driving up the Interstate. It took nearly three hours of
driving before

they finally saw a sign that read: "Harrisburg, Three miles." Nikki grabbed the map from the glove compartment and used its light to search out the directions to the house. When they circled the same 7-Eleven, Roto Rooters, and Telephone Company for the fifth time, Ricky became frustrated and pulled into the gas station for directions.

2615 Hemming Way Rd. a small one-story house that sat alone was more than fifty yards away from a neighbor on either side. Ricky turned the lights out and crept up on the lawn, only feet away from the porch and parked. Easing out of the car, Ricky and Nikki barely made a sound as they stepped up on the porch. Nikki was strapped with a buck knife in his pocket and a fishing line was wrapped around his gloves to strangle Hit Man. He graced the porch first. Ricky, strapped with a 38 Cal. revolver in his hand and a door jimmy in the other, stepped along side his brother and wedged the jimmy in the door crack.

"Wait a minute Ricky try this," he whispered, handing him a credit card. "We don't want to chance making a whole lot of noise." Ricky grabbed the card and instead of the jimmy he used it. He shook it gently against the lock and the door came right open. They stepped in…

+   +   +   +

Besides the sound of tractor-trailers flying up and down the Interstate, everything else was virtually quiet. The only sounds that Hit Man heard were the house settling in and a few crickets perched in the seams of the porch echoing mating calls to each other. The quiet noises that the house gave off gave Hit Man too much time to do exactly what he tried so desperately not to do; think. He sat in the Lazy Boy trying to make sense of the whole nutshell he was in, but nothing he could conceive justified him turning state's witness.

"Man, fuck dat! I ain't doin' no life bid for nobody! Then again, Rasul and them better be glad I'm doin' dis shit for them too! Shit if it wasn't for me turning states on Frankie and his Capelli Family we'd all be going to jail!" he said loudly, letting his voice carry throughout the house hoping that hearing the words instead of thinking them would make him feel better. Unfortunately, that wasn't the case because the truth fell upon his

shoulders like weights. The reality was that the 'Feds' didn't have anything on Rasul, Dog, or
Pretty E not to mention Frankie and he would have been safe too, had he kept his mouth shut instead of folding, but he did. The only thing they had was his blood at the scene, but he was shot too, so any good lawyer in his defense could have pleaded that he was a victim too. The more he thought about what he cold have done the more he could only blame himself. It was him who gave up the tapes to save his own ass and the guilt was beginning to crumble his mental. "Man, I'd rather be dead!" was the next thought to cross his mind as he rose from the Lazy Boy for the first time in hours.

Hit Man stumbled down the hallway into the bathroom and stood before the sink starring into the mirror. In just two weeks time he aged substantially and loss nearly thirty pounds from being shot. The deep bags that formed under his eyes gave him the look of a person mentally ill or one on the verge of becoming mentally ill. His hairline had receded an inch and there was something deep down inside him that needed to come out. He screamed, but that wasn't it, and the suicidal thoughts only grew stronger. "Damn!" he cried, pounding his fists down on the basin in disgust as he stared deep into the eyes of the man in the mirror. He leaned forward almost face to face in the mirror and just watched his breath steam up the glass. The Hit Man everyone knew had left the body of the man in the mirror only hours ago, after being forced out by insanity. He laughed uncontrollable at himself in the mirror and continued laughing when he stepped away. He turned the water on in the tub and undressed dropping his clothes in the middle of the floor. His thoughts were no longer rational, the laughs became more sinister, and wanting to be dead was the only thing that computed logics in his head.

Hit Man looked behind the mirror on the wall into the medicine cabinet and grabbed a box of BIC straight razors before sitting down in the hot water. He turned the spigot down and let the water continue to trickle down into the half filled tub as he laid back and rested his neck on the back of the tub. Closing his eyes, he listened to the water and let his mind take him on a journey to a far away place. Here he was stress free, guilt free, and all his regrets were gone. Only the sun shone in this place and the birds' chirped songs of love, while a steam of water trickled from some rocks into the clear blue river below. This place was paradise. Hit Man plucked a razor from the box with his eyes still shut as his other hand searched his neck for his jugular vein. He took a deep breath and in one swift motion paradise was real.

+ + + +

Ricky lead the way with his 38 revolver clutched tightly in his hand as they crept into the house and headed towards the sound of the running water. "What da fuck?" Ricky whispered to Nikki as he looked down and noticed the whole house flooded.

"I don't know?" Nikki replied, hunching his shoulders as they continued down the hallway.

Something just wasn't right about the whole thing, but they had to find out because the mark had to be whacked.

Hakeeme Stewart was the difference between their freedom and a life of confinement and no way were they going to jail. When they reached the bathroom door, they saw a steady flow of water coming from beneath the door. Ricky turned the knob and saw what was the most unexpected thing they'd ever come across. Hakeeme Stewart was literally floating on top of the water in the bathtub with one arm sprawled out and the other one at his side with nearly half his neck sliced through. Ricky turned to Nikki and said, "The firkin' Malian beat us to the punch," and smiled at his brother. Nikki reached in his pocket and pulled out his cell phone and called Frankie.

"Hey Boss, everything's taken care of. The fuckin' rat offed himself! You should fuckin' see this piece of shit rat! I ought' a put a slug in his ass for times sake!" he said.

"Nah, y'all get on back down here. I'll see you's when you's get here."

"O.K. Boss, see ya soon," Nikki said, then continued, "Come on Ricky let's get da fuck outta here!"

+ + + +

Chapter Sixteen

Congo's Funeral Home on the corner of 24th and Market St. was the location of Hit Man's going home services. The parking lot was filled with cars nearly stacked on top of one another, as was the streets on both sides for nearly two blocks in every direction. The only space left was directly in front of the parlor reserved for the family Limo's. People came in flocks to get their last glimpse of Hit Man and to verify his death, because him dying was just too hard to believe. There were just too many rumors floating around and even though they seen it in the newspaper they still couldn't believe it. Some said the mob killed him because he owed them half a million, others said the police killed him because he didn't want to testify against the mob, and the most unbelievable one was that he committed suicide. Whatever the cause, they knew he was gone for sure when they entered the funeral home and saw him in the casket.

The first of the family limo's pulled up in front of the funeral home and Trina, Ms. Veronica, and all four of Hit Man's sisters along with the kids got out and headed up the steps into the parlor. Rasul, Dog, and Pretty E accompanied by their women Tameeka, Kim, and Tammy pulled up in the other family car. They stepped out of the limo draped in all black Armani suits and Gator boots and their women complimented them to a tee as they stood at their sides diced out in all black Prada dresses and wide brimmed hats. Rasul, Dog, and Pretty E couldn't believe they were standing in front of a funeral home about to say goodbye to their brother and best friend. It seemed like yesterday when they were stealing candy out of the corner store and selling it in school to the suburban white kids for a profit, now one of them was dead. As they walked up the steps to the funeral home, they all took deep breaths and their hearts pounded the instant they heard the organs playing. Death was a part of life that no one wanted to encounter or accept, but it was a grim reality that everyone had to accept. They just wished that Hit Man didn't have to face it so early.

Inside the funeral home the custom made fourteen-carat gold-plated casket shined under the lights at the front of the parlor.

People stood in a line that stretched from inside the home to two blocks down the street, waiting patiently to pass the casket for one last look at Hit Man. Hit Man dressed in Burberry from head to toe looked peaceful and at ease, as if a burden had been lifted from his shoulders. Rasul, Dog, Pretty E and their women raised a brow and nodded their heads to people they knew as they were led to their seats at the front of the funeral home.

Once they were seated and all the mourners got a chance to view the body, the casket was closed, and the organs thundered back to life. The heavy bass tone to the hymn "Precious Lord" sent chills up the spines of the people in attendance, and the words sung by Ms. Congo from the funeral home choked out over the crowd
of mourners. It was filled with so many young lives she felt the urge boil up inside her to save their lives and spread the word of God. She touched base on everything from current events, to issues that meant absolutely nothing to the world, but everything she preached meant something to the soul.

"And yes he was a strong man, Ha! But when we living the devils life, we are all weak. Amen! That's why we need to accept Christ Jesus as our Lord and Savior! See it hurts an old lady like me, Ha! To see such a young man like Hakeeme, Ha! Called to go home so early, but this is a wake up call to all of y'all young folks out there, Ha! To get it together! Cause ain't no reason in the world it should be so many of y'all young folks up in here mourning. Y'all should be moving up the ladder in some careers, not filling up the re-habs and jail cells, not to mention the ground! See but it's the devils work! He don't care, Ha! He wants y'all out there selling drugs, killing one another, smoking all kinds of mess and puttin' dat junk up y'all's noses. That's his number one tool today, Ha! Drugs and alcohol, Ha! That's what keeps your minds cloudy and off of God, Ha! Got an ol'lady like me scared to go to the market. It's a shame, Ha! Cause I know y'all wasn't raised like dat! Whass' goin' on?! Somebody talk to me, ha!" She shouted through the claps and "aw'ight nows!" given by the mourners.

Every word she spoke cut right to the very core of Rasul's essence. He twitched in his seat and his conscience had him

believing the whole sermon was for him. With her shouting and
him staring at the casket that held his boy lying lifeless, he vowed
that now was the
time to get out of the game. As soon as Rev. Hackett finished the
service, the funeral director opened the casket for a final viewing
of the body and "Lea-Lea," the youngest of Hit Man's sisters sung
Yolanda Adams "Open My Heart." The way she sung the song
you would have swore an angel was amongst them as tears stained
everyone's faces.

Rasul walked up to the casket and gently in almost a
whisper asked him; "Is there a heaven for nigga's like us? Cause
cousin this sure feels like hell! But don't worry about nuffin'
cause I got Big Trina and the kids aw'ight?" he said, and swore he
seen Hit Man crack a smile. "I'm'ma miss you cousin," he
finished, and stepped away before the tears fell. Dog and Pretty E
said basically the same things, but more on the lines of "It's on!"
than anything else. The moment Trina walked up on the casket
and saw Hit Man lying there for the second time today she just
couldn't hold back the tears any longer. She looked at Hit Man
and screamed at the top of her lungs. "Oh my God! Why? Why?
Why God did you have to take my husband like that?" She yelled,
and collapsed over the casket nearly tipping it over.

"Mommy! Mommy!" Lil' Hakeeme yelled, "You scaring
me!," he said, and began to cry. He saw his daddy lying in that
casket too, but was too young to really understand that he would
never see his daddy again once that casket closed for the last time.
He was only crying now because his mom was.

"Come on now girl, you told me you was going to keep
yourself together," Ms. Veronica, Hit Man's mother said to Trina
who was kicking and screaming hysterically in the middle of the
isle. "Why Mom Ronnie, why?" Trina sobbed in the arms of Ms.
Veronica." Why did he take my husband like that?"

"Baby who knows? All we can do is except the Lords
work and know that he is the best of planners and the knower of all
things. I mean, I'm hurt too baby, he was my son my only son, but
I gotta stay strong for them lil' ones, " Ms. Veronica said, into
Trina's ear as

she rocked her back and forth in her arms sitting in the middle of the isle." "Now come on baby, let's get it together for them lil' ones."

"O.K.," Trina said, and nodded as she sniffled and tried to pull herself together under the eyes of all the mourners. It sure was good to have Ms. Veronica back and clean off drugs for the first time Trina thought, gaining her strength from her as she got up."

"O.K. Mom Ronnie, I'm alright," she said, as she stood on wobbly legs. When she turned to face the casket again everything she worked on so hard to do went right out the window and she crumpled back down to the ground. Rasul jumped up from his seat and ran over to Trina's side trying to pick her up as she lay limp in the isle. "Yo Dog, come on man. Help me get her up outta here," he said and they lifted her from the floor.

"Charmaine come get these babies." Ms. Veronica said to her eldest child then broke down herself unable to hold her tears any longer. She felt a pain and hurt that she didn't know existed as the years of guilt, shame, prostitution, and addiction fell upon her. "If only I would have been there for him," she thought, "I'd still have my baby today."

+   +   +   +

Det. Cohen sat parked in an unmarked car with tinted windows across the street from the funeral home. He watched with enjoyment as Rasul, Dog, and Pretty E led the pallbearers from the funeral home distraught. The looks on their faces were the same one's he had over two years ago, when his partner was shot dead. As he watched the mourners pile out of the funeral home he was glad that the "Feds" had dropped all charges against the Capelli family because now he could bust them all together. He knew that even if he did bust the Capelli's along with Rasul, Dog, and Pretty E the Feds would probably take over, but that didn't matter. The relief and satisfaction he was going to get from bringing down his partners killers would be far more rewarding than any recognition he could ever receive for the bust. Just seeing Rasul, Dog, and Pretty E go down forever was enough for him.

After the last car rolled out of the parking lot and the others cleared the street around the funeral home, Det. Cohen pulled off.

He had no idea where he was going or what he would do next because his
mind was too preoccupied with Rasul, Dog, and Pretty E, but he drove anyway. When he realized he was approaching the Maryland State Line his stomach reminded him that he hadn't ate all day long, as he smelled the aroma in the air from the McDonald's up ahead. He pulled into the drive-thru and said, "Yeah—I'll have a number three."

+   +   +   +

Rasul and Tameeka's house was where the mourners went after the funeral to wind down, relax, and celebrate the life of Hit Man over dinner. His death was a wake up call to each and everyone who knew him personally, just like the Reverend said. It made them all value and appreciate the things they didn't. Yes, Hit Man was gone, but his memories kept him well and very much alive in their hearts especially when they looked at Lil' Hakeeme.

"Yo! Don't dat lil' nigga look just like his pop?" Dog asked.

"Damn right! Dat's dat nigga's twin right there!" Rasul said then began to reminisce. "Yo! Remember that time we had them ex-lax gums?"

"Which time?" Pretty E and Dog asked in unison.

"The time we told Hit Man them shits was Chiclets gum and dat nigga shitted on himself!" Rasul said, bursting out laughing.

"Oh shit! Yeah! I remember dat shit! Dat nigga was ready to fight!" Pretty E said.

"Wasn't he? We probably would have had to pull his ass up off of you nigga!" Rasul said, still laughing at the memory.

"That's fucked up y'all! Why y'all do that to my baby? I should fuck one of y'all up for him." Trina said, and popped Dog in the back of the neck before laughing herself.

"Well since we all out here reminiscing about shit," Ms. Veronica said, "Did y'all used to steal my weed and my roaches off my shoe box top? And don't lie."

"Sometimes, but Charmaine and Lea-Lea turned us on to that, they stayed stealing your weed," Rasul said.

"Ooooo girl! You hear dat? Carmella yelled to her oldest sister Charmaine who was out in the kitchen." Rasul out here giving up the tapes to Mommy about how you and Lea-Lea used to steal her weed!"

"So what!? I ain't thinking about Rasul, I'm a grown ass woman!" she laughed from the kitchen.

"You ain't that damn grown!" Ms. Veronica said sharply.

"Yo, remember that night we got jammed up Chester with that stolen car and they took us to juvenile for the weekend?" Dog asked.

"Yeah I remember dat shit. But what about the time when we were walking home from the swimming pool and Tasha and them chased us, but caught Dog and Hit Man?" Pretty E asked Rasul.

"Yeah, when they pulled off their trunks?" Rasul asked.

"Yeah, that's the time! Them nigga's tried to blame it on the water!" Pretty E said holding up his pinky, and everyone bagged up laughing.

"Man fuck you two nigga's!" Dog said mad cause the joke was on him.

"Baby, forget them don't get mad! It's just right to me!" Kim said chuckling, adding insult to injury.

"Oh? It's like dat?"

"No baby, I'm just playing."

They continued on like that for several hours, each telling their own accounts of the times they had with Hit Man while chowing down on their food. The more they stuffed their stomachs with beef ribs, macaroni and cheese, potato salad, and greens while laughing, the better they began to feel. They knew they'd grieve some more later on, but the way they felt right now was an indicator that everything was going to be alright. After everyone finished eating, Tameeka and the rest of the women began cleaning up after the kids and their men, trying to bring the somber day to an end. Tameeka looked across the living room and stared at Trina who was cleaning extra hard and knew from experience that she was trying to relieve stress. She walked over to Trina and took the rag from her hand and pulled her to the side.

"Girl are you alright?" she asked.

215

"I'm fine," Trina replied.

"Are you sure? Matter of fact, why don't you and the kids stay here with me for a while. At least until you feel a little better," Tameeka asked, trying to support her friend.

Trina listened to Tameeka's invitation and entertained the idea for a moment before making her decision. She knew it would be a while before she'd be able to stay in her house because the memories her and Hit Man shared were still fresh. But the more she pondered the more she realized how important it was to have a real friend.

"Girl I really appreciate this here? Because I think I'm going crazy sometimes," Trina began.

"Girl! It's nuffin."

"Seriously, sometimes I do think I'm crazy. I swear to God I hear his voice sometimes, plus his smell is still in the house. Girl, I miss him so much that sometimes I just sit in the floor and smell his dirty clothes and cry. Girl, that's why I think I'm going crazy."

"Girl you ain't crazy, you just miss Hakeeme that's all. I can't begin to imagine how you feel right now, but I'm'ma let you know I'm here for you in anyway you need me to be O.K.?"

"Thank you Tameeka. Thank you so much," Trina said and the two embraced.

+   +   +   +

Rasul gathered Dog and Pretty E up while the people were leaving his house and led them into the game room for some privacy. It had been a long and stressed filled week for all of them and their bodies and minds were drained. They sat down in the leather recliners around the screen sized T.V. and took a long awaited rest. The burial of their brother from another mother and best friend was just too much mentally for them to have any type energy left. What they saw today was the most unimaginable thing they could have ever thought of, but it had become their reality. And still, after seeing the casket dropped down into the ground they couldn't believe it. Unconsciously, as if reading each other's minds, they turned and looked at the empty recliner where Hit Man sat and his absence sunk in.

"Yo Dog," Rasul said. " What'chu thinking about?"

216

"Man I'm fucked up right now. I can't believe Hit Man is gone," Dog answered.

"Me either," Pretty E added.

"I feel dat. But, whass' up? Where do we go from here?"

"What'chu mean where do we go from here?" Dog and Pretty E asked in unison.

"I mean, what we goin' to do about the game?"

"Da game? Shit don't stop cousin. Just because Hit Man ain't here no more don't mean it ain't still money to be made," Pretty E said.

"I heard dat. Plus who's goin' to look out for Trina and the kids?" Dog asked, knowing they all would.

"She is nigga. Wha'chu forgot Hit Man was a millionaire too? She got everything that nigga had, so she going to be straight. She got the businesses, the house, and the cars, all that shit. I'm sayin' what we going to do?" Rasul said.

"What'chu mean nigga?" they asked again, still not catching on.

"I mean I'm done nigga. Dat's what I mean! I just did eight years in the joint! Eight muthafuckin' years! I made plans, had goals I wanted to reach and I reached them all, but the shit ain't fun any more. We just lost our best muthafuckin' friend! I don't know about y'all two niggas, but I'm done! Y'all can have this shit! Fuck Frankie! Fuck da game! Fuck all dis shit! I got a wife and a kid on the way. Do you think Im'ma let a couple dollars take that away? Hell no!" he snapped.

Dog and Pretty E didn't respond. They knew their boy was emotionally fucked up about Hit Man's death because he was the closest one to him. They all were tight, but Rasul was closer because he knew Hit Man the longest. Dog looked at Pretty E and talked through his eyes, giving him the look that said don't comment. Rasul was venting and they figured they'd let him continue until it passes over. What they didn't know was that it wasn't going to pass over. Rasul's mind was made up. He would never play da game again.

+   +   +   +

It had been four days since Hit Man's funeral and Frankie still hadn't heard from Rasul. He was beginning to worry that their last conversation together had severed a nearly unbreakable bond. He thought back on the phone conversation trying to see where he went wrong if he went wrong at all, but couldn't come up with anything.

The only thing he did was, tell the truth as he explained to Rasul that he didn't kill Hit Man. He did tell him that he had ordered the hit on Hit Man, but he was already dead when Ricky and Nikki arrived to do the job. He also told Rasul that regardless of how much he loved Hit Man, Hit Man had become a snitch. He was no longer the person he knew and loved.

"I would have had to kill him Rasul. That's the way it goes in this lifestyle and you know that. You can't afford to let one rat get away because it opens up room for more rats to move in. Do you understand that? Did you want to spend the rest of your life in the can?" Frankie asked.

"Listen man that was my best friend, my brother and you're telling me you was just going to kill him without even letting me talk to him. I mean you did know where he was at right?" Rasul asked.

"Yeah I knew but..." Frankie said.

"But what? I coulda got him to recant. That nigga wasn't no police, that's why he killed himself! He thought he was alone man. I coulda stopped him man. I coulda stopped him! That's fucked up Frankie! And to think you care about me like a son. You don't care about me! All you care about is us making that money for you. You never cared about me cause if you did you would a at least let me try to talk to him."

"I couldn't take that chance." Frankie said.

"Whatever man. I gotta go I'll call you later."

That was almost a week ago and even at the funeral when Frankie saw Rasul he didn't speak he only nodded. Frankie remembered the look that turned his heart to mush as he handed Trina and Ms. Veronica envelopes of cash. Rasul gave him a look of betrayal and it crushed him. He wondered if he'd ever get Rasul's trust back again.

"Come on boss get it together. Rasul will come around just give him some time," Joey, The Fox, said as they sat around the bar at "Lil' Italy's" Bar & Lounge.

"I don't know Joey, I really disappointed him. Maybe I should have done things differently." Frankie said.

"You did the right thing Boss. There wasn't no two ways about it. The risk was too great, he coulda cost us life in the can!"

"Yeah, maybe your right. I'll just let him get over it first. Right now he's emotional and feels I betrayed him, but he'll see what I did was the right thing to do," Frankie said, but his words didn't even sound convincing to him. He wanted to explain to Joey the relationship he had with Rasul, but he knew he'd never understand. Nobody in regular society would understand unless they'd been in jail before. See because once your taken off the streets and you have to live, eat, sleep, cry, and share your most inner-thoughts and feelings with your cellmate you grow a bond like no other. Your cellmate becomes your family, friend, brother or son during your stay away from society and it's a friendship and bond that lasts forever. As Frankie thought about Rasul he fought the urge to call, but the love he had for him was too strong. Rasul was really like a son to him and not hearing from him was too much. He got up and walked around the bar to grab the phone as soon as he touched it rung.

"Lil' Italy's," Frankie answered.

"Frankie?" Rasul asked.

"Yes speaking."

"We need to talk." Rasul said.

"At my house, tomorrow at six," Frankie smiled.

"I'll be there," Rasul said and they hung up.

     +   +   +   +

Rasul arrived at Frankie's house six o'clock on the dot ready to sit down and talk about the future. He didn't know what to expect from Frankie after he told him he was done with the game, but either way he was done. Whether he gets mad or not wasn't the issue. The issue was his life and what he was going to do with it, not what Frankie, Dog, or Pretty E thought he should do with it. As he walked up the pavement and stepped up onto the porch, his heart raced with uncertainty. Frankie was a very powerful man and once you get involved with someone like him it always ends in death. The Mafia leaves no trails, no ties unknotted, no one behind to point a finger, so Rasul was nervous

about the outcome. If he loves me like a son then he'll understand.
If not then fuck him, he can get it too!" he said to himself, then
rung the bell.

Mrs. Maraachi answered the door with a smile on her face
as always, then, said gingerly, "Hello Rasul. Frankie's been
expecting
you." She led him down the hallway towards the kitchen and
stopped at the doorway. Inside there Frankie was standing over the
stove dropping garlic into a pot of sauce he was preparing. He
looked over his shoulder and lit up with satisfaction when he saw
his adopted son standing in the doorway.

"Hey Rasul! Glad you could make it," Frankie said, then,
continued, "Are you hungry?"

"No I'm cool. I just need to talk to you that's all."

"Well let me excuse myself then. If you need me baby I'll
be in the living room watching television," Mrs. Maraachi said and
left.

"What is it? Is everything alright?" Frankie said.
"Yeah everything's cool. I'm just, well, Rasul hesitated. I'm
ready to leave this game alone. Losing my best friend was a wake
up call for me. I have a wife now, and kids. I can't be selfish
anymore, especially not to them because they need me. I don't
ever want them to have to feel the way I did when I lost Hit Man,"
he finished.

"Is that all?" Frankie asked.

"Yeah that's all. I just thought I needed to tell you face to
face instead of over the phone. I didn't want you to think that I
was avoiding you or anything. I think I kinda gave you that
impression the last time we talked and I never got a chance to
apologize to you. It's just that I was emotional and my anger had
me not thinking straight. I realized after I thought about it that you
did what you had to do. It was true, Hit Man had turned, and I
apologize at the way I acted."

"I understood. I knew you'd come around, but I was
worried about our bond. You should have been able to talk to me.
Never give your power away to anything. Always be in control of
you. As for this game, it is what it is, a game. No game will or
could ever come between a bond like ours. If you want out of the

game, get out of the game. Im'ma support you in anything you do. Hey, I love you Rasul and not hearing from you showed me just how much I love you. You really are the son I never had. And just because there's no more game doesn't mean don't stay in contact." Frankie said. "Oh, I know that," Rasul said surprised at how supportive Frankie was. Everything he thought would happen, Frankie did the exact opposite. There was no anger, no explaining, nothing, and that was totally unexpected.

"So how's Dog and Pretty E? Are they alright?" "They're cool. I think they'll be in touch with you though, because there's still more work at the warehouse and the house on Vanderver Ave. Once that's done I'll bring you by the money, and then I think y'all should talk because they want to continue. Me, I'm done. I need to get away for a minute, get my mind right. I think Im'ma take a vacation."

"Where to? Do you have any idea?"

"Maybe Florida. My wife wants to go to Disney World and Universal Studios."

"Oh, well that's great! I have a Beach House in Orlando, right on the ocean. It's only twenty minutes away from all of that. Y'all can stay there instead of paying an arm and a leg on hotels and accommodations and crap like dat."

"Are you sure?" "Yeah I'm sure. No one is there this time of year. My wife didn't rent it out this year because I think she wants to go there for a few weeks. I'm still debating myself, so sure it's all right. Let me go get the keys from her. Do you have any idea when you want to go?"

"Maybe in a week. I have to straighten a few things out first," Rasul said, and then added,

"You know what Frankie? You really are like a father to me," and hugged him. Frankie was at a loss for words as he held Rasul in his arms. This was the same wild young boy who stepped foot in his cell at McKean Federal Prison nearly seven years ago, now he was a man. Members in the "Capelli Family" often questioned their Boss's decision to associate the young black men with the business, but Frankie had a vision. Now the entire "Capelli Family" saw it as Rasul, Dog, Pretty E, and Hit Man took the business to heights unthought of with the drug game. Frankie backed away from Rasul, but hung onto him by the shoulders at arms length and gave him a once over. For the first time in his sixty something years, he felt like a proud father standing before the son he never had.

Chapter Seventeen

Rasul helped Dog and Pretty E load the last of the luggage into the back of Dog's Escalade, as they waited for Tameeka, Tammy, and Jaquaan to come out of the house. The plane was to depart the Philadelphia International Airport at 1:30 p.m. and it was almost noon already. Rasul paced anxiously around the truck glancing at his watch as he checked the luggage making sure he wasn't forgetting anything. He shook his head disgusted at Tameeka for not being ready to leave yet, knowing she wasn't doing nothing but running her mouth to Tammy. "Man blow the muthafuckin' horn!" he said, impatiently. Pretty E stuck his hand in the window and blew the horn repeatedly while they stood outside of the jeep.

"Damn! Why is you blowin' the horn like you crazy or some'em?" Tameeka snapped, standing in the doorway to the house.

"What da fuck is you doin'? Damn! You shoulda been ready to go!" Rasul said.

"Boy why is you in a rush? I got a damn watch on too and that damn plane ain't going nowhere until one thirty. It's only twelve o'clock, so pump your brakes!" she stated.

"Man just come the fuck on. Always running your damn mouth to Tammy! Both of y'all do that same shit!" Rasul asked.

"And do! So now what!?" she barked, then mumbled under her breath. "Let me shut up before I really end up cussing his ass out," and turned to walk back in the house.

Rasul reached in his pocket and plucked a Newport from his pack to ease his nerves. He couldn't wait to be on the plane some 30,000 feet in the air on his way to relax in sunny Florida. Just the feel of the warm breeze blowing in from off the coast and the smell of Palm trees would be enough to help him forget this whole month; a month that changed his life forever. He let out a long smoke filled sigh as he remembered the mistakes they made that costs them their best friend, and it only made the vacation more inviting.

"Man blow the horn again," he said, his impatience becoming anger.

"I told you nigga! I told you before you done it that Tameeka would be wearing the pants in a month, I was wrong! She put them on that same day!" Dog said, sharing a laugh and a high five with Pretty E.

"Man fuck y'all!" he said and couldn't do nothing but laugh himself.

+   +   +   +

Det. Cohen had been following Dog and Pretty E since mid-night last night. He wrote down everything they did and every place they stopped the entire night, and in just two hours time he began to notice a pattern had formed. He watched them stop at four different houses and leave with duffle bags, but only after they returned to a house on Vanderver Ave. in between stops. It didn't take the brightest person in the world to realize something was going on. They were making some type of transaction and the house on Vanderver Ave. was the stash spot. He couldn't believe how boldly they went about their business and questioned himself on why they had been getting away with it this long.

Around nine o'clock that morning after Dog and Pretty E ate breakfast at the Post House their route changed. He realized then that they weren't going to settle in one spot so he continued to follow them. He stayed at least three cars behind them as they drove the Escalade out to Pennsylvania Ave. towards the upscale section of the city and wondered where they were going. "Maybe to Frankie's house, the MOB Boss," he thought. When they turned into Greenville, Delaware's richest neighborhood, where the most prominent people in the state settled down to raise families and retire he backed off. He parked a few houses away not to draw any attention to himself, and stared in awe at the immaculate homes surrounding him.

The Escalade pulled into the driveway of a mini-mansion that looked like it belonged in Beverly Hills, CA, as it stood proudly behind an iron gate. Det. Cohen knew this was the Mob Bosses house because there was no way any of the four "Young Punks" as he called them could afford a place like this. He looked through his binoculars
at Dog and Pretty E standing at the door to the house and couldn't believe his eyes. His chin literally dropped in his lap when he saw

Rasul answer the door in his robe. "Mother Fucker!" he said to himself; "This is Rasul's house!" The feeling Det. Cohen got after coming to realize he lived in a regular middle class two-story row home, and these four young punks were living like kings, was gut wrenching. Nothing he could think of added up to him. Maybe this was why his partner turned crooked after years and years of normal living. "Hell, I risk my life everyday and can't even afford a decent automobile." Det. Cohen thought. He entertained the thought of being crooked and even felt the benefits of it in his mind, but knew it was wrong. Nothing you do against the right things to do lasts forever and he knew that. There was no way in the world he was going to risk losing his newly wed wife or career job for instant gratification. He put the binoculars down on the passenger side seat and waited on their next move.

+   +   +   +

Dog and Pretty E dropped Tammy off at her Grandmother's home on Norris St. in North Philly, before heading back to Delaware. They were finally going to be able to relax in about another hour because everything was nearly done. Rasul, Tameeka, and Jaquaan had caught their 1:30 p.m., flight on time and would be landing in Florida within the next few hours, and all the work at the house on Vanderver Ave. was passed out except for two kilo's. That was the last thing on the agenda for the day and they were ready to get it done. Dog double parked the truck and cut on his hazard lights as Pretty E ran in the Vanderver Avenue house to grab the kilos. He laid his seat back and rubbed his eyes as he thought about what he needed to do before he went in the house for the day. He remembered her telling him earlier to stop and grab her some pads, so some Pussy was out. So he decided to make it a Blockbuster night. "Yeah that's what Im'ma do. Im'ma watch some movies. Lay the comforter out in the middle of the floor and eat some goodies," he said to himself with a smile, and then the passenger side door flew open.

"You ready Cousin? Let's go drop this shit off down Riverside and call it a day," Pretty E said.

"I heard dat!" Dog said.

+   +   +   +

Det. Cohen was on the C-B the moment he saw the
Escalade double park in front of the house on Vanderver Ave. He
called on every unit in the vicinity to post themselves eastbound
along Vanderver Ave. and wait for directions. "If they come out of
this house carrying anything, Im'ma swarm them," he said to
himself as his heart raced. He watched Pretty E jump from the
truck and run up the concrete steps onto the porch. "Please Mother
fucker! Please come out of there with something," he talked to
himself anticipating the bust. In an instant, all of his wishes came
true, as Pretty E looked up and down Vanderver Avenue in both
directions before running down the steps with a bag on his
shoulder. "Bingo!" he said and called the units back.

"10-6, 10-6. This is Det. Cohen calling all units advised to
stand by on Vanderver Ave. I'm in pursuit of two black males in a
black Cadillac Escalade suspected to be transporting a large
quantity of drugs into Riverside. I need some available units to set
up a checkpoint at the intersection of South Claymont St. and
Vanderver Ave. I want you to stop them before they enter the
Projects," he said, and moved out in pursuit of the Escalade. The
bust he realized probably wasn't the mother load, but judging by
the size of the duffle bag, it was enough to sit them down for ten to
twenty years. That was satisfying enough to Det. Cohen because
that would clear the way to Rasul, the one he really wanted.

+   +   +   +

Dog drove down Vanderver Ave. as normal as he always
did. He didn't do anything wrong at all, that's why it was puzzling
to him that a D.T. car was trailing him. He looked through the rear-
view mirror and smiled the minute he recognized who it was.

"Yo Pretty E. This nigga just don't stop do he?" Dog said,
referring to Det. Cohen.

Pretty E turned around in his seat and smiled too the minute
he saw Det. Cohen.

"If this muthafucka pulls us over and we still got all this
shit on us, Im'ma kill his punk ass!" Pretty E said, pulling his 40
Cal. from his waistline.

"Yeah cause I ain't going to jail for this coke!" Dog said.

Dog drove the Escalade through the intersection at
Governor Printz Blvd. and stayed eastbound on Vanderver Ave. a

block away from South Claymont St. He took his eyes off the road and glanced in
the mirror to check on Det. Cohen. When he looked back ahead of him it was too late to react. Blue and white patrol cars and unmarked ones came from everywhere blocking the street off. He slammed on brakes and threw the truck in reverse but to no avail because Det. Cohen and a stew of other patrol cars had boxed them in. They were trapped in the middle of a drug raid and there was nothing they could do about it, as they stared down the barrels of drawn guns. Nearly fifty officers in uniform and plain clothes surrounded them and moved in.

"GET OUT OF THE CAR! GET OUT!" one officer shouted.

"GET YOUR GOD DAMN HANDS UP NOOOWWW!" another one yelled.

Det. Cohen charged the truck like a wild man bo-guarding his way through the officers already at the truck. He reached through the window and snatched open the door, then dragged Dog out of the driver seat.

"I got your Punk Ass now don't I?" Det. Cohen said, and jumped on Dog's back.

"You ain't got shit Pussy!" Dog replied, then, felt the splitting headache instantly after Cohen slammed his face in the ground.

"We got it Detective, we got it!" one of the officers said from inside the truck holding the duffle bag.

"What is it?" Cohen asked.

"About two kilos!" the officer answered.

"Good! Hey Dog? You know your done right?" he teased.

"Like I said you ain't got shit pussy! I'll be on bail in minutes and gone by tomorrow, so fuck you!" he said looking over his shoulder at the Detective on his back.

"You alright over there Cousin?" Pretty E yelled from the other side of the truck.

"Yeah I'm straight, are you?" Dog yelled back.

"Yeah I'm cool. I'm just ready to fuck this pussy up on my back," Pretty E remarked.

"Me too," he said, and they were cuffed and thrown in the backseat of a patrol car.

+   +   +   +

They looked at each other and shook their heads in disgust, as they were driven to the police station on 4th and Walnut Street. They knew they made a major mistake the minute they saw the Detective behind them and wondered now if they'd ever see the streets again. Delaware did not play fair when it came to drugs but the money was so plentiful it was a risk that felt worth taking. Now, as they sat in the patrol car facing 20 to life for the drugs and weapons they found in the truck, the question again was was it worth it?? Everything they had worked so hard to get, all the money they had saved and everything that came with the game was taken away in minutes. The answer was simple, "Hell no!" it wasn't worth it.

+   +   +   +

Chapter Eighteen

The plane didn't take off down the runway until two o'clock, a whole half hour later than its scheduled time. Rasul was pleased when it finally did because Tameeka wouldn't stop. She complained from the moment she stepped on the plane till the moment they reached the sky. She just wouldn't let him live down the fact that he cussed her out and rushed her for nothing. He called the flight attendant as she strolled the isle and ordered two drinks.

"Can I get two shots of Jack Daniels," he said, hoping they would calm his nerves, as he fidgeted with the headset trying to tune in the television.

This vacation was the first of the many vacations he imagined taking while he lay awake at nights in his cell. The 6 by 9 cell was enough to rip the sanity from your mind after a period of time, not to mention the inch thick mattress you had to sleep on. Your imagination was one of the only things you were allowed to keep during your stay in jail whether it was as one day or ten years. It was all up to you and your mental strength whether you kept it or not. Rasul leaned back in his seat and tried to get comfortable as he stared out the window at the clouds. "This must be heaven," he thought, and then remembered all the brothers he met in jail that would never see the streets again. Imagination would be the only way they'd ever see a sight like this, and that's only if that 6 by 9 doesn't tear away their sanity by the time their released. With that thought fresh on his mind and the memories of keys jiggling, grown men crying, and walking the yard with murders, rapist, drug kingpins, and child molesters, Rasul turned and looked at his wife. He then looked across the isle at his stepson, then to Tameeka's stomach and really understood why he was done with the game. Nothing the game had to offer could make him feel the he felt right now, as he rubbed her belly.

"Baby whass wrong?" Tameeka asked, seeing the distant look in his eyes.

"Nuffin', I was just thinking about some shit, dat's all. I'm just glad I'm here and still living, you know? I got you, Jaquaan, and my baby on the way."

"You mean our baby," she cut in.

"Yeah, our baby and Baby I couldn't be happier," he said, and kissed her lips softly before saying, "Girl, I love you to death!"

"I love you too," she said, and meant it from the bottom of her heart.

The airplane's wheels screeched to a stop on the runway in Orlando at 4:30 p.m., bringing the almost three-hour flight to an end. The passengers exited the plane quickly, but fashionably, all in a hurry to beat the line at luggage claim. The instant Rasul stepped off the plane the Florida heat greeted him full fledged. The thermostat read 88 degrees, but it was a different 88 than he was used to in Delaware. The humidity was ridiculous and made it feel like he was stepping into an oven other than some 88-degree weather.

Damn it's hot out here! I need me a straw hat or some'em, plus these shoes I mean, these damn tennis shoes are hurtin' my feet! Baby I need some flip-flops," Tameeka complained already.

"Damn Baby, can't you stop bitchin' for one minute? I'll be so glad when you have dat baby, cause every since you got pregnant you been buggin'!" Rasul said, opening up a can of worms.

"What da fuck you mean bitchin! You walk around all day with a human being in your damn stomach and see how much you be bitchin'! You fuck me up wit dat shit!" Tameeka snapped, then under her breath said, "Done fucked my damn trip up already!"

"What'chu say?" Rasul asked.

"You heard me!" she replied, as she wobbled into the airport.

Inside the airport the hustle and bustle of passengers trying to catch flights, return from flights, and claim luggage was too chaotic. So to avoid the madness and keep from becoming more frustrated Tameeka went to sit down. "And hurry up and get the luggage, cause I'm ready to go!" she demanded before storming off. "Damn, Dog wasn't lying when he said she wore the pants," Rasul thought, as him and Jaquaan went to luggage claim and pick-up. Within minutes they were back and standing in front of Tameeka with the luggage on a handcart.

"Baby why don't you pull this luggage outside while me and Jaquaan go get the rental car," Rasul asked Tameeka.

"Why I can't go wit'chu to get the rental car?"

"Didn't you just say not too long ago that your feet hurt?"

"Just forget it! Cause see, all you want to do is argue," Tameeka said.

Rasul and Jaquaan grabbed the keys to the rental car from the rental office and drove around front. Traffic jammed the lanes and people were all over the sidewalk, but Rasul spotted Tameeka instantly. "Look at her," he said to himself, as she stood on the curb with her hands on her hips, tapping her foot on the ground.

"I should ride right past her ass, huh?" Rasul asked Jaquaan.

"I don't care, but you know she goin' snap!" he replied.

"Shit, she already snappin'," he said and rode right past her.

Tameeka couldn't believe her eyes when Rasul rode right by her. "I know damn well that muthafucka seen me standing here!" she told herself. Rasul and Jaquaan laughed their asses off as Tameeka stood in the middle of the street waving her hands in the air. He drove maybe two or three cars in front of her before putting it in reverse and backing up to where she stood. They tried their best to keep straight faces, and hold their laughs when she snatched the door open.

"I know y'all seen me standing there!" she bitched.

"We ain't see you girl," Rasul said, and he and Jaquaan bust out laughing.

"Oh, it's funny? Y'all think it's funny?" Tameeka said and laughed herself, before popping him in the back of the neck.

"About time, Damn! Put a smile on your face," Rasul said.

"Fuck you," she smiled and sucked her teeth.

+   +   +   +

The city of Orlando, Florida home to Disney World and Universal Studios was one of the most visited tourist attractions in the world. Huge palm trees blew in the summer breeze, tall buildings tickled the belly of clouds, and the sunshine could brighten up even your worst day. To a person with sore eyes, Orlando was Visine. The grass looked greener, the sky seemed bluer, and life just seemed to be more promising here. Rasul drove the rental car down the Interstate slow enough to take in the sights, as he headed towards Frankie's beach house. Being from a small state like Delaware made everything seem more spacious than he was used to, but he liked it. Orlando was the ideal city for dreamers, people on the verge of giving up, because it was almost a real life fantasy. It made you re-energized about life; made you want to get up off of that piss pot and do something different with yourself. The city was full of magic and it had already cast a spell on Rasul.

Rasul got off of the Interstate on Pacific Avenue and drove away from the city. By the directions Frankie had given him, the ocean was only about twenty minutes away from the airport and a hop, skip, and jump away from the Amusement Parks. Rasul looked at his wife then to his stepson and was glad she suggested this vacation. It was just what he needed to get his mind off of the death of Hit Man, and put him back in touch with reality. The game had made him totally forget about everything that was important to him. In jail he would have given anything to do what he was doing now, now he just took it for granted. The simple things like eating what you wanted, going and coming as you pleased, and showering everyday was a luxury in prison, and so easily how he forgot. But, Orlando made him remember. The atmosphere put him back in touch with all of that, and the space made him feel free. He didn't feel like a big fish in a little pond anymore. He didn't stick out like a sore thumb. Everything and everyone in Orlando looked like money. His Benz was normal here, his home was just average here, and he wouldn't have to worry about looking over his shoulder everyday. The closer he got to Frankie's beach house, the more he knew he had to leave Delaware. He had outgrown its small city and knew it wouldn't be long before he'd be back in jail, him and his boys Pretty E and Dog. That's why he took this trip. He needed time to think and contemplate his next move. He knew he wanted out of the game, but did he want out right now was the question.

"Baby look!" Tameeka said, excitedly as she snapped a picture at the Disney Castle off in a distance. "Ain't that beautiful?"

"Yeah Baby, that shit is pretty," he replied.

"Rasul look at this though," Jaquaan said from the back seat". Im'ma be playin there in three years watch!" he said, as they passed the Orlando Magic's Home Arena.

"In three years you'll only be a sophomore in college".

"I know, but I'm leaving early," he smiled.

"The hell if you are. Your ass is going to get a degree," Tameeka stated, reminding him who was really in charge.

"Im'ma still get one Mom. I can always go back," he said.

"Well, we'll talk about that when the time comes."

When Rasul pulled up to Frankie's oceanfront beach home, the normal twenty-minute drive from the airport had turned into a sixty-minute sight seeing adventure. The white-framed three-story beach house was stunning as were the others around it, but this one stood out. Frankie's beach house was actually seventy-five to eighty percent glass, and you could actually see the entire inside from outside of the house. White furniture in all different shapes occupied most of the first floor, and in the rear you could almost make out the kitchen. A white grand piano sat next to the bay window overlooking the beach, and the white marble swivel staircase went up in the center of the room. On the second level, you could only make out a few things with your eyesight, but the house was basically see-through. The only thing that could stop you from seeing inside the house were the white metal blinds that were pulled back to the edge of each window.

"Baby this house is the bomb!" Tameeka said, wide eyed from the car.

"I know man, this house is da shit!" Jaquaan added.

"Boy what da fuck did I tell you about your mouth? Don't get fucked-up! I ain't going to keep telling you that Rasul ain't none of your boys on the street. He's your step-dad and you goin' to start respecting him like one," Tameeka shouted.

"I do Mom. It just slipped out, dat's all." Jaquuan said.

"Well apologize then." Tameeka said.

"Rasul I'm sorry man, aw'iight?" Jaquaan said.

"Yeah you aw'iight. Don't even worry about it," Rasul said, and winked at him through the rear-view mirror.

Tameeka grabbed the keys to the house and went inside while Rasul and Jaquaan unloaded the car. The daylong trip of flying and driving had worn her out, and the pear shaped sofa looked more than
relaxing. Tameeka kicked off her shoes at the door, wiggled her toes, and made her way over to sit down. The marble floor felt cool on her
swollen feet and the sofa was more than satisfying to her tired body, as she flopped down on it. She was just getting comfortable when Rasul and Jaquaan came through the door and dropped the luggage right there.

"Ahn-Ahn. Why y'all drop the bags right there? Take that stuff upstairs while y'all are in the mood, cause you know later on y'all ain't goin' to feel like it," Tameeka said from the sofa.

"Why don't you get up and do it?" Rasul asked, knowing it would start something.

"Boy you must be crazy! I wish da fuck I would carry those heavy ass bags upstairs," she said sarcastically, then, continued, "You shouldn't want your pregnant wife carrying that shit no-way." Tameeka said.

"Damn, can't you take a joke? I was only bullshitin.'"

"If you wasn't, I wasn't doin' dat shit anyway." Tameeka said.

"If you say so," Rasul said.

After Rasul and Jaquaan carried the bags upstairs and unpacked them it was almost seven o'clock in the evening. Since it was mid-summer the sun didn't start setting until around eight. Jaquaan asked to leave and go down to the boardwalk for a couple of hours, so Rasul and Tameeka were alone. He sat down on the couch next to her and rubbed her feet, as they stared out the bay window at the beach. The once packed beach that was full of surfers and volleyball freaks now only inhabited a few people that were laid out on towels trying to catch the last rays of the sun until tomorrow. Rasul looked at Tameeka who was mesmerized at the sight of the sun starting to set at the ocean's edge, and said, "Come on Baby. Let's go watch it."

Tameeka went upstairs and slipped on her new bathing suit by Burberry, the one made for pregnant women with the stomach cut out. Then she wrapped a huge beach towel around her waist, put on her flip-flops, and grabbed her cell phone ready to leave. She stood in front of the body length mirror and stared at herself in approval then said, "Damn! Even pregnant I'm sharp as hell!"

"Come on Baby, you ready?" Rasul asked, carrying a towel and the cocoa butter lotion Tameeka used on her stomach to avoid getting stretch marks.

"Yeah I'm ready, but why you got that?" she asked of the lotion.

"So I can lotion my baby down while she watches the sun set, that's why," he answered, making her blush.

The cool breeze coming in off the ocean cut through the humidity sending a warm breeze into their faces, as they stepped onto the beach. Rasul grabbed Tameeka's hand and led her off to the most secluded spot he could find, and laid the towels down. There Tameeka stretched out and propped her head up on her beach bag to watch the sun set, while Rasul rubbed lotion on her stomach. The sight of the sun setting was absolutely astounding. In just a matter of minutes the sky went from a clear blue picture, into a red, orange, purple, and pink vision. Tameeka fumbled around through the bag until she found her disposable camera and started snapping shots. She needed these pictures to show Tammy because words wouldn't be enough to describe the sight. She would have to see it herself.

The sound of the water washing up on the beach and easing back into its resting spot in the ocean put Rasul's mind at ease. It sometimes wondered off to more places than one, but never stayed in one spot for long. It always came back to the reason why he was on this vacation in the first place. He wanted out. The stress of the game was beginning to take a toll on him and he needed to make a decision. It was either his life or the lives of his boys Pretty E and Dog, or the money, and that's what bothered him the most. There shouldn't have been any reason in the world that he couldn't make the decision, but it was. The money, the power, and the respect were an aspect of life that had hardened his heart to the point where he didn't know who he was anymore. It reminded him of this poem a sista named Shahida said at his Club during open mic night a few months ago. "The Game Is Over!" she shouted, and he

wondered if she knew how true her words were. Rasul stood up on that memory to stretch his legs out, and
Tameeka's cell phone came to life with a loud ring at the same time. "Hello," she answered, on the first ring, then, there was silence.

The look on his wife's face as the color flushed from her cheeks, spoke the inevitable. She didn't have to say one word, because Rasul already knew what happened. Everything that he felt
all day long, and for the past few weeks, led up to this phone call. He hoped like hell he was wrong, but more times than none his gut feeling was right. He knew Pretty E and Dog got busted, and when she confirmed it his mind was made up. The game was over. She hung up the phone and looked her husband square in the eye and said, "Baby they got Dog and Pretty E," and her tears started. They weren't the tears for them, they were the tears for her husband, and when he realized it he tried his best to comfort her.

"Baby whass' wrong?" he asked.

"I don't want you to go to jail. What am I going to do if you go to jail?" she cried even more at the thought.

"What do you mean go to jail? Baby, I ain't going to jail. I ain't never going back to that place!" he assured her, then asked, "Why would you think that?"

"Because Tammy said they were following them. If that's true, what makes you think they weren't following you? They could have been following y'all for I don't know how long. "

"Relax Baby didn't we already go through this with Hit Man?" Rasul said.

"Yeah." Tameeka said.

"Well relax then. I'm cool." Rasul said.

"O.K.," she mumbled.

"Did Tammy say what they got caught with? What's their bail?" Rasul asked.

"They got caught with a couple kilos and some guns, but they ain't get no bail yet. She said she'd call when they get one." Tameeka said.

"Alright, if she calls before I get back let me know what it is." Rasul said.

"Where you going?" Tameeka asked.

"I need to take a walk." Rasul said.

Rasul walked down to the edge of the beach where the water met the sand, and looked out over the sea. Huge waves arose and crashed down repeatedly only to reveal what was left of the sun when it fell. Half of it was still out and looked as if it was struggling to stay up, but it was no match for God's will. It was the exact same way he felt right now as he watched it fight. He stared out into space looking at nothing particularly and his mind traveled again. It took him right back to the place where he so desperately wanted to stay away from, the prison yard. As he thought, he remembered a brother named Sadiq, a good brother. No matter how much, or how good he made the game sound, Sadiq stood firm on his belief. He found Islam in prison and applied it to his everyday life without missing a beat. He received a twenty-five year prison term for the exact same shit Rasul was doing now, and Rasul remembered one of their conversations like it took place yesterday.

"Little Brother, all that shit you trying to do now, or planning on doing when you leave here, I already done. But the most valuable thing I've learned is that you always fail if you don't live in accordance with Allah. See that whole lifestyle is Haram, meaning it's forbidden to live that way. It goes against everything Allah has made good for us, and nothing good is going to come from it. Rasul, Allah will always beat the Shaitan at anything he tries to do, and if you're a part of it, then there's no secret, your going to lose too," he said, and Rasul answered, "Man, whatever." Now as he stood at the ocean's edge he ate every word.

Rasul kneeled down and grabbed a hand full of wet sand, letting it crumble through his fingers slowly. His world was falling apart at the seams and he wondered if it was too late to change it around. "Damn Brother Sadiq," he said, as if he could hear him, "You wasn't Bullshitin." Rasul stood up and walked down to the embankment that the boardwalk ran across, and bent down to pick up a couple of rocks. As he stood beneath the wooden structure he tossed them out into the ocean. He was about to kneel down and pick up a couple more, when he noticed a piece of silver buried under the sand. He bent and tried to grab it, but it was connected to something else, so he started moving the sand away. Once the piece of silver was fully exposed to the eye, he noticed it was a 'Chanel' symbol on a Coach

bag. For some odd reason he felt like he seen this bag somewhere before, but he couldn't place a finger on it. "Maybe Tameeka wanted one of these before," he thought, because the bag wasn't exactly up to

date. It looked like a model from a couple years ago, he reasoned. Rasul grabbed the label on the bag and pulled it up out of the sand, then checked it. He pulled the zipper back on it hoping to find something in it, but only seen a comb, some hair spray, and a dry rotted wallet. "Damn this shit look familiar," he thought again. Rasul grabbed the wallet and opened it up and his heart dropped, like he was on an elevator. Shelly's I.D. stared him right in the eyes and he dropped everything like it was a hot potato. With trembling hands he reached down to pick it up and put it back in the bag. He stood in shock for the next minute with the bag clutched tightly in his hand, trying to think of something to do with it. Those eyes, that smile, her long pretty hair, just seeing the oriental and black beauty's face again was unexplainable to Rasul. He cocked his arm back, and with all his might threw the bag as far as he could into the ocean and watched it sink. The mystery of where Shelly was at and what happened to her for the past two years was answered. He didn't have to guess anymore because now he knew. Ricky and Nikki, the cleanup crew, had disposed of Shelly and BoBo right here in this ocean probably with cement shoes on.

     "Damn Sadiq was right. This shit really ain't worth it. I lost the love of my life to this shit, my boy Hit Man is dead because of this shit, and Pretty E and Dog will probably get twenty-five to life for this shit! Man, I'm done wit all this shit!" Rasul said to himself, and turned to go back to his wife Tameeka.

     "Hey Baby!" She said cheerfully, feeling a whole lot better when he got back. "Are you O.K.?" she asked.

     "Yeah Baby, I'm fine now," he said.

THE END
"So real you'll feel you lived it!"

Next Books to be Released
The Tommy Good Story
"From ashy, To Nasty, To Classy"
&
Dope sick
"The other side of the Game"

Coming this Winter 2005!

Me & My Girls

A novel By: Leondrei Prince

Website: www.streetknowledgepublishing.com

Chapter One

Tish could hear her son Tymeere crying as she lie awake in bed. "Thank God it's Friday." She said to herself, as she glanced at the digital clock that read 5:45 A.M. "I'll be so glad when I graduate this year, I don't know what I'mma do?" She continued, before going to tend to her son. Tish got up, walked over to the crib and picked up her child. Using her index finger, she ran it across the edge of his diaper and he was wet. Tish laid Tymeere down at the foot of the bed and within seconds, before he could even roll over, she was back with a new diaper and baby wipes. "Hey stink butt don't you think it's about time for you to start asking for the potty?" She said playfully and poked a finger at his nose. When he smiled, Tish's stomach turned, and she literally almost threw-up because that's how much he resembled his father Saafie. Saafie was a small time drug dealer around the projects when they first met, but now he and his boy Tyaire ran the city. Tish couldn't stand him now, but she remembered the day they met like it was yesterday.

"Come here girl." A voice called, as Tish passed the corner she hated passing so much. This particular corner was where people did everything from shoot dice to sell drugs and it just so happened to be on the same route she had to take when walking home from her bus stop. Tish looked into the crowd of boys on the corner and tried to put a face with the voice, but to no avail. "I really don't need to know

1

who it is anyway if he's standing over there." She said to herself and
kept stepping.

"Oh, you ain't going to stop?" She heard the voice say again,
but this time she saw who it was.

"It's him! That cute boy I always see when I walk to the
corner store." She thought as he made his way over to her.

"I wasn't until I saw it was you." She answered.

"Whass your name?" The cute boy asked.

"My name is Tish. Whass yours?"

"Saafie." And from that very moment Tish knew Saafie
would be the one to steal her virginity.

On that note, Tish snapped back to reality from her daydream
and fastened Tymeere's diaper.

"Fuck your Daddy! We are goin' to be fine all by ourselves."
Tish said to Tymeere as he laid him on his side, and propped his
bottle up on the pillow. Tish looked up and the clock read 6:15 A.M.,
so she ran off to the shower. She put on her shower cap and lathered
up with Dove Body Wash, and stood under the hot spicket for what
seemed to be like 10 minutes, but when she saw the clock she
panicked.

"Damn, I only got 15 minutes to get me and him dressed."
She said.

Tish sat on the foot of her bed staring into the full length
mirror that covered her bedroom door and lotion up. Tish was tall,
around 6 feet and built like a goddess. If you didn't know her, you'd

2

never know she was a mother because her body showed no traces.

Many people said she resembled Tyra Banks, but she didn't think so,
she

thought more along the lines of a taller Lisa Raye. Tish stood up and
stepped into her matching pink polka-dot thong and bra set and
looked at herself in the mirror.

"Shit, Saafie don't know what he's missing." She said to
herself, as she continued to get dressed.

When she finished getting dressed, she couldn't do nuffin' but
shake her head. The powder blue Roca-Wear sweat suit fit her curves
to a tee, and her white Nike's set it all off, as her hair hung shoulder
length.

"A mutha-fucka can't say I ain't sharp!" She told herself as
she walked down the hallway to her mother's room.

"Mom" She said, as she knocked on the door instead of just
walking straight in. The thought of what happened just two days ago
made her smile with embarrassment, as she saw her Mom and Mr. Joe
getting it in.

"What?" Her Mom said.

"Can I come in?" Tish asked.

"Yeah, now what's the problem?" Her mom said.

"Can you please take Meere-Meere to daycare for me?" Tish
asked.

"Where's his no good ass daddy?" Her mom said.

"He has to go to court today, so he can't come." Tish said.

3

"It's always some'em! I'll do it, but this is the last time I take care of his so-called daddy's responsibility." Tish's mom said.

"Whatever!" Tish said, and left the room with a slam of door. "I'll be so glad when I get my own shit!"

"What you say? Don't get fucked up!" Ms. Carla, the older version of Tish, said.

Ms. Carla Wallace, a single mother of one and grandmother to another, sat up in bed and grabbed her robe from the whickered chair directly at her right. A sense of pride overcame her as she realized she managed to instill moral values in her only child and build an open and honest friendship with her at the same time. She remembered ever so clearly the news that literally broke her to her knees when Tish said "Momma, I'm pregnant." Even though the news was unexpected, Ms. Carla understood, and was proud that Tish could be so honest. When she was pregnant, she couldn't muster up the strength to tell her own parents, so hearing and seeing Tish tell her, she knew not only did she have a good daughter, she had a best friend.

*   *   *   *   *   *   *   *   *

"Beep-Beep" The horn sounded.

"Here I come, damn!" Tish said from her bedroom window.

"Come on Bitch, you always late!" Tasheena yelled from the passenger's side window.

"What you say girl?" Ms. Carla yelled back out of her window.

4

"Nuffin', Ms. Carla, Oooo I'm so sorry." Tasheena said embarrassingly.

"Hey Rayon, I knew your mouth wasn't that nasty." Ms. Carla said, knowing it could probably be, if not worse.

"Nope Mom Carla and never was." Rayon shot back.

"Bye Mom." Tish said as she locked the door behind her.

"Bye baby." Ms. Carla said and almost forgot about some key items. "Where are all of his things at?"

"Downstairs on the couch." Tish said and slid in the backseat of Tasheena's car. "Damn y'all, she gets on my nerves! I got to get my own shit and fast." Tish said to Tasheena and Rayon.

"Bitch stop crying! I know what you need early this morning," Tasheena said.

"Me too!" Rayon added, as they high fived and said in unison; "A blunt Bitch!" as they all fell out laughing.

"Well it looks like you two bitches already had one," Tish said.

"We wish, but bitch we only got 5 dollars we can spend. The rest of the money is for some gas and munchies." Tasheena said.

"I know that's right." Rayon added.

"Well who got it? Y'all wanna go see Ol' School on 2-4 or the young boys down on 27th street?" Tish asked.

"Let's go see the young boys 'cause we can work them. Ol' School ain't havin' it!" Tasheena said.

"Who you tellin'," Tish and Rayon said at the same time.

5

Rayon pulled her Honda Accord away from the curb in front of 2718 Bower Street and headed to 27th street. Tish looked around at the place she called home for her 18 years and was glad to be leaving the eye soaring slums, even if it was only to be going to school.

"Tasheena, do you feel the same way about this shit?" Tish asked.

"About what shit?"

"About the projects, like it ain't no way out of these muthafucka's"

"Hell no bitch, we ain't going to be here forever, we too damn sharp for dat shit. If anything, a nigga going' to get us up outta here." "Bitch that's your problem now. Deon done spoiled you and now since y'all ain't together, you just think a nigga posed to take care of you, huh?

"No, I ain't say dat. I'm just saying you can stay on the piss pot, but I'm not. I refuse to stay a project kid." Tasheena said.

"I heard dat," Rayon intervened.

"Bitch what you know about the projects and you live way out in the suburbs?" Tasheena shot back.

"Bitch I be in them around y'all so much, I might as well be from them! Put it this way, I know it ain't no place to want to be." She said as she crossed Market Street.

27th and West Street in Wilmington was a known drug spot for marijuana. Rayon pulled her car up to Fat Cat's corner store and parked, to avoid looking so obvious about buying weed because it

6

was hot. Not hot weather wise, but hot as far as the police were concerned. It seemed as though they frequented the block every five minutes.

"Who's getting out to get it?" Rayon asked, the suburban side of her starting to kick in. "cause I don't like it up here like dat," She finished.

"Bitch, you just scared." Tasheena said.

"Look just give me the money and I'll go get it." Tish said.

Tish strutted up the block like she was the baddest bitch in town and her tall stacked body shook in all the right places. It was too early in the morning for the block to be jammed packed, but for the couple of young boys that were out there, they got an eye full.

"Damn she phat as a mu'fucka!" One of them said.

"Yeah, she phat, but that's Saafie's baby's mom" The other one said.

"Oh shit! It is? She still phat dough."

"Whass' up y'all?" Tish said as she walked up on them. "Who got da dro?" She asked.

"Ain't no dro, but I got some blueberry," The first to speak said.

"Well I ain't got no blueberry money." Tish replied then heard someone call her name.

"Damn, did you have to call my whole government?" She said when she saw it was Tyaire.

"Girl shut up." He said smiling. "What'chu doing out here?"

7

"I'm trying to get some weed so we can get smoked before we go to school."

"Who's we? Is the babe Rayon with you?" Tyaire asked.

"Yeah she wit me, but she ain't thinking about you." Tish said.

"Yeah dats what your mouth says. Tell her I said whass'up. She know I been tryin' to smash dat for years."

"Yeah that's just why you haven't smashed it 'cause she know that's all you want to do," Tish said sarcastically, then continued, "Now who got da weed out here?"

"Here you can have my lil' personal sack," He said and pulled it from his back pocket.

"Damn cuz! I thought you was coming right back," Deon said.

"Deon, is that you?" Tish asked surprised, but more confused than anything.

"Oh shit! Hey sis, how you doin'?"

"I'm doing fine, how about you?" Deon said.

"I'm alright, I'm not like I used to be, but I'm alright," He said, yet his eyes told a very different story.

Deon looked bad! His hair wasn't cut and sharply lined like it usually was and his clothes weren't even right. His Timbs were leaning over and dirty and Tish just shook her head. She felt bad for Deon because he became like so many young boys in da hood, doped out. He literally looked like he gave up. She remembered when

8

Deon was the "Man" and when he and Tasheena were hot and heavy. In fact, he was the one who put Saafie and Tyaire on in the game, now it seemed as though he was on the verge of begging Tyaire for some'em.

"Deon if you ever need me, call me ok? You still got my number right" Tish asked.

"Yeah I got it," He answered with watery eyes. The pain Deon felt inside was almost too much bare, but he managed to fight back the tears. "Yo Tish, I love you sis. He said.

"I love you too Deon," Tish replied and hugged him tightly.

"Tell Tasheena I miss her and I love her to death."

"I will." Tasheena vowed.

"Don't forget to tell Rayon what I said," Tyaire interrupted.

"Whatever" Tish replied not paying him any attention and he knew it too.

Because of the situation that just occurred between Tish and Deon, he understood the cold shoulder. He also silently wished that his boy Deon could get it together and leave that dope alone. When Tish got back in the car, her whole demeanor had changed and her girls knew it. They waited until they pulled away from the corner store before asking her the reason for her strange mood.

"Nuffin." Tish said.

"Oh shit girl! Ain't dat the vice car?"

"Ooo yeah! Hurry up, roll down the window girl. Tyaire!"
Tish called. "5-0 coming around the corner." And with Deon on his
heels, Tyaire sprinted through the alley.

"Girl that looked like Deon." Tasheena said knowing it was
him. She had heard some rumors about how he was getting high, but
never actually saw him doing it, so she drew her own conclusions.
"Whatever he's doing," she thought on more than one occasion,
"must be more important than me."

"It was him girl and he looks a sight. I told him he really
needs to get it together, 'cause he's too good of peoples to be goin'
out like that." Tish said.

"For real?" Tasheena asked "What did he look like?"

"His hair was woofin' and his Timbs were ran over, but it
didn't look like he lost a whole bunch of weight or nuffin." She
answered.

"Oh," was all Tasheena said as she split the blunt to roll the
weed. She would have done anything to get her mind off of Deon
because she loved him and hearing of his condition only made things
worse. She wished like Hell she could help him, but she remembered
clearly what her aunt had said about addiction because her
uncle was addicted. "Baby don't worry about Deon, he will be fine.
He just has to hit rock bottom." So she figured that rock bottom
hadn't come yet.

"Bitch you ain't done twisting the weed yet?" Tish asked
from the back seat.

"Yeah, give me a lighter."

*   *   *   *   *   *   *   *   *

Howard High School, HCC, as it was known, was one of the only school's blacks were allowed to attend back in the in the 1930's through the 1950's. Now it was more like a popular career center known for its high fashion dress code and popular basketball teams. Howard was the school of choice for anyone wanting or trying to get noticed as someone of importance. People were willing to spend whatever on clothing, jewelry, and shoes and kept themselves manicured, pedicured, trimmed, dyed and blow-dried in hopes of being placed
on the school's most popular list. You could be or become whatever you wanted at Howard, if you were willing, but if you weren't careful and forgot the most important reason for being there, to get an education, you could find yourself on the long list of drop-outs.

Rayon pulled into HCC's parking lot and parked directly in the nurse's spot.

"Bitch you can't park here." Tasheena said.

"Girl I ain't thinking about these people. The only thing they can do is call my tags in over the intercom system and make me move it, that's when I usually go ride around and tell them I couldn't find a parking spot."

"Bitch you so petty."

"Ain't I though" Rayon said sarcastically.

11

"Look bitch, I'm high, and we almost late so I'll get wit' y'all later." Tish said.

"When?"

"Around lunch time," and she grabbed her bookbag and left.

Tish stopped in the ladies room and splashed some water on her face to make sure she looked presentable just in case she so happened to bump into Trans, her new boyfriend. And just like she figured, Trans was waiting at her locker, like he did every morning, in his usual pose, with his foot up on the wall.

"Hey Beauty," He said gingerly and gave her a warm hug and squeeze on the ass.

"Hey Boo," She replied and stood on her tip toes to give him a kiss.

Trans was tall, 6'6 to be exact, but the way he wore his clothes made him look like he was about 6'3. His tall stature, dark, chocolate skin, dimpled cheeks, white teeth, and temple tapered, baby Afro made him what the ladies called "the shit." Not only was he sharp as hell, but he was also the most talked about high school ball player in the country since LeBron "King" James and Tish loved him.

"You know I got some good news to tell you right?" Trans said.

"What news?" Tish asked.

"I just signed my letter of consent to U.C.L.A." Trans said.

"For real?"

12

"Yeah I'm for real and you can go out there with me to visit next month."

"I can't go."

"You can, I already arranged it. I told them if my girl can't come, than neither can I." Trans said. Tish could do nothing but blush. Trans always did sweet shit like that and that's what distinguished him from Saafie.

"Well I guess I can then, huh?" She answered then the bell rung.

"You better get to practice, right?"

"Yeah, the team has no classes today 'cause of the big game tonight up at Chester High. I know you coming, right?"

"I don't know baby? You know I ain't never see you play before except once and y'all lost, so I don't know. I might jinx you or some'em."

"Baby, I want you to come. How some'em that look as good as you be a jinx."

"Boy shut-up!" She blushed again. "Damn, he always knows what to say," She thought as he walked her to her cosmetology class.

Tish stepped through the door five minutes late, as usual, and Ms. Johnson didn't pay it one mind. Tish was her favorite student and the only one who actually worked at a real salon. When Tish saw Ms. Johnson she couldn't do anything but smile because she knew Ms. Johnson saw right through her. Tish didn't have to explain one thing, on the grounds that more than once she was caught necking in the hallway with Trans by Ms. Johnson.

13

"Good morning Ms. Tish and how are you today?" Ms. Johnson asked.

"I'm fine."

"Why are your eyes all chinky," Ms. Johnson asked knowing the reason. She just wanted to make Tish squirm a little bit; let her know that she was slipping.

"Um, um, no reason, why?"

"I'm just lettin' you know other people see you better than you see ya'self, remember that," And Tish smiled. Ms. Johnson was her girl.

"Whass up?"

"Ain't nuffin', just tired of this damn class girl. It's too much, but girl this is where the money is at."

"Who you tellin'? You know I know as much money as I be making down at Che-Che's shop."

"Huh? Girl what style are you getting ready to give that mannequin?" Renee, girl in her class, asked.

"Probably a lil' Bob or some'em. I'm just going to go light enough to keep Ms. Johnson straight, feel me?"

"I feel you. Oh by the way, how's my lil' boyfriend doin'?"

"Who Tymeere?"

"Yeah girl, who else. You know I'm waiting on his lil' behind. Shit when I'm 35 he'll be 21," Renee teased.

"He's alright. Bad as hell though. Done grew two more teeth and is tryin' to bite everything and everybody that picks him up."

"Awww, y'all better leave my baby alone."

"Damn!" Tish thought as Renee walked away. "Dat bitch will talk a bitch head off!" But before she could clear the thoughts from her head she was back.

"Oh, I almost forgot. Are you going to the game tonight? Girl it's sold out and everything, they said ESPN was shooting it live on TV tonight."

"Yeah I'm going. You know I ain't goin' to miss my personal Michael Jordan play in the biggest game of his life." Tish said making sure she rubbed it in at Renee. She knew deep down inside Renee had tried to fuck him a few months ago, but she felt they were both lying when they said nothing happened.

"I heard dat," Renee said and got the hint.

*   *   *   *   *   *   *   *   *

Trans bopped into the gym ten minutes late and not even dressed for practice. Coach Stormy blew his whistle and called a team huddle the moment he saw Trans. "Trans come here now!" He demanded.

"Who you talking to like that? My own pops don't even talk to me like that cuz!" Trans snapped, taking it harder than he usually would 'cause he was on the spot.

"I'm talking to you!" Coach Stormy didn't back down. "Just because you signed your letter to attend U.C.L.A., this morning don't make you exempt from being a part of this team! You need to be here like everyone else, who do you think you are?"

15

"Trans Owens."

"Well Mr. Owens, you won't start tonight!" Coach snapped. "Now everybody get back to practice!" He finished and walked away leaving Trans stunned.

*   *   *   *   *   *   *   *   *

Chapter Two

"Order in the court! Order in the court!" The judge spoke as
he rapped his gavel on the table, trying to silence the murmur that
overcame the courtroom when the jury returned unexpectedly fast.

"Has the jury reached a verdict?" He continued as the foreman
of the twelve jurors stood up. "Yes we have your honor." The
foreperson said.

Saafie looked over at his attorney puzzled, and then over his
shoulder to his boss, Pretty E. Pretty E looked at him with a smile
and a wink of reassurance. This was the same reaction the courtroom
had last year when him and Dog were on trial for more than a 15
brick indictment. Frankie, The Don, had done another favor for
Pretty E, and paid the jury off in Saafie's case.

"On counts one and two for drug possession and intent to
distribute and counts one and two for weapons possession, we the jury
find the defendant NOT GUILTY of all charges." The courtroom
erupted. Every police and vice officer present felt a slap in the face as
Saafie stood and hugged his attorney. "I told you baby boy
everything was going to be fine," Pretty E said. Then before he
stepped off, he looked over at Saafie and said "Call me."

Pumpkin stood dead center at the swinging gate in the
courtroom, which separated the spectators from the actual trial itself.
Saafie stepped through the wooden gate and received the kiss and hug
of a lifetime from his main girl.

"Hey baby!" Pumpkin said and puckered up.

17

"Hey." Saafie said disillusioned.

Saafie was still in awe every time he saw Pumpkin, but as he held her, he quickly discovered why she had that effect on him. Pumpkin was B-A-D, and as she stood before him in her Prada skirt set with the matching shoes and handbag, he literally shook with excitement. He knew from the moment he saw her he had to have her, and he went right at her. See Pumpkin was from South Bridge Projects, no better than Tish, but she was different. Pumpkin had to struggle to take care of her three little brothers and little sister while her mom smoked crack and drank Crystal Palace gin. In fact, when he met her, she was at the bus stop in a Burger King uniform headed to work. He had loved her from that moment, just off her strength alone and made a vow that he was one day going to get them out of the projects.

"I'm so glad you're coming home with me," Pumpkin said. "But baby if you wasn't, I was prepared," She finished and retrieved a $1,500 money order from her purse.

"See baby, that's why I love you. You don't just think about you." Saafie said.

"Of course not, that's why when I get off of work tonight I got some'em even more special for you." She said in a real sexually provocative way in his ear. "Now come on, I have to go to work. I told 'em I'd be there by twelve."

"O.K." Saafie said.

18

Saafie drove his convertible XJ8 Jaguar smoothly down King
St. with his baby in tow. He looked at the clock on the dashboard and
noticed that it was only a quarter of eleven, plenty of time for a
quickie. "Baby," he said excitedly, then touched her thigh. "Wanna
get a quickie?" Pumpkin looked at the clock and the thought crossed
her mind, but she quickly changed it when she saw her job, the bank
on 4th and Walnut.

"Nah baby, I have to take a rain check." She answered. "I got
you tonight," She said and sucked his ear lobe as he pulled up to her
job.

"Come on baaaby," He whined.

"Nope," She said full of energy and pecked his cheek, as she
got out of the car. Saafie didn't pull straight off, he watched as
Pumpkin swung her hips provocatively and then disappeared through
the revolving door. "Damn, I should call her back," he thought and
grabbed at his crotch at the thoughts of just how good his baby's
loving was. After pondering the thought and being snapped back to
reality by the long toot of the horn, he pulled off.

Saafie made a left off of 4th St. onto Walnut St. and made a
right on 9th. The jag rode so smoothly that he never felt a bump
beneath him and as he rode down the street, he fed off of the envious
looks he received. He only blew at a couple niggas from C.B.W., he
knew, but for the rest, he smiled a sinister smile. He remembered the
days all too fondly when people would tease him about being mixed,
but now he was up. It was his turn to get back because half of these

niggas out here were broke. On that note, he headed up Rt. 202
towards Faulk Rd. where his two-story duplex sat.

Saafie pulled the Jag into the driveway and pressed the
automatic garage door opener that was clipped onto the sun visor. He
parked in the two-car garage directly next to his new H-2 Hummer
and for the first time really looked at it since it came home from the
shop getting 24-inch shoes and a new system. "I'm pulling dat out
today." He said proudly as he went through the door leading into his
home. No sooner than he stepped foot
on the wall to wall blood red carpet, he was greeted by Pumpkin's
twin Szhit-zu's, Lady and Tramp. "Hey puppies," he said gingerly to
the little ones as they wagged their tails excitedly and spun around in
circles. "Damn, I gotta get my baby this operation," he thought sadly
about Pumpkin not being able to have kids. Just thinking about the
look on that sorry nigga's face when he said, "Remember Pumpkin
nigga" mad Saafie feel a certain kind of way. He had kept those
feelings he had buried, especially since he had murdered that nigga
that night, but it was different now. It
was really starting to get to Pumpkin, and he saw it every time he had
Tymeere with him. Saafie reached down and patted the two hairy
dogs on the head and made his way through the spacious home. The
all-white mesh furniture, matching lamp, and end tables set the carpet
off, as well as the paintings that hung on the walls throughout the
house.

Saafie stood next to the fireplace and looked up at his favorite poster, and like always felt good again. It was the one where Muhammad Ali stood dead center in the ring, arm folded to his chest, mouth open, and towering over a battered Sonny Liston.

"Ali-Ali-Ali," he chanted as he walked down the hallway towards his bedroom.

Saafie hit the switch on the wall and the beautiful 150 gallon fish tank built in to it, lit up like an aquarium. The huge piranhas swam back and forth aimlessly like they had chips on their shoulders and the algae eaters stayed stuck to the glass. Saafie reached into the small portable refrigerator that sat beneath the tank and grabbed two huge rats wrapped in wax paper. The moment he lifted the lids on the tank, the fish sat stark still facing the open tank. Before the first rat could even hit the water, one of the huge piranhas leaped from the tank. Saafie dropped the second rat and sat on the edge of his bed enjoying the frenzy. As he watched blood ooze and mix in with the now cloudy water, he made a sinister chuckle and thought; "This will happen to any nigga who tries to cross me" and then the phone rang.

"Hey nigga! Congratulations prick!" Tyaire shouted from the other end.

"Yeah nigga and fuck you too pussy!" Saafie shot back in their normal playful mode.

"Nah, whass'up though cousin? You know they got your shit on the twelve o'clock news."

"Yeah I know, them mu'fucka's was in the courtroom."

21

"Word?" Tyaire said.

"Yeah. Whass'up wit'chu, what you doin?"

"Nuffin."

"Why don't you ride down to Howard with me right quick, so I can go see Tish and see if I gotta pick up my son or not." Saafie said.

"Alright, come get me. I'm at the detail shop getting my car done."

"Oh, you know I went and got the H-2 from up in Philly last night. This mutha-fucka is sitting so pretty, I don't want to drive the mutha-fucka!"

"Say word."

"Word nigga! You'll see it. I'm on my way."

"Awight." Tyaire said.

*   *   *   *   *   *   *   *   *

Change clothes and go…

You know I stay-

Fresh to Death

Brought it from da projects

And I'mma take it to the top of the globe

Change Clothes

Jay-Z *The Black Album*

"Ya dude is back, Maybach coupe is back, tell the whole world the truth is back!" Saafie sung along as Jay-Z's Black Album pounded through the Hummer's new Alpine system. Tyaire cringed

22

up his face and stepped out the detail shop singing the hook, "Sexy, Sexy," when the black truck pulled up.

"Got damn baby boy, you know I'm jealous right?" Tyaire said as the Sprewell's spun endlessly.

"For what nigga?" Saafie asked.

"'Cause my shit ain't done yet, that's why nigga!" Tyaire responded and hopped in.

When Saafie turned out 12th St. from off of Pine St., the street was already starting to fill up with students going to lunch. He pulled directly across the street from the school and pumped the radio to its capacity, as the young girls shook their asses and did the latest dances.

"Damn these young bitches phat to def!" Saafie said discombobulated.

"Nigga you act like some ol'head nigga or some'em and you only like what? Twenty one?" Tyaire said.

"You too nigga."

"Oh I know nigga, but I ain't trying to act like some ol' nigga either. I'm trying to stay young forever nigga!"

"I heard that." Saafie said.

*   *   *   *   *   *   *   *   *

Tish and Trans left the school arm and arm and headed over to the corner store hugging. Just as they crossed the street, a black H-2 bent around the corner playing "Brush ya' shoulders off" by Jay-z and Tish nodded her head. When it came to a stop and Saafie hopped out, she spit on the ground, that's just how bitter it tasted in her mouth after she saw him.

"Ain't that Saafie, your baby's dad?" Trans asked.

"Yeah that's him, but so what?" She answered and cuddled up close to him, as if to insure his position as her man.

"No reason, I was just asking."

"Oh." Tish said.

*   *   *   *   *   *   *   *   *

"Man I know this bitch just seen me sittin' here," Saafie said to himself, as he watched Tish and that young nigga who stayed on the T.V., go in the corner store.

"Where you goin' cuz?" Tyaire asked, as Saafie stormed away.

"I'll be right back."

"I hope that nigga don't go do some'em stupid," Tyaire said to himself, then noticed Rayon across the street standing next to Tasheena.

"Rayon!" He called three times before she acknowledged him, even though he knew she saw him in this pretty Hummer when they first came outside.

"What?" She yelled from across the street.

"So you goin' to act like dat?"

"Like what?"

"Like that. Now come here." He demanded.

"Who you talking to," She rolled her eyes, but came anyway.

24

Rayon bopped across the street with her Louis Vuitton bag draped across her forearm swinging her keys in her hand. Her hip hugging Baby Phat jeans brought every curve out, and the half cut, v-neck matching Baby Phat t-shirt damn near pushed her titties out of the small V.

"I see why I been trying to fuck dis girl," He said imagining how phat her ass was just by looking at her waist from the front.

"What? Whass up?" She asked.

"What'chu mean whass'up? You know I been trying to see you about some'em for I don't know how long now."

"Me and how many other bitches? See that's why I ain't fuckin' wit you" She said, but visualized it like it already happened. See truth be told, she'd been having these same feelings about Tyaire that he had for her, but wasn't trying to just be fucked like the rest of the bitches, so she stayed away.

"Why not?" Tyaire asked.

"Because."

"Girl, let dat shit go whatever you holding on to. I know you feelin' a nigga, damn!" Tyaire said and he was right.

"How you know what I am feeling?"

"Cause I know," He replied.

"Know what," She asked.

"Are you coming wit me or not?" Tyaire asked.

"Where we goin'?"

"To my crib." Tyaire said.

"For what? We ain't doing nuffin'."

"Girl just come on." Tyaire pushed.

"Well at least let me go get some kind of fake pass or some'em"

"Alright, hurry up." Tyaire said with a smile on his face.

*   *   *   *   *   *   *   *   *

Tish and Trans were paying for their little snacks and soda's when Saafie walked in, so they never saw him coming. He walked straight up on her and grabbed her arm, spinning her towards him.

"Yo, I know you saw me out there sitting on my truck."

"Boy get your hands off me!" She yanked away.

"Bitch! I'll slap da shit out of you," He snapped as a crowd began to draw.

"Yo, who you callin' a bitch, nigga? Don't get your lil' pretty ass knocked out in here," Trans said and meant it.

"What nigga? Do you know who I am? I'll have your lil' bitch ass come up missing, how about that?" He said then stressed the word "pussy!"

"Whatever nigga. I just know if you call her another bitch, I'mma knock ya bitch ass out!" He said scared to death. He knew he could knock Saafie out, but he also knew Saafie had enough money to probably do what he said, so he held back. It was a threat that Trans would remember for a long time.

"Why are you always making a scene?" Tish asked.

26

"That's his young ass! I only came to ask if I had to go get my son or not."

"Don't you bring him home from daycare every day? Well what you think?"

"Man you ain't gotta be smart." Saafie said.

"Be smart? Be smart? For what? You already slapped us in the face, me and your son. All that mu'fuckin money you got and my son don't have any new Timbs and sneaks, but I see you gotta new truck for your fans though, huh? Nigga you ain't shit."

"Saafie was about to go haywire, but saw Trans looming over Tish in back of her and decided to step off."

She was really hurt, as was he, to think that's how Tish thought he felt about his son.

"You know what, you got dat." He said and left the store.

"You alright baby?" Trans asked.

"Yeah, as long as you are," She said and tried to smile.

*   *   *   *   *   *   *   *   *

"Man let's get the fuck away from here," Saafie said when he got back to his truck.

"Hold up cuz, I'm waiting on Rayon."

"Where she goin'?" Saafie asked.

"She goin' wit me nigga! What's wrong with you?" Tyaire asked.

"Nuffin man, I'm just ready to go." Saafie said.

27

"Yeah nigga, that young boy wearin' Tish ass out, ain't he?"

"Not now nigga, now is not the time." Saafie said pissed and hurt.

"I don't care nuffin' about you being mad nigga." Tyaire said then saw Rayon. "Hurry up baby, my boy trippin' again."

"Hey Saafie, whass' up?" Rayon said.

"Your mutha'fuckin girl keeps doing that bullshit, that's what's up."

"What'chu mean? I now you ain't talking about Trans are you? And you got a what? A wife at home!" Rayon said.

"That's what I told his ass," Tyaire added.

"Man, fuck both of you two mu'fucka's and get out my truck!" He said trying to hold back his smile as they reached the detail shop.

*   *   *   *   *   *   *   *   *

Tyaire disappeared into the detail shop leaving Rayon standing out front. When he came back, he was pulling his 500 SL from the back of the building as T.I. was screaming "24's are like 10's round here" on Memphis Bleek's new single "Round Here," as his Sprewell's spun oddly. He jumped out the car leaving the door open and told Rayon to get in as he walked back into the shop. Within minutes he returned with a man in a jumpsuit carrying a spray bottle. Rayon sat patiently and watched Tyaire, in his Jim Brown throwback and butter Timbs give the man instructions. "I guess he would want it done right, paying all that money," Rayon thought as the man sprayed

Armor All on his tires again. The man stood up after he hit the last
tire and Tyaire peeled him off a couple dollars, then got in the car.

"Was I too long baby?" Tyaire asked.

"No you wasn't too long, but can you play something else. Do
you have Alicia Keys?" And with one press of a button the sweet
sounds of "You don't know my name" poured through the system.

"That's what I'm talking bout," She said and reclined into the
soft leather.

Tyaire pulled up to his three-story home in Hockeson and
parked in the driveway. Rayon was shocked because he only lived
right around the corner, well five minutes away, from her.

"Who lives here? I mean, how long have you lived here?"
Rayon asked.

"For about six months now. See, my grandparents left me the
house in their will when they died last year. I only lived here for six
months because my peoples had fought the will saying my mom-mom
and pop-pop were incompetent when they left me everything, but I
won in court and got everything. I'm a millionaire."

"Well why do you still sell drugs?" She asked.

"I can't even answer that." He said and led her in the house.

Rayon walked into the house and was surprised at his set-up.
She had figured that the house would be more glamorous than it was,
but it wasn't. It looked as if older people still lived there. Don't get
me wrong, the house was not like Sanford and Son's, but it wasn't Al
Pacino's style either.

29

"You alright? I see you look a little puzzled." Tyaire asked.

"I was just thinking you would have done some things different to the house, that's all."

"Nah. I left it like my grandparents had it because it gives me that feel, you know?"

"I guess so." Rayon said.

"But if yo' ass was here a little more, then it probably would be decorated differently."

"What?" Rayon said hearing the unspoken words.

"You heard me," He said and headed upstairs. "Come on baby girl."

Rayon's heart pounded as she walked upstairs behind Tyaire. It had been over a year and a half since she'd had some and she's only did it with two people her whole 18 years. Her last boyfriend Joe and the person she'd never tell anyone about, Trans. They had made a promise to never tell anyone, besides, they were best friends. When they entered Tyaire's bedroom, she really began to tremble. Tyaire walked over to her and asked, "Are you alright,?" but her mouth was too dry to answer, so she just shook her head. "Come here," He whispered and took her into his arms.

The kiss was soft and their tongues twirled like they wanted to become one. Tyaire gently laid her across the bed and peeled her Baby Phat jeans off of her real easy. The way he moved, so patiently, had calmed Rayon's nerves to the point that she was starting to enjoy it. "You like that baby?" He asked and kissed her navel. "Um-Hmm"

She moaned and arched her ass up off the bed, so he could get the pants the rest of the way off. Rayon let out a soft cry and dug her manicured nails deep into his back, as he eased himself into her. Her prize was so wet and tight that Tyaire didn't want to move. "Damn," He said to himself, but Rayon was too far aroused to notice his reaction. She swiveled her hips like she was twirling a hoola-hoop and then it was on. In less than five minutes they both had came together and was starring into the ceiling, lost in thoughts.

*   *   *   *   *   *   *   *   *

Chapter Three

If it hadn't been for Rayon's cell phone ringing, she could have slept all day. She reached over and grabbed it from her purse and sat straight up. "Damn! It's 3:00 P.M.," She said to herself knowing school had let out at 2:50 P.M., and when she saw her 18 missed calls, she knew why. "Tyaire get up, I have to go," She said nudging him on the side. "Alright, here I come." Tyaire said. When they arrived at Howard High School, the street and parking lot was near empty. Just a few after school activities students lingered, along with a very pissed off Tish and Tasheena.

"Damn where's this girl at?" She know damn well I gotta go out here to grab this birth certificate, then go to work." Tish said anxiously.

"I don't know where the bitch at," Tasheena said, then remembered. "Girl I know where that bitch at, she's with Tyaire girl."

"No she ain't bitch." Tish said in disbelief.

"Word on everything, she is." Tasheena said.

"That's why she ain't been answering the phone." Tish said, then saw Tyaire's car turn the corner.

"Here da bitch come now." Tasheena said.

The moment Rayon pulled into the parking lot she saw her girls standing by the Honda, as they called it. She knew they'd be a little upset about her lateness, but they'd be alright once they got all the juicy info about her five minute escapade. Tyaire pulled up right

32

next to Rayon's Honda and parked. He rolled down his window and looked at Tish smiling from ear to ear.

"Hey sis! Thanks for putting the word in for me." He said knowing she didn't say anything.

"You're welcome," She said playing along while Rayon climbed out the passenger's side.

"Where you been at bitch?" Tasheena asked. "Oooh bitch, no you didn't!"

"No she didn't what?" Tyaire asked being nosy, and then called Rayon around the car to him.

"Give me a kiss baby and call me later," He said as they touched tongues one more time.

"Eeeewww bitch! Do you know where his mouth been?" Tish played.

"Fuck you," He responded with a chuckle and pulled off.

"Bitch what happened? And we want to know everything!" Tasheena asked as they piled into the car.

The whole ride from Howard High School to the Secretary of State office out on Limestone Rd., was filled with Tasheena and Tish laughing in stitches. Rayon had them laughing so hard their stomachs were hurting. It really got bad when Rayon was telling them about how much Tyaire was worried about his five minute performance.

"Baby look, I'mma make it up to you, o.k. baby?" Rayon mocked in her deepest voice.

"That bitch is crazy, ain't she?" Tish said still laughing.

"As a bed bug," Tasheena responded as Tish went into the office building to get her birth certificate.

After planning their every move out for the night, they dropped Tish off at Che-Che's shop to meet her only client for the day, Ms. Barber. It was exactly 4:30 on the dot, four hours away from the big game at Chester High and Ms. Barber wasn't there yet.

"I got the right mind to schedule her for tomorrow," She thought the same time Ms. Barber walked through the door.

"Hey baby, I ain't late am I?"

"No you're not Ms. Barber."

"O.k. baby, let's get started then o.k.?"

"How you want it Ms. Barber?"

"You know baby, like uh, what's that girl's name? You know, the one who sings that song, uh "Crazy in Love," oh I know now, the girl's name is Benonsay."

"You mean Beyonce."

"Yeah that's her name."

Tish couldn't do anything but grin as she walked Ms. Barber to her station.

"Now she now damn well she ain't goin' to look like Beyonce, when she already look like Florida Evans," She said to herself.

Ms. Barber was cool though and Tish liked her a lot. Her personality was animated and she always had something to say. Ms.

Barber was the walking Channel Six news van and kept up with the latest gossip.

"Girl, you know I missed the damn Powerball by one number." Ms. Barber started as soon as Tish laid her back in the hair washing sink.

"I know you were mad." Tish shot back.

"Not as mad my sister was when my niece, her daughter, left them kids on her and ain't been back in a week. I told my sister that damn girl got a problem; those drugs are killing her ass. See what we need to do is put her ass in rehab or jail, one or the other 'cause she need help! Anytime a mother can leave her children on someone, I don't care who it is and not check on them, some'em gotta be wrong!" Tish couldn't help but to think about Deon and how he looked earlier that morning.

"Dats a shame Ms. Barber," Tish replied.

"A shame it is baby, a shame it is." Ms. Barber finished and Tish sat her under the dryer.

By six-thirty Tish was finishing Ms. Barber up and Rayon and Tasheena were walking in.

"You almost done?" Rayon asked.

"Mmm-Hmm, all I got to do is clean my station," Tish answered.

"Damn Tasheena, that ass still phat," Che-Che said when he came downstairs.

"And is," She shot back, as they remembered the times.

35

"Tish, you don't have to come in tomorrow if you don't want to, unless you got some clients, alright?" Che-Che said and left out the door.

"Come on y'all, let's go." Tish said once she was done cleaning.

*   *   *   *   *   *   *   *   *

The Honda turned off of Todd's Lane onto Bower St. and headed down to 27th St. Veering through the front windshield, Tish saw Saafie's truck parked in front of her mom's house and became instantly agitated.

"What the fuck does he want?" She thought.

"Bitch don't get in here and start running your mouth." Tasheena said. "'Cause bitch we only got like an hour and some'em minutes until the game starts."

"I ain't, I ain't goin' to say a mutha-fuckin' thing to him," Tish said as the three walked up the busted sidewalk to the door.

When Tish saw the door knob, the first thing she saw was Saafie bouncin' his son on his knee saying; "Hey man!" Then at his side, and in front of him sat bags and bags of clothes and sneaker boxes.

"I ain't impressed!" She snapped looking Saafie dead in the face.

"It's always some'em wit'chu, ain't it?" Saafie responded.

"And mom, you fake!" She said as Ms. Carla sat across from Saafie smoking a Kool cigarette.

36

"Y'all can sit down." Tish said and walked upstairs.

"They know they can sit down. They're just as much welcomed as you," Ms. Carla responded.

"Hey Mom Carla. Whass'up Saafie?" Rayon and Tasheena said in unison.

"Whass'up wit'chall? Where y'all goin' looking all jazzy?" Saafie asked.

"To the game up in Chester," Rayon said.

"Oh, that's right," Saafie said and pulled out his Nextel. "Hey baby boy, what'chu doing tonight? You know the big game between the boah Shakim Shabazz from Chester and da boah, whass his name." He paused

then said, "Yeah dat nigga, is tonight. You tryin' to go? Yeah I'm goin' and I got a stack on da boah Shakim," He finished and hung up.

Tasheena, Rayon and Ms. Carla, all three were acting like they were in some deep conversation, but eavesdropping on Saafie's conversation the whole time. When he hung up the phone, he said, "Rayon, can you go get Tish for me?"

"Yeah, if you let me have a couple dollars 'cause a bitch is broke!" Rayon replied.

"Ahn-huh, I knew your mouth was just as filthy." Ms. Carla said, finally catching innocent Ms. Rayon swearing.

"I ain't say nuffin Mom Carla," She answered, busted.

"How much money you need?" Saafie said pulling out a sure enough hustler's knot.

"However much you goin' give a bitch, I mean, sista." Rayon said.

"Well you might as well hit us all off now!" Ms. Carla said and he did giving each one of them a half a man, fifty dollars, to those who don't know.

"I'll be right back," Rayon said and darted up the steps.

Tish, fresh out of the tub, stood in her matching new blue panty and bra set in front of her favorite mirror. Rayon opened the door and damn near hit Tish in the face because she didn't knock.

"Damn bitch, smash my toes under the door." Tish said holding her arms out to stop the door.

"My fault girl," Rayon said and eased in through the lil crack in the door.

"Whass'up," Tish asked as she sprayed Berry Island by Victoria's Secret over her most intimate parts.

"Nothing, Saafie down there talking 'bout how he need to see you, that's all." Rayon said.

"Fuck Saafie." Tish said.

"Can I ask you a question?" Rayon said.

"Shoot." Tish said.

"Why are you so mad at Saafie and that's your baby's daddy?" Rayon said.

"Because dat nigga deceived me, and lied to me too many times. Plus I love Trans now, that's my baby," Tish said and Rayon squirmed again. It happened every time Trans was mentioned and they were together. For some odd reason Rayon thought Tish knew

they had fucked or some'em.

"Oh I see." Rayon said.

"Ooo girl, grab dat shoe and kill dat roach right there," Tish

said as she looked at Rayon through the mirror.

"Eeew girl," Rayon said smashing it into the floor boards.

"Go get me some tissue."

"Does this look right?"

"Bitch you know it look right," Rayon said picking the roach up in the

tissue with her thumb and index finger and tossing it in the trash can.

"You sure?"

"Yeah bitch! And the way those jeans, what are they

Parasucos, are fitting your hips and ass, girl got damn you hurting

'um! I wish my hips were wide."

"Bitch they will be as soon as your ass drop a baby!" Tish

said.

"Not yet baby girl, not yet." Rayon said.

Rayon led the way downstairs and when she saw the look on

Saafie's face she said to herself, "Gosh, here she come." Tish stepped

off the last step in her blue Bebe sneakers, blue Parasuco jeans, white

long sleeve

t-shirt and Trans' varsity jacket. "What" She asked making her way

towards the kitchen. Saafie just stared for a moment as he took

inventory on Tish. He knew he loved Pumpkin, but was it wrong for him to still love Tish too? Those were his thoughts as he sat his son down and rose from the couch.

"She swears she slick," He said, finding it humorous to watch Tish trying to be smart.

Tish, who was at the refrigerator, bent down and looked into the fruit drawers, making her ass spread out. She knew he'd be looking so she wiggled it a little bit, and started singing the chorus to Master P's new song "Shake what you got in them jeans, them jeans." Saafie walked right up on her and smacked her ass and said, "Now touch the wall and shake," but before he could finish, she stood up and pushed him away.

"Nigga! Keep ya dusty ass hands off me!"

"Why are you fronting?"

"Saafie I don't even like you no more," She shot back, the words cutting him deep.

"Why would you say that," He asked, eyebrows frowned up.

"Look, I don't want to get into it right now, o.k.?"

"Come on Tish, we only got 15 minutes! You know we still gotta find a parking spot," Tasheena said.

"Here I come, I'm ready," She said and brushed right by Saafie. "Excuse me." Tish breezed by as Saafie stood dumbfounded. There was nothing left for him to do, so he said bye to Mom Carla and followed them out.

"So you are going to carry me like that huh?" Saafie asked.

"No, you carried yourself like that," Tish said and got in the Honda.

*   *   *   *   *   *   *   *   *

Chester High School's parking lot was filled to capacity. Everything from school buses to news vans lined the lot, as well as the streets around it. Frustrated, Rayon popped the curb and parked next to a school bus with Delaware tags and Howard Wildcats painted on the windows.

"Bitch I told you we was going to find a spot, didn't I?" She said while they exited.

Tish, Rayon, and Tasheena, the most popular girls at Howard, stepped in the gym and watched as girls from their school and Chester give them evil eyes.

"Hey jealous bitches," Tasheena said waving at them with her tongue out.

"Dats why I don't fuck wit these bitches now and I don't like coming out 'cause I'll beat a bitch down!" Tish said seriously. She and Tasheena really were fighters, but Rayon wasn't. She knew they would fight at the drop of a dime, so she knew Tish was for real.

The three of them managed to find somewhere to sit in the stands although it was really standing room only. Tish had called her girl Renee from shop class and she held it down, by getting them some seats, so they were straight. As soon as they were seated, Tish looked down on the court at Howard's lay-up line and couldn't find Trans anywhere. She

41

stood in bewilderment, looked harder, and then she saw him. There he was in the

center of media frenzy. There were countless reporters around, cameras were flashing, questions were coming a hundred miles an hour, and microphones lined his face.

"Trans, what do you think about going up against Shakim Shabazz?" A reporter from Fox News asked.

"You know he's number 5 in the nation on the list of top high school basketball players." Another reporter added.

"Well it should be a good game then. I mean, me and Shakim are good friends. We play one another all the time. I mean we even traveled together in the AAU league, so it'll be a good game." Trans answered.

"Trans, rumor has it that you'll forego college to play in the NBA. Is there any truth to that rumor?" One reporter from ESPN asked.

"As of now, I'm a UCLA Bruin," He replied.

"Do you have a prediction for tonight's game?" A local reporter asked.

"Yeah, Howard by 10!" He answered and jogged off.

"Trans wait!" The reporters called out, but he was gone.

The referee stood center court as the players from both Howard and Chester sought one another out to defend, but there was no Trans. Trans sat on the bench mad as he'd ever been, but he understood the disciplinary act. Coach Stormy saw the frustration on his face and walked down to comfort his star player; the nation's star player.

"The first three minutes Trans, that's all," and he turned his attention to the court when the crowd cheered.

Chester won the jump ball so their fans erupted in cheers. The center tipped it to Shakim Shabazz and he dazzled the gym with a no look pass on the break. The score was Chester with 2 points and Howard 0. Chester's full court press caused Howard to turn the ball over three times in a row, which led to 7 unanswered points all by Shakim.

"Hey Coach," Shakim yelled as he passed Howard's bench, "you better call a time out, 'cause I'mma kill your guard." He finished. Coach Stormy resisted, but had to do something because another turnover and another 3 pointer by Shakim gave Chester a 12-0 lead and only 2 and a half minutes had elapsed.

"Time out!" Coach Stormy yelled, and the chant of 'blow out' began in the gym.

"I told you nigga! Get dat money right!" Saafie yelled over the crowd to his boy Tyaire.

"Nigga, my man's ain't even hit the floor yet! You'll see when he gets in nigga!" Tyaire replied.

Howard huddled up around the bench and Coach Stormy stood in the center with a clipboard in his hand going crazy.

"What have we practiced all week long for? Yeah, that's right, the press! The press! I mean, y'all are panicking making

careless mistakes and we look nothing like the number one team in
the nation. This is the
only game y'all all been waiting on. Scouts from every major division
one college in the United States are in here, and y'all are performing
like freshmen. What scout would want to recruit anyone of y'all?"
Coach Stormy asked, then continued, "Trans it's your stage baby lead
your team!"

Trans stood up, snapped off his warm-ups and went to the
center of the circle.   "Look y'all these muthafuckas can't beat us!
We're the number one team in the country nigga's! Put ya hands in
here," Trans said as everyone put their hands on top of one another.

"One, two, three, fight!" They yelled raising their hands and
then dropping them down.

When the Howard fans saw number 21 step on the court, they
went cold blooded bananas. They were so loud that chill's shot up
Tish's back. The center for Howard got the ball and in-bounded it by
passing it to Trans. He caught it, stood straight up and with the ball
cradled under his arm waved three fingers to set up the offense before
starting his dribble. Shakim stood before the number one player in
the country and was determined to prove that he was better than his
number 5 ranking. Soon as Trans passed the half court line, Shakim
squatted down and smacked the palms of his hands on the floor as if
to say "I'mma steal that ball."

Trans smiled because he knew Shakim would play him to his
left, so he went left confusing him totally. With a hard power dribble

to the left and a quick stop, Shakim backed up like five steps. Trans
then quickly crossed
over to his right, looked down and stepped behind the three point line
for the jumper. The shot was nothing but net and it was on, Chester 12
points and Howard with 3.

By the middle of the second quarter, Howard had chipped
Chester's lead down to two and Trans had 19 points. The halftime
score read Chester 35, Howard 33. Shakim Shabazz led all scores
with 20 points and 6 assists.

*   *   *   *   *   *   *   *   *

"Girl we going to win this game." Rayon said as they headed
to the concession stands.

"Yeah we are, ain't we Tish?" Tasheena asked.

"I don't know girl, I think I'm jinxing the team or some'em,"
Tish answered while they made their way into the crowded cafeteria.

Tish, Rayon, and Tasheena stood in line waiting on their hot
dogs and shit for what seemed to be an eternity.

"They know damn well it don't take that long to put some
mustard on a hot dog!" Tasheena complained loud enough for
everyone to hear it.

"Girl chill out, 'cause if it was you you'd want to dress your
shit up too, right?" Tish spoke up for the people.

"Oh shit! Ain't that Tyaire?" Tasheena asked spotting him
through the crowd.

"It sure is bitch! Rayon you need to go cuss his ass out, I'll come with you."

"For what? He's not my man." She said, but was feeling some type of way about him being posted up like that. "I'mma get y'all's shit, y'all go handle dat!" Tish told them while she stayed in line.

Tyaire didn't see them coming as he talked shit to the broad Tamia from up in Chester. She was his role dog, his home girl, who he just so happened to fuck on occasion.

"I'm trying to see about some'em tonight, you hear me?" Tyaire said.

"Nigga do you got my money? 'Cause that shit been in my house for too long now," Tamia reminded him.

"Oh shit, I forgot all about that. I was wondering where that shit was at." He said and lost his train of thought when he heard Tasheena's voice.

"And who da fuck is she?" Tasheena asked with her hands on her hips.

"Hold up, Hold up! How you going to just walk up on me and ask me some shit like that? I mean I don't have a problem explaining it, but you ain't got to act all ghetto about it, feel me?"

"Well who is she 'cause your girl does want to know, right Rayon?" Rayon didn't answer.

"Oh shit, why haven't you introduced me to your girl Tyaire? Hi, I am his cousin Tamia." She said and held her hand out to Rayon.

"I'm Rayon," She replied and shook the girls hand.

46

"See you came over here on some dumb shit" Tyaire said.

"Call me tonight at Aunt Cat's house," Tamia said and smiled as she walked away hoping he would catch the usage of the word cat.

"I will, I just hope she got the house fresh 'cause I don't like coming over there when it's not." He said playing along.

"Well you know she always has that part of the house clean." She said over her shoulder.

"Hey baby! Come here and give me a hug," Tyaire said and grabbed Rayon in his arms.

"That's what the bitch betta had been, 'cause I woulda beat her ass!" Tasheena told Tyaire as he hugged Rayon.

By the time Tish reached where Rayon, Tyaire, and Tasheena were Saafie had accompanied them. She started to turn around, but remembered that she had their food.

"Here y'all" She said passing them their food.

Saafie looked over at his baby's mom again and tried to think of what he did that made her feel the way that she felt about him. He stepped over to her and asked, "Can I please say some'em to you?"

"I told you now was not the time," Tish said. The rejection from Tish, along with the weed and Belvedere he'd been drinking was too much for Saafie to handle.

"Bitch I said come here!" He snapped and damn near ripped her jacket off 'causing her to drop her food.

"Boy you better get da fuck..." She tried to say, but Saafie grabbed her by the neck.

Everything was happening so fast that Tyaire and them couldn't respond fast enough.

"Bitch you goin' to stop playin' wit me," He said, with his hands wrapped around Tish's neck squeezing the life out of her. Tish couldn't breathe as tears soaked her eyes. It wasn't the actual pain, it was the anger built up inside of her that 'caused them to fall and then she blanked out. Tish let out a loud scream and clutched Saafie's face as the few onlookers present said "Dats right girl, don't let dat nigga do that shit to you."

"Muthafucka I told you to keep your hands off of me," She shouted and dug her nails in his face.

When Tyaire finally gained his composure, he broke them apart. Tish had managed to leave a trail of scratches on Saafie's light skinned face.

"Bitch I'mma fuck you up!" Saafie threatened Tish.

"Why you mad nigga! Why you mad? What, 'cause I don't want you no more? Fuck you and you won't see ya son no more! He gotta a new daddy anyway." She barked.

"What bitch?" He said frantically as he tried to break Tyaire's grip.

"You heard me nigga loud and clear!" Tish said as the police were coming to break up the new main event.

*   *   *   *   *   *   *   *   *

Howard in-bounded the ball to start the second half. Trans, the 6'6" Phenom, dribbled the ball with grace, as if he had a string on

48

it and from the stands, you would have thought it was an oversized yo-yo. When he took the first shot of the third quarter, Chester knew they were in for a long night because the three pointer left the nets stuck on the rim and gave Howard their first lead.

"Wild Cats! Wild Cats! Wild Cats!" Tasheena started a chant and Chester could feel the momentum changing.

The whole entire third quarter belonged to Howard High School, as they began the fourth and final quarter with a seven point lead; Howard 60 and Chester 53. Shakim did everything he could do, from passing, scoring and rebounding to playing tenacious defense, but Trans and the Wild Cats were just too good. The entire fourth quarter Trans went unconscious and gave the entire world tuned into ESPN, a look at why he should forego college and enter the year's upcoming Draft. The final score was Howard 87 and Chester 70.

"Get my money nigga!" Tyaire yelled, as Saafie peeled off a quick 10 big faces.

"Got damn I ain't know that boy was like that. It's a shame he playing with his career like that." Saafie said referring to Trans dealing with Tish.

"Man leave dat nigga alone. You should be glad she fuckin' wit a nigga like dat anyway. At least you know ain't no dumb shit around your son or nuffin'," Tyaire said defending Trans.
"Man who you wit? Me or dat nigga?" Saafie said.

"I'm wit da young boah on this one," Tyaire answered and meant it. He liked Trans. He loved the idea of a young boy doing his thing and going somewhere. It kind of reminded him of himself and his days at M.C.I. prep school playing football. Tyaire had a great chance at playing in the NFL as a premiere running back, but a torn ACL took all his heart and glory away. He was forever scarred by the injury and was too scared to play on it again. So seeing Trans was like reliving his own dream through someone else.

"Man fuck dat nigga!" Saafie said.

*   *   *   *   *   *   *   *   *

Trans exited the gymnasium and Tish was waiting right there for him. She ran straight over to him and tried to hug the life out of him. The incident that occurred earlier in the cafeteria with Saafie had almost ruined her night, but as she hugged Trans, her man, she felt like she was melting in his arms and felt like a brand new person. "Damn baby! I need these kinds of hugs more often." Trans said.

"Me too," Tish responded and just like that their special moment was interrupted.

"Hey Trans! Hey Trans! Do you...? Are you...? You had a nice game!" Questions and comments were coming from all sorts of directions and they got caught up in another media frenzy.

"Here, here ask her," Trans said putting Tish on the forefront.

"Who is she?" A reporter asked.

"My good luck charm." Trans said with a smile.

"Oh, we see. She's the lucky lady." Another reporter said.

"Yeah, you got that right," He answered and Tish blushed.

Tish couldn't believe that Trans put her on the front line, but it was all good though. She felt real important giving up little intimate things the reporters wanted to know about Trans, because it gave him a life outside of basketball. Trans was impressed at how well Tish handled herself the first time under the gun and when the slew of questions was done he let her know.

"Baby I'm proud of you. I don't even act that calm yet." Trans said.

"Its nothing, all you have to do is tell the truth and answer the questions." She said when she heard Trans' coach call him as the team boarded the bus.

"Baby look I have to ride with the team. What are you doing tomorrow?" Trans asked.

"Nothing." Tish said.

"O.k. well look, I'mma probably get my peoples car and come and get you so we can do some'em special alright?" Trans said.

"Sounds good to me," She said giving him a kiss as he walked away. "Fuck this, its time for us to handle ours!" She thought to herself as she walked to the Honda.

Tish had been with Trans since the end of the last school year, which was around nine months ago and still hadn't given him any. It had been plenty of times when they came real close, but she'd always chicken out. See, Tish had never been with anyone outside of Saafie, so there was a fear factor involved in the long wait. Plus with Saafie, it was always rough, so she never really saw the joy in making love. I mean, sometimes it felt good and sometimes it was just painful. But the time had come, she wanted some, and she was tired of making her baby suffer.

When Tish finally reached the Honda, she saw a CLK 500 parked next to it and two guys leaning in both the driver's and passenger's side windows. They both raised their heads and spoke to her when they saw her approach, then went back to talking to Rayon and Tasheena.

"Girl you want to go with them to some bar?" Tasheena asked Tish as she closed the door.

"I don't know, you know my mom got Tymeere."

"Well call then, and tell Mom Carla its Friday night and you want to hang out for a little while."

"Who said I wanted to hang out?" Tish snapped.

"Bitch stop being a party pooper!" Tasheena snapped back.

Tish called her mom on the cell phone and told her she was hanging out tonight. Ms. Carla said she didn't mind and that Tymeere was already in bed, so it wasn't a problem.

"Just bring me some Kool's when you come in, that's all." Ms. Carla said and hung up the phone.

"Well bitch, is you coming or not?" Tasheena asked.

"Yeah I'm coming." Tish said unenthusiastically.

To be continued

"So real you'll feel you lived it!"

Street Knowledge Publishing

Order Form
Street Knowledge Publishing
P.O. Box 345, Wilmington, Delaware 19801
Email: jj@streetknowledgepublishing.com
Website: www.streetknowledgepublishing.com

Also by the Author:

Bloody Money
ISBN # 0-9746199-0-6   **$15.00**
Shipping/ Handling
Via U.S. Priority Mail   **$3.85**
Total   **$18.85**

Me & My Girls
ISBN # 0-9746199-1-4   **$15.00**
Shipping/ Handling
Via U.S. Priority Mail   **$3.85**
Total   **$18.85**

Bloody Money 2
ISBN # 0-9-746199-2-2   **$15.00**
Shipping/ Handling
Via U.S. Priority Mail   **$3.85**
Total   **$18.85**

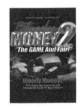

The Tommy Good Story
ISBN # 0-9746199-3-0   **$15.00**
Shipping/ Handling
Via U.S. Priority Mail   **$3.85**
Total   **$18.85**

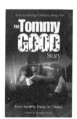

Purchaser Information

Name: _____

Address: _____

City: _____State: ___Zip Code: _____

Bloody Money ___

Me & My Girls ___

Bloody Money 2 ___

The Tommy Good Story ___

Quantity Of Books? _____

Make checks/money orders payable too:
Street Knowledge Publishing